THE
HELP

THE
HELP

Kathryn Stockett

AMY EINHORN BOOKS

PUBLISHED BY G. P. PUTNAM'S SONS

A MEMBER OF PENGUIN GROUP (USA) INC.

NEW YORK

AMY EINHORN BOOKS
Published by G. P. Putnam's Sons
Publishers Since 1838
Published by the Penguin Group
Penguin Group (USA) Inc., 375 Hudson Street, New York, New York 10014, USA • Penguin Group
(Canada), 90 Eglinton Avenue East, Suite 700, Toronto, Ontario M4P 2Y3, Canada (a division of
Pearson Canada Inc.) • Penguin Books Ltd, 80 Strand, London WC2R 0RL, England • Penguin
Ireland, 25 St Stephen's Green, Dublin 2, Ireland (a division of Penguin Books Ltd) • Penguin
Group (Australia), 250 Camberwell Road, Camberwell, Victoria 3124, Australia (a division
of Pearson Australia Group Pty Ltd) • Penguin Books India Pvt Ltd, 11 Community Centre,
Panchsheel Park, New Delhi–110 017, India • Penguin Group (NZ), 67 Apollo Drive, Rosedale,
North Shore 0632, New Zealand (a division of Pearson New Zealand Ltd) • Penguin Books
(South Africa) (Pty) Ltd, 24 Sturdee Avenue, Rosebank, Johannesburg 2196, South Africa

Penguin Books Ltd, Registered Offices: 80 Strand, London WC2R 0RL, England

ISBN-13: 978-1-61523-435-6

Printed in the United States of America

Book design by Stephanie Huntwork

This is a work of fiction. Names, characters, places, and incidents either are the product of the
author's imagination or are used fictitiously, and any resemblance to actual persons, living or dead,
businesses, companies, events, or locales is entirely coincidental.

While the author has made every effort to provide accurate telephone numbers and Internet addresses
at the time of publication, neither the publisher nor the author assumes any responsibility for errors,
or for changes that occur after publication. Further, the publisher does not have any control over
and does not assume any responsibility for author or third-party websites or their content.

To Grandaddy Stockett, the best storyteller of all

THE
HELP

AIBILEEN

CHAPTER 1

August 1962

MAE MOBLEY was born on a early Sunday morning in August, 1960. A church baby we like to call it. Taking care a white babies, that's what I do, along with all the cooking and the cleaning. I done raised seventeen kids in my lifetime. I know how to get them babies to sleep, stop crying, and go in the toilet bowl before they mamas even get out a bed in the morning.

But I ain't never seen a baby yell like Mae Mobley Leefolt. First day I walk in the door, there she be, red-hot and hollering with the colic, fighting that bottle like it's a rotten turnip. Miss Leefolt, she look terrified a her own child. "What am I doing wrong? Why can't I stop it?"

It? That was my first hint: something is wrong with this situation.

So I took that pink, screaming baby in my arms. Bounced her on my hip to get the gas moving and it didn't take two minutes fore Baby Girl stopped her crying, got to smiling up at me like she do. But Miss Leefolt, she don't pick up her own baby for the rest a the day. I seen plenty a womens get the baby blues after they done birthing. I reckon I thought that's what it was.

Here's something about Miss Leefolt: she not just frowning all the time, she skinny. Her legs is so spindly, she look like she done growed em last week. Twenty-three years old and she lanky as a fourteen-year-old boy. Even her hair is thin, brown, see-through. She try to tease it up, but it only make it look thinner. Her face be the same shape as that red devil on the redhot candy box, pointy chin and all. Fact, her whole body be so full a sharp knobs and corners, it's no wonder she can't soothe that baby. Babies like fat. Like to bury they face up in you armpit and go to sleep. They like big fat legs too. That I know.

By the time she a year old, Mae Mobley following me around everwhere I go. Five o'clock would come round and she'd be hanging on my Dr. Scholl shoe, dragging over the floor, crying like I weren't never coming back. Miss Leefolt, she'd narrow up her eyes at me like I done something wrong, unhitch that crying baby off my foot. I reckon that's the risk you run, letting somebody else raise you chilluns.

Mae Mobley two years old now. She got big brown eyes and honey-color curls. But the bald spot in the back of her hair kind a throw things off. She get the same wrinkle between her eyebrows when she worried, like her mama. They kind a favor except Mae Mobley so fat. She ain't gone be no beauty queen. I think it bother Miss Leefolt, but Mae Mobley my special baby.

I LOST MY OWN BOY, Treelore, right before I started waiting on Miss Leefolt. He was twenty-four years old. The best part of a person's life. It just wasn't enough time living in this world.

He had him a little apartment over on Foley Street. Seeing a real nice girl name Frances and I spec they was gone get married, but he was slow bout things like that. Not cause he looking for something better, just cause he the thinking kind. Wore big glasses and reading all the time. He even start writing his own book, bout being a colored man living and working in Mississippi. Law, that made me proud. But one night he working late at the Scanlon-Taylor mill, lugging two-by-fours to the truck, splinters slicing all the way through the glove. He too small for that kind a work, too skinny, but he needed the job. He was tired. It was raining. He slip off the loading dock, fell down on the drive. Tractor trailer didn't see him and crushed his lungs fore he could move. By the time I found out, he was dead.

That was the day my whole world went black. Air look black, sun look black. I laid up in bed and stared at the black walls a my house. Minny came ever day to make sure I was still breathing, feed me food to keep me living. Took three months fore I even look out the window, see if the world still there. I was surprise to see the world didn't stop just cause my boy did.

Five months after the funeral, I lifted myself up out a bed. I put on my white uniform and put my little gold cross back around my neck and I went to wait on Miss Leefolt cause she just have her baby girl. But it weren't too long before I seen something in me had changed. A bitter seed was planted inside a me. And I just didn't feel so accepting anymore.

"GET THE HOUSE straightened up and then go on and fix some of that chicken salad now," say Miss Leefolt.

It's bridge club day. Every fourth Wednesday a the month. A course I already got everthing ready to go—made the chicken salad this morning, ironed the tablecloths yesterday. Miss Leefolt seen me at it too. She ain't but twenty-three years old and she like hearing herself tell me what to do.

She already got the blue dress on I ironed this morning, the one with *sixty-five* pleats on the waist, so tiny I got to squint through my glasses to iron. I don't hate much in life, but me and that dress is *not* on good terms.

"And you make sure Mae Mobley's not coming in on us, now. I tell you, I am so burned up at her—tore up my good stationery into five thousand pieces and I've got fifteen thank-you notes for the Junior League to do…"

I arrange the-this and the-that for her lady friends. Set out the good crystal, put the silver service out. Miss Leefolt don't put up no dinky card table like the other ladies do. We set at the dining room table. Put a cloth on top to cover the big L-shaped crack, move that red flower centerpiece to the sideboard to hide where the wood all scratched. Miss Leefolt, she like it fancy when she do a luncheon. Maybe she trying to make up for her house being small. They ain't rich folk, that I know. Rich folk don't try so hard.

I'm used to working for young couples, but I spec this is the smallest house I ever worked in. It's just the one story. Her and Mister Leefolt's room in the back be a fair size, but Baby Girl's room be tiny. The dining room and the regular living room kind a join up. Only two bathrooms, which is a relief cause I worked in houses where they was five or six. Take a whole day just to clean toilets. Miss Leefolt don't pay but ninety-five cents an hour, less than I been paid in years. But after Treelore died, I took what I could. Landlord wasn't gone wait much longer. And even though it's small, Miss Leefolt done the house up nice as she can. She pretty good with the sewing machine. Anything she can't buy new of, she just get her some blue material and sew it a cover.

The doorbell ring and I open it up.

"Hey, Aibileen," Miss Skeeter say, cause she the kind that speak to the help. "How you?"

"Hey, Miss Skeeter. I'm alright. Law, it's hot out there."

Miss Skeeter real tall and skinny. Her hair be yellow and cut short above her shoulders cause she get the frizz year round. She twenty-three or so, same as Miss Leefolt and the rest of em. She set her pocketbook on the chair, kind a itch around in her clothes a second. She wearing a white lace blouse buttoned up like a nun, flat shoes so I reckon she don't look any taller. Her blue skirt gaps open in the waist. Miss Skeeter always look like somebody else told her what to wear.

I hear Miss Hilly and her mama, Miss Walter, pull up the driveway and toot the horn. Miss Hilly don't live but ten feet away, but she always drive over. I let her in and she go right past me and I figure it's a good time to get Mae Mobley up from her nap.

Soon as I walk in her nursery, Mae Mobley smile at me, reach out her fat little arms.

"You already up, Baby Girl? Why you didn't holler for me?"

She laugh, dance a little happy jig waiting on me to get her out. I give her a good hug. I reckon she don't get too many good hugs like this after I go home. Ever so often, I come to work and find her bawling in her crib, Miss Leefolt busy on the sewing machine rolling her eyes like it's a stray cat stuck in the screen door. See, Miss Leefolt, she dress up nice ever day. Always got her makeup on, got a carport, double-door Frigidaire with the built-in icebox. You see her in the Jitney 14 grocery, you never think she go and leave her baby crying in her crib like that. But the help always know.

Today is a good day though. That girl just grins.

I say, "Aibileen."

She say, "Aib-ee."

I say, "Love."

She say, "Love."

I say, "Mae Mobley."

She say, "Aib-ee." And then she laugh and laugh. She so tickled she talking and I got to say, it's about time. Treelore didn't say nothing till he two either. By the time he in third grade, though, he get to talking better than the President a the United States, coming home using words like *conjugation* and *parliamentary*. He get in junior high and we play this game where I give him a real simple word and he got to come up with a fancy one like it. I say *housecat*, he say *domesticized feline*, I say *mixer* and he say *motorized rotunda*. One day I say *Crisco*. He scratch his head. He just can't believe I done won the game with something simple as *Crisco*. Came to be a secret joke with us, meaning something you can't dress up no matter how you try. We start calling his daddy *Crisco* cause you can't fancy up a man done run off on his family. Plus he the greasiest no-count you ever known.

I tote Mae Mobley into the kitchen and put her in her high chair, thinking about two chores I need to finish today fore Miss Leefolt have a fit: separate the napkins that started to fray and straighten up the silver service in the cabinet. Law, I'm on have to do it while the ladies is here, I guess.

I take the tray a devil eggs out to the dining room. Miss Leefolt setting at the head and to her left be Miss Hilly Holbrook and Miss Hilly's mama, Miss Walter, who Miss Hilly don't treat with no respect. And then on Miss Leefolt's right be Miss Skeeter.

I make the egg rounds, starting with ole Miss Walter first cause she the elder. It's warm in here, but she got a thick brown sweater drooped around her shoulders. She scoop a egg up and near bout drop it cause she getting the palsy. Then I move over to Miss Hilly and she smile and take two. Miss Hilly got a round face and dark brown hair in the beehive. Her skin be olive color, with freckles and moles. She wear a lot a red plaid. And she getting heavy in the bottom. Today, since it's so hot, she wearing a red sleeveless dress with no waist to it. She one a those grown ladies that still dress like a little girl with big bows and matching hats and such. She ain't my favorite.

I move over to Miss Skeeter, but she wrinkle her nose up at me and say, "No, thanks," cause she don't eat no eggs. I tell Miss Leefolt ever time she have the bridge club and she make me do them eggs anyways. She scared Miss Hilly be disappointed.

Finally, I do Miss Leefolt. She the hostess so she got to pick up her eggs last. And soon as I'm done, Miss Hilly say, "Don't mind if I do," and snatch herself two more eggs, which don't surprise me.

"Guess who I ran into at the beauty parlor?" Miss Hilly say to the ladies.

"Who's that?" ask Miss Leefolt.

"Celia Foote. And do you know what she asked me? If she could help with the Benefit this year."

"Good," Miss Skeeter say. "We need it."

"Not that bad, we don't. I told her, I said, 'Celia, you have to be a League member or a sustainer to participate.' What does she think the Jackson League is? Open rush?"

"Aren't we taking nonmembers this year? Since the Benefit's gotten so big?" Miss Skeeter ask.

"Well, yes," Miss Hilly say. "But I wasn't about to tell *her* that."

"I can't believe Johnny married a girl so tacky like she is," Miss Leefolt say and Miss Hilly nod. She start dealing out the bridge cards.

I spoon out the congealed salad and the ham sandwiches, can't help but listen to the chatter. Only three things them ladies talk about: they kids, they clothes, and they friends. I hear the word *Kennedy*, I know they ain't discussing no politic. They talking about what Miss Jackie done wore on the tee-vee.

When I get around to Miss Walter, she don't take but one little old half a sandwich for herself.

"Mama," Miss Hilly yell at Miss Walter, "Take another sandwich. You are skinny as a telephone pole." Miss Hilly look over at the rest a the table. "I keep telling her, if that Minny can't cook she needs to just go on and fire her."

My ears perk up at this. They talking bout the help. I'm best friends with Minny.

"Minny cooks fine," say ole Miss Walter. "I'm just not so hungry like I used to be."

Minny near bout the best cook in Hinds County, maybe even all a Mississippi. The Junior League Benefit come around ever fall and they be wanting her to make ten caramel cakes to auction off. She ought a be the most sought-after help in the state. Problem is, Minny got a mouth on her. She always talking back. One day it be the white manager a the Jitney Jungle grocery, next day it be her husband, and ever day it's gone be the white lady she waiting on. The only reason she waiting on Miss Walter so long is Miss Walter be deaf as a doe-nob.

"I think you're malnutritioned, Mama," holler Miss Hilly. "That Minny isn't feeding you so that she can steal every last heirloom I have left." Miss Hilly huff out a her chair. "I'm going to the powder room. Y'all watch her in case she collapses dead of hunger."

When Miss Hilly gone, Miss Walter say real low, "I bet you'd love that." Everbody act like they didn't hear. I better call Minny tonight, tell her what Miss Hilly said.

In the kitchen, Baby Girl's up in her high chair, got purple juice all over her face. Soon as I walk in, she smile. She don't make no fuss being in here by herself, but I hate to leave her too long. I know she stare at that door real quiet till I come back.

I pat her little soft head and go back out to pour the ice tea. Miss Hilly's back in her chair looking all bowed up about something else now.

"Oh Hilly, I wish you'd use the guest bathroom," say Miss Leefolt, rearranging her cards. "Aibileen doesn't clean in the back until after lunch."

Hilly raise her chin up. Then she give one a her "ah-hem's." She got this way a clearing her throat real delicate-like that get everbody's attention without they even knowing she made em do it.

"But the guest bathroom's where the help goes," Miss Hilly say.

Nobody says anything for a second. Then Miss Walter nod, like she explaining it all. "She's upset cause the Nigra uses the inside bathroom and so do we."

Law, not this mess again. They all look over at me straightening the silver drawer in the sideboard and I know it's time for me to leave. But before

I can get the last spoon in there, Miss Leefolt give me the look, say, "Go get some more tea, Aibileen."

I go like she tell me to, even though they cups is full to the rim.

I stand around the kitchen a minute but I ain't got nothing left to do in there. I need to be in the dining room so I can finish my silver straightening. And I still got the napkin cabinet to sort through today but it's in the hall, right outside where they setting. I don't want a stay late just cause Miss Leefolt playing cards.

I wait a few minutes, wipe a counter. Give Baby Girl more ham and she gobble it up. Finally, I slip out to the hall, pray nobody see me.

All four of em got a cigarette in one hand, they cards in the other. "Elizabeth, if you had the choice," I hear Miss Hilly say, "wouldn't you rather them take their business outside?"

Real quiet, I open the napkin drawer, more concerned about Miss Leefolt seeing me than what they saying. This talk ain't news to me. Everwhere in town they got a colored bathroom, and most the houses do too. But I look over and Miss Skeeter's watching me and I freeze, thinking I'm about to get in trouble.

"I bid one heart," Miss Walter say.

"I don't know," Miss Leefolt say, frowning at her cards, "With Raleigh starting his own business and tax season not for six months…things are real tight for us right now."

Miss Hilly talk slow, like she spreading icing on a cake. "You just tell Raleigh every penny he spends on that bathroom he'll get back when y'all sell this house." She nod like she agreeing with herself. "All these houses they're building without maid's quarters? It's just plain dangerous. Everybody knows they carry different kinds of diseases than we do. I double."

I pick up a stack a napkins. I don't know why, but all a sudden I want a hear what Miss Leefolt gone say to this. She my boss. I guess everbody wonder what they boss think a them.

"It would be nice," Miss Leefolt say, taking a little puff a her cigarette, "not having her use the one in the house. I bid three spades."

"That's exactly why I've designed the Home Help Sanitation Initiative," Miss Hilly say. "As a disease-preventative measure."

I'm surprised by how tight my throat get. It's a shame I learned to keep down a long time ago.

Miss Skeeter look real confused. "The Home... the what?"

"A bill that requires every white home to have a separate bathroom for the colored help. I've even notified the surgeon general of Mississippi to see if he'll endorse the idea. I pass."

Miss Skeeter, she frowning at Miss Hilly. She set her cards down faceup and say real matter-a-fact, "Maybe we ought to just build you a bathroom outside, Hilly."

And Law, do that room get quiet.

Miss Hilly say, "I don't think you ought to be joking around about the colored situation. Not if you want to stay on as editor of the League, Skeeter Phelan."

Miss Skeeter kind a laugh, but I can tell she don't think it's funny. "What, you'd... kick me out? For disagreeing with you?"

Miss Hilly raise a eyebrow. "I will do whatever I have to do to protect our town. Your lead, Mama."

I go in the kitchen and don't come out again till I hear the door close after Miss Hilly's behind.

WHEN I KNOW MISS HILLY GONE, I put Mae Mobley in her playpen, drag the garbage bin out to the street cause the truck's coming by today. At the top a the driveway, Miss Hilly and her crazy mama near bout back over me in they car, then yell out all friendly how sorry they is. I walk in the house, glad I ain't got two new broken legs.

When I go in the kitchen, Miss Skeeter's in there. She leaning against the counter, got a serious look on her face, even more serious than usual. "Hey, Miss Skeeter. I get you something?"

She glance out at the drive where Miss Leefolt's talking to Miss Hilly through her car window. "No, I'm just... waiting."

I dry a tray with a towel. When I sneak a look over, she's still got her worried eyes on that window. She don't look like other ladies, being she so tall. She got real high cheekbones. Blue eyes that turn down, giving her a shy way about her. It's quiet, except for the little radio on the counter, play-ing the gospel station. I wish she'd go on out a here.

"Is that Preacher Green's sermon you're playing on the radio?" she ask.

"Yes ma'am, it is."

Miss Skeeter kind a smile. "That reminds me so much of my maid grow-ing up."

"Oh I knew Constantine," I say.

Miss Skeeter move her eyes from the window to me. "She raised me, did you know that?"

I nod, wishing I hadn't said nothing. I know too much about that situation.

"I've been trying to get an address for her family in Chicago," she say, "but nobody can tell me anything."

"I don't have it either, ma'am."

Miss Skeeter move her eyes back to the window, on Miss Hilly's Buick. She shake her head, just a little. "Aibileen, that talk in there...Hilly's talk, I mean..."

I pick up a coffee cup, start drying it real good with my cloth.

"Do you ever wish you could...change things?" she asks.

And I can't help myself. I look at her head on. Cause that's one a the stupidest questions I ever heard. She got a confused, disgusted look on her face, like she done salted her coffee instead a sugared it.

I turn back to my washing, so she don't see me rolling my eyes. "Oh no, ma'am, everthing's fine."

"But that talk in there, about the *bathroom*—" and smack on that word, Miss Leefolt walk in the kitchen.

"Oh, there you are, Skeeter." She look at us both kind a funny. "I'm sorry, did I...interrupt something?" We both stand there, wondering what she might a heard.

"I have to run," Miss Skeeter says. "See you tomorrow, Elizabeth." She open the back door, say, "Thanks, Aibileen, for lunch," and she gone.

I go in the dining room, start clearing the bridge table. And just like I knew she would, Miss Leefolt come in behind me wearing her upset smile. Her neck's sticking out like she fixing to ask me something. She don't like me talking to her friends when she ain't around, never has. Always wanting to know what we saying. I go right on past her into the kitchen. I put Baby Girl in her high chair and start cleaning the oven.

Miss Leefolt follow me in there, eyeball a bucket a Crisco, put it down. Baby Girl hold her arms out for her mama to pick her up, but Miss Leefolt open a cabinet, act like she don't see. Then she slam it close, open another one. Finally she just stand there. I'm down on my hands and knees. Pretty soon my head's so far in that oven I look like I'm trying to gas myself.

"You and Miss Skeeter looked like you were talking awful serious about something."

"No ma'am, she just...asking do I want some old clothes," I say and it sound like I'm down in a well-hole. Grease already working itself up my arms. Smell like a underarm in here. Don't take no time fore sweat's running down my nose and ever time I scratch at it, I get a plug a crud on my face. Got to be the worst place in the world, inside a oven. You in here, you either cleaning or you getting cooked. Tonight I just know I'm on have that dream I'm stuck inside and the gas gets turned on. But I keep my head in that awful place cause I'd rather be anywhere sides answering Miss Leefolt's questions about what Miss Skeeter was trying to say to me. Asking do I want to *change* things.

After while, Miss Leefolt huff and go out to the carport. I figure she looking at where she gone build me my new colored bathroom.

CHAPTER 2

You'd never know it living here, but Jackson, Mississippi, be filled with two hundred thousand peoples. I see them numbers in the paper and I got to wonder, where do them peoples live? Underground? Cause I know just about everbody on my side a the bridge and plenty a white families too, and that sure don't add up to be no two hundred thousand.

Six days a week, I take the bus across the Woodrow Wilson Bridge to where Miss Leefolt and all her white friends live, in a neighborhood call Belhaven. Right next to Belhaven be the downtown and the state capital. Capitol building is real big, pretty on the outside but I never been in it. I wonder what they pay to clean that place.

Down the road from Belhaven is white Woodland Hills, then Sherwood Forest, which is miles a big live oaks with the moss hanging down. Nobody living in it yet, but it's there for when the white folks is ready to move somewhere else new. Then it's the country, out where Miss Skeeter live on the Longleaf cotton plantation. She don't know it, but I picked cotton out there in 1931, during the Depression, when we didn't have nothing to eat but state cheese.

So Jackson's just one white neighborhood after the next and more springing up down the road. But the colored part a town, we one big anthill, surrounded by state land that ain't for sale. As our numbers get bigger, we can't spread out. Our part a town just gets thicker.

I get on the number six bus that afternoon, which goes from Belhaven to Farish Street. The bus today is nothing but maids heading home in our white uniforms. We all chatting and smiling at each other like we own it—not cause we mind if they's white people on here, we sit anywhere we want to now thanks to Miss Parks—just cause it's a friendly feeling.

I spot Minny in the back center seat. Minny short and big, got shiny black curls. She setting with her legs splayed, her thick arms crossed. She seventeen years younger than I am. Minny could probably lift this bus up over her head if she wanted to. Old lady like me's lucky to have her as a friend.

I take the seat in front a her, turn around and listen. Everbody like to listen to Minny.

"...so I said, Miss Walters, the world don't want a see your naked white behind any more than they want a see my black one. Now, get in this house and put your underpants and some clothes on."

"On the front porch? Naked?" Kiki Brown ask.

"Her behind hanging to her knees."

The bus is laughing and chuckling and shaking they heads.

"Law, that woman crazy," Kiki say. "I don't know how you always seem to get the crazy ones, Minny."

"Oh, like your Miss Patterson ain't?" Minny say to Kiki. "Shoot, she call the roll a the crazy lady club." The whole bus be laughing now cause Minny don't like nobody talking bad about her white lady except herself. That's her job and she own the rights.

The bus cross the bridge and make the first stop in the colored neighborhood. A dozen or so maids get off. I go set in the open seat next to Minny. She smile, bump me hello with her elbow. Then she relax back in her seat cause she don't have to put on no show for me.

"How you doing? You have to iron pleats this morning?"

I laugh, nod my head. "Took me a hour and a half."

"What you feed Miss Walters at bridge club today? I worked all morning making that fool a caramel cake and then she wouldn't eat a crumb."

That makes me remember what Miss Hilly say at the table today. Any other white lady and no one would care, but we'd all want a know if Miss Hilly after us. I just don't know how to put it.

I look out the window at the colored hospital go by, the fruit stand. "I think I heard Miss Hilly say something about that, bout her mama getting skinny." I say this careful as I can. "Say maybe she getting mal-nutritious."

Minny look at me. "She did, did she?" Just the name make her eyes narrow. "What else Miss Hilly say?"

I better just go on and say it. "I think she got her eye on you, Minny. Just...be extra careful around her."

"Miss Hilly ought to be extra careful around *me*. What she say, I can't cook? She say that old bag a bones ain't eating cause I can't feed her?" Minny stand up, throw her purse up on her arm.

"I'm sorry, Minny, I only told you so you stay out a her—"

"She ever say that to me, she gone get a piece a Minny for lunch." She huff down the steps.

I watch her through the window, stomping off toward her house. Miss Hilly ain't somebody to mess with. Law, maybe I should a just kept it to myself.

A COUPLE MORNINGS LATER, I get off the bus, walk the block to Miss Leefolt's house. Parked in front is a old lumber truck. They's two colored mens inside, one drinking a cup a coffee, the other asleep setting straight up. I go on past, into the kitchen.

Mister Raleigh Leefolt still at home this morning, which is rare. Whenever he here, he look like he just counting the minutes till he get to go back to his accounting job. Even on Saturday. But today he carrying on bout something.

"This is my damn house and I pay for what goddamn goes in it!" Mister Leefolt yell.

Miss Leefolt trying to keep up behind him with that smile that mean she ain't happy. I hide out in the washroom. It's been two days since the bathroom talk come up and I was hoping it was over. Mister Leefolt opens the back door to look at the truck setting there, slam it back close again.

"I put up with the new clothes, all the damn trips to New Orleans with your sorority sisters, but this takes the goddamn cake."

"But it'll increase the value of the house. Hilly said so!" I'm still in the washroom, but I can almost hear Miss Leefolt trying to keep that smile on her face.

"We can't afford it! And we do not take orders from the Holbrooks!"

Everthing get real quiet for a minute. Then I hear the *pap-pap* a little feetum pajamas.

"Da-dee?"

I come out the washroom and into the kitchen then cause Mae Mobley's my business.

Mister Leefolt already kneeling down to her. He's wearing a smile look like it's made out a rubber. "Guess what, honey?"

She smile back. She waiting for a good surprise.

"You're not going to college so your mama's friends don't have to use the same bathroom as the maid."

He stomp off and slam the door so hard it make Baby Girl blink.

Miss Leefolt look down at her, start shaking her finger. "Mae Mobley, you know you're not supposed to climb up out of your crib!"

Baby Girl, she looking at the door her daddy slammed, she looking at her mama frowning down at her. My baby, she swallowing it back, like she trying real hard not to cry.

I rush past Miss Leefolt, pick Baby Girl up. I whisper, "Let's go on in the living room and play with the talking toy. What that donkey say?"

"She keeps getting up. I put her back in bed three times this morning."

"Cause somebody needs changing. Whooooweeee."

Miss Leefolt tisk, say, "Well I didn't realize..." but she already staring out the window at the lumber truck.

I go on to the back, so mad I'm stomping. Baby Girl been in that bed since eight o'clock last night, a course she need changing! Miss Leefolt try to sit in twelve hours worth a bathroom mess without getting up!

I lay Baby Girl on the changing table, try to keep my mad inside. Baby Girl stare up at me while I take off her diaper. Then she reach out her little hand. She touch my mouth real soft.

"Mae Mo been bad," she say.

"No, baby, you ain't been bad," I say, smoothing her hair back. "You been good. Real good."

. . .

I LIVE ON GESSUM AVENUE, where I been renting since 1942. You could say Gessum got a lot a personality. The houses all be small, but every front yard's different—some scrubby and grassless like a bald-headed old man. Others got azalea bushes and roses and thick green grass. My yard, I reckon it be somewhere in between.

I got a few red camellia bushes out front a the house. My grass be kind a spotty and I still got a big yellow mark where Treelore's pickup sat for three months after the accident. I ain't got no trees. But the backyard, now it looks like the Garden of Eden. That's where my next-door neighbor, Ida Peek, got her vegetable patch.

Ida ain't got no backyard to speak of what with all her husband's junk—car engines and old refrigerators and tires. Stuff he say he gone fix but never do. So I tell Ida she come plant on my side. That way I don't have no mowing to tend to and she let me pick whatever I need, save me two or three dollars ever week. She put up what we don't eat, give me jars for the winter season. Good turnip greens, eggplant, okra by the bushel, all kind a gourds. I don't know how she keep them bugs out a her tomatoes, but she do. And they good.

That evening, it's raining hard outside. I pull out a jar a Ida Peek's cabbage and tomato, eat my last slice a leftover cornbread. Then I set down to look over my finances cause two things done happen: the bus gone up to fifteen cents a ride and my rent gone up to twenty-nine dollars a month. I work for Miss Leefolt eight to four, six days a week except Saturdays. I get paid forty-three dollars ever Friday, which come to $172 a month. That means after I pay the light bill, the water bill, the gas bill, and the telephone bill, I got thirteen dollars and fifty cents a week left for my groceries, my clothes, getting my hair done, and tithing to the church. Not to mention the cost to mail these bills done gone up to a nickel. And my work shoes is so thin, they look like they starving to death. New pair cost seven dollars though, which means I'm on be eating cabbage and tomato till I turn into Br'er Rabbit. Thank the Lord for Ida Peek, else I be eating nothing.

My phone ring, making me jump. Before I can even say hello, I hear Minny. She working late tonight.

"Miss Hilly sending Miss Walters to the old lady home. I got to find myself a new job. And you know when she going? Next *week*."

"Oh *no*, Minny."

"I been looking, call ten ladies today. Not even a speck a interest."

I am sorry to say I ain't surprised. "I ask Miss Leefolt first thing tomorrow do she know anybody need help."

"Hang on," Minny say. I hear old Miss Walter talking and Minny say, "What you think I am? A chauffeur? I ain't driving you to no country club in the pouring rain."

Sides stealing, worse thing you'n do for your career as a maid is have a smart mouth. Still, she such a good cook, sometimes it makes up for it.

"Don't you worry, Minny. We gone find you somebody deaf as a doe-knob, just like Miss Walter."

"Miss Hilly been hinting around for me to come work for her."

"What?" I talk stern as I can: "Now you look a here, Minny, I support you myself fore I let you work for that evil lady."

"Who you think you talking to, Aibileen? A monkey? I might as well go work for the KKK. And you know I never take Yule May's job away."

"I'm sorry, Lordy me." I just get so nervous when it come to Miss Hilly. "I call Miss Caroline over on Honeysuckle, see if she know somebody. And I call Miss Ruth, she so nice it near bout break your heart. Used to clean up the house ever morning so I didn't have nothing to do but keep her company. Her husband died a the scarlet fever, mm-hmm."

"Thank you, A. Now come on, Miss Walters, eat up a little green bean for me." Minny say goodbye and hang up the phone.

THE NEXT MORNING, there that old green lumber truck is again. Banging's already started but Mister Leefolt ain't stomping around today. I guess he know he done lost this one before it even started.

Miss Leefolt setting at the kitchen table in her blue-quilt bathrobe talking on the telephone. Baby Girl's got red sticky all over her face, hanging on to her mama's knees trying to get her look at her.

"Morning, Baby Girl," I say.

"Mama! Mama!" she say, trying to crawl up in Miss Leefolt's lap.

"No, Mae Mobley." Miss Leefolt nudge her down. "Mama's on the telephone. Let Mama talk."

"Mama, pick up," Mae Mobley whine and reach out her arms to her mama. "Pick Mae Mo up."

"Hush," Miss Leefolt whisper.

I scoop Baby Girl up right quick and take her over to the sink, but she keep craning her neck around, whining, "Mama, *Mama,*" trying to get her attention.

"Just like you told me to say it." Miss Leefolt nodding into the phone. "Someday when we move, it'll raise the value of the house."

"Come on, Baby Girl. Put your hands here, under the water."

But Baby Girl wriggling hard. I'm trying to get the soap on her fingers but she twisting and turning and she snake right out my arms. She run straight to her mama and stick out her chin and then she jerk the phone cord hard as she can. The receiver clatter out a Miss Leefolt's hand and hit the floor.

"Mae Mobley!" I say.

I rush to get her but Miss Leefolt get there first. Her lips is curled back from her teeth in a scary smile. Miss Leefolt slap Baby Girl on the back a her bare legs so hard I jump from the sting.

Then Miss Leefolt grab Mae Mobley by the arm, jerk it hard with ever word. "Don't you touch this phone again, Mae Mobley!" she say. "Aibileen, how many times do I have to tell you to keep her away from me when I am on the phone!"

"I'm sorry," I say and I pick up Mae Mobley, try to hug her to me, but she bawling and her face is red and she fighting me.

"Come on, Baby Girl, it's all right, everthing—"

Mae Mobley make an ugly face at me and then she rear back and *bowp*! She whack me right on the ear.

Miss Leefolt point at the door, yell, "Aibileen, you both just get *out.*"

I carry her out the kitchen. I'm so mad at Miss Leefolt, I'm biting my tongue. If the fool would just pay her child some attention, this wouldn't happen! When we make it to Mae Mobley's room, I set in the rocking chair. She sob on my shoulder and I rub her back, glad she can't see the mad on my face. I don't want her to think it's at her.

"You okay, Baby Girl?" I whisper. My ear smarting from her little fist. I'm so glad she hit me instead a her mama, cause I don't know what that woman would a done to her. I look down and see red fingermarks on the back a her legs.

"I'm here, baby, Aibee's here," I rock and soothe, rock and soothe.

But Baby Girl, she just cry and cry.

AROUND LUNCHTIME, when my stories come on tee-vee, it gets quiet out in the carport. Mae Mobley's in my lap helping me string the beans. She still kind a fussy from this morning. I reckon I am too, but I done pushed it down to a place where I don't have to worry with it.

We go in the kitchen and I fix her baloney sandwich. In the driveway, the workmen is setting in they truck, eating they own lunches. I'm glad for the peace. I smile over at Baby Girl, give her a strawberry, so grateful I was here during the trouble with her mama. I hate to think what would a happen if I wasn't. She stuff the strawberry in her mouth, smile back. I think she feel it too.

Miss Leefolt ain't here so I think about calling Minny at Miss Walter, see if she found any work yet. But before I get around to it, they's a knock on the back door. I open it to see one a the workmen standing there. He real old. Got coveralls on over a white collar shirt.

"Hidee, ma'am. Trouble you for some water?" he ask. I don't recognize him. Must live somewhere south a town.

"Sho nuff," I say.

I go get a paper cup from the cupboard. It's got happy birthday balloons on it from when Mae Mobley turn two. I know Miss Leefolt don't want me giving him one a the glasses.

He drink it in one long swallow and hand me the cup back. His face be real tired. Kind a lonesome in the eyes.

"How y'all coming along?" I ask.

"It's work," he say. "Still ain't no water to it. Reckon we run a pipe out yonder from the road."

"Other fella need a drink?" I ask.

"Be mighty nice." He nod and I go get his friend a little funny-looking cup too, fill it up from the sink.

He don't take it to his partner right away.

"Beg a pardon," he say, "but where…" He stand there a minute, look down at his feet. "Where might I go to make water?"

He look up and I look at him and for a minute we just be looking. I mean, it's one a them funny things. Not the ha-ha funny but the funny where you be thinking: Huh. Here we is with two in the house and one being built and they still ain't no place for this man to do his business.

"Well…" I ain't never been in this position before. The young'un, Robert, who do the yard ever two weeks, I guess he go fore he come over. But this fella, he a old man. Got heavy wrinkled hands. Seventy years a worry done put so many lines in his face, he like a roadmap.

"I spec you gone have to go in the bushes, back a the house," I hear myself say, but I wish it weren't me. "Dog's back there, but he won't bother you."

"Alright then," he say. "Thank ya."

I watch him walk back real slow with the cup a water for his partner.

The banging and the digging go on the rest a the afternoon.

ALL THE NEXT DAY LONG, they's hammering and digging going on in the front yard. I don't ask Miss Leefolt no questions about it and Miss Leefolt don't offer no explanation. She just peer out the back door ever hour to see what's going on.

Three o'clock the racket stops and the mens get in they truck and leave. Miss Leefolt, she watch em drive off, let out a big sigh. Then she get in her car and go do whatever it is she do when she ain't nervous bout a couple a colored mens hanging round her house.

After while, the phone ring.

"Miss Leef—"

"She telling everbody in town I'm stealing! That's why I can't get no work! That witch done turned me into the Smart-Mouthed Criminal Maid a Hinds County!"

"Hold on, Minny, get your breath—"

"Before work this morning, I go to the Renfroes' over on Sycamore and Miss Renfroe near bout chase me off the property. Say Miss Hilly told her about me, everbody know I stole a candelabra from Miss Walters!"

I can hear the grip she got on the phone, sound like she trying to crush it in her hand. I hear Kindra holler and I wonder why Minny already home. She usually don't leave work till four.

"I ain't done nothing but feed that old woman good food and look after her!"

"Minny, I know you honest. God know you honest."

Her voice dip down, like bees on a comb. "When I walk into Miss Walters', Miss Hilly be there and she try to give me twenty dollars. She say, 'Take it. I know you need it,' and I bout spit in her face. But I didn't. No sir." She start making this panting noise, she say, "I did *worse*."

"What you did?"

"I ain't telling. I ain't telling nobody about that pie. But I give her what she deserve!" She wailing now and I feel a real cold fear. Ain't no game crossing Miss Hilly. "I ain't never gone get no work again, Leroy gone kill me..."

Kindra gets to crying in the background. Minny hang up without even saying goodbye. I don't know what she talking about a pie. But Law, knowing Minny, it could not have been good.

THAT NIGHT, I pick me a poke salad and a tomato out a Ida's garden. I fry up some ham, make a little gravy for my biscuit. My wig been brushed out and put up, got my pink rollers in, already sprayed the Good Nuff on my hair. I been worried all afternoon, thinking bout Minny. I got to put it out a my mind if I'm on get some sleep tonight.

I set at my table to eat, turn on the kitchen radio. Little Stevie Wonder's singing "Fingertips." Being colored ain't nothing on that boy. He twelve years old, blind, and got a hit on the radio. When he done, I skip over Pastor Green playing his sermon and stop on WBLA. They play the juke joint blues.

I like them smoky, liquor-drinking sounds when it get dark. Makes me feel like my whole house is full a people. I can almost see em, swaying here in my kitchen, dancing to the blues. When I turn off the ceiling light, I pretend we at The Raven. They's little tables with red-covered lights. It's May or June and warm. My man Clyde flash me his white-toothed smile and say *Honey, you want you a drink?* And I say, *Black Mary straight up* and then I get to laughing at myself, setting in my kitchen having this daydream, cause the raciest thing I ever take is the purple Nehi.

Memphis Minny get to singing on the radio how lean meat won't fry, which is about how the love don't last. Time to time, I think I might find myself another man, one from my church. Problem is, much as I love the Lord, church-going man never do all that much for me. Kind a man I like ain't the kind that stays around when he done spending all you money. I made that mistake twenty years ago. When my husband Clyde left me for that no-count hussy up on Farish Street, one they call Cocoa, I figured I better shut the door for good on that kind a business.

A cat get to screeching outside and bring me back to my cold kitchen. I turn the radio off and the light back on, fish my prayer book out my purse. My prayer book is just a blue notepad I pick up at the Ben Franklin store. I use a pencil so I can erase till I get it right. I been writing my prayers since I was in junior high. When I tell my seventh-grade teacher I ain't coming back to school cause I got to help out my mama, Miss Ross just about cried.

"You're the smartest one in the class, Aibileen," she say. "And the only way you're going to keep sharp is to read *and write* every day."

So I started writing my prayers down instead a saying em. But nobody's called me smart since.

I turn the pages a my prayer book to see who I got tonight. A few times this week, I thought about maybe putting Miss Skeeter on my list. I'm not real sure why. She always nice when she come over. It makes me nervous, but I can't help but wonder what she was gone ask me in Miss Leefolt's kitchen, about do I want to change things. Not to mention her asking me the whereabouts a Constantine, her maid growing up. I know what happen between Constantine and Miss Skeeter's mama and ain't no way I'm on tell her that story.

The thing is though, if I start praying for Miss Skeeter, I know that conversation gone continue the next time I see her. And the next and the next. Cause that's the way prayer do. It's like electricity, it keeps things going. And the bathroom situation, it just ain't something I really want to discuss.

I scan down my prayer list. My Mae Mobley got the number one rung, then they's Fanny Lou at church, ailing from the rheumatism. My sisters Inez and Mable in Port Gibson that got eighteen kids between em and six with the flu. When the list be thin, I slip in that old stinky white fella that live behind the feed store, the one lost his mind from drinking the shoe polish. But the list be pretty full tonight.

And look a there who else I done put on this list. Bertrina Bessemer a all people! Everbody know Bertrina and me don't take to each other ever since she call me a nigga fool for marrying Clyde umpteen years ago.

"Minny," I say last Sunday, "why Bertrina ask *me* to pray for her?"

We walking home from the one o'clock service. Minny say, "Rumor is you got some kind a power prayer, gets better results than just the regular variety."

"Say what?"

"Eudora Green, when she broke her hip, went on your list, up walking in a week. Isaiah fell off the cotton truck, on your prayer list that night, back to work the next day."

Hearing this made me think about how I didn't even get the chance to pray for Treelore. Maybe that's why God took him so fast. He didn't want a have to argue with me.

"Snuff Washington," Minny say, "Lolly Jackson—heck, Lolly go on your list and two days later she pop up from her wheelchair like she touched Jesus. Everbody in Hinds County know about that one."

"But that ain't me," I say. "That's just prayer."

"But Bertrina—" Minny get to laughing, say, "You know Cocoa, the one Clyde run off with?"

"Phhh. You know I never forget her."

"Week after Clyde left you, I heard that Cocoa wake up to her cootchie spoilt like a rotten oyster. Didn't get better for three months. Bertrina, she good friends with Cocoa. She *know* your prayer works."

My mouth drop open. Why she never tell me this before? "You saying people think I got the black magic?"

"I knew it make you worry if I told you. They just think you got a better connection than most. We all on a party line to God, but you, you setting right in his ear."

My teapot start fussing on the stove, bringing me back to real life. Law, I reckon I just go ahead and put Miss Skeeter on the list, but how come, I don't know. Which reminds me a what I don't want a think about, that Miss Leefolt's building me a bathroom cause she think I'm diseased. And Miss Skeeter asking don't I want to change things, like changing Jackson, Mississippi, gone be like changing a lightbulb.

I'M STRINGING BEANS in Miss Leefolt's kitchen and the phone rings. I'm hoping it's Minny to say she found something. I done called everbody I ever waited on and they all told me the same thing: "We ain't hiring." But what they really mean is: "We ain't hiring *Minny*."

Even though Minny already had her last day a work three days ago, Miss Walter call Minny in secret last night, ask her to come in today cause the house feel too empty, what with most the furniture already taken away by Miss Hilly. I still don't know what happen with Minny and Miss Hilly. I reckon I don't really want to know.

"Leefolt residence."

"Um, hi. This is..." The lady stop, clear her throat. "Hello. May I...may I please speak to Elizabeth Leer-folt?"

"Miss Leefolt ain't home right now. May I take a message?"

"Oh," she say, like she got all excited over nothing.

"May I ask who calling?"

"This is . . . Celia Foote. My husband gave me this number here and I don't know Elizabeth, but . . . well, he said she knows all about the Children's Benefit and the Ladies League." I know this name, but I can't quite place it. This woman talk like she from so deep in the country she got corn growing in her shoes. Her voice is sweet though, high-pitch. Still, she don't sound like the ladies round here do.

"I give her your message," I say. "What's your number?"

"I'm kind of new here and, well, that's not true, I've been here a pretty good stretch, gosh, over a year now. I just don't really know anybody. I don't . . . get out too much."

She clear her throat again and I'm wondering why she telling me all this. I'm the maid, she ain't gone win no friends talking to me.

"I was thinking maybe I could help out with the Children's Benefit from home," she say.

I remember then who she is. She the one Miss Hilly and Miss Leefolt always talking trash on cause she marry Miss Hilly's old boyfriend.

"I give her the message. What you say your number is again?"

"Oh, but I'm fixing to scoot off to the grocery store. Oh, maybe I should sit and wait."

"She don't reach you, she leave a message with your help."

"I don't have any help. In fact, I was planning on asking her about that too, if she could pass along the name of somebody good."

"You looking for help?"

"I'm in a stitch trying to find somebody to come all the way out to Madison County."

Well, what do you know. "I know somebody real good. She known for her cooking and she look after you kids too. She even got her own car to drive out to you house."

"Oh, well . . . I'd still like to talk to Elizabeth about it. Did I already tell you my number?"

"No ma'am," I sigh. "Go head." Miss Leefolt never gone recommend Minny, not with all a Miss Hilly's lies.

She say, "It's Missus Johnny Foote and it's Emerson two-sixty-six-oh-nine."

Just in case I say, "And her name is Minny, she at Lakewood eight-four-four-three-two. You got that?"

Baby Girl tug on my dress, say, "Tum-my hurt," and she rubbing her belly.

I get an idea. I say, "Hold on, what's that Miss Leefolt? Uh-huh, I tell her." I put the phone back to my mouth and say, "Miss Celia, Miss Leefolt just walk in and she say she ain't feeling good but for you to go on and call Minny. She say she call you if she be needing help with the Benefit."

"Oh! Tell her I said thank you. And I sure do hope she gets to feeling better. And to call me up anytime."

"That's Minny Jackson at Lakewood eight-four-four-three-two. Hang on, what's that?" I get a cookie and give it to Mae Mobley, feel nothing but delight at the devil in me. I am lying and I don't even care.

I tell Miss Celia Foote, "She say don't tell nobody bout her tip on Minny, cause all her friends want a hire her and they be real upset if they find out she give her to somebody else."

"I won't tell her secret if she won't tell mine. I don't want my husband to know I'm hiring a maid."

Well, if that ain't perfect then I don't know what is.

Soon as we hang up, I dial Minny quick as I can. But just as I do, Miss Leefolt walk in the door.

This a real predicament, see. I gave this Miss Celia woman Minny's number at home, but Minny working today cause Miss Walter lonely. So when she call, Leroy gone give her Miss Walter number cause he a fool. If Miss Walter answer the phone when Miss Celia call, then the whole jig is up. Miss Walter gone tell this woman everthing Miss Hilly been spreading around. I got to get to Minny or Leroy before all this happen.

Miss Leefolt head back to her bedroom and, just like I figured, the first thing she do is tie up the phone. First she call Miss Hilly. Then she call the hairdresser. Then she call the store about a wedding present, talking, talking, talking. Soon as she hang up, she come out and ask what they having for supper this week. I pull out the notebook and go down the list. No, she don't want pork chops. She trying to get her husband to reduce. She want skillet steak and green salad. And how many calories do I spec them meringue thingies have? And don't give no more cookies to Mae Mobley cause she too fat and—and—and—

Law! For a woman who ain't said nothing to me but do this and use that bathroom, all a sudden she talking to me like I'm her best friend. Mae Mobley's dancing a hot-foot jig trying to get her mama to notice her. And just when Miss Leefolt about to bend down to pay her some attention, whoops! Miss Leefolt run out the door cause she forgot she got a errand to run and a blooming hour done passed already.

I can't make my fingers go round that dial fast enough.

"Minny! I got a job lined up. But you got to get to the phone—"

"She already call." Minny's voice is flat. "Leroy give her the number."

"So Miss Walter answer it," I say.

"Deaf as doo-doo and all a sudden it's like a miracle from God, she hear the phone ringing. I'm going in and out a the kitchen, not paying attention, but at the end I hear my name. Then Leroy call and I know that's what it was." Minny sound wore out, and she the kind that don't ever get tired.

"Well. Maybe Miss Walter didn't tell her them lies Miss Hilly started. You never know." But even I ain't fool enough to believe this.

"Even if she didn't, Miss Walters know all about how I got back at Miss Hilly. You don't know about the Terrible Awful Thing I did. I don't ever want you to know. I'm sure Miss Walters tell this woman I'm nothing short a the devil hisself." Her voice sound eerie. Like she a record player going too slow.

"I'm sorry. I wish I could a called you earlier so you could pick up that phone."

"You done what you can. Nothing nobody can do for me now."

"I be praying for you."

"Thank you," she say, and then her voice break down. "And I thank you for trying to help me."

We hang up and I go to mopping. The sound a Minny's voice scare me.

She always been a strong woman, always fighting. After Treelore died, she carry supper over to me ever night for three months straight. And ever day she say, "Nuh-uh, you ain't leaving me on this sorry earth without you," but I tell you, I was sure enough thinking about it.

I already had the rope tied when Minny found it. The coil was Treelore's, from back when he doing a science project with pulleys and rings. I don't know if I's gone use it, knowing it's a sin against God, but I wasn't in my right mind. Minny, though, she don't ask no questions about it, just pull it out from under the bed, put it in the can, take it to the street. When she come back in, she brush her hands together like she cleaning things up as usual. She all business, that Minny. But now, she sound bad. I got a mind to check under her bed tonight.

I put down the bucket a Sunshine cleaner them ladies is always smiling about on the tee-vee. I got to set down. Mae Mobley come up holding her tummy, say, "Make it not hurt."

She lay her face on my leg. I smooth her hair down over and over till she practically purring, feeling the love in my hand. And I think about all my friends, what they done for me. What they do ever day for the white women they waiting on. That pain in Minny's voice. Treelore dead in the ground. I look down at Baby Girl, who I know, deep down, I can't keep from turning out like her mama. And all of it together roll on top a me. I close my eyes, say the Lord's prayer to myself. But it don't make me feel any better.

Law help me, but something's gone have to be done.

BABY GIRL HUG ON MY LEGS all afternoon to where I bout fall over a few times. I don't mind. Miss Leefolt ain't said nothing to me or Mae Mobley since this morning. Been working so busy on that sewing machine in her bedroom. Trying to cover up something else she don't like the look of in the house.

After while me and Mae Mobley go in the regular living room. I got a load a Mister Leefolt's shirts to iron and after this I'm on get a pot roast going. I cleaned the bathrooms already, got the sheets changed, the rugs vacuumed. I always try to finish up early so me and Baby Girl can set together and play.

Miss Leefolt come in and watch me ironing. She do that sometimes. Frown and look. Then she smile real quick when I glance up. Pat up the back a her hair, trying to make it puffy.

"Aibileen, I have a surprise for you."

She smiling big now. She don't have no teeth showing, just a lip smile, kind you got to watch. "Mister Leefolt and I have decided to build you your very own bathroom." She clap her hands together, drop her chin at me. "It's right out there in the garage."

"Yes ma'am." Where she think I been all this time?

"So, from now on, instead of using the guest bathroom, you can use your own right out there. Won't that be nice?"

"Yes ma'am." I keep ironing. Tee-vee's on and my program's fixing to start. She keep standing there looking at me though.

"So you'll use that one out in the garage now, you understand?"

I don't look at her. I'm not trying to make no trouble, but she done made her point.

"Don't you want to get some tissue and go on out there and use it?"

"Miss Leefolt, I don't really have to go right this second."

Mae Mobley point at me from the playpen, say, "Mae Mo juice?"

"I get you some juice, baby," I say.

"Oh." Miss Leefolt lick her lips a few times. "But when you do, you'll go on back there and use that one now, I mean . . . only that one, right?"

Miss Leefolt wear a lot a makeup, creamy-looking stuff, thick. That yellowish makeup's spread across her lips too, so you can barely tell she even got a mouth. I say what I know she want to hear: "I use my colored bathroom from now on. And then I go on and Clorox the white bathroom again real good."

"Well, there's no hurry. Anytime today would be fine."

But by the way she standing there fiddling with her wedding ring, she really mean for me to do it right now.

I put the iron down real slow, feel that bitter seed grow in my chest, the one planted after Treelore died. My face goes hot, my tongue twitchy. I don't know what to say to her. All I know is, I ain't saying it. And I know she ain't saying what she want a say either and it's a strange thing happening here cause nobody saying nothing and we still managing to have us a conversation.

MINNY

CHAPTER 3

STANDING ON that white lady's back porch, I tell myself, *Tuck it in, Minny.* Tuck in whatever might fly out my mouth and tuck in my behind too. Look like a maid who does what she's told. Truth is, I'm so nervous right now, I'd never backtalk again if it meant I'd get this job.

I yank my hose up from sagging around my feet—the trouble of all fat, short women around the world. Then I rehearse what to say, what to keep to myself. I go ahead and punch the bell.

The doorbell rings a long *bing-bong*, fine and fancy for this big mansion out in the country. It looks like a castle, gray brick rising high in the sky and left and right too. Woods surround the lawn on every side. If this place was in a story book, there'd be witches in those woods. The kind that eat kids.

The back door opens and there stands Miss Marilyn Monroe. Or something kin to her.

"Hey there, you're right on time. I'm Celia. Celia Rae Foote."

The white lady sticks her hand out to me and I study her. She might be built like Marilyn, but she ain't ready for no screen test. She's got flour in her yellow hairdo. Flour in her glue-on eyelashes. And flour all over that tacky pink pantsuit. Her standing in a cloud of dust and that pantsuit being so tight, I wonder how she can breathe.

"Yes ma'am. I'm Minny Jackson." I smooth down my white uniform instead of shaking her hand. I don't want that mess on me. "You cooking something?"

"One of those upsidedown cakes from the magazine?" She sighs. "It ain't working out too good."

I follow her inside and that's when I see Miss Celia Rae Foote's suffered only a minor injury in the flour fiasco. The rest of the kitchen took the real hit. The countertops, the double-door refrigerator, the Kitchen-Aid mixer are all sitting in about a quarter-inch of snow flour. It's enough mess to drive me crazy. I ain't even got the job yet, and I'm already looking over at the sink for a sponge.

Miss Celia says, "I guess I have some learning to do."

"You sure do," I say. But I bite down hard on my tongue. *Don't you go sassing this white lady like you done the other. Sassed her all the way to the nursing home.*

But Miss Celia, she just smiles, washes the muck off her hands in a sink full of dishes. I wonder if maybe I've found myself another deaf one, like Miss Walters was. Let's hope so.

"I just can't seem to get the hang of kitchen work," she says and even with Marilyn's whispery Hollywood voice, I can tell right off, she's from *way* out in the country. I look down and see the fool doesn't have any shoes on, like some kind of white trash. Nice white ladies don't go around barefoot.

She's probably ten or fifteen years younger than me, twenty-two, twenty-three, and she's real pretty, but why's she wearing all that goo on her face? I'll bet she's got on double the makeup the other white ladies wear. She's got a lot more bosom to her, too. In fact, she's almost as big as me except she's skinny in all those places I ain't. I just hope she's an eater. Because I'm a cooker and that's why people hire me.

"Can I get you a cold drink?" she asks. "Set down and I'll bring you something."

And that's my clue: something funny's going on here.

"Leroy, she got to be crazy," I said when she called me up three days ago and asked if I'd come interview, "cause everbody in town think I stole Miss Walters' silver. And I know she do too cause she call Miss Walters up on the phone when I was there."

"White people strange," Leroy said. "Who knows, maybe that old woman give you a good word."

I look at Miss Celia Rae Foote hard. I've never in my life had a white woman tell me to sit down so she can serve me a cold drink. Shoot, now I'm wondering if this fool even plans on hiring a maid or if she just drug me all the way out here for sport.

"Maybe we better go on and see the house first, ma'am."

She smiles like the thought never entered that hairsprayed head of hers, letting me see the house I might be cleaning.

"Oh, of course. Come on in yonder, Maxie. I'll show you the fancy dining room first."

"The name," I say, "is Minny."

Maybe she's not deaf or crazy. Maybe she's just stupid. A shiny hope rises up in me again.

All over that big ole doodied up house she walks and talks and I follow. There are ten rooms downstairs and one with a stuffed grizzly bear that looks like it ate up the last maid and is biding for the next one. A burned-up Confederate flag is framed on the wall, and on the table is an old silver pistol with the name "Confederate General John Foote" engraved on it. I bet Great-Grandaddy Foote scared some slaves with that thing.

We move on and it starts to look like any nice white house. Except this one's the biggest I've ever been in and full of dirty floors and dusty rugs, the kind folks who don't know any better would say is worn out, but I know an antique when I see one. I've worked in some fine homes. I just hope she ain't so country she don't own a Hoover.

"Johnny's mama wouldn't let me decorate a thing. I had my way, there'd be wall-to-wall white carpet and gold trim and none of this old stuff."

"Where your people from?" I ask her.

"I'm from . . . Sugar Ditch." Her voice drops down a little. Sugar Ditch is as low as you can go in Mississippi, maybe the whole United States. It's up in Tunica County, almost to Memphis. I saw pictures in the paper one time, showing those tenant shacks. Even the white kids looked like they hadn't had a meal for a week.

Miss Celia tries to smile, says, "This is my first time hiring a maid."

"Well you sure need one." *Now, Minny—*

"I was real glad to get the recommendation from Missus Walters. She told me all about you. Said your cooking is the best in town."

That makes zero sense to me. After what I did to Miss Hilly, right in front of Miss Walters to see? "She say...anything else about me?"

But Miss Celia's already walking up a big curving staircase. I follow her upstairs, to a long hall with sun coming through the windows. Even though there are two yellow bedrooms for girls and a blue one and a green one for boys, it's clear there aren't any children living here. Just dust.

"We've got five bedrooms and five bathrooms over here in the main house." She points out the window and I see a big blue swimming pool, and behind that, *another* house. My heart thumps hard.

"And then there's the poolhouse out yonder," she sighs.

I'd take any job I can get at this point, but a big house like this should pay plenty. And I don't mind being busy. I ain't afraid to work. "When you gone have you some chilluns, start filling up all these beds?" I try to smile, look friendly.

"Oh, we're gonna have some kids." She clears her throat, fidgets. "I mean, kids is the only thing worth living for." She looks down at her feet. A second passes before she heads back to the stairs. I follow behind, noticing how she holds the stair rail tight on the way down, like she's afraid she might fall.

It's back in the dining room that Miss Celia starts shaking her head. "It's an awful lot to do," she says. "All the bedrooms and the floors..."

"Yes ma'am, it's big," I say, thinking if she saw my house with a cot in the hall and one toilet for six behinds, she'd probably run. "But I got lots a energy."

"...and then there's all this silver to clean."

She opens up a silver closet the size of my living room. She fixes a candle that's turned funny on the candelabra and I can see why she's looking so doubtful.

After the town got word of Miss Hilly's lies, three ladies in a row hung up on me the minute I said my name. I ready myself for the blow. *Say it, lady. Say what you thinking about me and your silver.* I feel like crying thinking about how this job would suit me fine and what Miss Hilly's done to keep me from getting it. I fix my eyes on the window, hoping and praying this isn't where the interview ends.

"I know, those windows are awful high. I never tried to clean them before."

I let my breath go. Windows are a heck of a lot better subject for me than silver. "I ain't afraid a no windows. I clean Miss Walters' top to bottom ever four weeks."

"Did she have just the one floor or a double decker?"

"Well, one... but they's a lot to it. Old houses got a lot a nooks and crannies, you know."

Finally, we go back in the kitchen. We both stare down at the breakfast table, but neither one of us sits. I'm getting so jittery wondering what she's thinking, my head starts to sweat.

"You got a big, pretty house," I say. "All the way out here in the country. Lot a work to be done."

She starts fiddling with her wedding ring. "I guess Missus Walters' was a lot easier than this would be. I mean, it's just us now, but when we get to having kids..."

"You, uh, got some other maids you considering?"

She sighs. "A bunch have come out here. I just haven't found... the right one yet." She bites on her fingernails, shifts her eyes away.

I wait for her to say I'm not the right one either, but we just stand there breathing in that flour. Finally, I play my last card, whisper it because it's all I got left.

"You know, I only left Miss Walters cause she going up to the rest home. She didn't fire me."

But she just stares down at her bare feet, black-soled because her floors haven't been scrubbed since she moved in this big old dirty house. And it's clear, this lady doesn't want me.

"Well," she says, "I appreciate you driving all this way. Can I at least give you some money for the gas?"

I pick up my pocketbook and thrust it up under my armpit. She gives me a cheery smile I could wipe off with one swat. *Damn* that Hilly Holbrook.

"No ma'am, no, you cannot."

"I knew it was gonna be a chore finding someone, but..."

I stand there listening to her acting all sorry but I just think, *Get it over with, lady, so I can tell Leroy we got to move all the way to the North Pole next to Santy Claus where nobody's heard Hilly's lies about me.*

"...and if I were you I wouldn't want to clean this big house either."

I look at her square on. Now that's just excusing herself a little too much, pretending Minny ain't getting the job cause Minny don't *want* the job.

"When you hear me say I don't want a clean this house?"

"It's alright, five maids have already told me it's too much work."

I look down at my hundred-and-sixty-five-pound, five-foot-zero self practically busting out of my uniform. "Too much for me?"

She blinks at me a second. "You...you'll do it?"

"Why you think I drove all the way out here to kingdom come, just to burn gas?" I clamp my mouth shut. *Don't go ruirning this now, she offering you a jay-o-bee.* "Miss Celia, I be happy to work for you."

She laughs and the crazy woman goes to hug me, but I step back a little, let her know that's not the kind of thing I do.

"Hang on now, we got to talk about some things first. You got to tell me what days you want me here and...and that kind a thing." *Like how much you paying.*

"I guess...whenever you feel like coming," she says.

"For Miss Walters I work Sunday through Friday."

Miss Celia chews some more on her pink pinky-nail. "You can't come here on weekends."

"Alright." I need the days, but maybe later on she'll let me do some party serving or whatnot. "Monday through Friday then. Now, what time you want me here in the morning?"

"What time do you want to come in?"

I've never had this choice before. I feel my eyes narrow up. "How bout eight. That's when Miss Walters used to get me in."

"Alright, eight's real good." Then she stands there like she's waiting for my next checker move.

"Now you supposed to tell me what time I got to leave."

"What time?" asks Celia.

I roll my eyes at her. "Miss Celia, you supposed to tell me that. That's the way it works."

She swallows, like she's trying real hard to get this down. I just want to get through this before she changes her mind about me.

"How bout four o'clock?" I say. "I work eight to four and I gets some time for lunch or what-have-you."

"That's just fine."

"Now...we got to talk bout pay," I say and my toes start wriggling in my shoes. It must not be much if five maids already said no.

Neither one of us says anything.

"Now come on, Miss Celia. What your husband say you can pay?"

She looks off at the Veg-O-Matic I bet she can't even use and says, "Johnny doesn't know."

"Alright then. Ask him tonight what he wants to pay."

"No, Johnny doesn't know I'm bringing in help."

My chin drops down to my chest. "What you mean he don't know?"

"I am *not* telling Johnny." Her blue eyes are big, like she's scared to death of him.

"And what's Mister Johnny gone do if he come home and find a colored woman up in his kitchen?"

"I'm sorry, I just can't—"

"I'll tell you what he's gone do, he's gone get that pistol and shoot Minny dead right here on this no-wax floor."

Miss Celia shakes her head. "I'm not telling him."

"Then I got to go," I say. *Shit. I knew it. I knew she was crazy when I walked in the door—*

"It's not that I'd be fibbing to him. I just need a maid—"

"A course you need a maid. Last one done got shot in the head."

"He never comes home during the day. Just do the heavy cleaning and teach me how to fix supper and it'll only take a few months—"

My nose prickles from something burning. I see a waft of smoke coming from the oven. "And then what, you gone fire me after them few months?"

"Then I'll...tell him," she say but she's frowning at the thought. "Please,

I want him to think I can do it on my own. I want him to think I'm...worth the trouble."

"Miss Celia..." I shake my head, not believing I'm already arguing with this lady and I haven't worked here two minutes. "I think you done burned up your cake."

She grabs a rag and rushes to the oven and jerks the cake out. "Oww! Dawgon it!"

I set my pocketbook down, sidle her out of the way. "You can't use no wet towel on a hot pan."

I grab a dry rag and take that black cake out the door, set it down on the concrete step.

Miss Celia stares down at her burned hand. "Missus Walters said you were a real good cook."

"That old woman eat two butterbeans and say she full. I couldn't get her to eat nothing."

"How much was she paying you?"

"Dollar an hour," I say, feeling kind of ashamed. Five years and not even minimum wage.

"Then I'll pay you two."

And I feel all the breath slip out of me.

"When Mister Johnny get out the house in the morning?" I ask, cleaning up the butterstick melting right on the counter, not even a plate under it.

"Six. He can't stand to do-dad around here very long. Then he heads back from his real estate office about five."

I do some figuring and even with the fewer hours it'd be more pay. But I can't get paid if I get shot dead. "I'll leave at three then. Give myself two hours coming and going so I can stay out a his way."

"Good." She nods. "It's best to be safe."

On the back step, Miss Celia dumps the cake in a paper sack. "I'll have to bury this in the waste bin so he won't know I've burned up another one."

I take the bag out of her hands. "Mister Johnny ain't seeing nothing. I'll throw it out at my house."

"Oh, *thank* you." Miss Celia shakes her head like that's the nicest thing anyone's ever done for her. She holds her hands in tight little fists under her chin. I walk out to my car.

I sit in the sagging seat of the Ford Leroy's still paying his boss twelve dollars every week for. Relief hits me. I have finally gotten myself a job. I don't have to move to the North Pole. Won't Santy Claus be disappointed.

"SIT DOWN ON YOUR BEHIND, Minny, because I'm about to tell you the rules for working in a White Lady's house."

I was fourteen years old to the day. I sat at the little wooden table in my mama's kitchen eyeing that caramel cake on the cooling rack, waiting to be iced. Birthdays were the only day of the year I was allowed to eat as much as I wanted.

I was about to quit school and start my first real job. Mama wanted me to stay on and go to ninth grade—she'd always wanted to be a school-teacher instead of working in Miss Woodra's house. But with my sister's heart problem and my no-good drunk daddy, it was up to me and Mama. I already knew about housework. After school, I did most of the cooking and the cleaning. But if I was going off to work in somebody else's house, who'd be looking after ours?

Mama turned me by the shoulders so I'd look at her instead of the cake. Mama was a crack-whip. She was proper. She took nothing from nobody. She shook her finger so close to my face, it made me cross-eyed.

"Rule Number One for working for a white lady, Minny: it is nobody's business. You keep your nose out of your White Lady's problems, you don't go crying to her with yours—you can't pay the light bill? Your feet are too sore? Remember one thing: white people are not your friends. They don't want to hear about it. And when Miss White Lady catches her man with the lady next door, you keep out of it, you hear me?

"Rule Number Two: don't you *ever* let that White Lady find you sitting on her toilet. I don't care if you've got to go so bad it's coming out of your hairbraids. If there's not one out back for the help, you find yourself a time when she's not there in a bathroom she doesn't use.

"Rule Number Three—" Mama jerked my chin back around to face her because that cake had lured me in again. "Rule Number Three: when you're cooking white people's food, you taste it with a different spoon. You put that spoon to your mouth, think nobody's looking, put it back in the pot, might as well throw it out.

"Rule Number Four: You use the same cup, same fork, same plate every day. Keep it in a separate cupboard and tell that white woman that's the one you'll use from here on out.

"Rule Number Five: you eat in the kitchen.

"Rule Number Six: you don't hit on her children. White people like to do their own spanking."

"Rule Number Seven: this is the last one, Minny. Are you listening to me? No sass-mouthing."

"Mama, I know how—"

"Oh, I hear you when you think I can't, muttering about having to clean the stovepipe, about the last little piece of chicken left for poor Minny. You sass a white woman in the morning, you'll be sassing out on the street in the afternoon."

I saw the way my mama acted when Miss Woodra brought her home, all Yes Ma'aming, No Ma'aming, I sure do thank you Ma'aming. *Why I got to be like that? I know how to stand up to people.*

"Now come here and give your mama a hug on your birthday—Lord, you are heavy as a house, Minny."

"I ain't eaten all day, when can I have my cake?"

"Don't say ain't, you speak properly now. I didn't raise you to talk like a mule."

First day at my White Lady's house, I ate my ham sandwich in the kitchen, put my plate up in my spot in the cupboard. When that little brat stole my pocketbook and hid it in the oven, I didn't whoop her on the behind.

But when the White Lady said: "Now I want you to be sure and handwash all the clothes first, then put them in the electric machine to finish up."

I said: "Why I got to handwash when the power washer gone do the job? That's the biggest waste a time I ever heard of."

That White Lady smiled at me, and five minutes later, I was out on the street.

WORKING FOR MISS CELIA, I'll get to see my kids off to Spann Elementary in the morning and still get home in the evening with time to myself. I haven't had a nap since Kindra was born in 1957, but with these hours—eight to three—I could have one every day if that was my idea of a fine time. Since no bus goes all the way out to Miss Celia's, I have to take Leroy's car.

"You ain't taking my car every day, woman, what if I get the day shift and need to—"

"She paying me seventy dollars cash every Friday, Leroy."

"Maybe I take Sugar's bike."

On Tuesday, the day after the interview, I park the car down the street from Miss Celia's house, around a curve so you can't see it. I walk fast on the empty road and up the drive. No other cars come by.

"I'm here, Miss Celia." I stick my head in her bedroom that first morning and there she is, propped up on the covers with her makeup perfect and her tight Friday-night clothes on even though it's Tuesday, reading the trash in the *Hollywood Digest* like it's the Holy B.

"Good morning, Minny! It's real good to see you," she says, and I bristle, hearing a white lady being so friendly.

I look around the bedroom, sizing up the job. It's big, with cream-colored carpet, a yellow king canopy bed, two fat yellow chairs. And it's neat, with no clothes on the floor. The spread's made up underneath her. The blanket on the chair's folded nice. But I watch, I look. I can feel it. Something's wrong.

"When can we get to our first cooking lesson?" she asks. "Can we start today?"

"I reckon in a few days, after you go to the store and pick up what we need."

She thinks about this a second, says, "Maybe you ought to go, Minny, since you know what to buy and all."

I look at her. Most white women like to do their own shopping. "Alright, I go in the morning, then."

I spot a small pink shag rug she's put on top of the carpet next to the bathroom door. Kind of catty-cornered. I'm no decorator, but I know a pink rug doesn't match a yellow room.

"Miss Celia, fore I get going here, I need to know. Exactly when you planning on telling Mister Johnny bout me?"

She eyes the magazine in her lap. "In a few months, I reckon. I ought to know how to cook and stuff by then."

"By a few, is you meaning two?"

She bites her lipsticky lips. "I was thinking more like...four."

Say what? I'm not working four months like an escaped criminal. "You ain't gone tell him till 1963? No ma'am, *before* Christmas."

She sighs. "Alright. But right before."

I do some figuring. "That's a hundred and...sixteen days then. You gone tell him. A hundred and sixteen days from now."

She gives me a worried frown. I guess she didn't expect the maid to be so good at math. Finally she says, "Okay."

Then I tell her she needs to go on in the living room, let me do my work in here. When she's gone, I eyeball the room, at how neat it all looks. Real slow, I open her closet and just like I thought, forty-five things fall down on my head. Then I look under the bed and find enough dirty clothes to where I bet she's hasn't washed in months.

Every drawer is a wreck, every hidden cranny full of dirty clothes and wadded-up stockings. I find fifteen boxes of new shirts for Mister Johnny so he won't know she can't wash and iron. Finally, I lift up that funny-looking pink shag rug. Underneath, there's a big, deep stain the color of rust. I shudder.

THAT AFTERNOON, Miss Celia and I make a list of what to cook that week, and the next morning I do the grocery shopping. But it takes me twice as long because I have to drive all the way to the white Jitney Jungle in town instead of the colored Piggly Wiggly by me since I figure she won't eat food from a colored grocery store and I reckon I don't blame her, with the potatoes having inch-long eyes and the milk almost sour. When I get to work, I'm ready to fight with her over all the reasons I'm late, but there Miss Celia is on the bed like before, smiling like it doesn't matter. All dressed up and going nowhere. For five hours she sits there, reading the magazines. The only time I see her get up is for a glass of milk or to pee. But I don't ask. I'm just the maid.

After I clean the kitchen, I go in the formal living room. I stop in the doorway and give that grizzly bear a good long stare. He's seven feet tall and baring his teeth. His claws are long, curled, witchy-looking. At his feet lays a bone-handled hunting knife. I get closer and see his fur's nappy with dust. There's a cobweb between his jaws.

First, I swat at the dust with my broom, but it's thick, matted up in his fur. All this does is move the dust around. So I take a cloth and try and wipe him down, but I squawk every time that wiry hair touches my hand. *White* people. I mean, I have cleaned everything from refrigerators to rear ends but what makes that lady think I know how to clean a damn grizzly bear?

I go get the Hoover. I suck the dirt off and except for a few spots where I sucked too hard and thinned him, I think it worked out pretty good.

After I'm done with the bear, I dust the fancy books nobody reads, the Confederate coat buttons, the silver pistol. On a table is a gold picture frame of Miss Celia and Mister Johnny at the altar and I look close to see what kind of man he is. I'm hoping he's fat and short-legged in case it comes to running, but he's not anywhere close. He's strong, tall, thick. And he's no stranger either. Lord. He's the one who went steady with Miss Hilly all those years when I first worked for Miss Walters. I never met him, but I saw him enough times to be sure. I shiver, my fears tripling. Because that alone says more about that man than anything.

AT ONE O'CLOCK, Miss Celia comes in the kitchen and says she's ready for her first cooking lesson. She settles on a stool. She's wearing a tight red sweater and a red skirt and enough makeup to scare a hooker.

"What you know how to cook already?" I ask.

She thinks this over, wrinkling her forehead. "Maybe we could just start at the beginning."

"Must be something you know. What your mama teach you growing up?"

She looks down at the webby feet of her panty hose, says, "I can cook corn pone."

I can't help but laugh. "What else you know how to do sides corn pone?"

"I can boil potatoes." Her voice drops even quieter. "And I can do grits. We didn't have electric current out where I lived. But I'm ready to learn right. On a real stovetop."

Lord. I've never met a white person worse off than me except for crazy Mister Wally, lives behind the Canton feed store and eats the cat food.

"You been feeding your husband grits and corn pone ever day?"

Miss Celia nods. "But you'll teach me to cook right, won't you?"

"I'll try," I say, even though I've never told a white woman what to do and I don't really know how to start. I pull up my hose, think about it. Finally, I point to the can on the counter.

"I reckon if there's anything you ought a know about cooking, it's this."

"That's just lard, ain't it?"

"No, it ain't just lard," I say. "It's the most important invention in the kitchen since jarred mayonnaise."

"What's so special about"—she wrinkles her nose at it—"pig fat?"

"Ain't *pig*, it's vegetable." Who in this world doesn't know what Crisco is? "You don't have a clue of all the things you can do with this here can."

She shrugs. "Fry?"

"Ain't just for frying. You ever get a sticky something stuck in your hair, like gum?" I jackhammer my finger on the Crisco can. "That's right, Crisco. Spread this on a baby's bottom, you won't even know what diaper rash is." I plop three scoops in the black skillet. "Shoot, I seen ladies rub it under they eyes and on they husband's scaly feet."

"Look how pretty it is," she says. "Like white cake frosting."

"Clean the goo from a price tag, take the squeak out a door hinge. Lights get cut off, stick a wick in it and burn it like a candle."

I turn on the flame and we watch it melt down in the pan. "And after all that, it'll still fry your chicken."

"Alright," she says, concentrating hard. "What's next?"

"Chicken's been soaking in the buttermilk," I say. "Now mix up the dry." I pour flour, salt, more salt, pepper, paprika, and a pinch of cayenne into a doubled paper sack.

"Now. Put the chicken parts in the bag and shake it."

Miss Celia puts a raw chicken thigh in, bumps the bag around. "Like this? Just like the Shake 'n Bake commercials on the tee-vee?"

"Yeah," I say and run my tongue up over my teeth because if that's not an insult, I don't know what is. "Just like the Shake 'n Bake." But then I freeze. I hear the sound of a car motor out on the road. I hold still and listen. I see Miss Celia's eyes are big and she's listening too. We're thinking the same thing: What if it's him and where will I hide?

The car motor passes. We both breathe again.

"Miss Celia," I grit my teeth, "how come you can't tell your husband about me? Ain't he gone know when the cooking gets good?"

"Oh, I didn't think of that! Maybe we ought to burn the chicken a little."

I look at her sideways. I ain't burning no chicken. She didn't answer the real question, but I'll get it out of her soon enough.

Real careful, I lay the dark meat in the pan. It bubbles up like a song and we watch the thighs and legs turn brown. I look over and Miss Celia's smiling at me.

"What? Something on my face?"

"No," she says, tears coming up in her eyes. She touches my arm. "I'm just real grateful you're here."

I move my arm back from under her hand. "Miss Celia, you got a lot more to be grateful for than me."

"I know." She looks at her fancy kitchen like it's something that tastes bad. "I never dreamed I'd have this much."

"Well, ain't you lucky."

"I've never been happier in my whole life."

I leave it at that. Underneath all that happy, she sure doesn't look happy.

. . .

THAT NIGHT, I CALL AIBILEEN.

"Miss Hilly was at Miss Leefolt's yesterday," Aibileen says. "She ask if anybody knew where you was working."

"Lordy, she find me out there, she ruirn it for sure." It's been two weeks since the Terrible Awful Thing I did to that woman. I know she'd just love to see me fired on the spot.

"What Leroy say when you told him you got the job?" Aibileen asks.

"Shoot. He strut around the kitchen like a plumed rooster cause he in front a the kids," I say. "Act like he the only one supporting the family and I'm just doing this to keep my poor self entertained. Later on though, we in bed and I thought my big old bull for a husband gone cry."

Aibileen laughs. "Leroy got a lot a pride."

"Yeah, I just got to make sure Mister Johnny don't catch up with me."

"And she ain't told you why she don't want him to know?"

"All she say is she want him to think she can do the cooking and the cleaning herself. But that ain't why. She hiding something from him."

"Ain't it funny how this worked out. Miss Celia can't tell nobody, else it'll get back to Mister Johnny. So Miss Hilly won't find out, cause Miss Celia can't tell nobody. You couldn't a fixed it up better yourself."

"Mm-hmm" is all I say. I don't want to sound ungrateful, since Aibileen's the one who got me the job. But I can't help but think that I've just doubled my trouble, what with Miss Hilly and now Mister Johnny too.

"Minny, I been meaning to ask you." Aibileen clears her throat. "You know that Miss Skeeter?"

"Tall one, used to come over to Miss Walters for bridge?"

"Yeah, what you think about her?"

"I don't know, she white just like the rest of em. Why? What she say about me?"

"Nothing about you," Aibileen says. "She just . . . a few weeks ago, I don't know why I keep thinking about it. She ask me something. Ask do I want to change things. White woman never asked—"

But then Leroy stumbles in from the bedroom wanting his coffee before his late shift.

"Shoot, he's up," I say. "Talk quick."

"Naw, never mind. It's nothing," Aibileen says.

"What? What's going on? What that lady tell you?"

"It was just jabber. It was nonsense."

CHAPTER 4

My first week at Miss Celia's, I scrub the house until there isn't a dust rag or a stripped sheet or even a run panty hose left to wipe with. Second week, I scrub the house again because it's like the dirt grew back. Third week, I am satisfied and settle in my ways.

Every day, Miss Celia looks like she just can't believe I've come back to work. I'm the only thing that interrupts all that quiet around her. My house is always full of five kids and neighbors and a husband. Most days when I come in to Miss Celia's, I am grateful for the peace.

My housekeeping tasks fall on the same day for every job I take: on Monday, I oil up the furniture. Tuesday, I wash and iron the damn sheets, the day I hate. Wednesday is for scrubbing the bathtub real good even though I wipe it down every morning. Thursday is for polishing floors and sucking rugs, minding the antique ones with a hand broom so they don't thread. Friday is heavy cooking for the weekend and what-have-you. And every day is mopping, washing clothes and ironing shirts so they don't go getting out of hand, and generally keeping things clean. Silver and windows, they're as needed. Since there aren't any kids to look after, there's ample time left for Miss Celia's so-called cooking lesson.

Miss Celia never does any entertaining, so we just fix whatever she and Mister Johnny are having for supper: pork chops, fried chicken, roast beef, chicken pie, lamb rack, baked ham, fried tomatoes, mashed potatoes, plus the vegetables. Or at least I cook and Miss Celia fidgets, looking more like a five-year-old than the rich lady paying my rent. When the lesson's over, she rushes back to laying down. In fact, the only time Miss Celia walks ten feet is to come in the kitchen for her lesson or to sneak upstairs every two or three days, up in the creepy rooms.

I don't know what she does for five minutes on the second floor. I don't like it up there though. Those bedrooms should be stacked full of kids laughing and hollering and pooping up the place. But it's none of my business what Miss Celia does with her day, and ask me, I'm glad she's staying out of my way. I've followed ladies around with a broom in one hand and a trash can in the other trying to keep up with their mess. As long as she stays in that bed, then I've got a job. Even though she has zero kids and nothing to do all day, she is the laziest woman I've ever seen. *Including* my sister Doreena who never lifted a royal finger growing up because she had the heart defect that we later found out was a fly on the X-ray machine.

And it's not just the bed. Miss Celia won't leave the *house* except to get her hair frosted and her ends trimmed. So far, that's only happened once in the three weeks I've been working. Thirty-six years old and I can still hear my mama telling me, *It ain't nobody's business.* But I want to know what that lady's so scared of outside this place.

EVERY PAYDAY, I give Miss Celia the count. "Ninety-nine more days till you tell Mister Johnny bout me."

"Golly, the time's going by quick," she'll say with kind of a sick look.

"Cat got on the porch this morning, bout give me a cadillac arrest thinking it was Mister Johnny."

Like me, Miss Celia gets a little more nervous the closer we get to the deadline. I don't know what that man will do when she tells him. Maybe he'll tell her to fire me.

"I hope that's enough time, Minny. Do you think I'm getting any better at cooking?" she says, and I look at her. She's got a pretty smile, white straight teeth, but she is the worst cook I have ever seen.

So I back up and teach her the simplest things because I want her to learn and learn it fast. See, I need her to explain to her husband why a hundred-and-sixty-five-pound Negro woman has keys to his house. I need him to know why I have his sterling silver and Miss Celia's zillion-karat ruby earrings in my hand every day. I *need* him to know this before he walks in one fine day and calls the police. Or saves a dime and takes care of business himself.

"Get the ham hock out, make sure you got enough water in there, that's right. Now turn up the flame. See that little bubble there, that means the water's happy."

Miss Celia stares down into the pot like she's looking for her future. "Are you happy, Minny?"

"Why you ask me funny questions like that?"

"But are you?"

"Course I's happy. You happy too. Big house, big yard, husband looking after you." I frown at Miss Celia and I make sure she can see it. Because ain't that white people for you, wondering if they are happy *enough*.

And when Miss Celia burns the beans, I try and use some of that self-control my mama swore I was born without. "Alright," I say through my teeth, "we'll do another batch fore Mister Johnny get home."

Any other woman I've worked for, I would've loved to have had just one hour of bossing them around, see how they like it. But Miss Celia, the way she stares at me with those big eyes like I'm the best thing since hairspray in the can, I almost rather she'd order me around like she's supposed to. I start to wonder if her laying down all the time has anything to do with her not telling Mister Johnny about me. I guess she can see the suspicious in my eye too, because one day, out of the blue she says:

"I get these nightmares a lot, that I have to go back to Sugar Ditch and live? That's why I lay down so much." Then she nods real fast, like she's been rehearsing this. "Cause I don't sleep real well at night."

I give her a stupid smile, like I really believe this, and go back to wiping the mirrors.

"Don't do it too good. Leave some smudges."

It's always something, mirrors, floors, a dirty glass in the sink or the trash can full. "We've got to make it believable," she'll say and I find myself reaching for that dirty glass a hundred times to wash it. I like things clean, put away.

"I wish I could tend to that azalea bush out there," Miss Celia says one day. She's taken to laying on the couch while my stories are on, interrupting the whole time. I've been tuned in to *The Guiding Light* for twenty-four years, since I was ten years old and listening to it on Mama's radio.

A Dreft commercial comes on and Miss Celia stares out the back window at the colored man raking up the leaves. She's got so many azalea bushes, her yard's going to look like *Gone With the Wind* come spring. I don't like azaleas and I sure didn't like that movie, the way they made slavery look like a big happy tea party. If I'd played Mammy, I'd of told Scarlett to stick those green draperies up her white little pooper. Make her own damn man-catching dress.

"And I know I could make that rose bush bloom if I pruned it back," Miss Celia says. "But the first thing I'd do is cut down that mimosa tree."

"What's wrong with that tree?" I press the corner of my iron into Mister Johnny's collar-point. I don't even have a shrub, much less a tree, in my entire yard.

"I don't like those hairy flowers." She gazes off like she's gone soft in the head. "They look like little baby hairs."

I get the creepers with her talking that way. "You know about flowers?"

She sighs. "I used to love to tend to my flowers back in Sugar Ditch. I learned to grow things hoping I could pretty up all that ugliness."

"Go head outside then," I say, trying not to sound too excited. "Take some exercise. Get some fresh air." *Get out a here.*

"No," Miss Celia sighs. "I shouldn't be running around out there. I need to be still."

It's really starting to irritate me how she never leaves the house, how she smiles like the maid walking in every morning is the best part of her day. It's like an itch. Every day I reach for it and can't quite scratch it. Every day, it itches a little worse. Every day she's *there*.

"Maybe you ought to go make some friends," I say. "Lot a ladies your age in town."

She frowns up at me. "I've been trying. I can't tell you the umpteen times I've called those ladies to see if I can help with the Children's Benefit or do something from home. But they won't call me back. None of them."

I don't say anything to this because ain't that a surprise. With her bosoms hanging out and her hair colored Gold Nugget.

"Go shopping then. Go get you some new clothes. Go do whatever white women do when the maid's home."

"No, I think I'll go rest awhile," she says and two minutes later I hear her creeping around upstairs in the empty bedrooms.

The mimosa branch knocks against the window and I jump, burn my thumb. I squeeze my eyes shut to slow my heart. Ninety-four more days of this mess and I don't know how I can take a minute more.

"Mama, fix me something to eat. I'm hungry." That's what my youngest girl, Kindra, who's five, said to me last night. With a hand on her hip and her foot stuck out.

I have five kids and I take pride that I taught them *yes ma'am* and *please* before they could even say *cookie*.

All except one.

"You ain't having nothing till supper," I told her.

"Why you so mean to me? I *hate* you," she yelled and ran out the door.

I set my eyes on the ceiling because that's a shock I will never get used to, even with four before her. The day your child says she hates you, and every child will go through the phase, it kicks like a foot in the stomach.

But Kindra, Lord. It's not just a phase I'm seeing. That girl is turning out just like me.

I'm standing in Miss Celia's kitchen thinking about last night, what with Kindra and her mouth, Benny and his asthma, my husband Leroy coming home drunk two times last week. He knows that's the one thing I can't stand after nursing my drunk daddy for ten years, me and Mama working ourselves to death so he had a full bottle. I guess I ought to be more upset about all this, but last night, as an *I'm sorry*, Leroy came home with a sack of early okra. He knows it's my favorite thing to eat. Tonight I'm going to fry up that okra in some cornmeal and eat like my mama never let me.

That's not the only treat to my day either. It's October first and here I am peeling peaches. Mister Johnny's mama brought back two crates from Mexico, heavy as baseballs. They are ripe and sweet and like cutting through butter. I don't take charity from white ladies because I *know* they just want me to owe them. But when Miss Celia told me to take a dozen peaches home I pulled out a sack and plopped twelve right in. When I get home tonight, I'm eating fried okra for supper and peach cobbler for dessert.

I'm watching the long, fuzzy peel fold down into Miss Celia's basin, paying no mind at all to the driveway. Usually when I'm standing at her kitchen sink, I map out my getaway from Mister Johnny. The kitchen's the best room for it because the front window looks out to the street. Tall azalea bushes hide my face, but I can see through enough to spot an approacher. If he came in the front door, the back door would escape me into the garage. If he came in the back, I could slip out the front. Another door in the kitchen leads out to the backyard, just in case. But what with the juice running down my hand and me nearabout drunk on the butter smell, I am lost in a peach-peeling reverie. I don't even notice the blue truck pull in.

The man's made it halfway up the walk by the time I look up. I catch a sliver of a white shirt, the variety of which I'm used to ironing every day, and the leg of a pair of khaki pants like I hang up in Mister Johnny's closet. I choke on a yelp. My knife clatters in the sink.

"Miss Celia!" I dash into her bedroom. "Mister Johnny *home*!"

Miss Celia jumps out of bed faster than I've seen her move before. I turn around in an idiot circle. *Where am I going? Which way do I go? What happened to my getaway plan?* And then I snap into decision—the guest bathroom!

I slip in and keep the door cracked. I crouch up on the toilet seat so he can't see my feet under the door. It's dark in here and hot. I feel like my head's on fire. Sweat drips off my chin and splats on the floor. I feel sick by the thick smell of gardenia soaps by the sink.

I hear footsteps. I hold my breath.

The footsteps stop. My heart is thumping like a cat in a clothes dryer. What if Miss Celia pretends she doesn't know me so she won't get in trouble? Acts like I'm a burglar? *Oh, I hate her! I hate that stupid woman!*

I listen, but all I can hear is my own panting. The thud-thud in my chest. My ankles hurt and creak, holding up my body like this.

My eyes grow sharper in the dark. After a minute, I see myself in the mirror over the sink. Crouched like a fool on top of a white lady's toilet.

Look at me. Look what it's come to for Minny Jackson to make a damn living.

MISS SKEETER

CHAPTER 5

I DRIVE MY MAMA'S CADILLAC fast on the gravel road, headed home. Patsy Cline can't even be heard on the radio anymore, for all the rocks banging the side of the car. Mother would be furious, but I just drive faster. I can't stop thinking about what Hilly said to me today at bridge club.

Hilly and Elizabeth and I have been best friends since Power Elementary. My favorite photograph is of the three of us sitting in the football stands in junior high, all jammed together, shoulder to shoulder. What makes the picture, though, is that the stands are completely empty around us. We sat close because we were close.

At Ole Miss, Hilly and I roomed together for two years before she left to get married and I stayed on to graduate. I rolled thirteen curlers in her hair every night at the Chi Omega house. But today, she threatened to throw me out of the League. Not that I care so much about the League, but I was hurt by how easily my friend would be willing to cast me aside.

I turn up the lane that leads to Longleaf, my family's cotton plantation. The gravel quiets to smooth, yellow dust and I slow down before Mother sees how fast I'm driving. I pull up to the house and get out. Mother is rocking on the front porch.

"Come sit, darling," she says, waving me toward a rocking chair beside her. "Pascagoula's just waxed the floors. Let them dry awhile."

"Alright, Mama." I kiss her powdery cheek. But I don't sit. I lean on the porch railing, look out on the three mossy oak trees in the front yard. Even though it's only five minutes outside of town, most people consider this the country out here. Surrounding our yard lie ten thousand acres of Daddy's cotton fields, the plants green and strong, tall as my waist. A few colored men sit under a distant shed, staring into the heat. Everyone is waiting for the same thing, for the cotton bolls to open.

I think about how things are different between Hilly and me, since I came home from school. But who is the different person, her or me?

"Did I tell you?" Mother says. "Fanny Peatrow got engaged."

"Good for Fanny."

"Not even a month after she got that teller job at the Farmer's Bank."

"That's great, Mother."

"*I* know," she says, and I turn to see one of those lightbulb-popping looks of hers. "Why don't you go down to the bank and apply for a teller job?"

"I don't want to be a bank teller, Mama."

Mother sighs, narrows her eyes at the spaniel, Shelby, licking his nether parts. I eye the front door, tempted to ruin the clean floors anyway. We've had this conversation so many times.

"Four years my daughter goes off to college and what does she come home with?" she asks.

"A diploma?"

"A pretty piece of paper," Mother says.

"I told you. I didn't meet anybody I wanted to marry," I say.

Mother rises from her chair, comes close so I'll look her in her smooth, pretty face. She's wearing a navy blue dress, narrow along her slim bones. As usual her lipstick is just so, but when she steps into the bright afternoon sun, I see dark stains, deep and dried, on the front of her clothes. I squint my eyes, trying to see if the stains are really there. "Mama? Are you feeling bad?"

"If you'd just show a little gumption, Eugenia—"

"Your dress is all dirty on the front."

Mother crosses her arms. "Now, I talked to Fanny's mother and she said Fanny was practically swimming in opportunities once she got that job."

I drop the dress issue. I'll never be able to tell Mother I want to be a writer. She'll only turn it into yet another thing that separates me from the married girls. Nor can I tell her about Charles Gray, my math study partner last spring, at Ole Miss. How he'd gotten drunk senior year and kissed me and then squeezed my hand so hard it should've hurt but it didn't, it felt wonderful the way he was holding me and looking into my eyes. And then he married five-foot Jenny Sprig.

What I needed to do was find an apartment in town, the kind of building where single, plain girls lived, spinsters, secretaries, teachers. But the one time I had mentioned using money from my trust fund, Mother had cried—real tears. "That is not what that money's for, Eugenia. To live in some rooming house with strange cooking smells and stockings hanging out the window. And when the money runs out, what then? What will you live on?" Then she'd draped a cold cloth on her head and gone to bed for the day.

And now she's gripping the rail, waiting to see if I'll do what fat Fanny Peatrow did to save herself. My own mother is looking at me as if I completely baffle her mind with my looks, my height, my hair. To say I have frizzy hair is an understatement. It is kinky, more pubic than cranial, and whitish blond, breaking off easily, like hay. My skin is fair and while some call this creamy, it can look downright deathly when I'm serious, which is all the time. Also, there's a slight bump of cartilage along the top of my nose. But my eyes are cornflower blue, like Mother's. I'm told that's my best feature.

"It's all about putting yourself in a man-meeting situation where you can—"

"Mama," I say, just wanting to end this conversation, "would it really be so terrible if I never met a husband?"

Mother clutches her bare arms as if made cold by the thought. "Don't. Don't say that, Eugenia. Why, every week I see another man in town over six feet and I think, *If Eugenia would just try...*" She presses her hand to her stomach, the very thought advancing her ulcers.

I slip off my flats and walk down the front porch steps, while Mother calls out for me to put my shoes back on, threatening ringworm, mosquito encephalitis. The inevitability of death by no shoes. Death by no husband. I shudder with the same left-behind feeling I've had since I graduated from college, three months ago. I've been dropped off in a place I do not belong anymore. Certainly not here with Mother and Daddy, maybe not even with Hilly and Elizabeth.

"...here you are twenty-three years old and I'd already had Carlton Jr. at your age..." Mother says.

I stand under the pink crepe myrtle tree, watching Mother on the porch. The day lilies have lost their blooms. It is nearly September.

I WAS NOT a cute baby. When I was born, my older brother, Carlton, looked at me and declared to the hospital room, "It's not a baby, it's a skeeter!" and from there the name stuck. I was long and leggy and mosquito-thin, a record-breaking twenty-five inches at Baptist Hospital. The name grew even more accurate with my pointy, beak-like nose when I was a child. Mother's spent my entire life trying to convince people to call me by my given name, Eugenia.

Mrs. Charlotte Boudreau Cantrelle Phelan does not like nicknames.

By sixteen I wasn't just not pretty, I was painfully tall. The kind of tall that puts a girl in the back row of class pictures with the boys. The kind of tall where your mother spends her nights taking down hems, yanking at sweater sleeves, flattening your hair for dances you hadn't been asked to, finally pressing the top of your head as if she could shrink you back to the years when she had to remind you to stand up straight. By the time I was seventeen, Mother would rather I suffered from apoplectic diarrhea than stand up straight. She was five-foot-four and first-runner-up as Miss South Carolina. She decided there was only one thing to do in a case like mine.

Mrs. Charlotte Phelan's Guide to Husband-Hunting, Rule Number One: a pretty, petite girl should accentuate with makeup and good posture. A tall plain one, with a trust fund.

I was five-foot-eleven but I had twenty-five thousand cotton dollars in my name and if the beauty in that was not apparent then, by God, he wasn't smart enough to be in the family anyway.

. . .

My childhood bedroom is the top floor of my parents' house. It has white-frosting chair rails and pink cherubs in the molding. It's papered in mint green rosebuds. It is actually the attic with long, sloping walls, and I cannot stand straight in many places. The box bay window makes the room look round. After Mother berates me about finding a husband every other day, I have to sleep in a wedding cake.

And yet, it is my sanctuary. The heat swells and gathers like a hot-air balloon up here, not exactly welcoming others. The stairs are narrow and difficult for parents to climb. Our previous maid, Constantine, used to stare those forward-sloping stairs down every day, like it was a battle between them. That was the only part I didn't like about having the top floor of the house, that it separated me from my Constantine.

Three days after my conversation with Mother on the porch, I spread out the help-wanted ads from the *Jackson Journal* on my desk. All morning, Mother's been following me around with a new hair-straightening thing while Daddy's been on the front porch growling and goddamning the cotton fields because they're melting like summer snow. Besides boll weevils, rain is just about the worst thing that can happen at harvest time. It's hardly September but the fall drenches have already begun.

My red pen in hand, I scan the squat, single column under HELP WANTED: FEMALE.

Kennington's Dept. Str. seeks salesgirls w/poise, manners & a smile!

Trim, young secretary wanted. Typing not nec. Call Mr. Sanders. Jesus, if he doesn't want her to type, what does he want her to do?

Jr. Stenographer wanted, Percy & Gray, LP, $1.25/hr. This is new. I draw a circle around it.

No one could argue that I hadn't worked hard at Ole Miss. While my friends were out drinking rum and Cokes at Phi Delta Theta parties and pinning on mum corsages, I sat in the study parlor and wrote for hours— mostly term papers but also short stories, bad poetry, episodes of *Dr. Kildare*, Pall Mall jingles, letters of complaint, ransom notes, love letters to boys I'd seen in class but hadn't had the nerve to speak to, all of which I never mailed. Sure, I dreamed of having football dates, but my real dream was that one day I would write something that people would actually read.

Fourth term of my senior year, I only applied to one job, but it was a good one, being six hundred miles away from Mississippi. Piling twenty-two dimes in the Oxford Mart pay phone, I'd inquired about an editor position at the Harper & Row publishing house on 33rd Street in Manhattan. I'd seen the ad in *The New York Times* down at the Ole Miss library and mailed them my résumé that very day. On a sprig of hope, I even called about an apartment listing on East 85th Street, a one-bedroom with hot plate for forty-five dollars a month. Delta Airlines told me a one-way ticket to Idlewild Airport would cost seventy-three dollars. I didn't have the sense to apply for more than one job at a time and I never even heard back from them.

My eyes drift down to HELP WANTED: MALE. There are at least four columns filled with bank managers, accountants, loan officers, cotton collate operators. On this side of the page, Percy & Gray, LP, is offering Jr. Stenographers fifty cents more an hour.

"MISS SKEETER, you got a phone call," I hear Pascagoula holler at the bottom of the stairs.

I go downstairs to the only phone in the house. Pascagoula holds the phone out to me. She is as tiny as a child, not even five feet tall, and black as night. Her hair is curly around her head and her white uniform dress has been tailored to fit her short arms and legs.

"Miss Hilly on the phone for you," she says, and hands it to me with a wet hand.

I sit at the white iron table. The kitchen is large and square and hot. Black-and-white linoleum tiles are cracked in places, worn thin in front of the sink. The new silver dishwashing machine sits in the middle of the room, attached to a hose stretched from the faucet.

"He's coming next weekend," Hilly says. "On Saturday night. You free?"

"Gee, let me check my calendar," I say. All traces of our bridge-club argument are gone from Hilly's voice. I'm suspicious but relieved.

"I can't believe this is *finally* going to happen," Hilly says, because she's been trying to set me up for months with her husband's cousin. She's intent on it even though he's much too good-looking for me, not to mention a state senator's son.

"Don't you think we should...meet first?" I ask. "I mean, before we go out on an actual date?"

"Don't be nervous. William and I will be right next to you the whole time."

I sigh. The date's been canceled twice already. I can only hope it'll be put off again. And yet I'm flattered that Hilly has so much faith that someone like him would be interested in someone like me.

"Oh, and I need you to come on by and pick up these notes," Hilly says. "I want my initiative in the next newsletter, a full page next to the photo ops."

I pause. "The bathroom thing?" Even though it was only a few days ago that she'd brought this up at bridge club, I'd hoped it was forgotten.

"It's called the Home Help Sanitation Initiative—*William Junior you get down or I will snatch you baldheaded Yule May get in here*—and I want it in this week."

I am editor of the League newsletter. But Hilly is president. And she's trying to tell me what to print.

"I'll see. I don't know if there's room," I lie.

From the sink, Pascagoula sneaks a look at me, as if she can hear what Hilly's saying. I look over at Constantine's bathroom, now Pascagoula's. It's off the kitchen. The door's half open and I can see a tiny room with a toilet, a pull string flusher at the top, a bulb with a yellowing plastic shade. The small corner sink hardly holds a glass of water. I've never once been inside. When we were kids, Mother told us she'd spank us if we went in Constantine's bathroom. I miss Constantine more than anything I've ever missed in my life.

"Then make room," Hilly says, "because this is pretty darn important."

CONSTANTINE LIVED ABOUT A MILE from our house, in a small Negro neighborhood called Hotstack, named after the tar plant that used to operate back there. The road to Hotstack runs along the north side of our farm, and for as long as I can remember, colored kids have walked and played along that mile stretch, kicking at the red dust, making their way toward the big County Road 49 to catch a ride.

I used to walk that hot mile myself, when I was a girl. If I begged and practiced my catechism, Mother would sometimes let me go home with Constantine on Friday afternoons. After twenty minutes of walking slow, we'd pass the colored five-and-dime store, then a grocer with hens laying in back, and all along the way, dozens of shacky-looking roadside houses with tin roofs and slanting porches, along with a yellow one that everybody said sold whiskey from the back door. It was a thrill to be in such a different world and I'd feel a prickly awareness of how good my shoes were, how clean my white pinafore dress that Constantine had ironed for me. The closer we got to Constantine's house, the more she'd smile.

"Hi-do, Carl Bird," Constantine'd holler at the root-selling man sitting in his rocking chair on the back of his pickup. Bags of sassafras and licorice root and birdeye vine sat open for bargaining, and by the time we poked around those a minute, Constantine's whole body'd be rambling and loose in the joints. Constantine wasn't just tall, she was stout. She was also wide in the hips and her knees gave her trouble all the time. At the stump on her corner, she would stick a pinch of Happy Days snuff in her lip and spit juice straight as an arrow. She'd let me look at the black powder in its round tin, but say, "Don't tell your mama, now."

There were always dogs, hollow-stomached and mangy, laid out in the road. From a porch a young colored woman named Cat-Bite would holler, "Miss Skeeter! Tell your daddy hey for me. Tell him I's doing fine." My own daddy gave her that name years ago. Drove by and saw a rabid cat attacking a little colored girl. "That cat near about ate her up," Daddy'd told me afterward. He'd killed the cat, carried the girl to the doctor, and set her up for the twenty-one days of rabies shots.

A little farther on, we'd get to Constantine's house. It had three rooms and no rugs and I'd look at the single photograph she had, of a white girl she told me she looked after for twenty years over in Port Gibson. I was pretty sure I knew everything about Constantine—she had one sister and grew up on a sharecropping farm in Corinth, Mississippi. Both her parents were dead. She didn't eat pork as a rule and wore a size sixteen dress and a size ten ladies' shoe. But I used to stare at the toothy smile of that child in the picture, a little jealous, wondering why she didn't have a picture of me up too.

Sometimes two girls from next door would come over to play with me, named Mary Nell and Mary Roan. They were so black I couldn't tell them apart and called them both just Mary.

"Be nice to the little colored girls when you're down there," Mother said to me one time and I remember looking at her funny, saying, "Why wouldn't I be?" But Mother never explained.

After an hour or so, Daddy would pull up, get out, hand Constantine a dollar. Not once did Constantine invite him inside. Even back then, I understood we were on Constantine's turf and she didn't have to be nice to anybody at her own house. Afterward, Daddy would let me go in the colored store for a cold drink and sucking candy.

"Don't tell your mama I gave Constantine a little extra, now."

"Okay, Daddy," I'd say. That's about the only secret my daddy and I have ever shared.

THE FIRST TIME I was ever called ugly, I was thirteen. It was a rich friend of my brother Carlton's, over to shoot guns in the field.

"Why you crying, girl?" Constantine asked me in the kitchen.

I told her what the boy had called me, tears streaming down my face.

"Well? Is you?"

I blinked, paused my crying. "Is I what?"

"Now you look a here, Eugenia"—because Constantine was the only one who'd occasionally follow Mama's rule. "Ugly live up on the inside. Ugly be a hurtful, mean person. Is you one a them peoples?"

"I don't know. I don't think so," I sobbed.

Constantine sat down next to me, at the kitchen table. I heard the cracking of her swollen joints. She pressed her thumb hard in the palm of my hand, something we both knew meant *Listen. Listen to me.*

"Ever morning, until you dead in the ground, you gone have to make this decision." Constantine was so close, I could see the blackness of her gums. "You gone have to ask yourself, *Am I gone believe what them fools say about me today?*"

She kept her thumb pressed hard in my hand. I nodded that I understood. I was just smart enough to realize she meant white people. And even though I still felt miserable, and knew that I was, most likely, ugly, it was the first time she ever talked to me like I was something besides my mother's white child. All my life I'd been told what to believe about politics, coloreds, being a girl. But with Constantine's thumb pressed in my hand, I realized I actually had a choice in what I could believe.

CONSTANTINE CAME TO WORK in our house at six in the morning, and at harvest time, she came at five. That way she could fix Daddy his biscuits and gravy before he headed to the field. I woke up nearly every day to her standing in the kitchen, Preacher Green playing on the radio that sat on the kitchen table. The minute she saw me, she smiled. "Good morning, beautiful girl!" I'd sit at the kitchen table and tell her what I'd dreamed. She claimed dreams told the future.

"I was in the attic, looking down at the farm," I'd tell her. "I could see the tops of the trees."

"You gone be a brain surgeon! Top a the house mean the head."

Mother ate her breakfast early in the dining room, then moved to the relaxing room to do needlepoint or write letters to missionaries in Africa. From her green wing chair, she could see everyone going almost anywhere in the house. It was shocking what she could process about my appearance in the split second it took for me to pass by that door. I used to dash by, feeling like a dartboard, a big red bull's-eye that Mother pinged darts at.

"Eugenia, you know there is no chewing gum in this house."

"Eugenia, go put alcohol on that blemish."

"Eugenia, march upstairs and brush your hair down, what if we have an unexpected visitor?"

I learned that socks are stealthier transportation than shoes. I learned to use the back door. I learned to wear hats, cover my face with my hands when I passed by. But mostly, I learned to just stay in the kitchen.

A SUMMER MONTH COULD STRETCH on for years, out on Longleaf. I didn't have friends coming over every day—we lived too far out to have any white neighbors. In town, Hilly and Elizabeth spent all weekend going to and from each other's houses, while I was only allowed to spend the night out or have company every other weekend. I grumbled over this plenty. I took Constantine for granted at times, but I think I knew, for the most part, how lucky I was to have her there.

When I was fourteen, I started smoking cigarettes. I'd sneak them from Carlton's packs of Marlboros he kept in his dresser drawer. He was almost eighteen and no one minded that he'd been smoking for years anywhere he wanted to in the house or out in the fields with Daddy. Sometimes Daddy smoked a pipe, but he wasn't a cigarette man and Mother didn't smoke anything at all, even though most of her friends did. Mother told me I wasn't allowed to smoke until I was seventeen.

So I'd slip into the backyard and sit in the tire swing, with the huge old oak tree concealing me. Or, late at night, I'd hang out of my bedroom window and smoke. Mother had eagle-eyes, but she had almost zero sense of smell. Constantine knew immediately, though. She narrowed her eyes, with a little smile, but said nothing. If Mother headed to the back porch while I was behind the tree, Constantine would rush out and bang her broom handle on the iron stair rail.

"Constantine, what are you doing?" Mother would ask her, but by then I would've stubbed it out and dropped the butt in the hole in the tree.

"Just cleaning this here old broom, Miss Charlotte."

"Well, find a way to do it a little quieter, please. Oh, Eugenia, what, did you grow another inch overnight? What am I going to do? Go…put on a dress that fits."

"Yes ma'am," Constantine and I would say at the same time and then pass each other a little smile.

Oh, it was delicious to have someone to keep secrets with. If I'd had a sister or a brother closer in age, I guessed that's what it would be like. But it wasn't just smoking or skirting around Mother. It was having someone look at you after your mother has nearly fretted herself to death because you are freakishly tall and frizzy and odd. Someone whose eyes simply said, without words, *You are fine with me.*

Still, it wasn't all sweet talk with her. When I was fifteen, a new girl had pointed at me and asked, "Who's the stork?" Even Hilly had tucked back a smile before steering me away, like we hadn't heard her.

"How tall are you, Constantine?" I asked, unable to hide my tears.

Constantine narrowed her eyes at me. "How tall is you?"

"Five-eleven," I cried. "I'm already taller than the boys' basketball coach."

"Well, I'm five-thirteen, so quit feeling sorry for yourself."

Constantine's the only woman I've ever had to look up to, to look her straight in the eye.

What you noticed first about Constantine, besides her tallness, were her eyes. They were light brown, strikingly honey-colored against her dark skin. I've never seen light brown eyes on a colored person. In fact, the shades of brown on Constantine were endless. Her elbows were absolutely black, with a dry white dust on them in the winter. The skin on her arms and neck and face was a dark ebony. The palms of her hands were orangey-tan and that made me wonder if the soles of her feet were too, but I never saw her barefooted.

"Just you and me this weekend," she said with a smile.

It was the weekend that Mother and Daddy were driving Carlton to look at LSU and Tulane. My brother was going to college next year. That morning, Daddy had moved the cot into the kitchen, next to her bathroom. That's where Constantine always slept when she spent the night.

"Go look what I got," she said, pointing to the broom closet. I went and opened it and saw, tucked in her bag, a five-hundred-piece puzzle with a picture of Mount Rushmore on it. It was our favorite thing to do when she stayed over.

That night, we sat for hours, munching on peanuts, sifting through the pieces spread out on the kitchen table. A storm raged outside, making the room cozy while we picked out the edges. The bulb in the kitchen dimmed then brightened again.

"Which one he?" Constantine asked, studying the puzzle box through her black-rimmed glasses.

"That's Jefferson."

"Oh it sure is. What about him?"

"That's—" I leaned over. "I think that's . . . Roosevelt."

"Only one I recognize is Lincoln. He look like my daddy."

I stopped, puzzle piece in hand. I was fourteen and had never made less than an A. I was smart, but I was as naïve as they come. Constantine put the box top down and looked over the pieces again.

"Because your daddy was so . . . tall?" I asked.

She chuckled. "Cause my daddy was white. I got the tall from my mama."

I put the piece down. "Your . . . father was white and your mother was . . . colored?"

"Yup," she said and smiled, snapping two pieces together. "Well, look a there. Got me a match."

I had so many questions—*Who* was he? *Where* was he? I knew he wasn't married to Constantine's mother, because that was against the law. I picked a cigarette from my stash I'd brought to the table. I was fourteen but, feeling very grown up, I lit it. As I did, the overhead light dimmed to a dull, dirty brown, buzzing softly.

"Oh, my daddy looooved me. Always said I was his favorite." She leaned back in her chair. "He used to come over to the house ever Saturday afternoon, and one time, he give me a set a ten hair ribbons, ten different colors. Brought em over from Paris, made out a Japanese silk. I sat in his lap from the minute he got there until he had to leave and Mama'd play Bessie Smith on the Victrola he brung her and he and me'd sing:

It's mighty strange, without a doubt
Nobody knows you when you're down and out

I listened wide-eyed, stupid. Glowing by her voice in the dim light. If chocolate was a sound, it would've been Constantine's voice singing. If singing was a color, it would've been the color of that chocolate.

"One time I was boo-hooing over hard feelings, I reckon I had a list a things to be upset about, being poor, cold baths, rotten tooth, I don't know. But he held me by the head, hugged me to him for the longest time. When I looked up, he was crying too and he...did that thing I do to you so you know I mean it. Press his thumb up in my hand and he say...he sorry."

We sat there, staring at the puzzle pieces. Mother wouldn't want me to know this, that Constantine's father was white, that he'd apologized to her for the way things were. It was something I wasn't supposed to know. I felt like Constantine had given me a gift.

I finished my cigarette, stubbed it out in the silver guest ashtray. The light brightened again. Constantine smiled at me and I smiled back.

"How come you never told me this before?" I said, looking into her light brown eyes.

"I can't tell you ever single thing, Skeeter."

"But why?" She knew everything about me, everything about my family. Why would I ever keep secrets from her?

She stared at me and I saw a deep, bleak sadness there, inside of her. After a while, she said, "Some things I just got to keep for myself."

WHEN IT WAS MY TURN to go off to college, Mother cried her eyes out when Daddy and I pulled away in the truck. But I felt free. I was off the farm, out from under the criticism. I wanted to ask Mother, *Aren't you glad? Aren't you relieved that you don't have to worry-wart over me every day anymore?* But Mother looked miserable.

I was the happiest person in my freshman dorm. I wrote Constantine a letter once a week, telling her about my room, the classes, the sorority. I had to mail her letters to the farm since the post didn't deliver to Hotstack and I had to trust that Mother wouldn't open them. Twice a month, Constantine wrote me back on parchment paper that folded into an envelope. Her handwriting was large and lovely, although it ran at a crooked angle down the page. She wrote me every mundane detail of Longleaf: *My back pains are bad but it's my feet that are worse,* or *The mixer broke off from the bowl and flew wild around the kitchen and the cat hollered and ran off. I haven't seen her since.* She'd tell me that Daddy had a chest cold or that Rosa Parks was coming to her church to speak. Often she demanded to know if I was happy and the details of this. Our letters were like a yearlong conversation, answering questions back and forth, continuing face-to-face at Christmas or between summer school sessions.

Mother's letters said, *Say your prayers* and *Don't wear heels because they make you too tall* clipped to a check for thirty-five dollars.

In April of my senior year, a letter came from Constantine that said, *I have a surprise for you, Skeeter. I am so excited I almost can't stand myself. And don't you go asking me about it neither. You will see for yourself when you come home.*

That was close to final exams, with graduation only a month away. And that was the last letter I ever got from Constantine.

I SKIPPED MY GRADUATION CEREMONY at Ole Miss. All my close friends had dropped out to get married and I didn't see the point in making Mama and Daddy drive three hours just to watch me walk across a stage, when what Mother really wanted was to watch me walk down the aisle. I still hadn't heard from Harper & Row, so instead of buying a plane ticket to New York, I rode home to Jackson in sophomore Kay Turner's Buick, squeezed in the front with my typewriter at my feet and her wedding dress between us. Kay Turner was marrying Percy Stanhope next month. For three hours I listened to her worry about cake flavors.

When I got home, Mother stepped back to get a better look at me. "Well, your skin looks beautiful," she said, "but your hair..." She sighed, shook her head.

"Where's Constantine?" I asked. "In the kitchen?"

And like she was delivering the weather, Mother said, "Constantine is no longer employed here. Now let's get all these trunks unpacked before you ruin your clothes."

I turned and blinked at her. I didn't think I'd heard her correctly. "What did you say?"

Mother stood straighter, smoothing down her dress. "Constantine's gone, Skeeter. She went to live with her people up in Chicago."

"But...what? She didn't say anything in her letters about Chicago." I knew that wasn't her surprise. She would've told me such terrible news immediately.

Mother took a deep breath, straightened her back. "I told Constantine she wasn't to write to you about leaving. Not in the middle of your final exams. What if you'd flunked and had to stay on another year? God knows, four years of college is more than enough."

"And she...agreed to that? Not to write me and tell me she was leaving?"

Mother looked off, sighed. "We'll discuss it later, Eugenia. Come on to the kitchen, let me introduce you to the new maid, Pascagoula."

But I didn't follow Mother to the kitchen. I stared down at my college trunks, terrified by the thought of unpacking here. The house felt vast, empty. Outside, a combine whirred in a cotton field.

By September, not only had I given up hope of ever hearing back from Harper & Row, I gave up on ever finding Constantine. No one seemed to know a thing or how I could reach her. I finally stopped asking people why Constantine had left. It was like she'd simply disappeared. I had to accept that Constantine, my one true ally, had left me to fend for myself with these people.

CHAPTER 6

O N A HOT SEPTEMBER MORNING, I wake up in my childhood bed, slip on the huarache shoes my brother, Carlton, brought me back from Mexico. A man's pair since, evidently, Mexican girls' feet don't grow to size nine-and-a-half. Mother hates them and says they're trashy-looking.

Over my nightgown, I put on one of Daddy's old button-down shirts and slip out the front door. Mother is on the back porch with Pascagoula and Jameso while they shuck oysters.

"You cannot leave a Negro and a Nigra together unchaperoned," Mother'd whispered to me, a long time ago. "It's not their fault, they just can't help it."

I head down the steps to see if my mail-order copy of *Catcher in the Rye* is in the box. I always order the banned books from a black market dealer in California, figuring if the State of Mississippi banned them, they must be good. By the time I reach the end of the drive, my huaraches and ankles are covered with fine yellow dust.

On either side of me, the cotton fields are a glaring green, fat with bolls. Daddy lost the back fields to the rain last month, but the majority bloomed unharmed. The leaves are just starting to spot brown with defoliant and I can still smell the sour chemical in the air. There are no cars on the County Road. I open the mailbox.

And there, underneath Mother's *Ladies' Home Journal*, is a letter addressed to Miss Eugenia Phelan. The red raised font in the corner says Harper & Row, Publishers. I tear it open right there in the lane, in nothing but my long nightgown and Daddy's old Brooks Brothers shirt.

September 4, 1962

Dear Miss Phelan,

I am responding personally to your résumé because I found it admirable that a young lady with absolutely no work experience would apply for an editing job at a publisher as prestigious as ours. A minimum of five years in the business is mandatory for such a job. You'd know this if you'd done any amount of research on the business.

Having once been an ambitious young lady myself, however, I've decided to offer you some advice: go to your local newspaper and get an entry-level job. You included in your letter that you "immensely enjoy writing." When you're not making mimeographs or fixing your boss's coffee, look around, investigate, and write. *Don't waste your time on the obvious things. Write about what disturbs you, particularly if it bothers no one else.*

Yours sincerely,

Elaine Stein, Senior Editor, Adult Book Division

Below the pica type is a handwritten note, in a choppy blue scrawl:

P.S. If you are truly serious, I'd be willing to look over your best *ideas and give my opinion. I offer this for no better reason, Miss Phelan, than someone once did it for me.*

A truck full of cotton rumbles by on the County Road. The Negro in the passenger side leans out and stares. I've forgotten I am a white girl in a thin nightgown. I have just received correspondence, maybe even encouragement, from New York City and I say the name aloud: "Elaine Stein." I've never met a Jewish person.

I race back up the lane, trying to keep the letter from flapping in my hand. I don't want it wrinkled. I dash up the stairs with Mother hollering to take off those tacky Mexican man shoes, and I get to work writing down every goddamn thing that bothers me in life, particularly those that do not seem to faze anyone else. Elaine Stein's words are running hot silver through my veins and I type as fast as I can. Turns out, it is a spectacularly long list.

By the next day, I am ready to mail my first letter to Elaine Stein, listing the ideas I thought worthy journalism material: the prevalence of illiteracy in Mississippi; the high number of drunk-driving accidents in our county; the limited job opportunities for women.

It's not until after I mail the letter that I realize I probably chose those ideas she would think impressive, rather than ones I was really interested in.

I TAKE A DEEP BREATH and pull open the heavy glass door. A feminine little bell tinkles hello. A not-so-feminine receptionist watches me. She is enormous and looks uncomfortable in the small wooden chair. "Welcome to the *Jackson Journal*. Can I help you?"

I had made my appointment day before yesterday, hardly an hour after I'd received Elaine Stein's letter. I asked for an interview for any position they might have. I was surprised they said they'd see me so soon.

"I'm here to see Mister Golden, please."

The receptionist waddles to the back in her tented dress. I try and calm my shaking hands. I peek through the open door to a small, wood-paneled room in the back. Inside, four men in suits bang away on typewriters and scratch with pencils. They are bent over, haggard, three with just a horseshoe of hair left. The room is gauzy with cigarette smoke.

The receptionist reappears, thumbs me to follow her, cigarette dangling in her hand. "Come on back." Despite my nerves, all I can think of is the old college rule, *A Chi Omega never walks with a cigarette.* I follow her through the desks of staring men, the haze of smoke, to an interior office.

"Close that thing back," Mister Golden hollers as soon as I've opened the door and stepped in. "Don't let all that damn smoke in here."

Mister Golden stands up behind his desk. He's about six inches shorter than me, trim, younger than my parents. He has long teeth and a sneer, the greased black hair of a mean man.

"Didn't you hear?" he said. "They announced last week cigarettes'll kill you."

"I hadn't heard that." I can only hope it hadn't been on the front page of his newspaper.

"Hell, I know niggers a hundred years old look younger than those idjits out there." He sits back down, but I keep standing because there are no other chairs in the room.

"Alright, let's see what you got." I hand him my résumé and sample articles I'd written in school. I grew up with the *Journal* sitting on our kitchen table, open to the farm report or the local sports page. I rarely had time to read it myself.

Mister Golden doesn't just look at my papers, he edits them with a red pencil. "Murrah High editor three years, *Rebel Rouser* editor two years, Chi Omega editor three years, double major English and journalism, graduated number four...*Damn*, girl," he mutters, "didn't you have *any* fun?"

I clear my throat. "Is...that important?"

He looks up at me. "You're peculiarly tall but I'd think a pretty girl like you'd be dating the whole goddamn basketball team."

I stare at him, not sure if he's making fun of me or paying me a compliment.

"I assume you know how to clean..." He looks back to my articles, strikes them with violent red marks.

My face flushes hot and quick. "Clean? I'm not here to clean. I'm here to *write*."

Cigarette smoke is bleeding under the door. It's like the entire place is on fire. I feel so stupid that I thought I could just walk in and get a job as a journalist.

He sighs heavily, hands me a thick folder of papers. "I guess you'll do. Miss Myrna's gone shit-house crazy on us, drunk hair spray or something. Read the articles, write the answers like she does, nobody'll know the damn difference."

"I...what?" And I take the folder because I don't know what else to do.

I have no idea who this Miss Myrna is. I ask the only safe question I can think of. "How much...did you say it pays?"

He gives me a surprisingly appreciative look, from my flat shoes to my flat hairstyle. Some dormant instinct tells me to smile, run my hand through my hair. I feel ridiculous, but I do it.

"Eight dollars, every Monday."

I nod, trying to figure out how to ask him what the job is without giving myself away.

He leans forward. "You do know who Miss Myrna is, don't you?"

"Of course. We...girls read her all the time," I say, and again we stare at each other long enough for a distant telephone to ring three times.

"What then? Eight's not enough? Jesus, woman, go clean your husband's toilet for free."

I bite my lip. But before I can utter anything, he rolls his eyes.

"Alright, *ten*. Copy's due on Thursdays. And if I don't like your style, I'm not printing it or paying you squat."

I take the folder, thank him more than I probably should. He ignores me and picks up his phone and makes a call before I'm even out the door. When I get to my car, I sink down into the soft Cadillac leather. I sit there smiling, reading the pages in the folder.

I just got a *job*.

I come home standing up straighter than I have since I was twelve, before my growth spurt. I am buzzing with pride. Even though every cell in my brain says do not, somehow I cannot resist telling Mother. I rush into the relaxing room and tell her everything about how I've gotten a job writing Miss Myrna, the weekly cleaning advice column.

"Oh the irony of it." She lets out a sigh that means life is hardly worth living under such conditions. Pascagoula freshens her iced tea.

"At least it's a start," I say.

"A start at what? Giving advice on how to keep up a home when..." She sighs again, long and slow like a deflating tire.

I look away, wondering if everyone in town will be thinking the same thing. Already the joy is fleeting.

"Eugenia, you don't even know how to polish silver, much less advise on how to keep a house clean."

I hug the folder to my chest. She's right, I won't know how to answer any of the questions. Still, I thought she'd at least be proud of me.

"And you will never meet anybody sitting at that typewriter. Eugenia, have some sense."

Anger works its way up my arms. I stand up straight again. "You think I *want* to live here? With *you?*" I laugh in a way I'm hoping will hurt her.

I see the quick pain in her eyes. She presses her lips together at the sting. Still, I have no desire to take back my words because finally, *finally*, I have said something she's listening to.

I stand there, refusing to leave. I want to hear what she'll say to this. I want to hear her say she's sorry.

"I need to...ask you something, Eugenia." She twists her handkerchief, grimaces. "I read the other day about how some...some girls get unbalanced, start thinking these—well, these un*natural* thoughts."

I have no idea what she's talking about. I look up at the ceiling fan. Someone's set it going too fast. *Clackety-clackety-clackety...*

"Are you...do you...find men attractive? Are you having unnatural thoughts about..." She shuts her eyes tight. "Girls or—or women?"

I stare at her, wishing the ceiling fan would fly from its post, crash down on us both.

"Because it said in this article there's a cure, a special root tea—"

"Mother," I say, shutting my eyes tight. "I want to be with girls as much as you'd like to be with...*Jameso*." I head for the door. But I glance behind me. "I mean, unless, of course, you do?"

Mother straightens, gasps. I pound up the stairs.

THE NEXT DAY, I stack the Miss Myrna letters in a neat pile. I have thirty-five dollars in my purse, the monthly allowance Mother still gives me. I go downstairs wearing a thick Christian smile. Living at home, whenever I want to leave Longleaf, I have to ask Mother if I can borrow her car. Which means she'll ask where I'm going. Which means I have to lie to her on a daily basis, which is in itself enjoyable but a little degrading at the same time.

"I'm going down to the church, see if they need any help getting ready for Sunday school."

"Oh, darling, that's just wonderful. Take your time with the car."

I decided, last night, what I need is a professional to help me with the column. My first idea was to ask Pascagoula, but I hardly know her. Plus I couldn't stand the thought of Mother nosing around, criticizing me all over again. Hilly's maid, Yule May, is so shy I doubt she'd want to help me. The only other maid I see often enough is Elizabeth's maid, Aibileen. Aibileen reminds me of Constantine in a way. Plus she's older and seems to have plenty of experience.

On my way to Elizabeth's, I go by the Ben Franklin store and buy a clipboard, a box of number two pencils, a blue-cloth notebook. My first column is due tomorrow, on Mister Golden's desk by two o'clock.

"Skeeter, come on in." Elizabeth opens her own front door and I fear Aibileen might not be working today. She has on a blue bathrobe and jumbo-sized rollers, making her head look huge, her body even more waif-like than it is. Elizabeth generally has rollers in all day, can never get her thin hair full enough.

"Sorry I'm such a mess. Mae Mobley kept me up half the night and now I don't even know where Aibileen's gotten off to."

I step inside the tiny foyer. It's a low-ceilinged house with small rooms. Everything has a secondhand look—the faded blue floral curtains, the crooked cover on the couch. I hear Raleigh's new accounting business isn't doing well. Maybe up in New York or somewhere it's a good thing, but in Jackson, Mississippi, people just don't care to do business with a rude, condescending asshole.

Hilly's car is out front, but she's nowhere to be seen. Elizabeth sits at the sewing machine she has on the dining room table. "I'm almost done," she says. "Let me just hem this last seam…" Elizabeth stands, holds up a green church dress with a round white collar. "Now be honest," she whispers with eyes that are pleading for me to be anything but. "Does it look homemade?"

The hem on one side hangs longer than the other. It's wrinkled and a cuff is already fraying. "One hundred percent store-bought. Straight from Maison Blanche's," I say because that is Elizabeth's dream store. It is five stories of expensive clothes on Canal Street in New Orleans, clothes that could never be found in Jackson. Elizabeth gives me a grateful smile.

"Mae Mobley's sleeping?" I ask.

"Finally." Elizabeth fiddles with a clump of hair that's slipped out of her roller, grimaces at its obstinacy. Sometimes her voice takes on a hard edge when she talks about her little girl.

The door to the guest bathroom in the hall opens and Hilly comes out talking, "...so much better. Everybody has their own place to go now."

Elizabeth fiddles with the machine needle, seems worried by it.

"You tell Raleigh I said *You are welcome*," Hilly adds, and it hits me, then, what's being said. Aibileen has her own bathroom in the garage now.

Hilly smiles at me and I realize she's about to bring up the initiative. "How's your mama?" I ask, even though I know this is her least favorite subject. "She get settled in the home alright?"

"I guess." Hilly pulls her red sweater down over the pudgy roll in her waist. She has on red-and-green plaid pants that seem to magnify her bottom, making it rounder and more forceful than ever. "Of course she doesn't appreciate a thing I do. I had to fire that maid for her, caught her trying to steal the damn silver right under my nose." Hilly narrows her eyes a bit. "Y'all haven't heard, by the way, if that Minny Jackson is working somewhere, have you?"

We shake our heads no.

"I doubt she'll find work in this town again," Elizabeth says.

Hilly nods, mulling this over. I take a deep breath, anxious to tell them my news.

"I just got a job at the *Jackson Journal*," I say.

There is quiet in the room. Suddenly Elizabeth squeals. Hilly smiles at me with such pride, I blush and shrug, like it's not that big of a deal.

"They'd be a fool not to hire you, Skeeter Phelan," Hilly says and raises her iced tea as a toast.

"So...um, have either of y'all actually read Miss Myrna?" I ask.

"Well no," Hilly says. "But I bet the poor white trash girls in South Jackson read it like the King James."

Elizabeth nods. "All those poor girls without help, I bet they do."

"Would you mind if I talked to Aibileen?" I ask Elizabeth. "To help me answer some of the letters?"

Elizabeth is very still a second. "Aibileen? *My* Aibileen?"

"*I* sure don't know the answers to these questions."

"Well...I mean, as long as it doesn't interfere with her work."

I pause, surprised by this attitude. But I remind myself that Elizabeth is paying her, after all.

"And not today with Mae Mobley about to get up or else I'll have to look after her myself."

"Okay. Maybe...maybe I'll come by tomorrow morning then?" I count the hours on my hand. If I finish talking to Aibileen by midmorning, I'll have time to rush home to type it up, then get it back to town by two.

Elizabeth frowns down at her spool of green thread. "And only for a few minutes. Tomorrow's silver-polishing day."

"It won't be long, I promise," I say.

Elizabeth is starting to sound just like my mother.

THE NEXT MORNING AT TEN, Elizabeth opens her door, nods at me like a schoolteacher. "Alright. Go on in. And not too long now. Mae Mobley'll be waking up any time."

I walk into the kitchen, my notebook and papers under my arm. Aibileen smiles at me from the sink, her gold tooth shining. She's a little plump in the middle, but it is a friendly softness. And she's much shorter than me, because who isn't? Her skin is dark brown and shiny against her starchy white uniform. Her eyebrows are gray even though her hair is black.

"Hey, Miss Skeeter. Miss Leefolt still at the machine?"

"Yes." It's strange, even after all these months home, to hear Elizabeth being called Miss Leefolt—not Miss Elizabeth or even her maiden name, Miss Fredericks.

"May I?" I point to the refrigerator. But before I can help myself, Aibileen's opened it for me.

"What you want? A Co-Cola?"

I nod and she pops the cap off with the opener mounted on the counter, pours it into a glass.

"Aibileen"—I take a deep breath—"I was wondering if I could get your help on something." I tell her about the column then, grateful when she nods that she knows who Miss Myrna is.

"So maybe I could read you some of the letters and you could...help me with the answers. After a while, maybe I'll catch on and..." I stop. There is no way I'll ever be able to answer cleaning questions myself. Honestly, I have no intention of learning how to clean. "It sounds unfair, doesn't it, me taking your answers and acting like they're mine. Or Myrna's, I mean." I sigh.

Aibileen shakes her head. "I don't mind that. I just ain't so sure Miss Leefolt gone approve."

"She said it was alright."

"During my regular hours working?"

I nod, remembering the propriety in Elizabeth's voice.

"Alright then." Aibileen shrugs. She looks up at the clock above the sink. "I probably have to stop when Mae Mobley gets up."

"Should we sit?" I point to the kitchen table.

Aibileen glances at the swinging door. "You go head, I'm fine standing."

I spent last night reading every Miss Myrna article from the previous five years, but I haven't had time to sort through the unanswered letters yet. I straighten my clipboard, pencil in hand. "Here's a letter from Rankin County.

"'Dear Miss Myrna,'" I read, "'how do I remove the rings from my fat slovenly husband's shirt collar when he is such a pig and...and sweats like one too...'"

Wonderful. A column on cleaning and relationships. *Two* things I know absolutely nothing about.

"Which one she want a get rid of?" Aibileen asks. "The rings or the husband?"

I stare at the page. I wouldn't know how to instruct her to do either one.

"Tell her a vinegar and Pine-Sol soak. Then let it set in the sun a little while."

I write it quickly on my pad. "Sit in the sun for how long?"

"Bout an hour. Let it dry."

I pull out the next letter and, just as quickly, she answers it. After four or five, I exhale, relieved.

"Thank you, Aibileen. You have no idea how much this helps."

"Ain't no trouble. Long as Miss Leefolt don't need me."

I gather up my papers and take a last sip of my Coke, letting myself relax for five seconds before I have to go write the article. Aibileen picks through a sack of green fiddleheads. The room is quiet except for the radio playing softly, Preacher Green again.

"How did you know Constantine? Were you related?"

"We...in the same church circle." Aibileen shifts her feet in front of the sink.

I feel what has become a familiar sting. "She didn't even leave an address. I just—I can't believe she quit like that."

Aibileen keeps her eyes down. She seems to be studying the fiddleheads very carefully. "No, I'm right sure she was let go."

"No, Mama said she quit. Back in April. Went to live up in Chicago with her people."

Aibileen picks up another fiddlehead, starts washing its long stem, the curly green ends. "No ma'am," she says after a pause.

It takes me a few seconds to realize what we're talking about here.

"Aibileen," I say, trying to catch her eye. "You really think Constantine was fired?"

But Aibileen's face has gone blank as the blue sky. "I must be misrememoring," she says and I can tell she thinks she's said too much to a white woman.

We hear Mae Mobley calling out and Aibileen excuses herself and heads through the swinging door. A few seconds pass before I have the sense to go home.

WHEN I WALK IN THE HOUSE ten minutes later, Mother is reading at the dining room table.

"Mother," I say, clutching my notebook to my chest, "did you *fire* Constantine?"

"Did I . . . *what*?" Mother asks. But I know she's heard me because she's set the DAR newsletter down. It takes a hard question to pull her eyes off that riveting material.

"Eugenia, I told you, her sister was sick so she went up to Chicago to live with her people," she says. "Why? Who told you different?"

I would never in a million years tell her it was Aibileen. "I heard it this afternoon. In town."

"Who would talk about such a thing?" Mother narrows her eyes behind her reading glasses. "It must've been one of the other Nigras."

"What did you *do* to her, Mother?"

Mother licks her lips, gives me a good, long look over her bifocals. "You wouldn't understand, Eugenia. Not until you've hired help of your own."

"You . . . *fired* her? For what?"

"It doesn't matter. It's behind me now and I just won't think about it another minute."

"Mother, she raised me. You tell me right now what happened!" I'm disgusted by the squeakiness of my voice, the childish sound of my demands.

Mother raises her eyebrows at my tone, takes her glasses off. "It was nothing but a colored thing. And that's all I'm saying." She puts her glasses back on and lifts her DAR sheet to her eyes.

I'm shaking, I'm so mad. I pound my way up the stairs. I sit at my typewriter, stunned that my mother could cast off someone who'd done her the biggest favor of her life, raise her children, teach me kindness and self-respect. I stare across my room at the rose wallpaper, the eyelet curtains, the yellowing photographs so familiar they are nearly contemptible. Constantine worked for our family for twenty-nine years.

FOR THE NEXT WEEK, Daddy rises before dawn. I wake to truck motors, the chug of the combines starting, the hollers to hurry. The fields are brown and crisp with dead cotton stalks, defoliated so the machines can get to the bolls. Cotton harvest is here.

Daddy doesn't even stop for church during harvest time, but on Sunday night, I catch him in the dusky hall, between his supper and sleep. "Daddy?" I ask. "Will you tell me what happened to Constantine?"

He is so dog-tired, he sighs before he answers.

"How could Mother fire her, Daddy?"

"What? Darlin', Constantine quit. You know your mother would never fire her." He looks disappointed in me for asking such a thing.

"Do you know where she went? Or have her address?"

He shakes his head no. "Ask your mama, she'll know." He pats my shoulder. "People move on, Skeeter. But I wish she'd stayed down here with us."

He wanders down the hall to bed. He is too honest a man to hide things so I know he doesn't have any more facts about it than I do.

That week and every week, sometimes twice, I stop by Elizabeth's to talk to Aibileen. Each time, Elizabeth looks a little warier. The longer I stay in the kitchen, the more chores Elizabeth comes up with until I leave: the doorknobs need polishing, the top of the refrigerator needs dusting, Mae Mobley's fingernails could use a trim. Aibileen is no more than cordial with me, nervous, stands at the kitchen sink and never stops working. It's not long before I am ahead of copy and Mister Golden seems pleased with the column, the first two of which only took me about twenty minutes to write.

And every week, I ask Aibileen about Constantine. Can't she get her address for me? Can't she tell me anything about why she got fired? Was there a big to-do, because I just can't imagine Constantine saying *yes ma'am* and walking out the back door. Mama'd get cross with her about a tarnished spoon and Constantine would serve her toast burned up for a week. I can only imagine how a firing would've gone.

It hardly matters, though, because all Aibileen will do is shrug at me, say she don't know nothing.

One afternoon, after asking Aibileen how to get out tough tub rings (never having scrubbed a bathtub in my life), I come home. I walk past the relaxing room. The television set is on and I glance at it. Pascagoula's standing about five inches away from the screen. I hear the words *Ole Miss* and on the fuzzy screen I see white men in dark suits crowding the camera, sweat running off their bald heads. I come closer and see a Negro man, about my age, standing in the middle of the white men, with Army men behind him. The picture pans back and there is my old administration building. Governor Ross Barnett stands with his arms crossed, looking the tall Negro in the eye. Next to the governor is our Senator Whitworth, whose son Hilly's been trying to set me up with on a blind date.

I watch the television, riveted. Yet I am neither thrilled nor disappointed by the news that they might let a colored man into Ole Miss, just surprised. Pascagoula, though, is breathing so loud I can hear her. She stands stock-still, not aware I am behind her. Roger Sticker, our local reporter, is nervous, smiling, talking fast. "President Kennedy has ordered the governor to step aside for James Meredith, I repeat, the President of the United—"

"Eugenia, Pascagoula! Turn that set off right this minute!"

Pascagoula jerks around to see me and Mother. She rushes out of the room, her eyes to the floor.

"Now, I won't have it, Eugenia," Mother whispers. "I won't have you encouraging them like that."

"Encouraging? It's nationwide news, Mama."

Mother sniffs. "It is not appropriate for the two of you to watch together," and she flips the channel, stops on an afternoon rerun of Lawrence Welk. "Look, isn't this so much nicer?"

ON A HOT SATURDAY in late September, the cotton fields chopped and empty, Daddy carries a new RCA color television set into the house. He moves the black-and-white one to the kitchen. Smiling and proud, he plugs the new TV into the wall of the relaxing room. The Ole Miss versus LSU football game blares through the house for the rest of the afternoon.

Mama, of course, is glued to the color picture, oohing and aahing at the vibrant reds and blues of the team. She and Daddy live by Rebel football. She's dressed up in red wool pants despite the sweltering heat and has Daddy's old Kappa Alpha blanket draped on the chair. No one mentions James Meredith, the colored student they let in.

I take the Cadillac and head into town. Mother finds it inexplicable that I don't want to watch my alma mater throw a ball around. But Elizabeth and her family are at Hilly's watching the game so Aibileen's working in the house alone. I'm hoping it'll be a little easier on Aibileen if Elizabeth's not there. Truth is, I'm hoping she'll tell me something, anything, about Constantine.

Aibileen lets me in and I follow her back to the kitchen. She seems only the smallest bit more relaxed in Elizabeth's empty house. She eyes the kitchen table, like she wants to sit today. But when I ask her, she answers, "No, I'm fine. You go head." She takes a tomato from a pan in the sink and starts to peel it with a knife.

So I lean against the counter and present the latest conundrum: how to keep the dogs from getting into your trashcans outside. Because your lazy husband forgets to put it out on the right pick-up day. Since he drinks all that damn beer.

"Just pour some pneumonia in that garbage. Dogs won't so much as wink at them cans." I jot it down, amending it to ammonia, and pick out the next letter. When I look up, Aibileen's kind of smiling at me.

"I don't mean nothing disrespectful, Miss Skeeter, but...ain't it kind a strange you being the new Miss Myrna when you don't know nothing about housekeeping?"

She didn't say it the way Mother did, a month ago. I find myself laughing instead, and I tell her what I've told no one else, about the phone calls and the résumé I'd sent to Harper & Row. That I want to be a writer. The advice I received from Elaine Stein. It's nice to tell somebody.

Aibileen nods, turns her knife around another soft red tomato. "My boy Treelore, he like to write."

"I didn't know you had a son."

"He dead. Two years now."

"Oh, I'm so sorry," I say and for a moment it's just Preacher Green in the room, the soft pat of tomato skins against the sink.

"Made straight As on ever English test he take. Then later, when he grown, he pick himself up a typewriter and start working on a idea..." The pin-tucked shoulders of her uniform slump down. "Say he gone write himself a book."

"What kind of idea?" I ask. "I mean, if you don't mind telling..."

Aibileen says nothing for a while. Keeps peeling tomatoes around and around. "He read this book call *Invisible Man*. When he done, he say he gone write down what it was like to be colored working for a white man in Mississippi."

I look away, knowing this is where my mother would stop the conversation. This is where she'd smile and change the subject to the price of silver polish or white rice.

"I read *Invisible Man*, too, after he did," Aibileen says. "I liked it alright."

I nod, even though I've never read it. I hadn't thought of Aibileen as a reader before.

"He wrote almost fifty pages," she says. "I let his girl Frances keep hold of em."

Aibileen stops peeling. I see her throat move when she swallows. "Please don't tell nobody that," she says, softer now, "him wanting to write about his white boss." She bites her lip and it strikes me then that she's still afraid for him. Even though he's dead, the instinct to be afraid for her son is still there.

"It's fine that you told me, Aibileen. I think it was...a brave idea."

Aibileen holds my gaze for a moment. Then she picks up another tomato and sets the knife against the skin. I watch, wait for the red juice to spill. But Aibileen stops before she cuts, glances at the kitchen door.

"I don't think it's fair, you not knowing what happen to Constantine. I just—I'm sorry, I don't feel right talking to you about it."

I stay quiet, not sure what's spurred this, not wanting to ruin it.

"I'll tell you though, it was something to do with her daughter. Coming to see your mama."

"Daughter? Constantine never told me she had a daughter." I knew Constantine for twenty-three years. Why would she keep this from me?

"It was hard for her. The baby come out real . . . pale."

I hold still, remembering what Constantine told me, years ago. "You mean, light? Like . . . white?"

Aibileen nods, keeping at her task in the sink. "Had to send her away, up north I think."

"Constantine's father was white," I say. "Oh . . . Aibileen . . . you don't think . . ." An ugly thought is running through my head. I am too shocked to finish my sentence.

Aibileen shakes her head. "No no, no ma'am. Not . . . that. Constantine's man, Connor, he was colored. But since Constantine had her daddy's blood in her, her baby come out a high yellow. It . . . happens."

I feel ashamed for having thought the worst. Still, I don't understand. "Why didn't Constantine ever tell me?" I ask, not really expecting an answer. "Why would she send her away?"

Aibileen nods to herself, like she understands. But I don't. "That was the worst off I ever seen her. Constantine must a said a thousand times, she couldn't wait for the day when she got her back."

"You said the daughter, she had something to do with Constantine getting fired? What happened?"

At this, Aibileen's face goes blank. The curtain has drawn. She nods toward the Miss Myrna letters, making it clear that's all she's willing to say. At least right now.

THAT AFTERNOON, I stop by Hilly's football party. The street is lined with station wagons and long Buicks. I force myself through the door, knowing I'll be the only single one there. Inside, the living room is full of couples on the sofas, the chaises, the arms of chairs. Wives sit straight with their legs crossed, while husbands lean forward. All eyes are on the wooden television set. I stand in the back, exchange a few smiles, silent hellos. Except for the announcer, the room is quiet.

"*Whoooooooa!*" they all yell and hands fly in the air and women stand and clap and clap. I chew at my cuticle.

"That's it, Rebels! You show those Tigers!"

"Go, Rebels!" cheers Mary Frances Truly, jumping up and down in her matching sweater set. I look at my nail where my cuticle hangs off, stinging and pink. The room is thick with bourbon-smell and red wool and diamond rings. I wonder if the girls really care about football, or if they just act this way to impress their husbands. In my four months of being in the League, I've never once had a girl ask me, "How bout them Rebs?"

I chat my way through some couples until I make it to the kitchen. Hilly's tall, thin maid, Yule May, is folding dough around tiny sausages. Another colored girl, younger, washes dishes at the sink. Hilly waves me over, where she's talking to Deena Doran.

"...best darn petit four I've ever tasted! Deena, you might be the most talented cook in the League!" Hilly stuffs the rest of the cake in her mouth, nodding and mm-mming.

"Why, thank you, Hilly, they're hard but I think they're worth it." Deena is beaming, looks like she might cry under Hilly's adoration.

"So you'll do it? Oh, I'm so glad. The bake sale committee *really* needs somebody like you."

"And how many did you need?"

"Five hundred, by tomorrow afternoon."

Deena's smile freezes. "Okay. I guess I can...work through the night."

"Skeeter, you made it," Hilly says and Deena wanders out of the kitchen.

"I can't stay long," I say, probably too quickly.

"Well, I found out." Hilly smirks. "He is definitely coming this time. Three weeks from today."

I watch Yule May's long fingers pinch the dough off a knife and I sigh, knowing right away who she means. "I don't know, Hilly. You've tried so many times. Maybe it's a sign." Last month, when he'd canceled the day before the date, I'd actually allowed myself a bit of excitement. I don't really feel like going through that again.

"What? Don't you dare say that."

"Hilly," I clench my teeth, because it's time I finally just said it, "you know I won't be his type."

"Look at me," she says. And I do as I'm told. Because that is what we do around Hilly.

"Hilly, you can't make me go—"

"It is *your time*, Skeeter." She reaches over and squeezes my hand, presses her thumb and fingers down as hard as Constantine ever did. "It is your turn. And damn it, I'm not going to let you miss this just because your mother convinced you you're not good enough for somebody like him."

I'm stung by her bitter, true words. And yet, I am awed by my friend, by her tenacity for me. Hilly and I've always been uncompromisingly honest with each other, even about the little things. With other people, Hilly hands out lies like the Presbyterians hand out guilt, but it's our own silent agreement, this strict honesty, perhaps the one thing that has kept us friends.

Elizabeth comes in the kitchen carrying an empty plate. She smiles, then stops, and we all three look at each other.

"What?" Elizabeth says. I can tell she thinks we've been talking about her.

"Three weeks then?" Hilly asks me. "You coming?"

"Oh yes you are! You most certainly are going!" Elizabeth says.

I look in their smiling faces, at their hope for me. It's not like Mother's meddling, but a clean hope, without strings or hurt. I hate that my friends have discussed this, my one night's fate, behind my back. I hate it and I love it too.

I HEAD BACK to the country before the game is over. Out the open window of the Cadillac, the fields look chopped and burned. Daddy finished the last harvest weeks ago, but the side of the road is still snowy with cotton stuck in the grass. Whiffs of it blow and float through the air.

I check the mailbox from the driver's seat. Inside is *The Farmer's Alma-*

nac and a single letter. It is from Harper & Row. I turn into the drive, throw the gear into Park. The letter is handwritten, on small square notepaper.

> *Miss Phelan,*
>
> *You certainly may hone your writing skills on such flat, passionless subjects as drunk driving and illiteracy. I'd hoped, however, you'd choose topics that actually had some punch to them. Keep looking. If you find something original, only then may you write me again.*

I slip past Mother in the dining room, invisible Pascagoula dusting pictures in the hall, up my steep, vicious stairs. My face burns. I fight the tears over Missus Stein's letter, tell myself to pull it together. The worst part is, I don't have any better ideas.

I bury myself in the next housekeeping article, then the League newsletter. For the second week in a row, I leave out Hilly's bathroom initiative. An hour later, I find myself staring off at the window. My copy of *Let Us Now Praise Famous Men* sits on the window ledge. I walk over and pick it up, afraid the light will fade the paper jacket, the black-and-white photo of the humble, impoverished family on the cover. The book is warm and heavy from the sun. I wonder if I'll ever write anything worth anything at all. I turn when I hear Pascagoula's knock on my door. That's when the idea comes to me.

No. I couldn't. That would be . . . crossing the line.

But the idea won't go away.

AIBILEEN

CHAPTER 7

THE HEAT WAVE finally passes round the middle a October and we get ourselves a cool fifty degrees. In the mornings, that bathroom seat get cold out there, give me a little start when I set down. It's just a little room they built inside the carport. Inside is a toilet and a little sink attached to the wall. A pull cord for the lightbulb. Paper have to set on the floor.

When I waited on Miss Caulier, her carport attach to the house so I didn't have to go outside. Place before that had a maid quarters. Plus my own little bedroom for when I sit at night. This one I got to cross through the weather to get there.

On a Tuesday noon, I carry my lunch on out to the back steps, set down on the cool concrete. Miss Leefolt's grass don't grow good back here. A big magnolia tree shades most a the yard. I already know that's the tree gone be Mae Mobley's hideout. In about five years, to hide from Miss Leefolt.

After a while, Mae Mobley waddle out on the back step. She got half her hamburger patty in her hand. She smile up at me and say, "Good."

"How come you not in there with your mama?" I ask, but I know why. She rather be setting out here with the help than in there watching her mama look anywhere but at her. She like one a them baby chickens that get confused and follow the ducks around instead.

Mae Mobley point at the bluebirds getting ready for winter, twittering in the little gray fountain. "Boo birds!" She point and drop her hamburger down on the step. Out a nowhere, that old bird dog Aubie they don't never pay no mind to come up and gobble it down. I don't take to dogs, but this one is just plain pitiful. I pet him on the head. I bet nobody petted that dog since Christmas.

When Mae Mobley see him, she squeal and grab at his tail. It whap her in the face a few times before she get holt. Poor thing, he whine and give her one a those pitiful people-dog looks, his head turned funny, his eyebrows up. I can almost hear him asking her to turn him loose. He ain't the biting kind.

So she'll let go, I say, "Mae Mobley, where your tail?"

Sho nuff, she let go and start looking at her rear. Her mouth's popped open like she just can't believe she done missed it all this time. She turning in wobbly circles trying to see it.

"You ain't got no tail." I laugh and catch her fore she fall off that step. Dog sniff around for more hamburger.

It always tickle me how these babies believe anything you tell em. Tate Forrest, one a my used-to-be babies long time ago, stop me on the way to the Jitney just last week, give me a big hug, so happy to see me. He a grown man now. I needed to get back to Miss Leefolt's, but he start laughing and memoring how I'd do him when he was a boy. How the first time his foot fell asleep and he say it tickle, I told him that was just his foot snoring. And how I told him don't drink coffee or he gone turn colored. He say he still ain't drunk a cup a coffee and he twenty-one years old. It's always nice seeing the kids grown up fine.

"Mae Mobley? Mae Mobley Leefolt!"

Miss Leefolt just now noticing her child ain't setting in the same room with her. "She out here with me, Miss Leefolt," I say through the screen door.

"I told you to eat in your high chair, Mae Mobley. How I ended up with you when all my friends have angels I just do not know…" But then the phone ring and I hear her stomping off to get it.

I look down at Baby Girl, see how her forehead's all wrinkled up between the eyes. She studying hard on something.

I touch her cheek. "You alright, baby?"

She say, "Mae Mo bad."

The way she say it, like it's a fact, make my insides hurt.

"Mae Mobley," I say cause I got a notion to try something. "You a smart girl?"

She just look at me, like she don't know.

"You a smart girl," I say again.

She say, "Mae Mo smart."

I say, "You a kind little girl?"

She just look at me. She two years old. She don't know what she is yet.

I say, "You a kind girl," and she nod, repeat it back to me. But before I can do another one, she get up and chase that poor dog around the yard and laugh and that's when I get to wondering, what would happen if I told her she something good, ever day?

She turn from the birdbath and smile and holler, "Hi, Aibee. I love you, Aibee," and I feel a tickly feeling, soft like the flap a butterfly wings, watching her play out there. The way I used to feel watching Treelore. And that makes me kind a sad, memoring.

After while, Mae Mobley come over and press her cheek up to mine and just hold it there, like she know I be hurting. I hold her tight, whisper, "You a *smart* girl. You a *kind* girl, Mae Mobley. You hear me?" And I keep saying it till she repeat it back to me.

THE NEXT FEW WEEKS is real important for Mae Mobley. You think on it, you probably don't remember the first time you went to the bathroom in the toilet bowl stead of a diaper. Probably don't give no credit to who taught you, neither. Never had a single baby I raise come up to me and say, *Aibileen, why I sure do thank you for showing me how to go in the pot.*

It's a tricky thing. You try and get a baby to go in the toilet before its time, it'll make em crazy. They can't get the hang of it and get to thinking low a theyselves. Baby Girl, though, I know she ready. And she know she ready. But, Law, if she ain't running my fool legs off. I set her on her wooden baby seat so her little hiney don't fall in and soon as I turn my back, she off that pot running.

"You got to go, Mae Mobley?"

"No."

"You drunk up two glasses a grape juice, I know you got to go."

"Nooo."

"I give you a cookie if you go for me."

We look at each other awhile. She start eyeing the door. I don't hear nothing happening in the bowl. Usually, I can get them going after about two weeks. But that's if I got they mamas helping me. Little boys got to see they daddy doing it standing-up style, little girls got to see they mama setting down. Miss Leefolt won't let that girl come near her when she going, and that's the trouble.

"Go just a little for me, Baby Girl."

She stick her lip out, shake her head.

Miss Leefolt gone to get her hair done, else I ask her again will she set the example even though that woman's already said *no* five times. Last time Miss Leefolt say no, I was fixing to tell her how many kids I raised in my lifetime and ask her what number she on, but I ended up saying *alright* like I always do.

"I give you *two* cookies," I say even though her mama always getting on me about making her fat.

Mae Mobley, she shake her head and say, "You go."

Now, I ain't saying I ain't heard this before, but usually I can get around it. I know, though, she got to see how it's done fore she gone get to business. I say, "I don't got to go."

We look at each other. She point again and say, "You go."

Then she get to crying and fidgeting cause that seat making a little indent on her behind and I know what I'm on have to do. I just don't know how to go about it. Should I take her out to the garage to mine or go here in this bathroom? What if Miss Leefolt come home and I'm setting up on this toilet? She have a fit.

I put her diaper back on and we go out to the garage. Rain make it smell a little swampy. Even with the light on it's dark, and they ain't no fancy wallpaper like inside the house. Fact, they really ain't no proper walls at all, just plyboard hammered together. I wonder if she gone be scared.

"Alright, Baby Girl, here tis. Aibileen's bathroom."

She stick her head in and her mouth make the shape of a Cheerio. She say, "Oooooo."

I take down my underthings and I tee-tee real fast, use the paper, and get it all back on before she can really see anything. Then I flush.

"And that's how you go in the toilet," I say.

Well, don't she look surprise. Got her mouth hanging open like she done seen a miracle. I step out and fore I know it, she got her diaper off and that little monkey done climbed on that toilet, holding herself up so she don't fall in, going tee-tee for herself.

"Mae Mobley! You going! That's real good!" She smile and I catches her fore she dip down in it. We run back inside and she get her two cookies.

Later on, I get her on her pot and she go for me again. That's the hardest part, those first couple a times. By the end a the day, I feel like I really done something. She getting to be a pretty good talker and you can guess what the new word a the day is.

"What Baby Girl do today?"

She say, "Tee-tee."

"What they gone put in the history books next to this day?"

She say, "Tee-tee."

I say, "What Miss Hilly smell like?"

She say, "Tee-tee."

But I get onto myself. It wasn't Christian, plus I'm afraid she repeat it.

LATE THAT AFTERNOON, Miss Leefolt come home with her hair all teased up. She got a permanent and she smell like pneumonia.

"Guess what Mae Mobley done today?" I say. "Went to the bathroom in the toilet bowl."

"Oh, that's wonderful!" She give her girl a hug, something I don't see enough of. I know she mean it, too, cause Miss Leefolt do *not* like changing diapers.

I say, "You got to make sure she go in the pot from now on. It's real confusing for her if you don't."

Miss Leefolt smile, say, "Alright."

"Let's see if she do it one more time fore I go home." We go in the bath-room. I get her diapers off and put her up on that toilet. But Baby Girl, she shaking her head.

"Come on, Mae Mobley, can't you go in the pot for your mama?"

"Noooo."

Finally I put her back down on her feet. "That's alright, you did real good today."

But Miss Leefolt, she got her lips sticking out and she hmphing and frowning down at her. Before I can get her diaper on again, Baby Girl run off fast as she can. Nekkid little white baby running through the house. She in the kitchen. She got the back door open, she in the garage, trying to reach the knob to *my* bathroom. We run after her and Miss Leefolt point-ing her finger. Her voice go about ten pitches too high. "This is not your bathroom!"

Baby Girl wagging her head. *"My bafroom!"*

Miss Leefolt snatch her up, give her a pop on the leg.

"Miss Leefolt, she don't know what she do—"

"Get back in the house, Aibileen!"

I hate it, but I go in the kitchen. I stand in the middle, leave the door open behind me.

"I did not raise you to use the colored bathroom!" I hear her hiss-whispering, thinking I can't hear, and I think, *Lady, you didn't raise your child* at all.

"This is dirty out here, Mae Mobley. You'll catch diseases! No no no!" And I hear her pop her again and again on her bare legs.

After a second, Miss Leefolt potato-sack her inside. There ain't nothing I can do but watch it happen. My heart feel like it's squeezing up into my throat-pipe. Miss Leefolt drop Mae Mobley in front a the tee-vee and she march to her bedroom and slam the door. I go give Baby Girl a hug. She still crying and she look awful confused.

"I'm real sorry, Mae Mobley," I whisper to her. I'm cussing myself for taking her out there in the first place. But I don't know what else to say, so I just hold her.

We set there watching *Li'l Rascals* until Miss Leefolt come out, ask ain't it past time for me to go. I tuck my bus dime in my pocket. Give Mae Mobley one more hug, whisper, "You a *smart* girl. You a *good* girl."

On the ride home, I don't see the big white houses passing outside the window. I don't talk to my maid friends. I see Baby Girl getting spanked cause a me. I see her listening to Miss Leefolt call me dirty, diseased.

The bus speeds up along State Street. We pass over the Woodrow Wilson Bridge and my jaw so tight I could break my teeth off. I feel that bitter seed growing inside a me, the one planted after Treelore died. I want to yell so loud that Baby Girl can hear me that dirty ain't a color, disease ain't the Negro side a town. I want to stop that moment from coming—and it come in ever white child's life—when they start to think that colored folks ain't as good as whites.

We turn on Farish and I stand up cause my stop be coming. I pray that wasn't her moment. Pray I still got time.

THINGS IS REAL QUIET the next few weeks. Mae Mobley's wearing big-girl panties now. She don't hardly ever have no accidents. After what happen in the garage, Miss Leefolt take a real interest in Mae Mobley's bathroom habits. She even let her watch her on the pot, set the white example. A few times, though, when her mama's gone, I still catch her trying to go in mine. Sometimes she do it fore I can tell her no.

"Hey, Miss Clark." Robert Brown, who do Miss Leefolt's yard, come up on her back steps. It's nice and cool out. I open the screen door.

"How you doing, son?" I say and pat him on the arm. "I hear you working ever yard on the street."

"Yes ma'am. Got two guys mowing for me." He grin. He a handsome boy, tall with short hair. Went to high school with Treelore. They was good friends, played baseball together. I touch him on the arm, just needing to feel it again.

"How your Granmama?" I ask. I love Louvenia, she is the sweetest person living. She and Robert came to the funeral together. This makes me remember what's coming next week. The worst day a the year.

"She stronger than me." He smile. "I be by your house on Saturday to mow."

Treelore always did my mowing for me. Now Robert does it without my even asking, never will take any money for it. "Thank you, Robert. I appreciate it."

"You need anything, you call me, alright, Miss Clark?"

"Thank you, son."

I hear the doorbell ring and I see Miss Skeeter's car out front. Miss Skeeter been coming over to Miss Leefolt's ever week this month, to ask me the Miss Myrna questions. She ask about hard water stains and I tell her cream of tartar. She ask how you unscrew a lightbulb that done broke off in the socket and I tell her a raw potato. She ask me what happen with her old maid Constantine and her mama, and I go cold. I thought if I told her a little, a few weeks ago, about Constantine having a daughter, she'd leave me alone about it after that. But Miss Skeeter just keep on asking me questions. I could tell she don't understand why a colored woman can't raise no white-skin baby in Mississippi. Be a hard, lonely life, not belonging here nor there.

Ever time Miss Skeeter finish asking me about how to clean the-this or fix the-that or where Constantine, we get to talking about other things too. That's not something I done a whole lot with my bosses or they friends. I find myself telling her how Treelore never made below a B+ or that the new church deacon get on my nerves cause he lisp. Little bits, but things I ordinarily wouldn't tell a white person.

Today, I'm trying to explain to her the difference between dipping and polishing the silver, how only the tacky houses do the dip cause it's faster, but it don't look good. Miss Skeeter cock her head to the side, wrinkle her forehead. "Aibileen, remember that...idea Treelore had?"

I nod, feel a prickle. I should a never shared that with a white woman.

Miss Skeeter squint her eyes like she did when she brung up the bathroom thing that time. "I've been thinking about it. I've been wanting to talk to you—"

But fore she can finish, Miss Leefolt come in the kitchen and catch Baby Girl playing with my comb in my pocketbook and say maybe Mae Mobley ought to have her bath early today. I tell Miss Skeeter goodbye, go start the tub.

AFTER I SPENT A YEAR dreading it, November eighth finally come. I spec I sleep about two hours the night before. I wake up at dawn and put a pot a Community coffee on the stovetop. My back hurts when I bend over to get my hose on. Fore I walk out the door, the phone ring.

"Just checking on you. You sleep?"

"I did alright."

"I'm on bring you a caramel cake tonight. And I don't want you to do nothing but set in your kitchen and eat the whole thing for supper." I try to smile, but nothing come out. I tell Minny thank you.

Three years ago today, Treelore died. But by Miss Leefolt's book it's still floor-cleaning day. Thanksgiving coming in two weeks and I got plenty to do to get ready. I scrub my way through the morning, through the twelve o'clock news. I miss my stories cause the ladies is in the dining room having a Benefit meeting and I ain't allowed to turn on the tee-vee when they's company. And that's fine. My muscles is shivering they so tired. But I don't want a stop moving.

About four o'clock, Miss Skeeter come in the kitchen. Before she can even say hello, Miss Leefolt rush in behind her. "Aibileen, I just found out Missus Fredericks is driving down from Greenwood tomorrow and staying through Thanksgiving. I want the silver service polished and all the guest towels washed. Tomorrow I'll give you the list of what else."

Miss Leefolt shake her head at Miss Skeeter like ain't she got the hardest life in town and walks out. I go on and get the silver service out the dining room. Law, I'm already tired and I got to be ready to work the Benefit next Saturday night. Minny ain't coming. She too scared she gone run into Miss Hilly.

Miss Skeeter still waiting on me in the kitchen when I come back in. She got a Miss Myrna letter in her hand.

"You got a cleaning question?" I sigh. "Go head."

"Not really. I just... I wanted to ask you... the other day..."

I take a plug a Pine-Ola cream and start rubbing it onto the silver, working the cloth around the rose design, the lip and the handle. God, please let tomorrow come soon. I ain't gone go to the gravesite. I can't, it'll be too hard—

"Aibileen? Are you feeling alright?"

I stop, look up. Realize Miss Skeeter been talking to me the whole time.

"I'm sorry I's just… thinking about something."

"You looked so sad."

"Miss Skeeter." I feel tears come up in my eyes, cause three years just ain't long enough. A hundred years ain't gone be long enough. "You mind if I help you with them questions tomorrow?"

Miss Skeeter start to say something, but then she stop herself. "Of course. I hope you feel better."

I finish the silver set and the towels and tell Miss Leefolt I got to go home even though it's half a hour early and she gone short my pay. She open her mouth like she want to protest and I whisper my lie, *I vomited*, and she say *go*. Cause besides her own mother, there ain't nothing Miss Leefolt scared of more than Negro diseases.

"ALRIGHT THEN. I'll be back in thirty minutes. I'll pull right up here at nine forty-five," Miss Leefolt say through the passenger car window. Miss Leefolt dropping me off at the Jitney 14 to pick up what else we need for Thanksgiving tomorrow.

"You bring her back that receipt, now," Miss Fredericks, Miss Leefolt's mean old mama, say. They all three in the front seat, Mae Mobley squeezed in the middle with a look so miserable you think she about to get a tetanus shot. Poor girl. Miss Fredericks supposed to stay two weeks this time.

"Don't forget the turkey, now," Miss Leefolt say. "And two cans of cranberry sauce."

I smile. I only been cooking white Thanksgivings since Calvin Coolidge was President.

"Quit squirming, Mae Mobley," Miss Fredericks snap, "or I'll pinch you."

"Miss Leefolt, lemme take her in the store with me. Help me with my shopping."

Miss Fredericks about to protest, but Miss Leefolt say, "*Take* her," and fore I know it, Baby Girl done wormed her way over Miss Fredericks' lap and is climbing out the window in my arms like I am the Lord Savior. I pull her up on my hip and they drive off toward Fortification Street, and Baby Girl and me, we giggle like a couple a schoolgirls.

I push open the metal door, get a cart, and put Mae Mobley up front, stick her legs through the holes. Long as I got my white uniform on, I'm allowed to shop in this Jitney. I miss the old days, when you just walk out to Fortification Street and there be the farmers with they wheelbarrows calling out, "Sweet potatoes, butter beans, string beans, okra. Fresh cream, buttermilk, yellow cheese, eggs." But the Jitney ain't so bad. Least they got the good air-condition.

"Alrighty, Baby Girl. Less see what we need."

In produce, I pick out six sweet potatoes, three handfuls a string beans. I get a smoked ham hock from the butcher. The store is bright, lined up neat. Nothing like the colored Piggly Wiggly with sawdust on the floor. It's mostly white ladies, smiling, got they hair already fixed and sprayed for tomorrow. Four or five maids is shopping, all in they uniforms.

"Purple stuff!" Mae Mobley say and I let her hold the can a cranberry. She smile at it like it's a old friend. She love the purple stuff. In dry goods, I heave the two-pound bag a salt in the cart, to brine the turkey in. I count the hours on my hands, ten, eleven, twelve. If I'm on soak the bird for fourteen hours in the salt water, I'll put it in the bucket around three this afternoon. Then I'll come in to Miss Leefolt's at five tomorrow morning and cook the turkey for the next six hours. I already baked two pans a cornbread, left it to stale on the counter today to give it some crunch. I got a apple pie ready to bake, gone do my biscuits in the morning.

"Ready for tomorrow, Aibileen?" I turn and see Franny Coots behind me. She go to my church, work for Miss Caroline on Manship. "Hey, cutie, look a them fat legs," she say to Mae Mobley. Mae Mobley lick the cranberry can.

Franny bend her head down, say, "You hear what happen to Louvenia Brown's grandson this morning?"

"Robert?" I say. "Who do the mowing?"

"Use the white bathroom at Pinchman Lawn and Garden. Say they wasn't a sign up saying so. Two white mens chased him and beat him with a tire iron."

Oh no. Not *Robert*. "He...is he...?"

Franny shake her head. "They don't know. He up at the hospital. I heard he blind."

"God, no." I close my eyes. Louvenia, she is the purest, kindest person they is. She raised Robert after her own daughter died.

"Poor Louvenia. I don't know why the bad have to happen to the good-est ones," Franny say.

THAT AFTERNOON, I work like a crazy woman, chopping onions and celery, mixing up my dressing, ricing sweet potatoes, stringing the beans, polishing silver. I heard folks is heading to Louvenia Brown's tonight at five-thirty to pray for Robert, but by the time I lift that twenty-pound turkey in the brine, I can't barely raise my arms.

I don't finish cooking till six o'clock that night, two hours later than usual. I know I ain't gone have the strength to go knock on Louvenia's door. I'll have to do it tomorrow after I'm done cleaning up the turkey. I waddle myself from the bus stop, hardly able to keep my eyes open. I turn the corner on Gessum. A big white Cadillac's parked in front a my house. And there be Miss Skeeter in a red dress and red shoes, setting on my front steps like a bullhorn.

I walk real slow through my yard, wondering what it's gone be now. Miss Skeeter stand up, holding her pocketbook tight like it might get snatched. White peoples don't come round my neighborhood less they toting the help to and fro, and that is just fine with me. I spend all day long tending to white peoples. I don't need em looking in on me at home.

"I hope you don't mind me coming by," she say. "I just...I didn't know where else we could talk."

I set down on the step and ever knob on my spine hurt. Baby Girl so nervous around her Granmama, she wet all over me and I smell like it.

The street's full a folks walking to sweet Louvenia's to pray for Robert, kids playing ball in the street. Everbody looking over at us thinking I must be getting fired or something.

"Yes ma'am," I sigh. "What can I do for you?"

"I have an idea. Something I want to write about. But I need your help."

I let all my breath out. I like Miss Skeeter, but come on. Sure, a phone call would a been nice. She never would a just shown up on some white lady's step without calling. But no, she done plopped herself down like she got ever right to barge in on me at home.

"I want to interview you. About what it's like to work as a maid."

A red ball roll a few feet in my yard. The little Jones boy run across the street to get it. When he see Miss Skeeter, he stop dead. Then he run and snatch it up. He turn and dash off like he scared she gone get him.

"Like the Miss Myrna column?" I say, flat as a pan. "Bout cleaning?"

"Not like Miss Myrna. I'm talking about a book," she say and her eyes is big. She excited. "Stories about what it's like to work for a white family. What it's like to work for, say…Elizabeth."

I turn and look at her. This what she been trying to ask me the past two weeks in Miss Leefolt kitchen. "You think Miss Leefolt gone agree to that? Me telling stories about her?"

Miss Skeeter's eyes drop down some. "Well, no. I was thinking we wouldn't tell her. I'll have to make sure the other maids will agree to keep it secret, too."

I scrunch up my forehead, just starting to get what she's asking. "Other maids?"

"I was hoping to get four or five. To really show what it's like to be a maid in Jackson."

I look around. We out here in the wide open. Don't she know how dangerous this could be, talking about this while the whole world can see us? "Exactly what kind a stories you think you gone hear?"

"What you get paid, how they treat you, the bathrooms, the babies, all the things you've seen, good and bad."

She looks excited, like this is some kind a game. For a second, I think I might be more mad than I am tired.

"Miss Skeeter," I whisper, "do that not sound kind a dangerous to you?"

"Not if we're careful—"

"Shhh, please. Do you know what would happen to me if Miss Leefolt find out I talked behind her back?"

"We won't tell her, or anyone." She lowers her voice some, but not enough. "These will be private interviews."

I just stare at her. Is she crazy? "Did you hear about the colored boy this morning? One they beat with a tire iron for *accidentally* using the white bathroom?"

She just look at me, blink a little. "I know things are unstable but this is—"

"And my cousin Shinelle in Cauter County? They burn up her car cause she went *down* to the voting station."

"No one's ever written a book like this," she say, finally whispering, finally starting to understand, I guess. "We'd be breaking new ground. It's a brand-new perspective."

I spot a flock a maids in they uniforms walking by my house. They look over, see me setting with a white woman on my front step. I grit my teeth, already know my phone gone be ringing tonight.

"Miss Skeeter," and I say it slow, try to make it count, "I do this with you, I might as well burn my *own* house down."

Miss Skeeter start biting her nail then. "But I've already..." She shut her eyes closed tight. I think about asking her, *Already what,* but I'm kind a scared to hear what she gone say. She reach in her pocketbook, pull out a scrap a paper and write her telephone number on it.

"Please, will you at least think about it?"

I sigh, stare out at the yard. Gentle as I can, I say, "No ma'am."

She set the scrap a paper between us on the step, then she get in her Cadillac. I'm too tired to get up. I just stay there, watch while she roll real slow down the road. The boys playing ball clear the street, stand on the side frozen, like it's a funeral car passing by.

MISS SKEETER

CHAPTER 8

I DRIVE DOWN Gessum Avenue in Mama's Cadillac. Up ahead, a little colored boy in overalls watches me, wide-eyed, gripping a red ball. I look into my rearview mirror. Aibileen is still on her front steps in her white uniform. She hadn't even looked at me when she said *No ma'am*. She just kept her eyes set on that yellow patch of grass in her yard.

I guess I thought it would be like visiting Constantine, where friendly colored people waved and smiled, happy to see the little white girl whose daddy owned the big farm. But here, narrow eyes watch me pass by. When my car gets close to him, the little colored boy turns and scats behind a house a few down from Aibileen's. Half-a-dozen colored people are gathered in the front yard of the house, holding trays and bags. I rub my temples. I try to think of something more that might convince Aibileen.

A WEEK AGO, Pascagoula knocked on my bedroom door.

"There's a long distance phone call for you, Miss Skeeter. From a Miss . . . Stern, she say?"

"Stern?" I thought out loud. Then I straightened. "Do you mean . . . *Stein?*"

"I . . . I reckon it could a been Stein. She talk kind a hard-sounding."

I rushed past Pascagoula, down the stairs. For some stupid reason, I kept smoothing my frizzy hair down as if it were a meeting and not a phone call. In the kitchen, I grabbed the phone dangling against the wall.

Three weeks earlier, I'd typed out the letter on Strathmore white. Three pages outlining the idea, the details, and the lie. Which was that a hard-working and respected colored maid has agreed to let me interview her and describe in specifics what it's like to work for the white women of our town. Weighing it against the alternative, that I *planned* to ask a colored woman for help, saying she'd already agreed to it seemed infinitely more attractive.

I stretched the cord into the pantry, pulled the string on the single bare bulb. The pantry is shelved floor to ceiling with pickles and soup jars, molasses, put-up vegetables, and preserves. This was my old high school trick to get some privacy.

"Hello? This is Eugenia speaking."

"Please hold, I'll put the call through." I heard a series of clicks and then a far, far away voice, almost as deep as a man's, say, "Elaine Stein."

"Hello? This is Skeet—Eugenia Phelan in Mississippi?"

"I know, Miss Phelan. I called you." I heard a match strike, a short, sharp inhale. "I received your letter last week. I have some comments."

"Yes ma'am." I sank down onto a tall tin can of King Biscuit flour. My heart thumped as I strained to hear her. A phone call from New York truly sounded as crackly as a thousand miles away ought to.

"What gave you this idea? About interviewing domestic housekeepers. I'm curious."

I sat paralyzed a second. She offered no chatting or hello, no introduction of herself. I realized it was best to answer her as instructed. "I was...well, I was raised by a colored woman. I've seen how simple it can be and—and how complex it can be between the families and the help." I cleared my throat. I sounded stiff, like I was talking to a teacher.

"Continue."

"Well," I took a deep breath, "I'd like to write this showing the point of view of the help. The colored women down here." I tried to picture Constantine's face, Aibileen's. "They raise a white child and then twenty years later the child becomes the employer. It's that irony, that we love them and they love us, yet..." I swallowed, my voice trembling. "We don't even allow them to use the toilet in the house."

Again there was silence.

"And," I felt compelled to continue, "everyone knows how we white people feel, the glorified Mammy figure who dedicates her whole life to a white family. Margaret Mitchell covered that. But no one ever asked Mammy how she felt about it." Sweat dripped down my chest, blotting the front of my cotton blouse.

"So you want to show a side that's never been examined before," Missus Stein said.

"Yes. Because no one ever talks about it. No one talks about anything down here."

Elaine Stein laughed like a growl. Her accent was tight, Yankee. "Miss Phelan, I lived in Atlanta. For six years with my first husband."

I latched on to this small connection. "So...you know what it's like then."

"Enough to get me out of there," she said, and I heard her exhale her smoke. "Look, I read your outline. It's certainly...original, but it won't work. What maid in her right mind would ever tell you the truth?"

I could see Mother's pink slippers pass by the door. I tried to ignore them. I couldn't believe Missus Stein was already calling my bluff. "The first interviewee is...eager to tell her story."

"Miss Phelan," Elaine Stein said, and I knew it wasn't a question, "this Negro actually agreed to talk to you candidly? About working for a white family? Because that seems like a hell of a risk in a place like Jackson, Mississippi."

I sat blinking. I felt the first fingers of worry that Aibileen might not be as easy to convince as I'd thought. Little did I know what she would say to me on her front steps the next week.

"I watched them try to integrate your bus station on the news," Missus Stein continued. "They jammed fifty-five Negroes in a jail cell built for four."

I pursed my lips. "She has agreed. Yes, she has."

"Well. That is impressive. But after her, you really think other maids will talk to you? What if the employers find out?"

"The interviews would be conducted secretly. Since, as you know, things are a little dangerous down here right now." The truth was, I had very little idea how dangerous things were. I'd spent the past four years locked away in the padded room of college, reading Keats and Eudora Welty and worrying over term papers.

"A little dangerous?" She laughed. "The marches in Birmingham, Martin Luther King. Dogs attacking colored children. Darling, it's the hottest topic in the nation. But, I'm sorry, this will never work. Not as an article, because no Southern newspaper would publish it. And certainly not as a book. A book of *interviews* would never sell."

"Oh," I heard myself say. I closed my eyes, feeling all the excitement drain out of me. I heard myself say again, "Oh."

"I called because, frankly, it's a good idea. But... there's no possible way to take it to print."

"But... what if..." My eyes started darting around the pantry, looking for something to bring back her interest. Maybe I *should* talk about it as an article, maybe a magazine, but she said no—

"Eugenia, who are you talking to in there?" Mother's voice cut though the crack. She inched the door open and I yanked it closed again. I covered the receiver, hissed, "I'm talking to *Hilly*, Mother—"

"In the pantry? You're like a teenager again—"

"I mean—" Missus Stein let out a sharp tsk. "I suppose I could read what you get. God knows, the book business could use some rattling."

"You'd do that? Oh Missus Stein..."

"I'm not saying I'm considering it. But... do the interview and I'll let you know if it's worth pursuing."

I stuttered a few unintelligible sounds, finally coming out with, "*Thank* you. Missus Stein, I can't tell you how much I appreciate your help."

"Don't thank me yet. Call Ruth, my secretary, if you need to get in touch." And she hung up.

I lug an old satchel to bridge club at Elizabeth's on Wednesday. It is red. It is ugly. And for today, at least, it is a prop.

It's the only bag in Mother's house I could find large enough to carry the Miss Myrna letters. The leather is cracked and flaking, the thick shoulder strap leaves a brown mark on my blouse where the leather stain is rubbing off. It was my Grandmother Claire's gardening bag. She used to carry her garden tools around the yard in it and the bottom is still lined with sunflower seeds. It matches absolutely nothing I own and I don't care.

"Two weeks," Hilly says to me, holding up two fingers. "He's coming." She smiles and I smile back. "I'll be right back," I say and I slip into the kitchen, carrying my satchel with me.

Aibileen is standing at the sink. "Afternoon," she says quietly. It was a week ago that I visited her at her house.

I stand there a minute, watching her stir the iced tea, feeling the discomfort in her posture, her dread that I might be about to ask for her help on the book again. I pull a few housekeeping letters out and, seeing this, Aibileen's shoulders relax a little. As I read her a question about mold stains, she pours a little tea in a glass, tastes it. She spoons more sugar in the pitcher.

"Oh, fore I forget, I got the answer on that water ring question. Minny say just rub you a little mayonnaise on it." Aibileen squeezes half a lemon in the tea. "Then go on and throw that no-good husband out the door." She stirs, tastes. "Minny don't take too well to husbands."

"Thanks, I'll put that down," I say. As casually as I can, I pull an envelope from my bag. "And here. I've been meaning to give you this."

Aibileen stiffens back into her cautious pose, the one she had when I walked in. "What you got there?" she says without reaching for it.

"For your help," I say quietly. "I've put away five dollars for every article. It's up to thirty-five dollars now."

Aibileen's eyes move quickly back to her tea. "No thank you, ma'am."

"Please take it, you've earned it."

I hear chairs scraping on wood in the dining room, Elizabeth's voice.

"Please, Miss Skeeter. Miss Leefolt have a fit if she find you giving me cash," Aibileen whispers.

"She doesn't have to know."

Aibileen looks up at me. The whites of her eyes are yellowed, tired. I know what she's thinking.

"I already told you, I'm sorry, I can't help you with that book, Miss Skeeter."

I set the envelope on the counter, knowing I've made a terrible mistake.

"Please. Find you another colored maid. A young'un. Somebody… else."

"But I don't know any others well enough." I am tempted to bring up the word *friends,* but I'm not that naïve. I know we're not friends.

Hilly's head pops through the door. "Come on, Skeeter, I'm fixing to deal," and she disappears.

"I'm begging you," Aibileen says, "put that money away so Miss Leefolt don't see it."

I nod, embarrassed. I tuck the envelope in my bag, knowing we're worse off than ever. It's a bribe, she thinks, to get her to let me interview her. A bribe disguised as goodwill and thanks. I'd been waiting to give her the money anyway, once it added up to something, but it's true, my timing today had been deliberately planned. And now I've scared her off for good.

"DARLING, just try it on your head. It cost eleven dollars. It must be good."

Mother has me cornered in the kitchen. I glance at the door to the hall, the door to the side porch. Mother comes closer, the thing in hand, and I'm distracted by how thin her wrists look, how frail her arms are carrying the heavy gray machine. She pushes me down into a chair, not so frail after all, and squeezes a noisy, farty tube of goo on my head. Mother's been chasing me with the Magic Soft & Silky Shinalator for two days now.

She rubs the cream in my hair with both hands. I can practically feel the hope in her fingers. A cream will not straighten my nose or take a foot off my height. It won't add distinction to my almost translucent eyebrows, nor add weight to my bony frame. And my teeth are already perfectly straight. So this is all she has left to fix, my hair.

Mother covers my dripping head with a plastic cap. She fastens a hose from the cap into a square machine.

"How long does this take, Mother?"

She picks up the booklet with a sticky finger. "It says here, 'Cover with the Miracle Straightening Cap, then turn on the machine and wait for the miraculous—'"

"Ten minutes? Fifteen?"

I hear a click, a rising rumble, then feel a slow, intense warmth on my head. But suddenly there's a *pop!* The tube is loose from the machine and jerking around like a mad firehose. Mother shrieks, grabs at it and misses. Finally, she snatches it and reattaches it.

She takes a deep breath and picks up the booklet again. "The Miracle Cap must remain on the head for two hours without removal or results—"

"Two *hours?*"

"I'll have Pascagoula fix you a glass of tea, dear." Mother pats me on the shoulder and swishes out through the kitchen door.

For two hours, I smoke cigarettes and read *Life* magazine. I finish *To Kill a Mockingbird.* Finally, I pick up the *Jackson Journal*, pick through it. It's Friday, so there won't be a Miss Myrna column. On page four, I read: *Boy blinded over segregated bathroom, suspects questioned.* It sounds . . . familiar. I remember then. This must be Aibileen's neighbor.

Twice this week, I've gone by Elizabeth's house hoping she wouldn't be home, so I could talk to Aibileen, try to find some way to convince her to help me. Elizabeth was hunched over her sewing machine, intent on getting a new dress ready for the Christmas season, and it is yet another green gown, cheap and frail. She must've gotten a steal at the bargain bin on green material. I wish I could go down to Kennington's and charge her something new but just the offer would embarrass her to death.

"So, do you know what you're wearing for the date?" Hilly'd asked the second time I came by. "Next Saturday?"

I'd shrugged. "I guess I have to go shopping."

Just then Aibileen brought a tray of coffee out and set it on the table.

"Thank you." Elizabeth nodded to her.

"Why, thank you, Aibileen," Hilly said, sugaring her cup. "I tell you, you make the best colored coffee in town."

"Thank you, ma'am."

"Aibileen," Hilly continued, "how do you like your new bathroom out there? It's nice to have a place of your own, now isn't it?"

Aibileen stared at the crack in the dining table. "Yes ma'am."

"You know, Mister Holbrook arranged for that bathroom, Aibileen. Sent the boys over and the equipment, too." Hilly smiled.

Aibileen just stood there and I wished I wasn't in the room. *Please,* I thought, *please don't say thank you.*

"Yes ma'am." Aibileen opened a drawer and reached inside, but Hilly kept looking at her. It was so obvious what she wanted.

Another second passed with no one moving. Hilly cleared her throat and finally Aibileen lowered her head. "Thank you, ma'am," she whispered. She walked back into the kitchen. It's no wonder she doesn't want to talk to me.

At noon, Mother removes the vibrating cap from my head, washes the goo from my hair while I lean back in the kitchen sink. She quickly rolls up a dozen curlers, puts me under her hair dryer hood in her bathroom.

An hour later, I emerge pink and soreheaded and thirsty. Mother stands me in front of the mirror, pulling out curlers. She brushes out the giant circular mounds on my head.

We stare, dumbfounded.

"Ho-ly shit," I say. All I'm thinking is, *The date. The blind date is next weekend.*

Mother smiles, shocked. She doesn't even scold me for cursing. My hair looks great. The Shinalator actually worked.

CHAPTER 9

O n Saturday, the day of my date with Stuart Whitworth, I sit for two hours under the Shinalator (results, it seems, only last until the next wash). When I'm dry, I go to Kennington's and buy the flattest shoes I can find and a slim black crepe dress. I hate shopping, but I'm glad for the distraction, to not have to worry about Missus Stein or Aibileen for an afternoon. I charge the eighty-five dollars to Mother's account since she's always begging me to go buy new clothes. ("Something flattering for your *size.*") I know Mother would profoundly disapprove of the cleavage the dress enables me to have. I've never owned a dress like this.

In the Kennington's parking lot I start the car, but cannot drive for the sudden pains in my stomach. I grip the white padded steering wheel, telling myself for the tenth time that it's ridiculous to wish for something I'll never have. To think I know the color blue his eyes are from a black-and-white photograph. To consider something a chance that is nothing but paper and filament and postponed dinners. But the dress, with my new hair, it actually looks pretty good on me. And I can't help but hope.

It was four months ago when Hilly showed me the picture, out back by her swimming pool. Hilly was tanning in the sun, I was fanning in the murky shade. My heat rash had flared in July and hadn't subsided.

"I'm busy," I said. Hilly sat on the edge of the pool, saggy and post-pregnant fat, inexplicably confident in her black swimsuit. Her stomach was paunchy, but her legs, as always, were thin and pretty.

"I haven't even told you when he's coming," she said. "And he comes from such a good family." She was, of course, talking about her own. He was William's second cousin removed. "Just meet him and see what you think."

I looked down at the picture again. He had clear open eyes, light brown curly hair, was the tallest in a group of men by a lake. But his body was half-hidden by the others. He must not have all his limbs.

"There's nothing *wrong* with him," Hilly said. "Ask Elizabeth, she met him at the Benefit last year while you were up at school. Not to mention, he dated Patricia van Devender for forever."

"Patricia van Devender?" Most Beautiful at Ole Miss, two years in a row?

"Plus he started his own oil business over in Vicksburg. So if it doesn't work out, it's not like you'll be running into him every day in town."

"Alright," I finally sighed, more than anything to get Hilly off my back.

It's past three o'clock by the time I get back home from buying the dress. I'm supposed to be at Hilly's at six to meet Stuart. I check the mirror. The curls are starting to fray on the ends, but rest of my hair is still smooth. Mother was thrilled when I told her I wanted to try the Shinalator again and wasn't even suspicious of why. She doesn't know about my date tonight and if she somehow finds out, the next three months will be full of excruciating questions like "Did he call?" and "What did you do wrong?" when it doesn't work out.

Mother's downstairs in the relaxing room with Daddy, hollering at the Rebel basketball team. My brother, Carlton, is on the sofa with his shiny new girlfriend. They drove up this afternoon from LSU. She has a dark straight ponytail and wears a red blouse.

When I get Carlton alone in the kitchen, he laughs, yanks my hair like we're kids again. "So how are you, sister?"

I tell him about the job at the paper, that I'm editor of the League news-letter. I also tell him he better be moving back home after law school. "You deserve some of Mother's time too. I'm taking more than my fair share here," I say through gritted teeth.

He laughs like he understands, but how could he really? He's three years older than me and great-looking, tall with wavy blond hair, finishing LSU law school, protected by a hundred and seventy miles of badly paved roads.

When he goes back to his girlfriend, I search for Mother's car keys, but I can't find them anywhere. It's already a quarter to five. I go and stand in the doorway, try to catch Mother's attention. I have to wait for her to fin-ish firing questions at Ponytail Girl about her people and where she's from, but Mother will not let up until she finds at least one person they have in common. After that, it's what sorority the girl was in at Vanderbilt, and she finally concludes by asking what her silver pattern is. It's better than a horo-scope, Mother always says.

Ponytail Girl says her family pattern is Chantilly, but she'll be pick-ing out her own new pattern when she gets married. "Since I consider myself an independent thinker and all." Carlton pets her on the head and she nudges against his hand like a cat. They both look up at me and smile.

"Skeeter," Ponytail Girl says to me across the room, "you're so lucky to come from a Francis the First family pattern. Will you keep it when you get married?"

"Francis the First is just dreamy," I beam. "Why, I pull those forks out all the time just to look at them."

Mother narrows her eyes at me. I motion her to the kitchen, but another ten minutes pass until she comes in.

"Where in the world are your keys, Mama? I'm late for Hilly's. I'm stay-ing there tonight."

"What? But Carlton's home. What's his new friend going to think if you leave for something better to do?"

I've put off telling her this because I knew, whether Carlton was home or not, it would turn into an argument.

"And Pascagoula made a roast and Daddy's got the wood all ready for a fire tonight in the relaxing room."

"It's eighty-five degrees outside, Mama."

"Now look. Your brother is home and I expect you to behave like a good sister. I don't want you leaving until you've had a nice long visit with this girl." She's looking at her watch while I remind myself I'm twenty-three years old. "Please, darling," she says and I sigh and carry a damn tray of mint juleps out to the others.

"Mama," I say back in the kitchen at five twenty-eight. "I've got to go. Where are your keys? Hilly's waiting on me."

"But we haven't even had the pigs in a blanket yet."

"Hilly's got...a stomach bug," I whisper. "And her help doesn't come in tomorrow. She needs me to watch the kids."

Mother sighs. "I guess that means you're going to church with them too. And I thought we could all go tomorrow as a family. Have Sunday dinner together."

"Mama, please," I say, rummaging through a basket where she keeps her keys. "I can't find your keys *anywhere.*"

"You can't take the Cadillac overnight. That's our good Sunday church car."

He's going to be at Hilly's in thirty minutes. I'm supposed to dress and do my makeup at Hilly's so Mother won't suspect anything. I can't take Daddy's new truck. It's full of fertilizer and I know he'll need it at dawn tomorrow.

"Alright, I'll take the old truck, then."

"I believe it has a trailer on it. Go ask your daddy."

But I can't ask Daddy because I can't go through this in front of three other people who will look all hurt that I'm leaving, so I grab the old truck keys and say, "It doesn't matter. I'm just going straight to Hilly's," and I huff outside only to find that not only does the old truck have a trailer hitched to it, but a half-ton tractor on top of that trailer.

So I drive into town for my first date in two years in a red 1941 Chevrolet four-on-the-floor with a John Deere motor grader hooked behind me. The engine sputters and churns and I wonder if the truck will make it. Chunks of mud spray behind me off the tires. The engine stalls on the main road, sending my dress and bag flying onto the dirty floor. I have to restart twice.

At five forty-five, a black thing streaks out in front of me and I feel a thunk. I try to stop but braking's just not something you can do very quickly with a 10,000-pound piece of machinery behind you. I groan and pull over. I have to go check. Remarkably, the cat stands up, looks around stunned, and shoots back into the woods as quickly as it came.

At three minutes to six, after doing twenty in a fifty with horns honking and teenagers hollering at me, I park down the street from Hilly's house since Hilly's cul-de-sac doesn't provide adequate parking for farm equipment. I grab my bag and run inside without even knocking, all out of breath and sweaty and windblown and there they are, the three of them, including my date. Having highballs in the front living room.

I freeze in the entrance hall with all of them looking at me. William and Stuart both stand up. God, he's tall, has at least four inches over me. Hilly's eyes are big when she grabs my arm. "Boys, we'll be right back. Y'all just sit tight and talk about quarterbacks or something."

Hilly whisks me off to her dressing room and we both start groaning. It's just so goddamn awful.

"Skeeter, you don't even have lipstick on! Your hair looks like a rat's nest!"

"I know, look at me!" All traces of the Shinalator's miracle are gone. "There's no air-conditioning in the truck. I had to ride with the damn windows down."

I scrub my face and Hilly sits me in her dressing room chair. She starts combing my hair out the way my mother used to do, twisting it into these giant rollers, spraying it with Final Net.

"Well? What did you think of him?" she asks.

I sigh and close my unmascaraed eyes. "He looks handsome."

I smear the makeup on, something I hardly even know how to do. Hilly looks at me and smudges it off with a tissue, reapplies it. I slip into the black dress with the deep V in the front, the black Delman flats. Hilly quickly brushes out my hair. I wash my armpits with a wet rag and she rolls her eyes at me.

"I hit a *cat*," I say.

"He's already had two drinks waiting on you."

I stand up and smooth my dress down. "Alright," I say, "give it to me. One to ten."

Hilly looks me up and down, stops on the dip in the front of the dress. She raises her eyebrows. I've never shown cleavage before in my life; kind of forgot I had it.

"Six," she says, like she is surprised herself.

We just look at each other a second. Hilly lets out a little squeal and I smile back. Hilly's never given me higher than a four.

When we come back into the front living room, William's pointing his finger at Stuart. "I'm going to run for that seat and by God, with your daddy's—"

"Stuart Whitworth," Hilly announces, "I'd like to introduce Skeeter Phelan."

He stands up, and for a minute my head is perfectly quiet inside. I make myself look, like self-inflicted torture, as he takes me in.

"Stuart here went to school over at the University of Alabama," William says, adding, "Roll Tide."

"Nice to meet you." Stuart flips me a brief smile. Then he takes a long slurp of his drink until I hear the ice clink against his teeth. "So where we off to?" he asks William.

We take William's Oldsmobile to the Robert E. Lee Hotel. Stuart opens my door and sits beside me in the back, but then leans over the seat talking to William about deer season the rest of the ride.

At the table, he pulls out my chair for me and I sit, smile, say thank you.

"You want a drink?" he asks me, not looking my way.

"No, thanks. Just water, please."

He turns to the waiter and says, "Double Old Kentucky straight with a water back."

I guess it's some time after his fifth bourbon, I say, "So Hilly tells me you're in the oil business. That must be interesting."

"The money's good. If that's what you really want to know."

"Oh, I didn't..." But I stop because he's craning his neck at something. I look up and see he's staring at a woman who's at the door, a busty blonde with red lipstick and a tight green dress.

William turns to see what Stuart's looking at, but he swings back around quickly. He shakes his head no, very slightly, at Stuart and I see, heading out the door, it's Hilly's old boyfriend, Johnny Foote, with his new wife, Celia. They leave and William and I glance at each other, sharing our relief that Hilly didn't see them.

"Lord, that girl's hot as Tunica blacktop," Stuart says under his breath and I suppose that's when I just stop caring what happens.

At some point, Hilly looks at me to see what's going on. I smile like everything's fine and she smiles back, happy to see it's all working out. "William! The lieutenant governor just walked in. Let's go speak before he sits down."

They go off together, leaving us, the two lovebirds sitting on the same side of the table, staring at all the happy couples in the room.

"So," he says, hardly turning his head. "You ever go to any of the Alabama football games?"

I never even made it to Colonel Field and that was five thousand yards from my bed. "No, I'm not really a football fan." I look at my watch. It's hardly seven fifteen.

"That so." He eyes the drink the waiter has handed him like he'd really enjoy downing it. "Well, what do you do with your time?"

"I write a...domestic maintenance column for the *Jackson Journal*."

He wrinkles his brow, then laughs. "Domestic maintenance. You mean...housekeeping?"

I nod.

"Jesus." He stirs his drink. "I can't think of anything worse than reading a column on how to clean house," he says, and I notice that his front tooth is the slightest bit crooked. I long to point this imperfection out to him, but he finishes his thought with, "Except maybe writing it."

I just stare at him.

"Sounds like a ploy to me, to find a husband. Becoming an expert on keeping house."

"Well, you must be a genius. You've figured out my whole scheme."

"Isn't that what you women from Ole Miss major in? Professional husband hunting?"

I watch him, dumbfounded. I may not've had a date in umpteen years, but who does he think he is?

"I'm sorry, but were you dropped on your head as an infant?"

He blinks at me, then laughs for the first time all night.

"Not that it's any of your business," I say, "but I had to start somewhere if I plan on being a journalist." I think I've actually impressed him. But then he throws back the drink and the look is gone.

We eat dinner, and from his profile I can see his nose is a little pointy. His eyebrows are too thick, and his light brown hair too coarse. We say little else, to each other at least. Hilly chats, throwing things our way like, "Stuart, Skeeter here lives on a plantation just north of town. Didn't the senator grow up on a peanut farm?"

Stuart orders yet another drink.

When Hilly and I go to the bathroom, she gives me a hopeful smile. "What do you think?"

"He's...tall," I say, surprised she hasn't noticed that not only is my date inexplicably rude, but drop-dead drunk.

The end of the meal finally comes and he and William split the check. Stuart stands up and helps me with my jacket. At least he has nice manners.

"Jesus, I've never met a woman with such long arms," he says.

"Well, I've never met anybody with such a drinking problem."

"Your coat smells like—" He leans down and sniffs it, grimacing. "*Fertilizer.*"

He strides off to the men's room and I wish I could disappear.

The car ride, all three minutes of it, is impossibly silent. And long.

We go back inside Hilly's house. Yule May comes out in her white uniform, says, "They all fine, went to bed good," and she slips out through the kitchen door. I excuse myself to the bathroom.

"Skeeter, why don't you drive Stuart home?" William says when I come out. "I'm bushed, aren't you, Hilly?"

Hilly's looking at me like she's trying to figure out what I want to do. I thought I'd made it obvious when I stayed in the bathroom for ten minutes.

"Your…car's not here?" I ask the air in front of Stuart.

"I don't believe my cousin's in a position to drive." William laughs. Everyone's quiet again.

"I came in a truck," I say. "I'd hate for you to…"

"Shoot," William says, slapping Stuart on the back. "Stuart doesn't mind riding in a truck, do you, buddy?"

"William," Hilly says, "why don't you drive and, Skeeter, you can ride along."

"Not me, I'm too boozed up myself," William says even though he just drove us home.

Finally, I just walk out the door. Stuart follows me, doesn't comment that I didn't park in front of Hilly's house or in Hilly's driveway. When we get to my truck, we both stop, stare at the fifteen-foot tractor hooked behind my vehicle.

"You pulled that thing all by yourself?"

I sigh. I guess it's because I'm a big person and have never felt petite or particularly feminine or girly, but that tractor. It just seems to sum up so much.

"That is the funniest damn looking thing I have ever seen," he says.

I step away from him. "Hilly can take you," I say. "Hilly will drive you."

He turns and focuses on me for what, I'm pretty sure, is the first time all night. After several long moments of standing there being looked at, my eyes fill with tears. I'm just so tired.

"Ah, shit," he says and his body loosens. "Look, I told Hilly I wasn't ready for any damn date."

"Don't…" I say, backing away from him, and I head back to the house.

Sunday morning I get up early, before Hilly and William, before the kids and the church traffic. I drive home with the tractor rumbling behind me. The fertilizer smell gives me a hangover even though I had nothing but water last night.

I'd gone back in Hilly's house last night, Stuart trailing behind me. Knocking on Hilly's bedroom door, I asked William, who already had a mouth full of toothpaste, would he mind driving Stuart home. I'd walked upstairs to the guest room before he even answered.

I step over Daddy's dogs on the porch, go into my parents' house. As soon as I see Mother, I give her a hug. When she tries to let go, I can't let her.

"What is it, Skeeter? You didn't catch Hilly's stomach bug, did you?"

"No, I'm fine." I wish I could tell her about my night. I feel guilty for not being nicer to her, for not needing her until my own life turns bad. I feel bad for wishing Constantine was here instead.

Mother pats my windblown hair down since it must be adding at least two inches to my height. "You sure you're not feeling bad?"

"I'm alright, Mama." I am too tired to resist. I ache like someone kicked me in the stomach. With boots on. It won't go away.

"You know," she says, smiling, "I think this might be the one for Carlton."

"Good, Mama," I say. "I'm really glad for him."

AT ELEVEN O'CLOCK the next morning, the phone rings. Luckily, I'm in the kitchen and pick it up.

"Miss Skeeter?"

I stand very still, then look out at Mother examining her checkbook at the dining room table. Pascagoula is pulling a roast out of the oven. I go into the pantry and shut the door.

"Aibileen?" I whisper.

She's quiet a second and then she blurts it out. "What if—what if you don't like what I got to say? I mean, about white peoples."

"I—I . . . this isn't about my opinion," I say. "It doesn't matter how I feel."

"But how I know you ain't gone get mad, turn around on me?"

"I don't . . . I guess you'll just have to . . . trust me." I hold my breath, hoping, waiting. There is a long pause.

"Law have mercy. I reckon I'm on do it."

"*Aibileen.*" My heart is pounding. "You have no idea how much I appreciate—"

"Miss Skeeter, we gone have to be real careful."

"We will, I *promise*."

"And you gone have to change my name. Mine, Miss Leefolt's, everbody's."

"Of course." I should've mentioned this. "When can we meet? *Where* can we meet?"

"Can't do it in the white neighborhood, that's for sure. I guess...we gone have to do it over at my house."

"Do you know any other maids who might be interested?" I ask, even though Missus Stein has only agreed to read one. But I have to be ready, on the slim chance she likes it.

Aibileen is quiet a moment. "I guess I could ask Minny. But she ain't real keen on talking to white peoples."

"Minny? You mean...Missus Walters' old maid," I say, feeling suddenly how incestuous this is turning. I wouldn't just be peering into Elizabeth's life, but Hilly's too.

"Minny got her some stories. Sho nuff."

"Aibileen," I say. "Thank you. Oh, thank you."

"Yes ma'am."

"I just...I have to ask you. What changed your mind?"

Aibileen doesn't even pause. "Miss Hilly," she says.

I go quiet, thinking of Hilly's bathroom plan and accusing the maid of stealing and her talk of diseases. The name comes out flat, bitter as a bad pecan.

MINNY

CHAPTER 10

I WALK INTO WORK with one thing on my mind. Today is the first day of December and while the rest of the United States is dusting off their manger scenes and pulling out their old stinky stockings, I've got another man I'm waiting on. And it's not Santy Claus and it's not the Baby Jesus. It's Mister Johnny Foote, Jr., who will learn that Minny Jackson is his maid on Christmas Eve.

I am waiting on the twenty-fourth like a court date. I don't know what Mister Johnny's going to do when he finds out I'm working here. Maybe he'll say, Good! Come clean my kitchen anytime! Here's some money! But I'm not that stupid. This secret-keeping is way too fishy for him to be some smiling whitey wanting to give me a raise. There's a good chance I might not have a job come Christmas Day.

It's eating me up, not knowing, but what I do know is, a month ago, I decided there had to be a more dignified way to die than having a heart attack squatting on top of a white lady's toilet lid. And after all that, it wasn't even Mister Johnny that came home, it was just the damn meter man.

But there wasn't much relief when it was over. What scared me worse was Miss Celia. Afterwards, during her cooking lesson, she was still shaking so bad, she couldn't even measure the salt in a spoon.

. . .

MONDAY COMES AND I CAN'T stop thinking about Louvenia Brown's grandson, Robert. He got out of the hospital this weekend, went to live with Louvenia, what with his parents already dead and all. Last night, when I went over there to take them a caramel cake, Robert had a cast on his arm and bandages over his eyes. "Oh, *Louvenia*," was all I could say when I saw him. Robert was laid up on the sofa asleep. They'd shaved half his head to operate. Louvenia, with all her troubles, still wanted to know how each and every person in my family was doing. And when Robert started to stir, she asked if I wouldn't mind going on home because Robert wakes up screaming. Terrified and remembering all over again that he's blind. She thought it might bother me. I can't stop thinking about it.

"I'm going to the store after while," I say to Miss Celia. I hold the grocery list out for her to see. Every Monday we do this. She gives me the grocery cash and when I get home I push the receipt in her face. I want her to see that every penny of change matches the paper. Miss Celia just shrugs but I keep those tickets safe in a drawer in case there's ever any question.

Minny cooking:
1. Ham with pineapples
2. Black-eyed peas
3. Sweet potatoes
4. Apple pie
5. Biscuits

Miss Celia cooking:
1. Butter beans

"But I did butter beans last week."

"Learn those, everything else come easy."

"I guess it's better anyway," she says. "I can sit down and be still when I'm shelling."

Almost three months and the fool still can't boil coffee. I pull out my pie dough, want to get it ready before I go to the store.

"Can we do a chocolate pie this time? I love chocolate pie."

I grit my teeth. "I don't know how to cook no chocolate pie," I lie. *Never. Never again after Miss Hilly.*

"You can't? Gosh, I thought you could cook anything. Maybe we ought to get us a recipe."

"What else kind a pie you thinking about?"

"Well, what about that peach pie you did that time?" she says, pouring a glass of milk. "That was real good."

"Them peaches from Mexico. Peaches ain't in season around here yet."

"But I saw them advertised in the paper."

I sigh. Nothing is easy with her, but at least she's off the chocolate. "One thing you got to know, things is best when they in season. You don't cook pumpkins in the summer, you don't cook peaches in the fall. You can't find it selling on the side a the road, it ain't in. Let's just do us a nice pecan pie instead."

"And Johnny loved those pralines you did. He thought I was the smartest girl he'd ever met when I gave him those."

I turn back to my dough so she can't see my face. Twice in a minute she's managed to irritate me. "Anything else you want Mister Johnny to think you did?" Besides being scared out of my wits, I am sick and tired of passing off my cooking for somebody else's. Except my kids, my cooking's the only thing I'm proud of.

"No, that's all." Miss Celia smiles, doesn't notice I've stretched my pie crust to where five holes rip through. Just twenty-four more days of this shit. I am praying to the Lord and the devil on the side that Mister Johnny doesn't come home before then.

EVERY OTHER DAY, I hear Miss Celia on the phone in her room, calling and calling the society ladies. The Benefit was three weeks ago and here she is already gunning up for next year. She and Mister Johnny didn't go or I would've heard plenty about it.

I didn't work the Benefit this year, first time in a decade. The money's pretty good, but I just couldn't risk running into Miss Hilly.

"Could you tell her Celia Foote called again? I left her a message a few days back…"

Miss Celia's voice is chipper, like she's peddling something on the tee-vee. Every time I hear it, I want to jerk the phone out of her hand, tell her to quit wasting her time. Because never mind she looks like a hussy. There's a bigger reason why Miss Celia doesn't have any friends and I knew it the minute I saw that picture of Mister Johnny. I've served enough bridge club luncheons to know something about every white woman in this town. Mister Johnny dumped Miss Hilly for Miss Celia back in college, and Miss Hilly never got over him.

I WALK IN THE CHURCH on Wednesday night. It's not but half full since it's only a quarter to seven and the choir doesn't start singing until seven thirty. But Aibileen asked me to come early so here I am. I'm curious what she has to say. Plus Leroy was in a good mood and playing with the kids so I figure, if he wants them, he can have them.

I see Aibileen in our usual pew, left side, fourth from the front, right by the window fan. We're prime members and we deserve a prime spot. She's got her hair smoothed back, a little roll of pencil curls around her neck. She's wearing a blue dress with big white buttons that I've never seen before. Aibileen has white lady clothes out the wazoo. White ladies love giving her their old stuff. As usual, she looks plump and respectable, but for all her prim and proper, Aibileen can still tell a dirty joke that'll make you tinkle in your pants.

I walk up the aisle, see Aibileen frown at something, creasing her forehead. For a second I can see the fifteen-odd years between us. But then she smiles and her face goes young and fat again.

"Lord," I say as soon as I'm settled in.

"I know. Somebody got to tell her." Aibileen fans her face with her hanky. It was Kiki Brown's morning for cleaning and the whole church is gaudied up with her lemon smell-good she makes and tries to sell for twenty-five cents a bottle. We have a sign-up sheet for cleaning the church.

Ask me, Kiki Brown ought to sign a little less and the men ought to sign a lot more. Far as I know, no man has signed that sheet once.

Besides the smell, the church looks pretty good. Kiki shined the pews to where you could pick your teeth looking at them. The Christmas tree's already up, next to the altar, full of tinsel and a shiny gold star on top. Three windows of the church have stained glass—the birth of Christ, Lazarus raised from the dead, and the teaching of those fool Pharisees. The other seven are filled with regular clear panes. We're still raising money for those.

"How Benny's asthma?" Aibileen asks.

"Had a little spell yesterday. Leroy dropping him and the rest a the kids by in a while. Let's hope the lemon don't kill him."

"Leroy." Aibileen shakes her head and laughs. "Tell him I said he better behave. Or I put him on my prayer list."

"I wish you would. Oh Lord, hide the food."

Hoity-toity Bertrina Bessemer waddles toward us. She leans over the pew in front of us, smilling with a big, tacky blue-bird hat on. Bertrina, she's the one who called Aibileen a fool for all those years.

"Minny," Bertrina says, "I sure was glad to hear about your new job."

"Thank you, Bertrina."

"And Aibileen, I thank you for putting me on your prayer list. My angina sure is better now. I call you this weekend and we catch up."

Aibileen smiles, nods. Bertrina waddles off to her pew.

"Maybe you ought a be a little pickier who you pray for," I say.

"Aw, I ain't mad at her no more," says Aibileen. "And look a there, she done lost some weight."

"She telling everybody she lost forty pounds," I say.

"Lord a mercy."

"Only got two hundred more to go."

Aibileen tries not to smile, acts like she's waving away the lemon smell.

"So what you want me to come early for?" I ask. "You miss me or something?"

"Naw, it's no big deal. Just something somebody said."

"What?"

Aibileen takes a breath, looks around for anybody listening. We're like royalty here. Folks are always hemming in on us.

"You know that Miss Skeeter?" she asks.

"I told you I did the other day."

She quiets her voice, says, "Well, remember how I slipped up and told her about Treelore writing colored things down?"

"I remember. She want a sue you for that?"

"No, no. She nice. But she had the gall to ask if me and some a my maid friends might want a put down on paper what it's like to tend for white people. Say she writing a book."

"Say what?"

Aibileen nods, raises her eyebrows. "Mm-hmm."

"Phhh. Well, you tell her it's a real Fourth of July picnic. It's what we dream a doing all weekend, get back in they houses to polish they silver," I say.

"I told her, let the regular old history books tell it. White people been representing colored opinions since the beginning a time."

"That's right. You tell her."

"I did. I tell her she crazy," Aibileen says. "I ask her, what if we told the truth? How we too scared to ask for minimum wage. How nobody gets paid they Social Security. How it feel when your own boss be calling you..." Aibileen shakes her head. I'm glad she doesn't say it.

"How we love they kids when they little..." she says and I see Aibileen's lip tremble a little. "And then they turn out just like they mamas."

I look down and see Aibileen's gripping her black pocketbook like it's the only thing she has left in this world. Aibileen, she moves on to another job when the babies get too old and stop being color-blind. We don't talk about it.

"Even if she is changing all the names a the help and the white ladies," she sniff.

"She crazy if she think we do something dangerous as that. For *her*."

"We don't want a bring all that mess up." Aibileen wipes her nose with a hankie. "Tell people the truth."

"No, we don't," I say, but I stop. It's something about that word *truth*.

I've been trying to tell white women the truth about working for them since I was fourteen years old.

"We don't want a change nothing around here," Aibileen says and we're both quiet, thinking about all the things we don't want to change. But then Aibileen narrows her eyes at me, asks, "What. You don't think it's a crazy idea?"

"I do, I just..." And that's when I see it. We've been friends for sixteen years, since the day I moved from Greenwood to Jackson and we met at the bus stop. I can read Aibileen like the Sunday paper. "You thinking about it, ain't you," I say. "You want a talk to Miss Skeeter."

She shrugs and I know I'm right. But before Aibileen can confess, Reverend Johnson comes and sits down in the pew behind us, leans between our shoulders. "Minny, I'm sorry I haven't had the chance to tell you congratulations on your new job."

I smooth my dress down. "Why, thank you, Reverend Minister."

"You must of been on Aibileen's prayer list," he says, patting Aibileen on the shoulder.

"Sure was. I told Aibileen, at this rate, she needs to start charging."

The Reverend laughs. He gets up and treads slowly to the pulpit. Everything goes still. I can't believe Aibileen wants to tell Miss Skeeter the truth.

Truth.

It feels cool, like water washing over my sticky-hot body. Cooling a heat that's been burning me up all my life.

Truth, I say inside my head again, just for that feeling.

Reverend Johnson raises his hands and speaks in a soft, deep voice. The choir behind him begins to hum "Talking to Jesus" and we all stand up. In half a minute I'm sweating.

"Think you might be interested? In talking to Miss Skeeter?" whispers Aibileen.

I look back and there's Leroy with the kids, late as usual. "Who, me?" I say and my voice is loud against the soft music. I tamp it down, but not by much.

"Ain't no way I'm gonna do something crazy as that."

. . .

For no reason but to irritate me, we get a heat wave in December. In forty degrees, I sweat like iced tea in August and here I woke up this morning to eighty-three on the dial. I've spent half my life trying not to sweat so much: Dainty Lady sweat cream, frozen potatoes in my pockets, ice pack tied to my head (I actually paid a doctor for that fool advice), and I still soak my sweat pads through in five minutes. I tote my Fairley Funeral Home fan every place I go. Works good and it was free.

Miss Celia takes to the week of warm weather, though, and actually goes outside and sits by the pool in these tacky white sunglasses and a fuzzy bathrobe. Thank the Lord she's out of the house. At first I thought maybe she was sick in the body, but now I'm wondering if she's sick in the head. I don't mean the talking to yourself variety you see in old ladies like Miss Walters where you know it's just the old timers disease, but the capital C crazy where you get hauled to Whitfield in a straitjacket.

I catch her slipping upstairs to the empty bedrooms almost every day now. I hear her sneaky little feet walking down the hall, passing over that little squeak in the floor. I don't think much of it—heck, it's her house. But then one day, she does it again, and then again, and it's the fact that she's so darn *sneaky* about it, waiting until I turn on the Hoover or get busy on a cake, that makes me suspicious. She spends about seven or eight minutes up there and then pokes her little head around to make sure I don't see her come down again.

"Don't go getting in her business," Leroy says. "You just make sure she tells her mister you cleaning his house." Leroy's been on the damn Crow the past couple of nights, drinking behind the power plant after his shift. He's no fool. He knows if I'm dead, that paycheck won't be showing up on its own.

After she makes her trip upstairs, Miss Celia comes to the kitchen table instead of going back to bed. I wish she'd get on out of here. I'm pulling chicken off the bone. I've got the broth boiling and the dumplings already cut. I don't want her trying to help with this.

"Just thirteen more days before you tell Mister Johnny about me," I say, and like I knew she would, Miss Celia gets up from the kitchen table and heads for her bedroom. But before she makes it out the door she mutters, "Do you have to remind me of that fact every day of my life?"

I stand up straighter. That's the first time Miss Celia's ever gotten cross with me. "Mm-hmm," I tell her, not even looking up because I will remind her until Mister Johnny's shook my hand and said nice to meet you, Minny.

But then I look over and see Miss Celia still standing there. She's holding on to the doorframe. Her face has gone flat white, like cheap wall paint.

"You been fooling with the raw chicken again?"

"No, I'm...just tired."

But the pricks of sweat on her makeup—that now's gone gray—tell me she's not fine. I help her to bed and bring her the Lady-a-Pinkam to drink. The pink label has a picture of a real proper lady on it with a turban on her head, smiling like she feels better. I hand Miss Celia the spoon to measure it out, but that tacky woman just drinks it straight from the bottle.

Afterward, I wash my hands. Whatever it is she's got, I hope it ain't catching.

THE DAY AFTER MISS CELIA's face goes funny is change-the-damn-sheets day and the day I hate the most. Sheets are just too personal a thing for folks who aren't kin to be fooling with. They are full of hair and scabs and snot and the signs of jelly-rolling. But it's the blood stains that are the worst. Scrubbing those out with my bare hands, I gag over the sink. That goes for blood anywhere and anything with a suspicious resemblance. A stepped-on strawberry can hang me over the toilet bowl for the rest of the day.

Miss Celia knows about Tuesdays and usually she moves out to the sofa so I can do my work. A cold front started in this morning, so she can't go out to the swimming pool, and they say the weather's going to get worse. But at nine, then ten, then eleven the bedroom door's still closed. Finally, I knock.

"Yes?" she says. I open the door.

"Morning, Miss Celia."

"Hey, Minny."

"It's Tuesday."

Not only is Miss Celia still in bed, she's curled up on top of the covers in her nightgown without a drop of her makeup on.

"I got to get them sheets washed and ironed and then I got to get to this old chiffarobe you done let go dry as Texas. And then we cooking—"

"No learning lesson today, Minny." She isn't smiling either, like she usually does when she sees me.

"You feeling bad?"

"Fetch me some water, will you?"

"Yes'm." I go in the kitchen and fill up a glass from the sink. She must be feeling bad because she's never asked me to serve her anything before.

When I walk back in the bedroom though, Miss Celia's not in bed and the bathroom door's closed. Now why'd she ask me to go get her water if she's got the means to get up and go to the bathroom? At least she's out of my way. I pick Mister Johnny's pants up off the floor, toss them over my shoulder. Ask me, this woman doesn't take enough exercise, sitting around the house all day. Oh now, Minny, don't go on that way. If she's sick, she's sick.

"You sick?" I holler outside the bathroom door.

"I'm...fine."

"While you in there, I'm on go head and change these sheets."

"No, I want you to go on," she says through the door. "Go on home for the day, Minny."

I stand there and tap my foot on her yellow rug. I don't want to go on home. It's Tuesday, change-the-damn-sheets day. If I don't do it today, that makes Wednesday change-the-damn-sheets day too.

"What Mister Johnny gone do if he come home and the house's a mess?"

"He's at the deer camp tonight. Minny, I need you to bring me the phone over—" her voice breaks into a trembly wail. "Drag it on over and fetch my phone book that's setting in the kitchen."

"You sick, Miss Celia?"

But she doesn't answer so I go get the book and stretch the phone over to the bathroom door and tap on it.

"Just leave it there." Miss Celia sounds like she's crying now. "I want you to go on home now."

"But I just gots—"

"I said go home, Minny!"

I step back from that closed door. Heat rises up my face. And it stings, not because I haven't been yelled at before. I just haven't been yelled at by Miss Celia yet.

THE NEXT MORNING, Woody Asap on Channel Twelve is waving his white scaly hands all over the state map. Jackson, Mississippi, is frozen like an ice pop. First it rained, then it froze, then anything with more than a half-inch extending broke off to the ground by this morning. Tree branches, power lines, porch awnings collapsed like they'd plumb given up. Outside's been dunked in a shiny clear bucket of shellac.

My kids glue their sleepy faces to the radio and when the box says the roads are frozen and school is closed, they all jump around and whoop and whistle and run outside to look at the ice with nothing on but their long johns.

"Get back in this house and put some shoes on!" I holler out the door. Not one of them does. I call Miss Celia to tell her I can't drive in the ice and to find out if she's got power out there. After she yelled at me like I was a nigger in the road yesterday, you'd think I wouldn't give a hoot about her.

When I call, I hear, "Yeeello."

My heart hiccups.

"Who is this? Who's calling here?"

Real careful I hang up that phone. I guess Mister Johnny's not working today either. I don't know how he made it home with the storm. All I know is, even on a day off, I can't escape the fear of that man. But in eleven days, that's all going to be over.

MOST OF THE TOWN THAWS in a day. Miss Celia's not in bed when I walk in. She's sitting at the white kitchen table staring out the window with an ugly look on her face like her poor fancy life is just too hot a hell to live in. It's the mimosa tree she's eyeing out there. It took the ice pretty hard. Half of the branches broke off and all the spindly leaves are brown and soggy.

"Morning, Minny," she says, not even looking my way.

But I just nod. I have nothing to say to her, not after the way she treated me day before yesterday.

"We can finally cut that old ugly thing down now," says Miss Celia.

"Go ahead. Cut em all down." Just like me, cut me down for no reason at all.

Miss Celia gets up and comes over to the sink where I'm standing. She grabs hold of my arm. "I'm sorry I hollered at you like I did." Tears brim up in her eyes when she says it.

"Mm-hmm."

"I was sick and I know that's no excuse, but I was feeling real poor and..." She starts sobbing then, like the worst thing she's ever done in her life is yell at her maid.

"Alright," I say. "Ain't nothing to boo-hoo over."

And then she hugs me tight around the neck until I kind of pat her on the back and peel her off. "Go on, set down," I say. "I'll fix you some coffee."

I guess we all get a little snippy when we're not feeling good.

BY THE NEXT MONDAY, the leaves on that mimosa tree have turned black like it burned instead of froze. I come in the kitchen ready to tell her how many days we have left, but Miss Celia's staring at that tree, hating it with her eyes the same way she hates the stove. She's pale, won't eat anything I put in front of her.

All day, instead of laying up in bed, she works on decorating the ten-foot Christmas tree in the foyer, making my life a vacuuming hell with all the needles flying around. Then she goes in the backyard, starts clipping the rose bushes and digging the tulip bulbs. I've never seen her move that much, ever. She comes in for her cooking lesson afterward with dirt under her nails but she's still not smiling.

"Six more days before we tell Mister Johnny," I say.

She doesn't say anything for a while, then her voice comes out flat as a pan. "Are you sure I have to? I was thinking maybe we could wait."

I stop where I am, with buttermilk dripping off my hands. "Ask me how sure I am again."

"Alright, alright." And then she goes outside again to take up her new favorite pastime, staring down that mimosa tree with the axe in her hand. But she never takes a chop.

Wednesday night all I can think is just ninety-six more hours. Knowing I might not have a job after Christmas gnaws at my stomach. I'll have a lot more to worry about than just being shot dead. Miss Celia's supposed to tell him on Christmas Eve, after I leave, before they go over to Mister Johnny's mama's house. But Miss Celia's acting so strange, I wonder if she's going to try and back out. No ma'am, I say to myself all day. I intend to stay on her like hair on soap.

When I walk in Thursday morning though, Miss Celia's not even home. I can't believe she's actually left the house. I sit at the table and pour myself a cup of coffee.

I look out at the backyard. It's bright, sunny. That black mimosa tree sure is ugly. I wonder why Mister Johnny doesn't just go ahead and cut that thing down.

I lean in a little closer to the windowsill. "Well look a there." Down around the bottom, some green fronds are still hanging on, perking up a little in the sun.

"That old tree just playing possum."

I pull a pad out of my pocketbook where I keep a list of what needs to be tended to, not for Miss Celia, but my own groceries, Christmas presents, things for my kids. Benny's asthma has gotten a little better but Leroy came home last night smelling like Old Crow again. He pushed me hard and I bumped my thigh on the kitchen table. He comes home like that tonight, I'll fix him a knuckle sandwich for supper.

I sigh. Seventy-two more hours and I'm a free woman. Maybe fired, maybe dead after Leroy finds out, but free.

I try to concentrate on the week. Tomorrow's heavy cooking and I've got the church supper Saturday night and the service on Sunday. When am I going to clean my own house? Wash my own kids' clothes? My oldest girl, Sugar, is sixteen and pretty good about keeping things neat, but I like to help her out on the weekends the way my mama never helped me. And Aibileen. She called me again last night, asked if I'd help her and Miss Skeeter with the stories. I love Aibileen, I do. But I think she's making a king-sized mistake trusting a white lady. And I told her, too. She's risking her job, her safety. Not to mention why anyone would want to help a friend of Miss Hilly's.

Lord, I better get on with my work.

I pineapple the ham and get it in the oven. Then I dust the shelves in the hunting room, vacuum the bear while he stares at me like I'm a snack. "Just you and me today," I tell him. As usual he doesn't say much. I get my rag and my oil soap, work my way up the staircase, polishing each spoke on the banister as I go. When I make it to the top, I head into bedroom number one.

I clean upstairs for about an hour. It's chilly up here, no bodies to warm it up. I work my arm back and forth, back and forth across everything wood. Between the second and third bedrooms, I go downstairs to Miss Celia's room before she comes back.

I get that eerie prickle, of being in a house so empty. Where'd she go? After working here all this time and her only leaving three times and always telling me when and where and why she's leaving, like I care anyway, now she's gone like the wind. I ought to be happy. I ought to be glad that fool's out of my hair. But being here by myself, I feel like an intruder. I look down at the little pink rug that covers the bloodstain by the bathroom. Today I was going to take another crack at it. A chill blows through the room, like a ghost passing by. I shiver.

Maybe I won't work on that bloodstain today.

On the bed the covers, as usual, have been thrown off. The sheets are twisted and turned around the wrong way. It always looks like a wrestling match has gone on in here. I stop myself from wondering. You start to wonder about people in the bedroom, before you know it you're all wrapped up in their business.

I strip off one of the pillowcases. Miss Celia's mascara smudged little charcoal butterflies all over it. The clothes on the floor I stuff into the pillowcase to make it easier to carry. I pick up Mister Johnny's folded pants off the yellow ottoman.

"Now how'm I sposed to know if these is clean or dirty?" I stick them in the sack anyway. My motto on housekeeping: when in doubt, wash it out.

I tote the bag over to the bureau. The bruise on my thigh burns when I bend down to pick up a pair of Miss Celia's silky stockings.

"Who are *you*?"

I drop the sack.

Slowly, I back away until my bottom bumps the bureau. He's standing in the doorway, eyes narrowed. Real slow, I look down at the axe hanging from his hand.

Oh Lord. I can't get to the bathroom because he's too close and he'd get in there with me. I can't make it past him out the door unless I pummel him, and the man has an axe. My head throbs hot I'm so panicked. I'm *cornered*.

Mister Johnny stares down at me. He swings the axe a little. Tilts his head and smiles.

I do the only thing I can do. I wrinkle my face as mean as I can and pull my lips across my teeth and yell: *"You and your axe better get out a my way."*

Mister Johnny looks down at the axe, like he forgot he had it. Then back up at me. We stare at each other a second. I don't move and I don't breathe.

He sneaks a look over at the sack I've dropped to see what I was stealing. The leg of his khakis is poking out the top. "Now, listen," I say, and tears spring up in my eyes. "Mister Johnny, I told Miss Celia to tell you about me. I must a asked her a thousand times—"

But he just laughs. He shakes his head. He thinks it's funny he's about to chop me up.

"Just listen to me, I told her—"

But he's still chuckling. "Calm down, girl. I'm not going to get you," he says. "You surprised me, that's all."

I'm panting, easing my way toward the bathroom. He still has the axe in his hand, swinging it a little.

"What's your name, anyway?"

"Minny," I whisper. I've still got five feet to go.

"How long have you been coming, Minny?"

"Not long." I jiggle my head no.

"*How* long?"

"Few…weeks," I say. I bite down on my lip. *Three months.*

He shakes his head. "Now, I know it's been longer than that."

I look at the bathroom door. What good would it do to be in a bathroom where the door won't even lock? When the man's got an axe to hack the door down with?

"I swear I'm not mad," he says.

"What about that axe?" I say, my teeth gritted.

He rolls his eyes, then he sets it on the carpet, kicks it to the side.

"Come on, let's go have us a talk in the kitchen."

He turns and walks away. I look down at the axe, wondering if I should take it. Just the sight of it scares me. I push it under the bed and follow him.

In the kitchen, I edge myself close to the back door, check the knob to make sure it's unlocked.

"Minny, I promise. It's fine that you're here," he says.

I watch his eyes, trying to see if he's lying. He's a big man, six-two at least. A little paunch in the front, but strong looking. "I reckon you gone fire me, then."

"Fire you?" He laughs. "You're the best cook I've ever known. Look what you've done to me." He frowns down at his stomach that's just starting to poke out. "Hell, I haven't eaten like this since Cora Blue was around. She practically raised me."

I take a deep breath because his knowing Cora Blue seems to safen things up a little. "Her kids went to my church. I knew her."

"I sure do miss her." He turns, opens the refrigerator, stares in, closes it.

"When's Celia coming back? You know?" Mister Johnny asks.

"I don't know. I spec she went to get her hair done."

"I thought for a while there, when we were eating your food, she really did learn how to cook. Until that Saturday, when you weren't here, and she tried to make hamburgers."

He leans against the sink board, sighs. "Why doesn't she want me to know about you?"

"I don't know. She won't tell me."

He shakes his head, looks up at the black mark on the ceiling from where Miss Celia burned up the turkey that time. "Minny, I don't care if Celia never lifts another finger for the rest of her life. But she says she wants to do things for me herself." He raises his eyebrows a little. "I mean, do you understand what I was eating before you got here?"

"She learning. Least she . . . trying to learn," but I kind of snort at this. Some things you just can't lie about.

"I don't *care* if she can cook. I just want her here"—he shrugs—"with me."

He rubs his brow with his white shirtsleeve and I see why his shirts are always so dirty. And he *is* sort of handsome. For a white man.

"She just doesn't seem happy," he says. "Is it me? Is it the house? Are we too far away from town?"

"I don't know, Mister Johnny."

"Then what's going on?" He props his hands down on the counter behind him, grabs hold. "Just tell me. Is she"—he swallows hard—"is she seeing somebody else?"

I try not to, but I feel kind of sorry for him then, seeing he's just as confused as I am about all this mess.

"Mister Johnny, this ain't none a my business. But I can tell you Miss Celia ain't having no relations outside a this house."

He nods. "You're right. That was a stupid thing to ask."

I eye the door, wondering when Miss Celia's going to be home. I don't know what she'd do if she found Mister Johnny here.

"Look," he says, "don't say anything about meeting me. I'm going to let her tell me when she's ready."

I manage my first real smile. "So you want me to just go on like I been doing?"

"Look after her. I don't like her in this big house by herself."

"Yessuh. Whatever you say."

"I came by today to surprise her. I was going to cut down that mimosa tree she hates so much, then take her into town for lunch. Pick out some jewelry for her Christmas present." Mister Johnny walks to the window, looks out, and sighs. "I guess I'll go get lunch in town somewhere."

"I fix you something. What you want?"

He turns around, grinning like a kid. I start going through the refrigerator, pulling things out.

"Remember those pork chops we had that time?" He starts nibbling on his fingernail. "Will you make those for us this week?"

"I fix em for supper tonight. Got some in the freezer. And tomorrow night you having chicken and dumplings."

"Oh, Cora Blue used to make us those."

"Sit up there at the table and I'm on do you a good BLT to take with you in the truck."

"And will you toast the bread?"

"A course. Can't have no proper sandwich on no raw bread. And this afternoon I'll make one a Minny's famous caramel cakes. And next week we gone do you a fried catfish..."

I pull out the bacon for Mister Johnny's lunch, get the skillet out to fry. Mister Johnny's eyes are clear and wide. He's smiling with every part of his face. I fix his sandwich and wrap it in waxed paper. Finally, somebody I get the satisfaction of feeding.

"Minny, I have to ask, if *you're* here...what in the world is Celia doing all day?"

I shrug. "I ain't never seen a white woman sit there like she do. Most of em is busy-busy, running errands, acting like they busier than me."

"She needs some friends. I asked my buddy Will if he'd get his wife to come out and teach her to play bridge, get her in a group. I know Hilly's the ringleader of all that stuff."

I stare at him, like if I kept real still, maybe it wouldn't be true. Finally I ask, "That Miss Hilly Holbrook you talking about?"

"You know her?" he asks.

"Mm-hmm." I swallow the tire iron that's rising up in my throat at the thought of Miss Hilly hanging around this house. Miss Celia finding out the truth about the Terrible Awful. There's no way those two could be friends. But I bet Miss Hilly would do anything for Mister Johnny.

"I'll call Will tonight and ask him again." He pats me on my shoulder and I find myself thinking about that word again, *truth*. And Aibileen's telling Miss Skeeter all about it. If the truth gets out on me, I'm done. I crossed the wrong person, and that's all it takes.

"I'm going to give you my number at the office. Call me if you ever run into trouble, alright?"

"Yessuh," I say, feeling my dread erase any relief I had coming to me today.

MISS SKEETER

CHAPTER 11

IT'S TECHNICALLY WINTER in most of the nation, but already there is gnashing of teeth and wringing of hands in my mother's house. Signs of spring have come too early. Daddy's in a cotton-planting frenzy, had to hire ten extra field workers to till and drive tractors to get the seed in the ground. Mother's been studying *The Farmer's Almanac*, but she's hardly concerned with planting. She delivers the bad news to me with a hand on her forehead.

"They say this'll be the most humid one in years." She sighs. The Shinalator never did much good after those first few times. "I'd pick up some more spray cans down at Beemon's, the new extra-heavy kind."

She looks up from the *Almanac*, narrows her eyes at me. "What are you dressed that way for?"

I have on my darkest dress, dark stockings. The black scarf over my hair probably makes me look more like Peter O'Toole in *Lawrence of Arabia* than Marlene Dietrich. The ugly red satchel hangs from my shoulder.

"I have some errands to run tonight. Then I'm meeting...some girls. At church."

"On a Saturday night?"

"Mama, God doesn't care what day of the week it is," I say and make for the car before she can ask any more questions. Tonight, I'm going to Aibileen's for her first interview.

My heart racing, I drive fast on the paved town roads, heading for the colored part of town. I've never even sat at the same table with a Negro who wasn't paid to do so. The interview has been delayed by over a month. First, the holidays came and Aibileen had to work late almost every night, wrapping presents and cooking for Elizabeth's Christmas party. In January, I started to panic when Aibileen got the flu. I'm afraid I've waited so long, Missus Stein will have lost interest or forgotten why she even agreed to read it.

I drive the Cadillac through the darkness, turning on Gessum Avenue, Aibileen's Street. I'd rather be in the old truck, but Mother would've been too suspicious and Daddy was using it in the fields. I stop in front of an abandoned, haunted-looking house three down from Aibileen's, as we planned. The front porch of the spooky house is sagging, the windows have no panes. I step into the dark, lock the doors and walk quickly. I keep my head lowered, my noisy heels clicking on the pavement.

A dog barks and my keys jangle to the pavement. I glimpse around, pick them up. Two sets of colored people sit on porches, watching, rocking. There are no streetlights so it's hard to say who else sees me. I keep walking, feeling as obvious as my vehicle: large and white.

I reach number twenty-five, Aibileen's house. I give one last look around, wishing I wasn't ten minutes early. The colored part of town seems so far away when, evidently, it's only a few miles from the white part of town.

I knock softly. There are footsteps, and something inside slams closed. Aibileen opens the door. "Come on in," she whispers and quickly shuts it behind me and locks it.

I've never seen Aibileen in anything but her whites. Tonight she has on a green dress with black piping. I can't help but notice, she stands a little taller in her own house.

"Make yourself comfortable. I be back real quick."

Even with the single lamp on, the front room is dark, full of browns and shadows. The curtains are pulled and pinned together so there's no gap. I don't know if they're like that all the time, or just for me. I lower myself onto the narrow sofa. There's a wooden coffee table with hand-tatted lace draped over the top. The floors are bare. I wish I hadn't worn such an expensive-looking dress.

A few minutes later, Aibileen comes back with a tray holding a teapot and two cups that don't match, paper napkins folded into triangles. I smell the cinnamon cookies she's made. As she pours the tea, the top to the pot rattles.

"Sorry," she says and holds the top down. "I ain't never had a white person in my house before."

I smile, even though I know it wasn't meant to be funny. I drink a sip of tea. It is bitter and strong. "Thank you," I say. "The tea is nice."

She sits and folds her hands in her lap, looks at me expectantly.

"I thought we'd do a little background work and then just jump right in with the questions," I say. I pull out my notebook and scan the questions I've prepared. They suddenly seem obvious, amateur.

"Alright," she says. She is sitting up very straight, on the sofa, turned toward me.

"Well, to start, um, when and where were you born?"

She swallows, nods. "Nineteen o-nine. Piedmont Plantation down in Cherokee County."

"Did you know when you were a girl, growing up, that one day you'd be a maid?"

"Yes ma'am. Yes, I did."

I smile, wait for her to elucidate. There is nothing.

"And you knew that...because...?"

"Mama was a maid. My granmama was a house slave."

"A house slave. Uh-huh," I say, but she only nods. Her hands stay folded in her lap. She's watching the words I'm writing on the page.

"Did you...ever have dreams of being something else?"

"No," she says. "No ma'am, I didn't." It's so quiet, I can hear both of us breathing.

"Alright. Then...what does it feel like, to raise a white child when your own child's at home, being…" I swallow, embarrassed by the question, "…looked after by someone else?"

"It feel…" She's still sitting up so straight it looks painful. "Um, maybe…we could go on to the next one."

"Oh. Alright." I stare at my questions. "What do you like best about being a maid and what do you like least?"

She looks up at me, like I've asked her to define a dirty word.

"I—I spec I like looking after the kids best," she whispers.

"Anything…you'd like to add…about that?"

"No ma'am."

"Aibileen, you don't have to call me 'ma'am.' Not here."

"Yes ma'am. Oh. Sorry." She covers her mouth.

Loud voices shout in the street and both our eyes dart toward the window. We are quiet, stock-still. What would happen if someone white found out I was here on a Saturday night talking to Aibileen in her regular clothes? Would they call the police, to report a suspicious meeting? I'm suddenly sure they would. We'd be arrested because that is what they do. They'd charge us with integration violation—I read about it in the paper all the time—they despise the whites that meet with the coloreds to help with the civil rights movement. This has nothing to do with integration, but why else would we be meeting? I didn't even bring any Miss Myrna letters as backup.

I see open, honest fear on Aibileen's face. Slowly the voices outside dissipate down the road. I exhale but Aibileen stays tense. She keeps her eyes on the curtains.

I look down at my list of questions, searching for something to draw this nervousness out of her, out of myself. I keep thinking about how much time I've lost already.

"And what…did you say you disliked about your job?"

Aibileen swallows hard.

"I mean, do you want to talk about the bathroom? Or about Eliz—Miss Leefolt? Anything about the way she pays you? Has she ever yelled at you in front of Mae Mobley?"

Aibileen takes a napkin and dabs it to her forehead. She starts to speak, but stops herself.

"We've talked plenty of times, Aibileen…"

She puts her hand to her mouth. "I'm sorry, I—" She gets up and walks quickly down the narrow hall. A door closes, rattling the teapot and the cups on the tray.

Five minutes pass. When she comes back, she holds a towel to her front, the way I've seen Mother do after she vomits, when she doesn't make it to her toilet in time.

"I'm sorry. I thought I was…ready to talk."

I nod, not sure what to do.

"I just…I know you already told that lady in New York I's gone do this but…" She closes her eyes. "I'm sorry. I don't think I can. I think I need to lay down."

"Tomorrow night. I'll…come up with a better way. Let's just try again and…"

She shakes her head, clutches her towel.

On my drive home, I want to kick myself. For thinking I could just waltz in and demand answers. For thinking she'd stop feeling like the maid just because we were at her house, because she wasn't wearing a uniform.

I look over at my notebook on the white leather seat. Besides where she grew up, I've gotten a total of twelve words. And four of them are *yes ma'am* and *no ma'am.*

PATSY CLINE'S VOICE DRIFTS out of WJDX radio. As I drive down the County Road, they're playing "Walking After Midnight." When I pull into Hilly's driveway, they're on "Three Cigarettes in an Ashtray." Her plane crashed this morning and everyone from New York to Mississippi to Seattle is in mourning, singing her songs. I park the Cadillac and stare out at Hilly's rambling white house. It's been four days since Aibileen vomited in the middle of our interview and I've heard nothing from her.

I go inside. The bridge table is set up in Hilly's antebellum-style parlor with its deafening grandfather clock and gold swag curtains. Everyone is seated—Hilly, Elizabeth, and Lou Anne Templeton, who has replaced Missus Walters. Lou Anne is one of those girls who wears a big eager smile—*all* the time, and it never stops. It makes me want to stick a straight pin in her. And when you're not looking, she stares at you with that vapid, toothy smile. And she agrees with every single little thing Hilly says.

Hilly holds up a *Life* magazine, points to a spread of a house in California. "A den they're calling it, like wild animals are living there."

"Oh, isn't that dreadful!" Lou Anne beams.

The picture shows wall-to-wall shag carpet and low, streamlined sofas, egg-shaped chairs and televisions that look like flying saucers. In Hilly's parlor, a portrait of a Confederate general hangs eight feet tall. It is as prominent as if he were a grandfather and not a third cousin removed.

"That's it. Trudy's house looks just like that," Elizabeth says. I've been so wrapped up in the interview with Aibileen, I'd almost forgotten Elizabeth's trip last week to see her older sister. Trudy married a banker and they moved to Hollywood. Elizabeth went out there for four days to see her new house.

"Well, that's just bad taste, is what it is," Hilly says. "No offense to your family, Elizabeth."

"What was Hollywood like?" Lou Anne asks.

"Oh, it was like a dream. And Trudy's house—T.V. sets in every room. That same crazy space-age furniture you could hardly even sit in. We went to all these fancy restaurants, where the movie stars eat, and drank martinis and burgundy wine. And one night Max Factor himself came over to the table, spoke to Trudy like they're just old friends"—she shakes her head—"like they were just passing by in the grocery store." Elizabeth sighs.

"Well, if you ask me, you're still the prettiest in the family," Hilly says. "Not that Trudy's unattractive, but you're the one with the poise and the real style."

Elizabeth smiles at this, but then drifts back to frowning. "Not to mention she has live-in help, every day, every *hour*. I hardly had to see Mae Mobley at all."

I cringe at this comment, but no one else seems to notice. Hilly's watching her maid, Yule May, refill our tea glasses. She's tall, slender, almost regal-looking and has a much better figure than Hilly. Seeing her makes me worry about Aibileen. I've called Aibileen's house twice this week, but there wasn't any answer. I'm sure she's avoiding me. I guess I'll have to go to Elizabeth's house to talk to her whether Elizabeth likes it or not.

"I was thinking next year we might do a *Gone With the Wind* theme for the Benefit," Hilly says, "maybe rent the old Fairview Mansion?"

"What a great idea!" Lou Anne says.

"Oh Skeeter," Hilly says, "I know you just hated missing it this year." I nod, give a pitiful frown. I'd pretended to have the flu to avoid going alone.

"I'll tell you one thing," Hilly says, "I won't be hiring that rock-and-roll band again, playing all that fast dance music..."

Elizabeth taps my arm. She has her handbag in her lap. "I almost forgot to give this to you. From Aibileen, for the Miss Myrna thing? I told her though, y'all cannot powwow on this today, not after all that time she missed in January."

I open the folded piece of paper. The words are in blue ink, in a lovely cursive hand.

I know how to make the teapot stop rattling.

"And who in the world cares about how to make a teapot not rattle?" Elizabeth says. Because of course she read it.

It takes me two seconds and a drink of iced tea to understand. "You wouldn't believe how hard it is," I tell her.

TWO DAYS LATER, I sit in my parents' kitchen, waiting for dusk to fall. I give in and light another cigarette even though last night the surgeon general came on the television set and shook his finger at everybody, trying to convince us that smoking will kill us. But Mother once told me tongue kissing would turn me blind and I'm starting to think it's all just a big plot between the surgeon general and Mother to make sure no one ever has any fun.

At eight o'clock that same night, I'm stumbling down Aibileen's street as discreetly as one can carrying a fifty-pound Corona typewriter. I knock softly, already dying for another cigarette to calm my nerves. Aibileen answers and I slip inside. She's wearing the same green dress and stiff black shoes as last time.

I try to smile, like I'm confident it will work this time, despite the idea she explained over the phone. "Could we...sit in the kitchen this time?" I ask. "Would you mind?"

"Alright. Ain't nothing to look at, but come on back."

The kitchen is about half the size of the living room, and warmer. It smells like tea and lemons. The black-and-white linoleum floor has been scrubbed thin. There's just enough counter for the china tea set.

I set the typewriter on a scratched red table under the window. Aibileen starts to pour the hot water into the teapot.

"Oh, none for me, thanks," I say and reach in my bag. "I brought us some Co-Colas if you want one." I've tried to come up with ways to make Aibileen more comfortable. Number One: don't make her feel like she has to serve me.

"Well, ain't that nice. I usually don't take my tea till later anyway." She brings over an opener and two glasses. I drink mine straight from the bottle and, seeing this, she pushes the glasses aside, does the same.

I called Aibileen after Elizabeth gave me the note, and listened hopefully as Aibileen told me her idea—for her to write her own words down and then show me what she's written. I tried to act excited. But I know I'll have to rewrite everything she's written, wasting even more time. I thought it might make it easier if she could see it in typeface instead of me reading it and telling her it can't work this way.

We smile at each other. I take a sip of my Coke, smooth my blouse. "So..." I say.

Aibileen has a wire-ringed notebook in front of her. "Want me to...just go head and read?"

"Sure," I say.

We both take deep breaths and she begins reading in a slow, steady voice.

"My first white baby to ever look after was named Alton Carrington Speers. It was 1924 and I'd just turned fifteen years old. Alton was a long, skinny baby with hair fine as silk on a corn..."

I begin typing as she reads, her words rhythmic, pronounced more clearly than her usual talk. "Every window in that filthy house was painted shut on the inside, even though the house was big with a wide green lawn. I knew the air was bad, felt sick myself…"

"Hang on," I say. I've typed *wide greem.* I blow on the typing fluid, retype it. "Okay, go ahead."

"When the mama died, six months later," she reads, "of the lung disease, they kept me on to raise Alton until they moved away to Memphis. I loved that baby and he loved me and that's when I knew I was good at making children feel proud of themselves…"

I hadn't wanted to insult Aibileen when she told me her idea. I tried to urge her out of it, over the phone. "Writing isn't that easy. And you wouldn't have time for this anyway, Aibileen, not with a full-time job."

"Can't be much different than writing my prayers every night."

It was the first interesting thing she'd told me about herself since we'd started the project, so I'd grabbed the shopping pad in the pantry. "You don't say your prayers, then?"

"I never told nobody that before. Not even Minny. Find I can get my point across a lot better writing em down."

"So this is what you do on the weekends?" I asked. "In your spare time?" I liked the idea of capturing her life outside of work, when she wasn't under the eye of Elizabeth Leefolt.

"Oh no, I write a hour, sometimes two ever day. Lot a ailing, sick peoples in this town."

I was impressed. That was more than I wrote on some days. I told her we'd try it just to get the project going again.

Aibileen takes a breath, a swallow of Coke, and reads on.

She backtracks to her first job at thirteen, cleaning the Francis the First silver service at the governor's mansion. She reads how on her first morning, she made a mistake on the chart where you filled in the number of pieces so they'd know you hadn't stolen anything.

"I come home that morning, after I been fired, and stood outside my house with my new work shoes on. The shoes my mama paid a month's worth a light bill for. I guess that's when I understood what shame was and the color of it too. Shame ain't black, like dirt, like I always thought it was. Shame be the color of a new white uniform your mother ironed all night to pay for, white without a smudge or a speck a work-dirt on it."

Aibileen looks up to see what I think. I stop typing. I'd expected the stories to be sweet, glossy. I realize I might be getting more than I'd bargained for. She reads on.

"...so I go on and get the chiffarobe straightened out and before I know it, that little white boy done cut his fingers clean off in that window fan I asked her to take out ten times. I never seen that much red come out a person and I grab the boy, I grab them four fingers. Tote him to the colored hospital cause I didn't know where the white one was. But when I got there, a colored man stop me and say, *Is this boy white?*" The typewriter keys are clacking like hail on a roof. Aibileen is reading faster and I am ignoring my mistakes, stopping her only to put in another page. Every eight seconds, I fling the carriage aside.

"And I say, *Yessuh,* and he say, *Is them his white fingers?* And I say, *Yessuh,* and he say, *Well, you better tell em he your high yellow cause that colored doctor won't operate on a white boy in a Negro hospital.* And then a white policeman grab me and he say, *Now you look a here—*"

She stops. Looks up. The clacking ceases.

"What? The policeman said *look a here* what?"

"Well, that's all I put down. Had to catch the bus for work this morning."

I hit the return and the typewriter dings. Aibileen and I look each other straight in the eye. I think this might actually work.

CHAPTER 12

EVERY OTHER NIGHT for the next two weeks, I tell Mother I'm off to feed the hungry at the Canton Presbyterian Church, where we, fortunately, know not a soul. Of course she'd rather I go down to the First Presbyterian, but Mother's not one to argue with Christian works and she nods approvingly, tells me on the side to make sure I wash my hands thoroughly with soap afterward.

Hour after hour, in Aibileen's kitchen, she reads her writing and I type, the details thickening, the babies' faces sliding into focus. At first, I'm disappointed that Aibileen is doing most of the writing, with me just editing. But if Missus Stein likes it, I'll be writing the other maids' stories and that will be more than enough work. *If she likes it* . . . I find myself saying this over and over in my head, hoping it might make it so.

Aibileen's writing is clear, honest. I tell her so.

"Well, look who I been writing to." She chuckles. "Can't lie to God."

Before I was born, she actually picked cotton for a week at Longleaf, my own family's farm. Once she lapses into talking about Constantine without my even asking.

"Law, that Constantine could sing. Like a purebred angel standing in the front a the church. Give everbody chills, listening to that silky voice a hers and when she wouldn't sing no more after she had to give her baby to—" She stops. Looks at me.

She says, "Anyway."

I tell myself not to press her. I wish I could hear everything she knows about Constantine, but I'll wait until we've finished her interviews. I don't want to put anything between us now.

"Any word from Minny yet?" I ask. "If Missus Stein likes it," I say, practically chanting the familiar words, "I just want to have the next interview set up and ready."

Aibileen shakes her head. "I asked Minny three times and she still say she ain't gone do it. I spec it's time I believed her."

I try not to show my worry. "Maybe you could ask some others? See if they're interested?" I am positive that Aibileen would have better luck convincing someone than I would.

Aibileen nods. "I got some more I can ask. But how long you think it's gone take for this lady to tell you if she like it?"

I shrug. "I don't know. If we mail it next week, maybe we'll hear from her by mid-February. But I can't say for sure."

Aibileen presses her lips together, looks down at her pages. I see something that I haven't noticed before. Anticipation, a glint of excitement. I've been so wrapped up in my own self, it hasn't occurred to me that Aibileen might be as thrilled as I am that an editor in New York is going to read her story. I smile and take a deep breath, my hope growing stronger.

On our fifth session, Aibileen reads to me about the day Treelore died. She reads about how his broken body was thrown on the back of a pickup by the white foreman. "And then they dropped him off at the colored hospital. That's what the nurse told me, who was standing outside. They rolled him off the truck bed and the white men drove away." Aibileen doesn't cry, just lets a parcel of time pass while I stare at the typewriter, she at the worn black tiles.

On the sixth session, Aibileen says, "I went to work for Miss Leefolt in 1960. When Mae Mobley two weeks old," and I feel I've passed through a leaden gate of confidence. She describes the building of the garage bathroom, admits she is glad it is there now. It's easier than listening to Hilly complain about sharing a toilet with the maid. She tells me that I once commented that colored people attend too much church. That stuck with her. I cringe, wondering what else I've said, never suspecting the help was listening or cared.

One night she says, "I was thinking..." But then she stops.

I look up from the typewriter, wait. It took Aibileen vomiting on herself for me to learn to let her take her time.

"I's thinking I ought to do some reading. Might help me with my own writing."

"Go down to the State Street Library. They have a whole room full of Southern writers. Faulkner, Eudora Welty—"

Aibileen gives me a dry cough. "You know colored folks ain't allowed in that library."

I sit there a second, feeling stupid. "I can't believe I forgot that." The colored library must be pretty bad. There was a sit-in at the white library a few years ago and it made the papers. When the colored crowd showed up for the sit-in trial, the police department simply stepped back and turned the German shepherds loose. I look at Aibileen and am reminded, once again, the risk she's taking talking to me. "I'll be glad to pick the books up for you," I say.

Aibileen hurries to the bedroom and comes back with a list. "I better mark the ones I want first. I been on the waiting list for *To Kill a Mockingbird* at the Carver Library near bout three months now. Less see..."

I watch as she puts checkmarks next to the books: *The Souls of Black Folk* by W. E. B. Du Bois, poems by Emily Dickinson (any), *The Adventures of Huckleberry Finn*.

"I read some a that back in school, but I didn't get to finish." She keeps marking, stopping to think which one she wants next.

"You want a book by...Sigmund Freud?"

"Oh, people crazy." She nods. "I love reading about how the head work. You ever dream you fall in a lake? He say you dreaming about your own self being born. Miss Frances, who I work for in 1957, she had all them books."

On her twelfth title, I have to know. "Aibileen, how long have you been wanting to ask me this? If I'd check these books out for you?"

"A while." She shrugs. "I guess I's afraid to mention it."

"Did you...think I'd say no?"

"These is white rules. I don't know which ones you following and which ones you ain't."

We look at each other a second. "I'm tired of the rules," I say.

Aibileen chuckles and looks out the window. I realize how thin this revelation must sound to her.

FOR FOUR DAYS STRAIGHT, I sit at my typewriter in my bedroom. Twenty of my typed pages, full of slashes and red-circled edits, become thirty-one on thick Strathmore white. I write a short biography of Sarah Ross, the name Aibileen chose, after her sixth-grade teacher who died years ago. I include her age, what her parents did for a living. I follow this with Aibileen's own stories, just as she wrote them, simple, straightforward.

On day three, Mother calls up the stairs to ask what in the world I'm doing up there all day and I holler down, *Just typing up some notes from the Bible study. Just writing down all the things I love about Jesus.* I hear her tell Daddy, in the kitchen after supper, "She's up to something." I carry my little white baptism Bible around the house, to make it more believable.

I read and re-read and then take the pages to Aibileen in the evenings and she does the same. She smiles and nods over the nice parts where everyone gets along fine but on the bad parts she takes off her black reading glasses and says, "I know I wrote it, but you really want to put that in about the—"

And I say, "Yes, I do." But I am surprised myself by what's in these stories, of separate colored refrigerators at the governor's mansion, of white women throwing two-year-old fits over wrinkled napkins, white babies calling Aibileen "Mama."

At three a.m., with only two white correction marks on what is now twenty-seven pages, I slide the manuscript into a yellow envelope. Yesterday, I made a long-distance phone call to Missus Stein's office. Her secretary, Ruth, said she was in a meeting. She took down my message, that the interview is on its way. There was no call back from Missus Stein today.

I hold the envelope to my heart and almost weep from exhaustion, doubt. I mail it at the Canton P. O. the next morning. I come home and lie down on my old iron bed, worrying over what will happen...*if she likes it.* What if Elizabeth or Hilly catches us at what we're doing? What if Aibileen gets fired, sent to jail? I feel like I'm falling down a long spiral tunnel. God, would they beat her the way they beat the colored boy who used the white bathroom? What am I doing? Why am I putting her at such risk?

I go to sleep. I have nightmares for the next fifteen hours straight.

It's a quarter past one and Hilly and Elizabeth and I are sitting at Elizabeth's dining room table waiting on Lou Anne to show up. I've had nothing to eat today except Mother's sexual-correction tea and I feel nauseous, jumpy. My foot is wagging under the table. I've been like this for ten days, ever since I mailed Aibileen's stories to Elaine Stein. I called once and Ruth said she passed it on to her four days ago, but still I've heard nothing.

"Is this not just the rudest thing you've ever heard of?" Hilly looks at her watch and scowls. This is Lou Anne's second time to be late. She won't last long in our group with Hilly around.

Aibileen walks in the dining room and I do my best not to look at her for too long. I am afraid Hilly or Elizabeth will see something in my eyes.

"Stop jiggling your foot, Skeeter. You're shaking the whole entire table," Hilly says.

Aibileen moves around the room in her easy, white-uniformed stride, not showing even a hint of what we've done. I guess she's grown deft at hiding her feelings.

Hilly shuffles and deals out a hand of gin rummy. I try to concentrate on the game, but little facts keep jumping in my head every time I look at Elizabeth. About Mae Mobley using the garage bathroom, how Aibileen can't keep her lunch in the Leefolts' refrigerator. Small details I'm privy to now.

Aibileen offers me a biscuit from a silver tray. She fills my iced tea like we are the strangers we were meant to be. I've been to her house twice since I mailed the package to New York, both times to trade out her library books.

She still wears the green dress with black piping when I come over. Sometimes she'll slip off her shoes under the table. Last time, she pulled out a pack of Montclairs and smoked right there with me in the room and that was kind of something, the casualness of it. I had one too. Now she is clearing away my crumbs with the sterling silver scraper I gave to Elizabeth and Raleigh for their wedding.

"Well, while we wait, I have some news," Elizabeth says and I recognize the look on her face already, the secretive nod, one hand on her stomach.

"I'm pregnant." She smiles, her mouth trembling a little.

"That's great," I say. I put down my cards and touch her arm. She truly looks like she might cry. "When are you due?"

"October."

"Well, it's about time," Hilly says, giving her a hug. "Mae Mobley's practically grown."

Elizabeth lights a cigarette, sighs. She looks down at her cards. "We're all real excited."

While we play a few practice hands, Hilly and Elizabeth talk about baby names. I try to contribute to the conversation. "Definitely Raleigh, if it's a boy," I add. Hilly talks about William's campaign. He's running for state senate next year, even though he has no political experience. I'm grateful when Elizabeth tells Aibileen to go ahead and serve lunch.

When Aibileen comes back in with the gelatin salad, Hilly straightens in her chair. "Aibileen, I have an old coat for you and a sack of clothes from Missus Walters' house." She dabs her mouth with her napkin. "So you come on out to the car after lunch and pick it all up, alright?"

"Yes ma'am."

"Don't forget now. I can't worry with bringing them by again."

"Oh now isn't that nice of Miss Hilly, Aibileen?" Elizabeth nods. "You go on and get those clothes right after we're done."

"Yes ma'am."

Hilly raises her voice about three octaves higher when she talks to colored people. Elizabeth smiles like she's talking to a child, although certainly not her own. I am starting to notice things.

By the time Lou Anne Templeton shows up, we've finished our shrimp and grits and are just starting on dessert. Hilly is amazingly forgiving. Lou Anne was late, after all, because of a League duty.

Afterward, I tell Elizabeth congratulations again, walk out to my car. Aibileen is outside collecting her gently used coat from 1942 and old clothes that, for some reason, Hilly won't give to her own maid, Yule May. Hilly strides over to me, hands me an envelope.

"For the newsletter next week. You'll be sure and get it in for me?"

I nod and Hilly walks back to her car. Just as Aibileen opens the front door to go back in the house, she glances back my way. I shake my head, mouth the word *Nothing.* She nods and goes on in the house.

That night, I work on the newsletter, wishing I was working on the stories instead. I go through the notes from the last League meeting, and come across Hilly's envelope. I open it. It is one page, written in Hilly's fat, curly pen:

Hilly Holbrook introduces the Home Help Sanitation Initiative. A disease preventative measure. Low-cost bathroom installation in your garage or shed, for homes without such an important fixture.
Ladies, did you know that:
- *99% of all colored diseases are carried in the urine*
- *Whites can become permanently disabled by nearly all of these diseases because we lack immunities coloreds carry in their darker pigmentation*
- *Some germs carried by whites can also be harmful to coloreds too*

Protect yourself. Protect your children. Protect your help.
From the Holbrooks, we say, You're welcome!

THE PHONE RINGS IN THE kitchen and I practically fall over myself racing to it. But Pascagoula has already answered it.

"Miss Charlotte residence."

I stare her down, watch as tiny Pascagoula nods, says, "Yes ma'am, she here," and hands me the phone.

"This is Eugenia," I say quickly. Daddy's in the fields and Mother's at a doctor's appointment in town, so I stretch the black, twisting phone cord to the kitchen table.

"Elaine Stein here."

I breathe deep. "Yes ma'am. Did you receive my package?"

"I did," she says and then breathes into the phone a few seconds.

"This Sarah Ross. I like her stories. She likes to kvetch without complaining too much."

I nod. I don't know what *kvetch* means, but I think it must be good.

"But I still stand by my opinion that a book of interviews...ordinarily wouldn't work. It's not fiction, but it's not nonfiction either. Perhaps it's anthropological but that's a ghastly category to be in."

"But you...liked it?"

"Eugenia," she says, exhaling her cigarette smoke into the phone. "Have you seen the cover of *Life* magazine this week?"

I haven't seen the cover of my *Life* magazine in a month, I've been so busy.

"Martin Luther King, dear. He just announced a march on D.C. and invited every Negro in America to join him. Every white person, for that matter. This many Negro and white people haven't worked together since *Gone With the Wind.*"

"Yes, I did hear about the...marching...event," I lie. I cover my eyes, wishing I'd read the paper this week. I sound like an idiot.

"My advice to you is, write it and write it fast. The march is in August. You should have it written by New Year's."

I gasp. She's telling me to write it! She's telling me... "Are you saying you'll publish it? If I can write it by—"

"I said nothing of the sort," she snaps. "I will read it. I look at a hundred manuscripts a month and reject nearly all of them."

"Sorry, I just...I'll write it," I say. "I'll have it finished in January."

"And four or five interviews won't be enough for a book. You'll need a dozen, maybe more. You have more interviews set up, I assume?"

I press my lips together. "Some...more."

"Good. Then get going. Before this civil rights thing blows over."

. . .

THAT EVENING, I go to Aibileen's. I hand her three more books from her list. My back hurts from leaning over the typewriter. This afternoon, I wrote down everyone I know who has a maid (which is everyone I know), and their maid's name. But some of the names I can't remember.

"Thank you, oh Law, look at this." She smiles and flips to the first page of *Walden,* looks like she wants to start reading it right there.

"I spoke to Missus Stein this afternoon," I say.

Aibileen's hands freeze on the book. "I knew something was wrong. I seen it on your face."

I take a deep breath. "She said she likes your stories very much. But...she won't say if she'll publish it until we've written the whole thing." I try to look optimistic. "We have to be finished just after the new year."

"But that's good news, ain't it?"

I nod, try to smile.

"*January,*" Aibileen whispers and she gets up and leaves the kitchen. She comes back with a Tom's candy wall calendar. She sets it down on the table, flips through the months.

"Seem a long ways off now, but January ain't but...two...four... six...ten pages away. Gone be here before we know it." She grins.

"She said we have to interview at least twelve maids for her to consider it," I say. The strain in my voice is starting to really come through.

"But...you ain't got any other maids to talk to, Miss Skeeter."

I clench my hands. I close my eyes. "I don't have anyone I can ask, Aibileen," I say, my voice rising. I've spent the last four hours poring over this very fact. "I mean, who is there? Pascagoula? If I talk to her, Mama will find out. I'm not the one who knows the other maids."

Aibileen's eyes drop from mine so fast I want to cry. *Damn it, Skeeter.* Any barrier that had eroded between us these past few months, I've just built back up in a matter of seconds. "I'm sorry," I say quickly. "I'm sorry I raised my voice."

"No, no, it's alright. That was my job, to get the others."

"What about...Lou Anne's maid," I say quietly, pulling out my list. "What's her name...Louvenia? Do you know her?"

Aibileen nods. "I asked Louvenia." Her eyes are still on her lap. "Her grandson the one got blinded. She say she real sorry, but she have to keep her mind on him."

"And Hilly's maid, Yule May? You've asked her?"

"She say she too busy trying to get her boys into college next year."

"Any other maids that go to your church? Have you asked them?"

Aibileen nods. "They all got excuses. But really, they just too scared."

"But how many? How many have you asked?"

Aibileen picks up her notebook, flips though a few pages. Her lips move, counting silently.

"Thirty-one," Aibileen says.

I let out my breath. I didn't know I'd been holding it.

"That's...a lot," I say.

Aibileen finally meets my look. "I didn't want a tell you," she says and her forehead wrinkles. "Until we heard from the lady..." She takes off her glasses. I see the deep worry in her face. She tries to hide it with a trembling smile.

"I'm on ask em again," she says, leaning forward.

"Alright," I sigh.

She swallows hard, nods rapidly to make me understand how much she means it. "Please, don't give up on me. Let me stay on the project with you."

I close my eyes. I need a break from seeing her worried face. How could I have raised my voice to her? "Aibileen, it's alright. We're...together on this."

A FEW DAYS LATER, I sit in the hot kitchen, bored, smoking a cigarette, something I can't seem to stop doing lately. I think I might be "addicted." That's a word Mister Golden likes to use. *The idjits are all addicts.* He calls me in his office every once in a while, scans the month's articles with a red pencil, marking and slashing and grunting.

"That's fine," he'll say. "You fine?"

"I'm fine," I say.

"Fine, then." Before I leave, the fat receptionist hands me my ten-dollar check and that's pretty much it for my Miss Myrna job.

The kitchen is hot, but I have to get out of my room, where all I do is worry because no other maids have agreed to work with us. Plus, I have to smoke in here because it's about the only room in the house without a ceiling fan to blow ashes everywhere. When I was ten, Daddy tried to install one in the tin kitchen ceiling without asking Constantine. She'd pointed to it like he'd parked the Ford on the ceiling.

"It's for you, Constantine, so you don't get so hot being up in the kitchen all the time."

"I ain't working in no kitchen with no ceiling fan, Mister Carlton."

"Sure you will. I'm just hooking up the current to it now."

Daddy climbed down the ladder. Constantine filled a pot with water. "Go head," she sighed. "Turn it on then."

Daddy flipped the switch. In the seconds it took to really get going, cake flour blew up from the mixing bowl and swirled around the room, recipes flapped off the counter and caught fire on the stovetop. Constantine snatched the burning roll of parchment paper, quickly dipped it in the bucket of water. There's still a hole where the ceiling fan hung for ten minutes.

In the newspaper, I see State Senator Whitworth pointing to an empty lot of land where they plan to build a new city coliseum. I turn the page. I hate being reminded of my date with Stuart Whitworth.

Pascagoula pads into the kitchen. I watch as she cuts out biscuits with a shot glass that's never shot a thing but short dough. Behind me, the kitchen windows are propped open with Sears, Roebuck & Co. catalogues. Pictures of two-dollar hand mixers and mail-order toys flutter in a breeze, swollen and puckered from a decade of rain.

Maybe I should just ask Pascagoula. Maybe Mother won't find out. But who am I kidding? Mother watches her every move and Pascagoula seems afraid of me anyway, like I might tell on her if she does something wrong. It could take years to break through that fear. My best sense tells me, leave Pascagoula out of this.

The phone rings like a fire alarm. Pascagoula clangs her spoon on the bowl and I grab the receiver before she can.

"Minny gone help us," Aibileen whispers.

I slip into the pantry and sit on my flour can. I can't speak for about five seconds. "When? When can she start?"

"Next Thursday. But she got some...requirements."

"What are they?"

Aibileen pauses a moment. "She say she don't want your Cadillac anywhere this side a the Woodrow Wilson bridge."

"Alright," I say. "I guess I could...drive the truck in."

"And she say...she say you can't set on the same side a the room as her. She want a be able to see you square on at all times."

"I'll...sit wherever she wants me to."

Aibileen's voice softens. "She just don't know you, is all. Plus she ain't got a real good history with white ladies."

"Whatever I have to do, I'll do it."

I walk out of the pantry beaming, hang the phone up on the wall. Pascagoula is watching me, the shot glass in one hand, a raw biscuit in the other. She looks down quickly and goes back to her work.

Two days later, I tell Mother I'm going to pick up a new copy of the King James Bible since I've worn mine so thin and all. I also tell her I feel guilty driving the Cadillac what with all those poor starving babies in Africa and I've decided to take the old truck today. She narrows her eyes at me from her porch rocker. "Where exactly do you plan on buying this new Bible?"

I blink. "The...they ordered it for me. At the Canton church."

She nods, watches me the entire time it takes to start the old truck.

I drive to Farish Street with a lawn mower in the back and a rusted-out floorboard. Under my feet, I can see flashes of pavement whiz by. But at least I'm not pulling a tractor.

Aibileen opens the door and I come in. In the back corner of the living room, Minny stands with her arms crossed over her huge bosom. I've met her the few times Hilly allowed Missus Walters to host bridge club. Minny and Aibileen are both still in their white uniforms.

"Hello," I say from my side of the room. "Good to see you again."

"Miss Skeeter." Minny nods. She settles in a wooden chair Aibileen has brought out from the kitchen, and the frame creaks. I sit on the far end of the sofa. Aibileen sits on the other end of the sofa, between us.

I clear my throat, produce a nervous smile. Minny doesn't smile back. She is fat and short and strong. Her skin is blacker than Aibileen's by ten shades, and shiny and taut, like a pair of new patent shoes.

"I already told Minny how we doing the stories," Aibileen says to me. "You helping me write mine. And hers she gone tell you, while you write it down."

"And Minny, everything you say here is in confidence," I say. "You'll get to read everything we—"

"What makes you think colored people need your help?" Minny stands up, chair scraping. "Why you even care about this? You *white*."

I look at Aibileen. I've never had a colored person speak to me this way.

"We all working for the same thing here, Minny," Aibileen says. "We just talking."

"And what thing is that?" Minny says to me. "Maybe you just want me to tell you all this stuff so I get in trouble." Minny points to the window. "Medgar Evers, the NAACP officer who live five minutes away, they blew up his carport last night. For *talking*."

My face is burning red. I speak slowly. "We want to show your perspective...so people might understand what it's like from your side. We—we hope it might change some things around here."

"What you think you gone change with this? What law you want to reform so it say you got to be nice to your maid?"

"Now hold on," I say, "I'm not trying to change any laws here. I'm just talking about attitudes and—"

"You know what'll happen if people catch us? Forget the time I accidentally use the wrong changing room down at McRae's women's wear, I'd have *guns* pointing at my house."

There's a still, tight moment in the room with just the sound of the brown Timex clock ticking on the shelf.

"You don't have to do this, Minny," Aibileen says. "It's alright if you want a change your mind."

Slowly, warily, Minny settles again in her chair. "I do it. I just want a make sure she understand, this ain't no *game* we playing here."

I glance at Aibileen. She nods at me. I take a deep breath. My hands are shaking.

I start with the background questions and somehow we back our way into talking about Minny's work. She looks at Aibileen as she talks, like she's trying to forget I'm even in the room. I record everything she says, my pencil scratching as fast as I can move it. We thought it might be less formal than using the typewriter.

"Then they's one job where I work late ever night. And you know what happened?"

"What's...that?" I ask, even though she's looking at Aibileen.

"*Oh, Minny,*" she cat-calls, "*you the best help we ever had. Big Minny, we gone keep you on forever.* Then one day she say she gone give me a week a paid vacation. I ain't had no vacation, paid or unpaid, in my entire life. And when I pull up a week later to go back to work, they gone. Moved to Mobile. She tell somebody she scared I'd find new work before she move. Miss Lazy Fingers couldn't go a day without having a maid waiting on her."

She suddenly stands up, throws her bag on her arm. "I got to go. You giving me the heart palpitations talking bout this." And out she goes, slamming the door behind her.

I look up, wipe the sweat off my temple.

"And that was a good mood," Aibileen says.

CHAPTER 13

FOR THE NEXT TWO WEEKS, the three of us arrange ourselves in the same seats in Aibileen's small, warm living room. Minny storms in mad, quiets down as she tells Aibileen her story, then rushes out in a rage as fast as she came in. I write down as much as I can.

When Minny lapses into news about Miss Celia—"She sneaking upstairs, think I don't see her, but I know, that crazy lady up to something"—she always stops herself, the way Aibileen does when she speaks of Constantine. "That ain't part a my story. You leave Miss Celia out a this." She watches me until my writing stops.

Besides her furiousness at white people, Minny likes to talk about food. "Let's see, I put the green beans in first, then I go on and get the pork chops going cause, mmm-mmm, I like my chops hot out the pan, you know."

One day, while she's saying, "...got a white baby on one arm, green beans in the pot—" she stops. Cocks her jaw at me. Taps her foot.

"Half this stuff don't have nothing to do with colored rights. Ain't but day-to-day business." She eyes me up and down. "Look to me like you just writing *life*."

I stop my pencil. She's right. I realize that's just what I wanted to do. I tell her, "I hope so." She gets up and says she's got more important things to worry about than what I'm hoping for.

. . .

THE NEXT EVENING, I'm working upstairs in my room, banging the keys on my Corona. Suddenly I hear Mother hit the stairs running. In two seconds she's made it in my room. "Eugenia!" she whispers.

I stand so fast my chair teeters, trying to guard the contents of my typewriter. "Yes ma'am?"

"Now don't panic but there is a man—a very *tall* man—downstairs to see you."

"Who?"

"He says his name is Stuart *Whit*worth."

"What?"

"He said y'all spent an evening together awhile back but how can that be, I didn't know anything—"

"Christ."

"Don't take the Lord's name in vain, Eugenia Phelan. Just put some lipstick on."

"Believe me, Mama," I say, putting on lipstick anyway. "Jesus wouldn't like him either."

I brush my hair because I know it's awful. I even wash the typewriter ink and correcting fluid off my hands and elbows. But I won't change clothes, not for him.

Mother gives me a quick up and down in my dungarees and Daddy's old button-up white shirt. "Is he a Greenwood Whitworth or a Natchez?"

"He's the state senator's son."

Mother's jaw drops so far it hits her string of pearls. I go down the stairs, past the assembly of our childhood portraits. Pictures of Carlton line the wall, taken up until about the day before yesterday. Pictures of me stop when I was twelve. "Mother, give us some privacy." I watch as she slowly drags herself back to her room, glancing over her shoulder before she disappears.

I walk out onto the porch, and there he is. Three months after our date, there is Stuart Whitworth himself, standing on my front porch in khaki pants and a blue coat and a red tie like he's ready for Sunday dinner.

Asshole.

"What brings you here?" I ask. I don't smile though. I'm not smiling at him.

"I just...I wanted to drop by."

"Well. Can I get you a drink?" I ask. "Or should I just get you the entire bottle of Old Kentucky?"

He frowns. His nose and forehead are pink, like he's been working in the sun. "Look, I know it was...a long while back, but I came out here to say I'm sorry."

"Who sent you—Hilly? William?" There are eight empty rocking chairs on my porch. I don't ask him to sit in any of them.

He looks off at the west cotton field where the sun is dipping into the dirt. He shoves his hands down in his front pockets like a twelve-year-old boy. "I know I was...rude that night, and I've been thinking about it a lot and..."

I laugh then. I'm just so embarrassed that he would come out here and have me relive it.

"Now look," he says, "I told Hilly ten times I wasn't ready to go out on any date. I wasn't even close to being ready..."

I grit my teeth. I can't *believe* I feel the heat of tears; the date was months ago. But I remember how secondhand I'd felt that night, how ridiculously fixed up I'd gotten for him. "Then why'd you even show up?"

"I don't know." He shakes his head. "You know how Hilly can be."

I stand there waiting for whatever it is he's here for. He runs a hand through his light brown hair. It is almost wiry it's so thick. He looks tired.

I look away because he's cute in an overgrown boy kind of way and it's not something I want to be thinking right now. I want him to leave—I don't want to feel this awful feeling again, yet I hear myself saying, "What do you mean, not ready?"

"Just not ready. Not after what happened."

I stare at him. "You want me to guess?"

"Me and Patricia van Devender. We got engaged last year and then...I thought you knew."

He sinks down in a rocking chair. I don't sit next to him. But I don't tell him to leave either.

"What, she ran off with someone else?"

"Shoot." He drops his head down into his hands, mumbles, "That'd be a goddamn Mardi Gras party compared to what happened."

I don't let myself say to him what I'd like to, that he probably deserved whatever she did, but he's just too pathetic-looking. Now that all his good ole boy, tough bourbon talk has evaporated, I wonder if he's this pathetic all the time.

"We'd been dating since we were fifteen. You know how it is, when you've been steady with somebody that long."

And I don't know why I admit this, except that I simply have nothing to lose. "Actually, I wouldn't know," I say. "I've never dated anybody."

He looks up at me, kind of laughs. "Well, that must be it, then."

"Be what?" I steel myself, recalling fertilizer and tractor references.

"You're...different. I've never met anybody that said exactly what they were thinking. Not a woman, anyway."

"Believe me, I had a lot *more* to say."

He sighs. "When I saw your face, out there by the truck...I'm not that guy. I'm really not such a jerk."

I look away, embarrassed. It's just starting to hit me what he said, that even though I'm different, maybe it's not in a strange way or an abnormal, tall-girl way. But maybe in a good way.

"I came by to see if you'd like to come downtown with me for supper. We could talk," he says and stands up. "We could...I don't know, listen to each other this time."

I stand there, shocked. His eyes are blue and clear and fixed on me like my answer might really mean something to him. I take in a deep breath, about to say yes—I mean, why would I of all people refuse—and he bites his bottom lip, waiting.

And then I think about how he treated me like I was nothing. How he got shit-dog drunk he was so miserable to be stuck with me. I think about how he told me I smelled like fertilizer. It took me three months to stop thinking about that comment.

"No," I blurt out. "Thank you. But I really can't imagine anything worse."

He nods, looks down at his feet. Then he goes down the porch steps.

"I'm sorry," he says, the door to his car open. "That's what I came to say and, well, I guess I said it."

I stand on the porch, listening to the hollow sounds of the evening, gravel under Stuart's shifting feet, dogs moving in the early darkness. For a second, I remember Charles Gray, my only kiss in a lifetime. How I'd pulled away, somehow sure the kiss hadn't been intended for me.

Stuart gets in his car and his door clicks shut. He props his arm up so his elbow pokes through the open window. But he keeps his eyes turned down.

"Just give me a minute," I holler out to him. "Let me get my sweater."

No one tells us, girls who don't go on dates, that remembering can be almost as good as what actually happens. Mother climbs all the way to the third floor and stands over me in my bed, but I act like I'm still asleep. Because I just want to remember it awhile.

We'd driven to the Robert E. Lee for dinner last night. I'd thrown on a light blue sweater and a slim white skirt. I'd even let Mother brush out my hair, trying to drown out her nervous, complicated instructions.

"And don't forget to smile. Men don't want a girl who's moping around all night, and don't sit like some squaw Indian, cross your—"

"Wait, my legs or my ank—"

"Your ankles. Don't you remember anything from Missus Rheimer's etiquette class? And just go ahead and lie and tell him you go to church every Sunday, and whatever you do, do not crunch your ice at the table, it's awful. Oh, and if the conversation starts to lag, you tell him about our second cousin who's a city councilman in Kosciusko..."

As she brushed and smoothed and brushed and smoothed, Mother kept asking how I'd met him and what happened on our last date, but I managed to scoot out from under her and dash down the stairs, shaking with wonder and nervousness of my own. By the time Stuart and I walked into the hotel and sat down and put our napkins in our lap, the waiter said they'd be closing soon. All they'd serve us was dessert.

Then Stuart had gotten quiet.

"What…do you want, Skeeter?" he'd asked and I'd sort of tensed up then, hoping he wasn't planning on getting drunk again.

"I'll have a Co-Cola. Lots of ice."

"No." He smiled. "I mean…in life. What do you want?"

I took a deep breath, knowing what Mother would advise me to say: fine, strong kids, a husband to take care of, shiny new appliances to cook tasty yet healthful meals in. "I want to be a writer," I said. "A journalist. Maybe a novelist. Maybe both."

He lifted his chin and looked at me then, right in the eye.

"I like that," he said, and then he just kept staring. "I've been thinking about you. You're smart, you're pretty, you're"—he smiled—"tall."

Pretty?

We ate strawberry soufflés and had one glass of Chablis apiece. He talked about how to tell if there's oil underneath a cotton field and I talked about how the receptionist and I were the only females working for the paper.

"I hope you write something really good. Something you believe in."

"Thank you. I…hope so too." I don't say anything about Aibileen or Missus Stein.

I haven't had the chance to look at too many men's faces up close and I noticed how his skin was thicker than mine and a gorgeous shade of toast; the stiff blond hairs on his cheeks and chin seemed to be growing before my eyes. He smelled like starch. Like pine. His nose wasn't so pointy after all.

The waiter yawned in the corner but we both ignored him and stayed and talked some more. And by the time I was wishing I'd washed my hair this morning instead of just bathed and was practically doubled over with gratefulness that I'd at least brushed my teeth, out of the blue, he kissed me. Right in the middle of the Robert E. Lee Hotel Restaurant, he kissed me so slowly with an open mouth and every single thing in my body—my skin, my collarbone, the hollow backs of my knees, everything inside of me filled up with light.

ON A MONDAY AFTERNOON, a few weeks after my date with Stuart, I stop by the library before going to the League meeting. Inside, it smells like grade school—boredom, paste, Lysoled vomit. I've come to get more books for Aibileen and check if anything's ever been written about domestic help.

"Well hey there, Skeeter!"

Jesus. It's Susie Pernell. In high school, she could've been voted most likely to talk too much. "Hey...Susie. What are you doing here?"

"I'm working here for the League committee, remember? You really ought to get on it, Skeeter, it's real fun! You get to read all the latest magazines and file things and even laminate the library cards." Susie poses by the giant brown machine like she's on *The Price Is Right* television show.

"How new and exciting."

"So, what may I help you find today, ma'am? We have murder mysteries, romance novels, how-to makeup books, how-to *hair* books," she pauses, jerks out a smile, "rose gardening, home decorating—"

"I'm just browsing, thanks." I hurry off. I'll fend for myself in the stacks. There is no way I can tell her what I'm looking for. I can already hear her whispering at the League meetings, *I knew there was something not right about that Skeeter Phelan, hunting for those Negro materials...*

I search through card catalogues and scan the shelves, but find nothing about domestic workers. In nonfiction, I spot a single copy of *Frederick Douglass, an American Slave.* I grab it, excited to deliver it to Aibileen, but when I open it, I see the middle section has been ripped out. Inside, someone has written NIGGER BOOK in purple crayon. I am not as disturbed by the words as by the fact that the handwriting looks like a third grader's. I glance around, push the book in my satchel. It seems better than putting it back on the shelf.

In the Mississippi History room, I search for anything remotely resembling race relations. I find only Civil War books, maps, and old phone books. I stand on tiptoe to see what's on the high shelf. That's when I spot a booklet, laid sideways across the top of the *Mississippi River Valley Flood Index.* A regular-sized person would never have seen it. I slide it down to glance at the cover. The booklet is thin, printed on onionskin paper, curling, bound with staples. "Compilation of Jim Crow Laws of the South," the cover reads. I open the noisy cover page.

The booklet is simply a list of laws stating what colored people can and cannot do, in an assortment of Southern states. I skim the first page, puzzled why this is here. The laws are neither threatening nor friendly, just citing the facts:

> *No person shall require any white female to nurse in wards or rooms in which negro men are placed.*
> *It shall be unlawful for a white person to marry anyone except a white person. Any marriage in violation of this section shall be void.*
> *No colored barber shall serve as a barber to white women or girls.*
> *The officer in charge shall not bury any colored persons upon ground used for the burial of white persons.*
> *Books shall not be interchangeable between the white and colored schools, but shall continue to be used by the race first using them.*

I read through four of the twenty-five pages, mesmerized by how many laws exist to separate us. Negroes and whites are not allowed to share water fountains, movie houses, public restrooms, ballparks, phone booths, circus shows. Negroes cannot use the same pharmacy or buy postage stamps at the same window as me. I think about Constantine, the time my family took her to Memphis with us and the highway had mostly washed out, but we had to drive straight on through because we knew the hotels wouldn't let her in. I think about how no one in the car would come out and say it. We all know about these laws, we live here, but we don't talk about them. This is the first time I've ever seen them written down.

Lunch counters, the state fair, pool tables, hospitals. Number forty-seven I have to read twice, for its irony.

> *The Board shall maintain a separate building on separate grounds for the instruction of all blind persons of the colored race.*

After several minutes, I make myself stop. I start to put the booklet back, telling myself I'm not writing a book about Southern legislation, this is a waste of my time. But then I realize, like a shell cracking open in my head, there's no difference between these government laws and Hilly building

Aibileen a bathroom in the garage, except ten minutes' worth of signatures in the state capital.

On the last page, I see the pica type that reads *Property of Mississippi Law Library*. The booklet was returned to the wrong building. I scratch my revelation on a piece of paper and tuck it inside the booklet: *Jim Crow or Hilly's bathroom plan—what's the difference?* I slip it in my bag. Susie sneezes behind the desk across the room.

I head for the doors. I have a League meeting in thirty minutes. I give Susie an extra friendly smile. She's whispering into the phone. The stolen books in my bag feel like they're pulsing with heat.

"Skeeter," Susie hisses from the desk, eyes wide. "Did I really hear *you* have been seeing Stuart Whitworth?" She puts a bit too much emphasis on the *you* for me to keep up my smile. I act like I don't hear her and walk out into the bright sunshine. I've never stolen a thing in my life before today. I'm a little satisfied it was on Susie's watch.

OUR PLACES OF COMFORT ARE expectedly different, my friends and I. Elizabeth's is hunched over her sewing machine trying to make her life look seamless, store-bought. Mine is at my typewriter writing pithy things I'll never have the guts to say out loud. And Hilly's is behind a podium telling sixty-five women that three cans apiece isn't enough to feed all those PSCAs. The Poor Starving Children of Africa, that is. Mary Joline Walker, however, thinks three is plenty.

"And isn't it kind of expensive, carting all this tin across the world to Ethiopia?" Mary Joline asks. "Doesn't it make more sense just to send them a check?"

The meeting has not officially started, but Hilly's already behind her podium. There's a franticness in her eyes. This isn't our normal evening time, but an extra afternoon session Hilly's called. In June, many of the members are going out of town for summer vacations. Then, in July, Hilly leaves for her annual trip down to the coast for three weeks. It's going to be hard for her to trust an entire town to operate properly without her here.

Hilly rolls her eyes. "You cannot give these tribal people money, Mary Joline. There is no Jitney 14 Grocery in the Ogaden Desert. And how would we know if they're even feeding their kids with it? They're likely to go to the local voodoo tent and get a satanic tattoo with our money."

"Alright." Mary Joline teeters off, flat-faced, brainwashed-looking. "I guess you know best." It is this bug-eyed effect Hilly has on people that makes her such a successful League president.

I make my way across the crowded meeting room, feeling the warmth of attention, as if a beam of light is shining down on my head. The room is full of cake-eating, Tab-drinking, cigarette-smoking women all about my age. Some are whispering to each other, glancing my way.

"*Skeeter,*" Liza Presley says before I make it past the coffee urns, "did I hear you were at the Robert E. Lee a few weeks ago?"

"Is that right? Are you really seeing Stuart Whitworth?" says Frances Greenbow.

Most of the questions are not unkind, not like Susie's at the library. Still, I shrug, try not to notice how when a regular girl gets asked out, it's information, but when Skeeter Phelan gets asked out, it's *news.*

But it's true. I am seeing Stuart Whitworth and have been for three weeks now. Twice at the Robert E. Lee if you include the disaster date, and three more times sitting on my front porch for drinks before he drove home to Vicksburg. My father even stayed up past eight o'clock to speak to him. "Night, son. You tell the Senator we sure do appreciate him stomping out that farm tax bill." Mother's been trembling, torn between the terror that I'll screw it up and glee that I actually like men.

The white spotlight of wonder follows me as I make my way to Hilly. Girls are smiling and nodding at me.

"When will y'all see each other again?" This is Elizabeth now, twisting a napkin, eyes wide like she's staring at a car accident. "Did he say?"

"Tomorrow night. As soon as he can drive over."

"Good." Hilly's smile is a fat child's at the Seale-Lily Ice Cream window. The button on her red suitcoat bulges. "We'll make it a double date, then."

I don't answer. I don't want Hilly and William coming along. I just want to sit with Stuart, have him look at me and only me. Twice, when we were alone, he brushed my hair back when it fell in my eyes. He might not brush my hair back if they're around.

"William'll telephone Stuart tonight. Let's go to the picture show."

"Alright," I sigh.

"I'm just dying to see *It's a Mad, Mad, Mad, Mad World*. Won't this be fun," Hilly says. "You and me and William and Stuart."

It strikes me as suspicious, the way she's arranged the names. As if the point were for William and Stuart to be together instead of me and Stuart. I know I'm being paranoid. But everything makes me wary now. Two nights ago, as soon as I crossed over the colored bridge, I was stopped by a policeman. He shone his flashlight in the truck, let it shine on the satchel. He asked for my license and where I was going. "I'm taking a check to my maid...Constantine. I forgot to pay her." Another cop pulled up, came to my window. "Why did you stop me?" I asked, my voice sounding about ten pitches too high. "Did something happen?" I asked. My heart was slamming against my chest. What if they looked in my satchel?

"Some Yankee trash stirring up trouble. We'll catch em, ma'am," he said, patting his billy club. "Do your business and get back over the bridge."

When I got to Aibileen's street, I parked even farther down the block. I walked around to her back door instead of using the front. I shook so bad for the first hour, I could hardly read the questions I'd written for Minny.

Hilly gives the five-minute-till bang with her gavel. I make my way to my chair, lug my satchel onto my lap. I tick through the contents, suddenly conscious of the Jim Crow booklet I stole from the library. In fact, my satchel holds all the work we've done—Aibileen and Minny's interviews, the book outline, a list of potential maids, a scathing, unmailed response I wrote to Hilly's bathroom initiative—everything I can't leave at home for fear Mother will snoop through my things. I keep it all in a side zip-pocket with a flap over it. It bulges unevenly.

"Skeeter, those poplin pants are just the cutest thing, why haven't I seen those before?" Carroll Ringer says a few chairs away and I look up at her and smile, thinking *Because I wouldn't dare wear old clothes to a meeting and neither would you.* Clothing questions irritate me after so many years of Mother hounding me.

I feel a hand on my other shoulder and turn to find Hilly with her finger in my satchel, right on the booklet. "Do you have the notes for next week's newsletter? Are these them?" I hadn't even seen her coming.

"No, wait!" I say and ease the booklet back into my papers. "I need to . . . to correct one thing. I'll bring them to you a little later."

I take a deep breath.

At the podium, Hilly looks at her watch, toying with the gavel like she's just dying to bang it. I push my satchel under my chair. Finally, the meeting begins.

I record the PSCA news, who's on the trouble list, who's not brought in their cans. The calendar of events is full of committee meetings and baby showers, and I shift around in my wooden chair, hoping the meeting will end soon. I have to get Mother's car back to her by three.

It's not until a quarter till, an hour and a half later, that I rush out of the hot room toward the Cadillac. I'll be on the trouble list for leaving early, but Jesus Christ, what's worse, the wrath of Mother or the wrath of Hilly?

I WALK INTO THE HOUSE five minutes early, humming "Love Me Do," thinking I ought to go buy a short skirt like Jenny Foushee wore today. She said she'd gotten it up in New York City at Bergdorf Goodman's. Mother would keel over if I showed up with a skirt above the knee when Stuart picks me up on Saturday.

"Mama, I'm home," I call down the hallway.

I pull a Co-Cola from the fridge, sigh and smile, feeling good, strong. I head to the front door for my satchel, ready to thread together more of Minny's stories. I can tell she is itching to talk about Celia Foote, but she always stops after a minute of it and changes the subject. The phone rings and I answer it, but it's for Pascagoula. I take a message on the pad. It's Yule May, Hilly's maid.

"Hey, Yule May," I say, thinking what a small town this is. "I'll give her the message when she gets back." I lean a minute against the counter, wishing

Constantine was here like it used to be. How I'd love to share every single thing about my day with her.

I sigh and finish my Coke and then go to the front door for my satchel. It's not there. I go outside and look in the car but it's not there either. *Huh,* I think and head up the stairs, feeling less pink now and more of a pale yellow. Did I go upstairs yet? I scour my room, but it's nowhere to be found. Finally, I stand still in my quiet bedroom, a slow tingle of panic working its way up my spine. The satchel, it has *everything* in it.

Mother, I think and I dash downstairs and look in the relaxing room. But suddenly I realize it's not Mother who has it—the answer has come to me, numbing my entire body. I left my satchel at the League House. I was in such a hurry to get Mother's car home. And even as the phone is ringing, I already know it is Hilly on the end of that line.

I grab the phone from the wall. Mother calls goodbye from the front door.

"Hello?"

"How could you leave this heavy thing behind?" Hilly asks. Hilly never has had a problem with going through other people's things. In fact, she enjoys it.

"Mother, wait a second!" I holler from the kitchen.

"Good Lord, Skeeter, what's in here?" Hilly says. I've got to catch Mother, but Hilly's voice is muffled, like she's bending down, opening it.

"Nothing! Just...all those Miss Myrna letters, you know."

"Well, I've lugged it back to my house so come on by and get it when you can."

Mother is starting the car outside. "Just...keep it there. I'll be by as soon as I can get there."

I race outside but Mother's already down the lane. I look over and the old truck's gone too, toting cotton seed somewhere in the fields. The dread in my stomach is flat and hard and hot, like a brick in the sun.

Down by the road, I watch the Cadillac slow, then jerk to a stop. Then it goes again. Then stops. Then slowly reverses and zigzags its way back up the hill. By the grace of a god I never really liked, much less believed in, my mother is actually coming *back.*

"I can't believe I forgot Sue Anne's casserole dish…"

I jump in the front passenger seat, wait until she climbs back into the car. She puts her hands on the wheel.

"Drive me by Hilly's? I need to pick something up." I press my hand to my forehead. "Oh God, hurry, Mother. Before I'm too late."

Mother's car hasn't moved. "Skeeter, I have a million things to do today—"

The panic is rising up in my throat. "Mama, please, just *drive*…"

But the Deville sits in the gravel, ticking like a time bomb.

"Now look," Mother says, "I have some personal errands to run and I just don't think it's a good time to have you tagging along."

"It'll take you five minutes. Just drive, Mama!"

Mother keeps her white-gloved hands on the steering wheel, her lips pressed together.

"I happen to have something confidential and important to do today."

I can't imagine my mother has anything more important to do than what I'm staring down the throat of. "What? A Mexican's trying to join the DAR? Somebody got caught reading the *New American Dictionary*?"

Mother sighs, says, "Fine," and moves the gear shift carefully into drive. "Alright, here we go." We roll down the lane at about one-tenth of a mile an hour, putting along so the gravel won't knock at the paint job. At the end of the lane, she puts on her blinker like she's doing brain surgery and creeps the Cadillac out onto the County Road. My fists are clenched. I press my imaginary accelerator. Every time's Mother's first time to drive.

On the County Road, she speeds up to fifteen and grips the wheel like we're doing a hundred and five.

"Mama," I finally say, "just let me drive the car."

She sighs. I'm surprised that she pulls over into the tall grass.

I get out and run around the car while she slides over. I put the car in D and press it to seventy, praying, *Please, Hilly, resist the temptation to rummage through my personal business….*

"So what's the big secret, what do you have to do today?" I ask.

"I'm…I'm going to see Doctor Neal for some tests. It's just routine, but

I don't want your daddy to know. You know how upset he gets every time somebody goes to the doctor."

"What kind of tests?"

"It's just an iodine test for my ulcers, same as I have every year. Drop me at the Baptist and then you can take yourself to Hilly's. At least I won't have to worry over parking."

I glance at her to see if there's more to this, but she's sitting straight and starched in her light blue dress, her legs crossed at the ankles. I don't remember her having these tests last year. Even with me being up at school, Constantine would've written to me about them. Mother must've kept them secret.

Five minutes later, at the Baptist Hospital, I come around and help her out of the car.

"Eugenia, please. Just because this is a hospital doesn't mean I'm an invalid."

I open the glass door for her and she walks in, head held high.

"Mother, do you...want me to come with you?" I ask, knowing I can't—I have to deal with Hilly, but suddenly I don't want to drop her off here, like this.

"It's *routine.* Go on to Hilly's and come back in an hour."

I watch her grow smaller down the long hall, clutching her handbag, knowing I should turn and run. But before I do, I wonder at how frail and inconsequential my mother has become. She used to fill a room by just breathing and now there seems to be...less of her. She turns a corner and disappears behind the pale yellow walls. I watch a second longer before I rush back to the car.

A MINUTE AND A HALF LATER, I'm ringing Hilly's bell. If these were regular times, I'd talk to Hilly about Mama. But I can't distract her. It is the first moment that will tell me everything. Hilly is an exceptional liar, except for the moment right before she speaks.

Hilly opens the door. Her mouth is tight and red. I look down at her hands. They are knotted together like ropes. I've arrived too late.

"Well, that was quick," she says and I follow her inside. My heart is seizing inside my chest. I'm not sure I'm breathing at all.

"There it is, that ugly thing. I hope you don't mind, I had to check something in the minutes from the meeting."

I stare at her, my best friend, trying to see just what she's read in my things. But her smile is professional if not sparkling. The telling moments are gone.

"Can I get you something to sip on?"

"No, I'm fine." Then I add, "Want to hit balls at the club later? It's so gorgeous out."

"William's got a campaign meeting and then we're going to see *It's a Mad, Mad, Mad, Mad World*."

I study her. Didn't she ask me, just two hours ago, to double-date to this movie tomorrow night? Slowly, I move down to the end of the dining table, like she might pounce on me if I move too fast. She picks up a sterling fork from the sideboard, thrums her index finger along the tines.

"Yes, um, I heard Spencer Tracy's supposed to be divine," I say. Casually, I tick through the papers in my satchel. Aibileen and Minny's notes are still tucked deep in the side pocket, the flap closed, the latch snapped. But Hilly's bathroom initiative is in the open center section with the paper where I wrote *Jim Crow or Hilly's bathroom plan—what's the difference?* Besides this is the draft of the newsletter that Hilly has examined already. But the booklet—the laws—I tick through again—they are gone.

Hilly tilts her head, narrows her eyes at me. "You know, I was just thinking about how Stuart's daddy stood right next to Ross Barnett when they fought that colored boy walking into Ole Miss. They're awfully close, Senator Whitworth and Governor Barnett."

I open my mouth to say something, anything, but then two-year-old William, Jr., totters in.

"There you are." Hilly picks him up, nuzzles his neck. "You are perfect, my perfect boy!" she says. William looks at me and screams.

"Well, enjoy the picture show," I say, going for the front door.

"Alright," she says. I walk down the steps. From her doorway, Hilly waves, flaps William's hand bye-bye. She slams the door before I've even made it to my car.

AIBILEEN

CHAPTER 14

I BEEN IN SOME tense situations, but to have Minny on one side a my living room and Miss Skeeter on the other, and the topic at hand be what it feel like being Negro and working for a white woman. Law, it's a wonder they hadn't been a injury.

We had some close calls though.

Like last week, when Miss Skeeter showed me Miss Hilly's reasons why colored folk need they own bathroom.

"Feel like I'm looking at something from the KKK," I said to Miss Skeeter. We was in my living room and the nights had started to get warm. Minny'd gone in the kitchen to stand in front a the icebox. Minny don't stop sweating but for five minutes in January and maybe not even then.

"Hilly wants me to print it in the League newsletter," Miss Skeeter said, shaking her head disgusted. "I'm sorry, I probably shouldn't have shown it to you. But there's no one else I can tell."

A minute later, Minny come back from the kitchen. I gave Miss Skeeter a look, so she slid the list under her notebook. Minny didn't look much cooler. Fact, she looked hotter than ever.

"Minny, do you and Leroy ever talk about civil rights?" Miss Skeeter ask. "When he comes home from work?"

Minny had that big bruise on her arm cause that's what Leroy do when he come home from work. He push her around.

"Nope" was all Minny said. Minny do not like people up in her business.

"Really? He doesn't share the way he feels about the marches and the segregation? Maybe at work, his bo—"

"Move off a Leroy." Minny crossed her arms up so that bruise wouldn't show.

I gave Skeeter a nudge on the foot. But Miss Skeeter, she had that look she gets when she's all up in something.

"Aibileen, don't you think it would be interesting if we could show a little of the husbands' perspective? Minny, maybe—"

Minny stood so quick the lightshade rattled. "I ain't doing this no more. You making this too personal. I don't care about telling white people how it feel."

"Minny, okay, I'm sorry," Miss Skeeter said. "We don't have to talk about your family."

"No. I change my mind. You find somebody else to spill the beans." We been through this before. But this time, Minny snatched up her pocket-book, grabbed her funeral fan that fell under the chair, and said, "I'm sorry, Aib. But I just can't do this no more."

I got a panicky feeling then. She really gone leave. Minny can't quit. She the only maid besides me who agreed to do it.

So I leant up, slipped Hilly's piece a paper out from under Miss Skeeter's notebook. My fingers stopped right in front a Minny.

She look down at it. "What that?"

I put on my blank face. Shrugged my shoulders. Couldn't act like I really wanted her to read it cause then she wouldn't.

Minny picked it up and started skimming. Pretty soon, I could see all her front teeth. But she wasn't smiling.

Then she looked at Miss Skeeter, long and heavy. She said, "Maybe we keep going then. But you stay out a my personal business, you hear?"

Miss Skeeter nodded. She learning.

. . .

I MIX A EGG SALAD for Miss Leefolt and Baby Girl's lunch, put them little pickles on the side to fancy it up. Miss Leefolt set at the kitchen table with Mae Mobley, start telling her how the baby's gone be here in October, how she hope she don't have to be in the hospital for the Ole Miss homecoming game, how she might have her a little sister or a little brother and wonder what they gone name it. It's nice, seeing them talking like this. Half the morning, Miss Leefolt been on the phone with Miss Hilly gossiping about something, hardly noticing Baby Girl at all. And once the new baby come, Mae Mobley ain't gone get so much as a swat from her mama.

After lunch, I take Baby Girl out to the backyard and fill up the green plastic pool. It's already ninety-five degrees outside. Mississippi got the most unorganized weather in the nation. In February, it'll be fifteen degrees and you be wishing spring would come on, and the next day it's ninety degrees for the next nine months.

The sun shining. Mae Mobley's setting in the middle a that pool in bathing bottoms. First thing she do is take off that top. Miss Leefolt come outside and say, "That looks like fun! I'm fixing to call Hilly, tell her to bring Heather and little Will over here."

And fore I know it, all three kids is playing in there, splashing around, having a good old time.

Heather, Miss Hilly's girl, she pretty cute. She six months older than Mae Mobley and Mae Mobley just love her. Heather got dark, shiny curls all over her head and some little freckles, and she real talkative. She pretty much just a short version a Miss Hilly, only it look better on a child. Little William, Jr., he two. He tow-headed and he don't say nothing. Just waddle around like a duck, following them girls to the high monkey grass on the edge a the yard, to the swingset that hitch up on one side if you swing too high and scare me to death, and back into the baby pool.

One thing I got to say about Miss Hilly, she love her children. About every five minutes, she kiss little Will on the head. Or she ask Heather, is she having fun? Or come here and give Mama a hug. Always telling her she the most beautiful girl in the world. And Heather love her mama too. She look at Miss Hilly like she looking up at the Statue a Liberty. That kind a love always make me want a cry. Even when it going to Miss Hilly. Cause it makes me think about Treelore, how much he love me. I appreciate seeing a child adoring they mama.

We grown-ups is setting in the shade a the magnolia tree while the kids play. I put a few feet between me and the ladies so it's proper. They got towels down in them black iron chairs that gets so hot. I like to sit in the plastic green folding chair. Keep my legs cool.

I watch Mae Mobley make Barbie Doll do the skinny dip, jumping off the side a the pool. But I got my eye on the ladies too. I been noticing how Miss Hilly act all sweet and happy when she talk to Heather and William, but ever time she turn to Miss Leefolt, she get a sneer on her face.

"Aibileen, get me a little more iced tea, would you, please?" Hilly ask. I go and get the pitcher from the refrigerator.

"See, that's what I don't understand," I hear Miss Hilly say when I'm close enough. "Nobody wants to sit down on a toilet seat they have to share with them."

"It does make sense," Miss Leefolt say, but then she hush up when I come over to fill up they glasses.

"Why, thank you," Miss Hilly say. Then she give me a real perplexed look, say, "Aibileen, you like having your own toilet, don't you?"

"Yes ma'am." She still talking about that pot even though it's been in there six months.

"Separate but equal," Miss Hilly say back to Miss Leefolt. "That's what Governor Ross Barnett says is right, and you can't argue with the *government*."

Miss Leefolt clap her hand on her thigh like she got the most interesting thing to change the subject to. I'm with her. Let's discuss something else. "Did I tell you what Raleigh said the other day?"

But Miss Hilly shaking her head. "Aibileen, you wouldn't want to go to a school full of white people, would you?"

"No ma'am," I mumble. I get up and pull the ponytail holder out a Baby Girl's head. Them green plastic balls get all tangly when her hair get wet. But what I really want to do is put my hands up over her ears so she can't hear this talk. And worse, hear me agreeing.

But then I think: Why? Why I have to stand here and agree with her? And if Mae Mobley gone hear it, she gone hear some sense. I get my breath. My heart beating hard. And I say polite as I can, "Not a school full a just white people. But where the colored and the white folks is together."

Hilly and Miss Leefolt both look at me. I look back down at the kids.

"But *Aibileen*"—Miss Hilly smile real cold—"colored people and white people are just so...*different*." She wrinkle up her nose.

I feel my lip curling. A course we different! Everybody know colored people and white people ain't the same. But we still just people! Shoot, I even been hearing Jesus had colored skin living out there in the desert. I press my lips together.

It don't matter though, cause Miss Hilly already moved on. Ain't nothing to her. She back to her low-down talk with Miss Leefolt. Out a nowhere, a big heavy cloud cover the sun. I spec we about to get a shower.

"...government knows best and if Skeeter thinks she's going to get away with this colored non—"

"Mama! Mama! Look at me!" holler Heather from the pool. "Look at my pigtails!"

"I see you! I do! What with William running for office next—"

"Mama, give me your comb! I want to do beauty parlor!"

"—cannot have colored-supporting friends in my closet—"

"Mamaaaaa! Gimme your comb. Get your comb for me!"

"I read it. I found it in her satchel and I intend to take action."

And then Miss Hilly quiet, hunting for her comb in her pocketbook. Thunder boom over in South Jackson and way off we hear the wail a the tornado bell. I'm trying to make sense a what Miss Hilly just said: *Miss Skeeter. Her satchel. I read it.*

I get the kids out the pool, swaddle em up in towels. The thunder come crashing out the sky.

A MINUTE AFTER DARK, I'm setting at my kitchen table, twirling my pencil. My white-library copy a *Huckleberry Finn*'s in front a me, but I can't read it. I got a bad taste in my mouth, bitter, like coffee grounds in the last sip. I need to talk to Miss Skeeter.

I ain't never called her house except two times cause I had no choice, when I told her I'd work on the stories, and then to tell her Minny would too. I know it's risky. Still, I get up, put my hand on the wall phone. But what if her mama answer, or her daddy? I bet their maid gone home hours ago. How Miss Skeeter gone explain a colored woman calling her up on the telephone?

I set back down. Miss Skeeter come over here three days ago to talk to Minny. Seemed like everthing was fine. Nothing like when the police pull her over a few weeks ago. She didn't say nothing about Miss Hilly.

I huff in my chair awhile, wishing the phone would ring. I shoot up and race a cockroach across the floor with my workshoe. Cockroach win. He crawl under that grocery bag a clothes Miss Hilly give me, been setting there for months.

I stare at the sack, start twirling that pencil in my hand again. I got to do something with that bag. I'm used to ladies giving me clothes—got white lady clothes out the wazoo, ain't had to buy my own clothes in thirty years. It always takes a while till they feel like mine. When Treelore was a little thing, I put on a old coat from some lady I's waiting on and Treelore, he look at me funny, back away. Say I smell white.

But this bag is different. Even what would fit me in that paper sack, I can't wear. Can't give to my friends either. Ever piece in that bag—the culotte pants, the shirt with the Peter Pan collar, the pink jacket with the gravy stain on it, even the socks—they all got the letters *H.W.H.* sewn in. Red thread, pretty little cursive letters. I reckon Yule May had to sew them letters. Wearing those, I'd feel like I's personal-owned property a Hilly W. Holbrook.

I get up and kick at the bag, but the cockroach don't come out. So I take out my notebook, intending to start on my prayers, but I'm just too deep worrying about Miss Hilly. Wondering what she meant when she said *Read it.*

After while, my mind done drifted to where I wish it wouldn't. I reckon I know pretty well what would happen if the white ladies found out we was writing about them, telling the truth a what they really like. Womens, they ain't like men. A woman ain't gone beat you with a stick. Miss Hilly wouldn't pull no pistol on me. Miss Leefolt wouldn't come burn my house down.

No, white womens like to keep they hands clean. They got a shiny little set a tools they use, sharp as witches' fingernails, tidy and laid out neat, like the picks on a dentist tray. They gone take they time with em.

First thing a white lady gone do is fire you. You upset, but you figure you'll find another job, when things settle down, when the white lady get around to forgetting. You got a month a rent saved. People bring you squash casseroles.

But then a week after you lost your job, you get this little yellow envelope stuck in your screen door. Paper inside say NOTICE OF EVICTION. Ever landlord in Jackson be white and ever one got a white wife that's friends with somebody. You start to panic some then. You still ain't got no job prospects. Everwhere you try, the door slams in your face. And now you ain't got a place to live.

Then it starts to come a little faster.

If you got a note on your car, they gone repossess it.

If you got a parking ticket you ain't paid, you going to jail.

If you got a daughter, maybe you go live with her. She tend to a white family a her own. But a few days later she come home, say, "Mama? I just got fired." She look hurt, scared. She don't understand why. You got to tell her it's cause a you.

Least her husband still working. Least they can feed the baby.

Then they fire her husband. Just another little sharp tool, shiny and fine.

They both pointing at you, crying, wondering why you done it. You can't even remember why. Weeks pass and nothing, no jobs, no money, no house. You hope this is the end of it, that she done enough, she ready to forget.

It'll be a knock on the door, late at night. It won't be the white lady at the door. She don't do that kind a thing herself. But while the nightmare's happening, the burning or the cutting or the beating, you realize something you known all your life: the white lady don't *ever* forget.

And she ain't gone stop till you dead.

. . .

THE NEXT MORNING, Miss Skeeter pull her Cadillac up in Miss Leefolt's driveway. I got raw chicken on my hands and a flame on the stovetop and Mae Mobley whining cause she starving to death but I can't stand it another second. I walk in the dining room with my dirty hands up in the air.

Miss Skeeter, she asking Miss Leefolt about a list a girls who serving on a committee and Miss Leefolt say, "The head of the cupcake committee is Eileen," and Miss Skeeter say, "But the cupcake committee chairman is Roxanne," and Miss Leefolt say, "No, the cupcake co-chair is Roxanne and Eileen is the cupcake head," and I'm getting so peckertated over this cupcake talk I want to poke Miss Skeeter with my raw-chicken finger but I know better than to interrupt so I don't. There ain't no talk at all about the satchel.

Before I know it, Miss Skeeter out the door.

Law.

That night after supper, me and that cockroach stare each other down across the kitchen floor. He big, inch, inch an a half. He black. Blacker than me. He making a crackling sound with his wings. I got my shoe in my hand.

The phone ring and we both jump.

"Hey, Aibileen," Miss Skeeter say and I hear a door shut. "Sorry to call so late."

I breathe out. "I'm glad you did."

"I was just calling to see if you had any...word. From any other maids, I mean."

Miss Skeeter sound strange. Tight in the jaw. Lately, she been glowing like a firefly she so in love. My heart start drumming. Still, I don't jump right in with my questions. I ain't sure why.

"I asked Corrine who work at the Cooleys. She say no. Then Rhonda, and Rhonda's sister who wait on the Millers...but both a them say no too."

"What about Yule May? Have you...talked to her recently?"

I wonder then if that's why Miss Skeeter acting strange. See, I told Miss Skeeter a fib. I told her a month ago I asked Yule May, but I didn't. It's not just that I don't know Yule May well. It's that she Miss Hilly Holbrook's maid, and anything having to do with that name make me nervous.

"Not real recent. Maybe...I try her again," I lie, hating it.

Then I get back to jiggling my pencil. Ready to tell her what Miss Hilly said.

"Aibileen," Miss Skeeter voice gone all shaky, "I have to tell you something."

Miss Skeeter get quiet and it's like them eerie seconds before a funnel cloud drop.

"What happen, Miss Skeeter?"

"I...left my satchel. At the League. Hilly picked it up."

I squint my eyes, feel like I ain't hearing too good. "The red one?"

She don't reply.

"Aw...*Law.*" This all starting to make a sick sense.

"The stories were in a flap pocket. On the side, in another folder. I think all she saw were Jim Crow laws, some...booklet I'd picked up at the library but...I can't say for sure."

"Oh Miss *Skeeter*," I say and shut my eyes. God help me, God help *Minny*...

"I know. I *know*," Miss Skeeter say and start to cry into the phone.

"Alright. Alright, now." I try to make myself swallow my anger down. It was a accident, I tell myself. Kicking her ain't gone do us no good.

But *still.*

"Aibileen, I am so *so* sorry."

There's a few seconds a nothing but heart-pumping. Real slow and scary, my brain start ticking through the few facts she given me, what I know myself.

"How long ago this happen?" I ask.

"Three days ago. I wanted to find out what she knew before I told you."

"You talked to Miss Hilly?"

"Just for a second when I picked it up. But I've talked to Elizabeth and Lou Anne and probably four other girls who know Hilly. Nobody's said anything about it. That was...that was why I asked about Yule May," she say. "I was wondering if she'd heard anything at work."

I draw in a breath, hating what I have to tell her. "I heard it. Yesterday. Miss Hilly was talking to Miss Leefolt about it."

Miss Skeeter don't say nothing. I feel like I'm waiting for a brick to come slamming through my window.

"She talking about Mister Holbrook running for office and how you supporting colored people and she say...she read something." Saying it out loud now, I'm shaking. And still bobbing the pencil between my fingers.

"Did she say anything about maids?" Miss Skeeter ask. "I mean, was she only upset with me or did she mention you or Minny?"

"No, just...you."

"Okay." Miss Skeeter blow air into the phone. She sound upset, but she don't know what could happen to me, to Minny. She don't know about them sharp, shiny utensils a white lady use. About that knock on the door, late at night. That there are white men out there *hungry* to hear about a colored person crossing whites, ready with they wooden bats, matchsticks. Any little thing'll do.

"I-I can't say a hundred percent, but..." Miss Skeeter say, "if Hilly knew anything about the book or you or *especially* Minny, she'd be spreading it all over town."

I think on this, wanting so hard to believe her. "It's true, she do not like Minny Jackson."

"Aibileen," Miss Skeeter say, and I hear her start to break down again. That calm-down in her voice is cracking. "We can stop. I understand completely if you want to stop working on it."

If I say I don't want a do it anymore, then everthing I been writing and still have to write ain't gone get to be said. *No,* I think. I *don't* want a stop. I'm surprised by how loud I think it.

"If Miss Hilly know, she know," I say. "Stopping ain't gone save us now."

I DON'T SEE, hear, or smell Miss Hilly for two days. Even when I ain't holding a pencil, my fingers is jiggling it, in my pocket, on the kitchen counter, thumping like drumsticks. I got to find out what's inside Miss Hilly's head.

Miss Leefolt leave Yule May three messages for Miss Hilly, but she always at Mister Holbrook's office—the "campaign H.Q." is what Miss Hilly been calling it. Miss Leefolt sigh, hang up the phone like she just don't know how her brain gone operate without Miss Hilly coming over to push the Think buttons. Ten times Baby Girl ask when little Heather gone come play in the plastic pool again. I reckon they'll be good friends growing up, with Miss Hilly teaching them both how things is. By that afternoon, we all wandering around the house, jiggling our fingers, wondering when Miss Hilly gone show up again.

After while, Miss Leefolt go to the material store. Say she gone make a cover for something. She don't know what. Mae Mobley look at me and I reckon we thinking the same thing: that woman'd cover us both up if she could.

I HAVE TO WORK REAL LATE that evening. I feed Baby Girl supper and put her to bed, cause Mister and Miss Leefolt gone to see a picture at the Lamar. Mister Leefolt promise he take her and she hold him to it, even though it's only the late show left. When they get home, they yawning, crickets is cricking. Other houses, I'd sleep in the maid's room, but they ain't one here. I kind a hang around thinking Mister Leefolt gone offer to drive me home, but he just go right to bed.

Outside, in the dark, I walk all the way up to Riverside, about ten minutes away, where they run a late bus for the nighttime water-plant workers. The breeze is good enough keep the mosquitoes off. I sit on the edge a the park, in the grass under the streetlight. Bus come after while. Ain't but four people on there, two colored, two white, all mens. I don't know any of em. I take a window seat behind a thin colored fella. He got on a brown suit and a brown hat, be about my age.

We cross the bridge, head in the direction a the colored hospital, where the bus make its turn. I got my prayer book out so I can write some things down. I concentrate on Mae Mobley, try to keep my mind off Miss Hilly. *Show me how to teach Baby Girl to be kind, to love herself; to love others, while I got time with her...*

I look up. The bus done stopped in the middle a the road. I lean over into the aisle, see a few blocks up they's blue lights flashing in the dark, people standing around, a road block.

White driver stare ahead. He turn off the motor and my seat go still, feel strange. He straighten his driver's hat, hop out the seat. "Y'all stay put. Let me find out what's going on."

So we all set there in the quiet, waiting. I hear a dog barking, not a house dog, but the kind that sound like he yelling at you. After a full five minutes, driver get back on the bus, start the motor again. He toot his horn, wave his hand out the window, and start backing up real slow.

"Wha happen up there?" colored man in front a me call to the driver.

Driver don't answer. He keep backing up. The flashing lights is getting smaller, the dog barking fading off. Driver turn the bus around on Farish Street. At the next corner, he stop. "Colored people off, last stop for you," he holler in the rearview. "White people lemme know where y'all need to get to. I'll get you close as I can."

The colored man look back at me. I guess we both ain't got a good feeling. He stand up so I do too. I follow him to the front door. It's eerie quiet, just the sound a our feets.

White man lean up to the driver, say, "What's going on?"

I follow the colored man down the steps a the bus. Behind me, I hear the driver say, "I don't know, some nigger got shot. Where you headed?"

The door swish closed. Oh Law, I think, please don't let this be any a my peoples.

Ain't a sound on Farish Street, or a person, cept us two. The man look at me. "You alright? You close to home?"

"I be alright. I'm close." My house is seven blocks from here.

"Want me to walk you?"

I kind a do, but I shake my head. "Naw, thank you. I be fine."

A news truck whiz by, way down at the intersection the bus turned off of. Big WLBT-TV letters on the side.

"Law, I hope this ain't as bad as it—" but the man gone. They ain't a soul now but me. I get that feeling people talk about, right before they get mugged. In two seconds, my stockings is rubbing together so fast I sound like zippers zipping. Up ahead I see three people walking fast like me. All of em turn off, go into houses, shut the door.

I'm real sure I don't want to be alone another second. I cut between Mule Cato's house and the back a the auto repair, then through Oney Black's yard, trip on a hose-pipe in the dark. I feel like a burglar. Can see lights on inside the houses, heads bent down, lights that should be off this time a night. Whatever going on, everbody either talking about it or listening to it.

Finally, up ahead I see Minny's kitchen light, back door open, screen door closed. The door make a whine when I push it. Minny setting at the table with all five kids: Leroy Junior, Sugar, Felicia, Kindra, and Benny. I guess Leroy Senior gone to work. They all staring at the big radio in the middle a the table. A wave a static come in with me.

"What is it?" I say. Minny frown, fiddle with the dial. In a second I take in the room: a ham slice curled and red in a skillet. A tin can on the counter, lid open. Dirty plates in the sink. Ain't Minny's kitchen at all.

"What happen?" I ask again.

The radio man come into tune, hollering, "—*almost ten years serving as the Field Secretary for the N-double-A-C-P. Still no word from the hospital but wounds are said to be—*"

"*Who?*" I say.

Minny stare at me like I ain't got my head on. "Medgar Evers. Where you been?"

"Medgar Evers? What happen?" I met Myrlie Evers, his wife, last fall, when she visit our church with Mary Bone's family. She wore this smart red-and-black scarf tied on her neck. I remember how she looked me in the eye, smiled like she was real glad to meet me. Medgar Evers like a celebrity around here, being so high in the NAACP.

"Set down," Minny say. I set in a wooden chair. They all ghost-faced, staring at the radio. It's about half the size of a car engine, wood, four knobs on it. Even Kindra quiet in Sugar's lap.

"KKK shot him. Front a his house. A hour ago."

I feel a prickle creep up my spine. "Where he live?"

"On Guynes," Minny say. "The doctors got him at our hospital."

"I...saw," I say, thinking a the bus. Guynes ain't but five minutes away from here if you got a car.

"...*witnesses say it was a single man, a white male, who jumped from the bushes. Rumors of KKK involvement are...*"

Now they's some unorganized talking on the radio, some people yelling, some fumbling round. I tense up like somebody watching us from outside. Somebody white. The KKK was here, five minutes away, to hunt down a colored man. I want a close that back door.

"*I was just informed,*" the announcer say, panting, "*that Medgar Evers is dead.*"

"*Medgar Evers,*" he sound like he getting pushed around, voices round him, "*I was just told. Has died.*"

Oh *Law*.

Minny turn to Leroy Junior. Her voice low, steady.

"Take your brothers and your sisters in the bedroom. Get in bed. And stay back there." It always sound scarier when a hollerer talk soft.

Even though I know Leroy Junior want a stay, he give em a look and they all disappear, quiet, quick. The radio man go quiet too. For a second, that box nothing but brown wood and wires. "*Medgar Evers,*" he say, his voice sound like it's rolling backwards, "*NAACP Field Secretary, is dead.*" He sigh. "*Medgar Evers is dead.*"

I swallow back a mouthful a spit and stare at Minny's wallpaint that's gone yellow with bacon grease, baby hands, Leroy's Pall Malls. No pictures or calendars on Minny's walls. I'm trying not to think. I don't want a think about a colored man dying. It'll make me remember Treelore.

Minny's hands is in fists. She gritting her teeth. "Shot him right in front a his *children*, Aibileen."

"We gone pray for the Everses, we gone pray for Myrlie..." but it just sound so empty, so I stop.

"Radio say his family run out the house when they heard the shots. Say he bloody, stumbling round, all the kids with blood all over em..." She slap her hand on the table, rattling the wood radio.

I hold my breath, but I feel dizzy. I got to be the one who's strong. I got to keep my friend here from losing it.

"Things ain't never gone change in this town, Aibileen. We living in hell, we *trapped*. Our *kids* is trapped."

Radio man get loud again, say, "*...policemen everywhere, blocking the road. Mayor Thompson is expected to hold a press conference shortly—*"

I choke then. The tears roll down. It's all them white peoples that breaks me, standing around the colored neighborhood. White peoples with guns, pointed at colored peoples. Cause who gone protect our peoples? Ain't no colored policemans.

Minny stare at the door the kids went through. Sweat's drilling down the sides a her face.

"What they gone do to us, Aibileen? If they catch us..."

I take a deep breath. She talking about the stories. "We both know. It be bad."

"But what would they do? Hitch us to a pickup and drag us behind? Shoot me in my yard front a my kids? Or just starve us to death?"

Mayor Thompson come on the radio, say how sorry he is for the Evers family. I look at the open back door and get that watched feeling again, with a white man's voice in the room.

"This ain't...we ain't doing civil rights here. We just telling stories like they really happen."

I turn off the radio, take Minny's hand in mine. We set like that, Minny staring at the brown moth pressed up on the wall, me staring at that flap a red meat, left dry in the pan.

Minny got the most lonesome look in her eyes. "I wish Leroy was home," she whisper.

I doubt if them words ever been said in this house before.

FOR DAYS AND DAYS, Jackson, Mississippi's like a pot a boiling water. On Miss Leefolt's tee-vee, flocks a colored people march up High Street the day after Mister Evers' funeral. Three hundred arrested. Colored paper say thousands a people came to the service, but you could count the whites on one hand. The police know who did it, but they ain't telling nobody his name.

I come to find that the Evers family ain't burying Medgar in Mississippi. His body's going to Washington, to the Arlington Cemetery, and I reckon Myrlie real proud a that. She should be. But I'd want him here, close by. In the newspaper, I read how even the President a the United States telling Mayor Thompson he need to do better. Put a committee together with blacks and whites and work things out down here. But Mayor Thompson, he say—to *President Kennedy*—"I am not going to appoint a bi-racial committee. Let's not kid ourselves. I believe in the separation of the races, and that's the way it's going to be."

Few days later, the mayor come on the radio again. "Jackson, Mississippi, is the closest place to heaven there is," he say. "And it's going to be like this for the rest of our lives."

For the second time in two months, Jackson, Mississippi's in the *Life* magazine. This time, though, we make the cover.

CHAPTER 15

Nᴏɴᴇ ᴀ ᴛʜᴇ Mᴇᴅɢᴀʀ Eᴠᴇʀs talk come up in Miss Leefolt's house. I
change the station when she come back from her lunch meeting. We
go on like it's a nice summer afternoon. I still ain't heard hide nor hair from
Miss Hilly and I'm sick a the worry that's always in my head.

A day after the Evers funeral, Miss Leefolt's mama stop by for a visit. She
live up in Greenwood, Mississippi, and she driving down to New Orleans. She
don't knock, Miss Fredericks just waltz on in the living room where I'm ironing. She give me a lemony smile. I go tell Miss Leefolt who here.

"Mama! You're so early! You must've gotten up at the crack of dawn this
morning, I hope you didn't tire yourself out!" Miss Leefolt say, rushing into
the living room, picking up toys fast as she can. She shoot me a look that
say, *now*. I put Mister Leefolt's wrinkled shirts in a basket, get a cloth for
Baby Girl's face to wipe off the jelly.

"And you look so fresh and stylish this morning, Mama." Miss Leefolt
smiling so hard she getting bug-eyed. "Are you excited about your shopping
trip?"

From the good Buick she drive and her nice buckle shoes, I spec Miss
Fredericks got a lot more money than Mister and Miss Leefolt do.

"I wanted to break up the drive. And I was hoping you'd take me to the
Robert E. Lee for lunch," Miss Fredericks say. I don't know how this woman

can stand her own self. I heard Mister and Miss Leefolt arguing about how evertime she come to town, she make Miss Leefolt take her to the fanciest place in town and then sit back and make Miss Leefolt pay the bill.

Miss Leefolt say, "Oh, why don't we have Aibileen fix us lunch here? We have a real nice ham and some—"

"I stopped by to go out to lunch. Not to eat here."

"Alright. Alright, Mama, let me just go get my handbag."

Miss Fredericks look down at Mae Mobley playing with her baby doll, Claudia, on the floor. She bend down and give her a hug, say, "Mae Mobley, did you like that smocked dress I sent over last week?"

"Yeah," Baby Girl say to her Granmama. I hated showing Miss Leefolt how tight that dress was around the middle. Baby Girl getting plumper.

Miss Fredericks, she scowl down at Mae Mobley. "You say *yes ma'am*, young lady. Do you hear me?"

Mae Mobley, she get a dull look on her face, say, "Yes ma'am." But I know what she thinking. She thinking, *Great. Just what I need today. Another lady in this house who don't like me.*

They head out the door with Miss Fredericks pinching the back a Miss Leefolt's arm. "You don't know how to hire proper help, Elizabeth. It is her job to make sure Mae Mobley has good *manners*."

"Alright, Mama, we'll work on it."

"You can't just hire anybody and hope you get lucky."

After while, I fix Baby Girl that ham sandwich Miss Fredericks too good to eat. But Mae Mobley only take one bite, push it away.

"I don't feel good. My froat hurts, Aibee."

I know what a froat is and I know how to fix it. Baby Girl getting a summer cold. I heat her up a cup a honey water, little lemon in it to make it good. But what this girl really needs is a story so she can go to sleep. I lift her up in my arms. Law, she getting big. Gone be three years old in a few months, and pudgy as a punkin.

Ever afternoon, me and Baby Girl set in the rocking chair before her nap. Ever afternoon, I tell her: *You kind, you smart, you important.* But she growing up and I know, soon, them few words ain't gone be enough.

"Aibee? Read me a story?"

I look through the books to see what I'm on read to her. I can't read that *Curious George* one more time cause she don't want a hear it. Or *Chicken Little* or *Madeline* neither.

So we just rock in the chair awhile. Mae Mobley lean her head against my uniform. We watch the rain dripping on the water left in the green plastic pool. I say a prayer for Myrlie Evers, wishing I'd had work off to go to the funeral. I think on how her ten-year-old son, somebody told me, had cried so quiet through the whole thing. I rock and pray, feeling so sad, I don't know, something just come over me. The words just come out.

"Once upon a time they was two little girls," I say. "One girl had black skin, one girl had white."

Mae Mobley look up at me. She listening.

"Little colored girl say to the little white girl, 'How come your skin be so pale?' White girl say, 'I don't know. How come your skin be so black? What you think that mean?'

"But neither one a them little girls knew. So little white girl say, 'Well, let's see. You got hair, I got hair.'" I gives Mae Mobley a little tousle on her head.

"Little colored girl say 'I got a nose, you got a nose.'" I gives her little snout a tweak. She got to reach up and do the same to me.

"Little white girl say, 'I got toes, you got toes.' And I do the little thing with her toes, but she can't get to mine cause I got my white work shoes on.

"'So we's the same. Just a different color,' say that little colored girl. The little white girl she agreed and they was friends. The End."

Baby Girl just look at me. Law, that was a sorry story if I ever heard one. Wasn't even no plot to it. But Mae Mobley, she smile and say, "Tell it again."

So I do. By the fourth time, she asleep. I whisper, "I'm on tell you a better one next time."

"Don't we have more towels, Aibileen? This one's fine, but we can't take this old ratty thing, I'd be embarrassed to death. I guess we'll just take the one, then."

Miss Leefolt all in a tizzy. She and Mister Leefolt don't belong to no swim club, not even the dinky Broadmoore pool. Miss Hilly call this morning and ask if she and Baby Girl want to go swimming at the Jackson Country Club and that's a invitation Miss Leefolt ain't had but once or twice. I probably been there more times than she has.

You can't use paper money there, you got to be a member and charge it to your account and one thing I know about Miss Hilly is, she don't like to carry nobody's costs. I reckon Miss Hilly got other ladies she go to the Country Club with, ones who got the memberships.

We still ain't heard another word about the satchel. Ain't even seen Miss Hilly in five days. Neither has Miss Skeeter, which is bad. They sposed to be best friends. Miss Skeeter, she brung over the first Minny chapter last night. Miss Walter was no cup a tea and if Miss Hilly saw anything relating to that, I don't know what's gone happen to us. I just hope Miss Skeeter ain't too scared to tell me if she heard anything new.

I put Baby Girl's yellow bikini on. "You got to keep you top on, now. They don't let no nekkid babies swim at the country club." Nor Negroes nor Jews. I used to work for the Goldmans. The Jackson Jews got to swim at the Colonial Country Club, the Negroes, in May's Lake.

I feed Baby Girl a peanut butter sandwich and the phone ring.

"Miss Leefolt residence."

"Aibileen, hey, it's Skeeter. Is Elizabeth there?"

"Hey Miss Skeeter..." I look over at Miss Leefolt, about to hand her the phone, but she wave her hands. She shake her head and mouth, *No. Tell her I'm not here.*

"She...she gone, Miss Skeeter," I say and I look Miss Leefolt right in the eye while I tell her lie. I don't understand it. Miss Skeeter a member a the club, wouldn't be no trouble inviting her.

At noontime, we all three get in Miss Leefolt's blue Ford Fairlane. On the back seat next to us, I got a bag with a Thermos a apple juice, cheese nabs, peanuts, and two Co-Cola bottles that's gone be like drinking coffee they gone be so hot. I spec Miss Leefolt know Miss Hilly ain't gone be pushing us to the snack bar. Law knows why she invite her today.

Baby Girl ride in my lap in the back seat. I crank the window down, let the warm air blow on our faces. Miss Leefolt keep poofing her hair up. She a stop-and-go driver and I feel nauseous, wish she'd just keep both hands on the wheel.

We pass the Ben Franklin Five and Dime, the Seale-Lily Ice Cream drive-thru. They got a sliding window on the back side so colored folk can get our ice cream too. My legs is sweating with Baby Girl setting on me. After while, we on a long, bumpy road with pasture on both sides, cows flapping at the flies with they tails. We count us twenty-six cows but Mae Mobley just call out "*Ten*" after the first nine. That's high as she know.

Bout fifteen minutes later, we pull onto a paved drive. The club's a low, white building with prickle bushes around it, not nearly so fancy as folks talk about it. They's plenty a parking places up front, but Miss Leefolt think on it a second, park a ways back.

We step out onto the blacktop, feel the heat cover us. I got the paper sack in one hand, Mae Mobley's hand in the other and we trudge across the steaming black lot. Gridlines make it like we on a charcoal grill, roasting like corncobs. My face getting tight, burning in the sun. Baby Girl lagging back on my hand looking stunned like she just got slapped. Miss Leefolt panting and frowning at the door, still twenty yards away, wondering, I reckon, why she park so far. The part in my hair get to burning, then itching, but I can't scratch at it cause both hands is full then *whoo!* somebody blow out the flame. The lobby's dark, cool, heaven. We blink awhile.

Miss Leefolt look around, blind and shy, so I point to the side door. "Pool that a way, ma'am."

She look grateful I know my way around so she don't have to ask like poor folk.

We push open the door and the sun flash in our eyes again, but it's nice, cooler. The swimming pool shining blue. The black-and-white stripe awnings look clean. The air smell like laundry soap. Kids is laughing and splashing and ladies is laying around in they swimsuits and sunglasses reading magazines.

Miss Leefolt roof her eyes and spy around for Miss Hilly. She got a white floppy hat on, black-and-white polky-dot dress, clonky white buckle sandals a size too big for her feet. She frowning cause she feel out a place, but smiling cause she don't want nobody to know it.

"*There* she is." We follow Miss Leefolt around the pool to where Miss Hilly is in a red bathing suit. She laid out on a lounge chair, watching her kids swim. I see two maids I don't know with other families, but not Yule May.

"There y'all are," Miss Hilly say. "Why, Mae Mobley, don't you look like a little butterball in that bikini. Aibileen, the kids are right there in the baby pool. You can sit in the shade back yonder and look after them. Don't let William splash the girls, now."

Miss Leefolt lay down on the lounge chair next to Miss Hilly and I set at the table under a umbrella, few feet behind the ladies. I pop my hose away from my legs to dry the sweat. I'm in a pretty good position for hearing what they say.

"Yule May," Miss Hilly shake her head at Miss Leefolt. "Another day off. I tell you, that girl is pushing it with me." Well, that's one mystery solved. Miss Hilly invite Miss Leefolt to the pool cause she know she bring me.

Miss Hilly pour more cocoa butter on her plump, tan legs, rub it around. She already so greasy she shining. "I am so ready to get down to the coast," Miss Hilly say. "Three weeks at the beach."

"I wish Raleigh's family had a house down there." Miss Leefolt sigh. She pull her dress up a little to sun her white knees. She can't wear no bathing suit since she pregnant.

"Of course we have to pay the bus fare to get Yule May back up here on the weekends. *Eight* dollars. I ought to take it out of her pay."

The kids yell they want to get in the big pool now. I pull Mae Mobley's Styrofoam bubble out the bag, fasten it around her tummy. Miss Hilly hand me two more and I put one on William and Heather too. They get in the big pool and float around like a bunch a fishing corks. Miss Hilly look at me, say, "Aren't they the cutest things?" and I nod. They sure is. Even Miss Leefolt nodding.

They talk and I listen, but they ain't no mention a Miss Skeeter or a satchel. After while, Miss Hilly send me to the snack window to get cherry Co-Colas for everone, even myself. After while, the locusts in the trees start humming, the shade get cooler and I feel my eyes, trained on the kids in the pool, start to sag.

"Aibee, watch me! Looky at me!" I focus my eyes, smile at Mae Mobley funning around.

And that's when I see Miss Skeeter, back behind the pool, outside the fence. She got on her tennis skirt and her racquet in her hand. She staring at Miss Hilly and Miss Leefolt, tilting her head like she sorting something out. Miss Hilly and Miss Leefolt, they don't see her, they still talking about Biloxi. I watch Miss Skeeter come in the gate, walk around the pool. Pretty soon, she standing right in front a them and they still don't see her.

"Hey y'all," Miss Skeeter say. She got sweat running down her arms. Her face is pink and swolled up in the sun.

Miss Hilly look up, but she stay stretched out on her pool chair, magazine in her hand. Miss Leefolt jump up off her chair and stand up.

"Hey, Skeeter! Why—I didn't...we tried to call..." Her teeth just about chattering she smiling so big.

"Hey, Elizabeth."

"Tennis?" Miss Leefolt ask, nodding her head like she a doll on a dashboard. "Who're you playing with?"

"I was hitting balls on the backboard by myself," Miss Skeeter say. She blow a thicket a hair off her forehead, but it's stuck. She don't move out the sun, though.

"Hilly," Miss Skeeter say, "did Yule May tell you I called?"

Hilly smile kind a tight. "She's off today."

"I called you yesterday too."

"Look, Skeeter, I didn't have time. I have been at the campaign H.Q. since Wednesday addressing envelopes to practically every white person in Jackson."

"Alright." Miss Skeeter nod. Then she squint, say, "Hilly, are we...did I...do something to upset you?" and I feel my fingers jiggling again, twirling that dumb invisible pencil.

Miss Hilly close her magazine, put it on the concrete so she don't get her grease on it. "This should be discussed at a later time, Skeeter."

Miss Leefolt sit back down real quick. She pick up Miss Hilly's *Good Housekeeping*, start reading it like she ain't ever seen nothing so important.

"Alright." Miss Skeeter shrug. "I just thought we could talk about . . . whatever this is before you go out of town."

Miss Hilly bout to protest, but then she let out a long sigh. "Why don't you just tell me the truth, Skeeter?"

"The truth about wh—"

"Look, I found that *paraphernalia* of yours." I swallow hard. Miss Hilly trying to whisper but she really ain't no good at it.

Miss Skeeter keep her eyes on Hilly. She real calm, don't look up at me at all. "What paraphernalia do you mean?"

"In your satchel when I was hunting for the minutes? And Skeeter"— she flash her eyes up at the sky and back down—"I don't know. I just do not know anymore."

"Hilly, what are you talking about? What did you see in my satchel?"

I look out at the kids, Law, I almost forgot about em. I feel like I'm gone faint listening to this.

"Those *laws* you were carrying around? About what the—" Miss Hilly look back at me. I keep my eyes trained on the pool. "What those *other* people can and cannot do and frankly," she hiss, "I think it's downright pig-headed of you. To think you know better than our government? Than Ross Barnett?"

"When did I ever say a word about Ross Barnett?" Miss Skeeter say.

Miss Hilly wag her finger up at Miss Skeeter. Miss Leefolt staring at the same page, same line, same word. I got the whole scene fixed in the corner a my eye.

"You are not a politician, Skeeter Phelan."

"Well, neither are you, Hilly."

Miss Hilly stand up then. She point her finger to the ground. "I am about to be a politician's wife, unless you have anything to do with it. How is William ever going to get elected in Washington, D.C., one day if we have integrational friends in our closet?"

"Washington?" Miss Skeeter roll her eyes. "William's running for the local senate, Hilly. And he might not win."

Oh Law. I finally let myself look at Miss Skeeter. Why you doing this? Why you pushing her hot button?

Oh, Miss Hilly mad now. She snap her head straight. "You know well as I do, there are good, tax-paying white people in this town who would fight you to the death on this. You want to let them get in our swimming pools? Let them put their hands on everything in our grocery stores?"

Miss Skeeter stare long and hard at Miss Hilly. Then, for one-half a second, Miss Skeeter glance at me, see the pleading in my eyes. Her shoulders ease back some. "Oh Hilly, it's just a booklet. I found it at the darn library. I'm not trying to change any laws, I just took it home to *read*."

Miss Hilly take this in a second. "But if you're looking at those *laws*," Miss Hilly snap the leg a her bathing suit that's crept up her behind, "I have to wonder, what *else* are you up to?"

Miss Skeeter shift her eyes away, lick her lips. "*Hilly*. You know me better than anybody else in this world. If I was up to something, you'd have me figured out in half a second."

Miss Hilly just watch her. Then Miss Skeeter grab Miss Hilly's hand and squeeze it. "I am worried about you. You disappear for an entire week, you're working yourself to death on this campaign. Look at that." Miss Skeeter turn Miss Hilly's palm over. "You have a blister from addressing all those envelopes."

And real slow, I watch Miss Hilly's body slump down, start to give in on itself. She look to make sure Miss Leefolt ain't listening.

"I'm just so scared," Miss Hilly whisper through her teeth. I can't hear much. "...piled so much money in this campaign, if William doesn't win...been working day and..."

Miss Skeeter lay a hand on Miss Hilly's shoulder, say something to her. Miss Hilly nod and give her a tired smile.

After while, Miss Skeeter tell them she got to go. She head off through the sunbathers, winding through the chairs and the towels. Miss Leefolt look over at Miss Hilly with big eyes, like she scared to ask any questions.

I lean back in my chair, wave to Mae Mobley making twirlies in the water. I try to rub the headache out my temples. Across the way, Miss Skeeter look back at me. Everbody around us is sunning and laughing and squinting, not a soul guessing that the colored woman and the white woman with the tennis racquet is wondering the same thing: is we fools to feel some relief?

CHAPTER 16

ABOUT A YEAR AFTER Treelore died, I started going to the Community
Concerns Meeting at my church. I reckon I started doing it to fill
time. Keep the evenings from getting so lonely. Even though Shirley Boon,
with her big know-it-all smile, kind a irritate me. Minny don't like Shirley
neither, but she usually come anyway to get out the house. But Benny got
the asthma tonight, so Minny ain't gone make it.

Lately, the meetings is more about civil rights than keeping the streets
clean and who gone work at the clothing exchange. It ain't aggressive,
mostly people just talking things out, praying about it. But after Mr. Evers
got shot a week ago, lot a colored folks is frustrated in this town. Especially
the younger ones, who ain't built up a callus to it yet. They done had meetings all week over the killing. I hear folks was angry, yelling, crying. This
the first one I come to since the shooting.

I walk down the steps to the basement. Generally, it's cooler than up in
the church, but it's warm down here tonight. Folks is putting ice cubes in
they coffee. I look around to see who's here, reckoning I better ask some
more maids to help us, now that it look like we squeaked by Miss Hilly.
Thirty-five maids done said no and I feel like I'm selling something nobody
want to buy. Something big and stinky, like Kiki Brown and her lemon
smell-good polish. But what really makes me and Kiki the same is, I'm

proud a what I'm selling. I can't help it. We telling stories that need to be told.

I wish Minny could help me ask people. Minny know how to put a sell on. But we decided from the start, nobody needs to know Minny's a part a this. It's just too risky for her family. We felt like we had to tell folks it was Miss Skeeter, though. Nobody would agree if they didn't know who the white lady was, wondering if they knew her or had worked for her. But Miss Skeeter can't do the front sell. She'd scare em off before she even opened her mouth. So it's up to me and it didn't take but five or six maids before everbody already know what I'm on ask before I get three words out my mouth. They say it ain't worth it. They ask me why I'd put my own self at risk when it ain't gone do no good. I reckon peoples is starting to think old Aibileen's basket ain't got many pawpaws left in it.

All the wooden fold-chairs is full tonight. They's over fifty people here, mostly womens.

"Sit down by me, Aibileen," Bertrina Bessemer say. "Goldella, let the older folk have the chairs."

Goldella jump up, motion me down. Least Bertrina still treating me like I ain't crazy.

I settle in. Tonight, Shirley Boon's sitting down and the Deacon standing at the front. He say we need a quiet prayer meeting tonight. Say we need to heal. I'm glad for it. We close our eyes and the Deacon leads us in a prayer for the Everses, for Myrlie, for the sons. Some folks is whispering, murmuring to God, and a quiet power fill up the room, like bees buzzing on a comb. I say my prayers to myself. When I'm done, I take a deep breath, wait for the others to finish. When I get home tonight, I'll write my prayers too. This is worth the double time.

Yule May, Miss Hilly's maid, setting in front a me. Yule May easy to recognize from the back cause she got such good hair, smooth, no nap to it. I hear she educated, went through most a college. Course we got plenty a smart people in our church with they college degrees. Doctors, lawyers, Mr. Cross who own *The Southern Times*, the colored newspaper that come out ever week. But Yule May, she probably the most educated maid we got in our parish. Seeing her makes me think again about the wrong I need to right.

The Deacon open his eyes, look out on us all real quiet. "The prayers we are say—"

"Deacon Thoroughgood," a deep voice boom through stillness. I turn—everbody turn—and there's Jessup, Plantain Fidelia's grandson, standing in the doorway. He twenty-two, twenty-three. He got his hands in thick fists.

"What I want to know is," he say slow, angry, "what we plan to *do* about it."

Deacon got a stern look on his face like he done talked with Jessup before. "Tonight, we are going to lift our prayers to God. We will march peacefully down the streets of Jackson next Tuesday. And in August, I will see you in Washington to march with Doctor King."

"That is not enough!" Jessup say, banging his fist on his hand. "They shot him in the back like a dog!"

"Jessup." Deacon raise his hand. "Tonight is for prayer. For the family. For the lawyers on the case. I understand your anger, but, son—"

"Prayer? You mean y'all just gonna sit around and pray about it?"

He look around at all a us in our chairs.

"Y'all think *prayer's* going to keep white people from killing us?"

No one answer, not even the Deacon. Jessup just turn and leave. We all hear his feet stomping up the stairs and then over our heads out the church.

The room is real quiet. Deacon Thoroughgood got his eyes locked a few inches above our heads. It's strange. He ain't a man not to look you in the eye. Everbody staring at him, everbody wondering what he thinking so that he can't look in our faces. Then I see Yule May shaking her head, real small, but like she mean it and I reckon the Deacon and Yule May is thinking the same thing. They thinking about what Jessup ask. And Yule May, she just answering the question.

THE MEETING ENDS around eight o'clock. The ones who got kids go on, others get ourselves coffee from the table in the back. They ain't much chatter. People quiet. I take a breath, go to Yule May standing at the coffee urn. I just want to get this lie off that's stuck on me like a cocklebur. I ain't gone ask nobody else at the meeting. Ain't nobody gone buy my stinky smell-good tonight.

Yule May nod at me, smile polite. She about forty and tall and thin. She done kept her figure nice. She still wearing her white uniform and it fit trim on her waist. She always wear earrings, tiny gold loops.

"I hear the twins is going to Tougaloo College next year. Congratulations."

"We hope so. We've still got a little more to save. Two at once's a lot."

"You went to a good bit college yourself, didn't you?"

She nod, say, "Jackson College."

"I loved school. The reading and the writing. Cept the rithmatic. I didn't take to that."

Yule May smiles. "The English was my favorite too. The writing."

"I been . . . writing some myself."

Yule May look me in the eye and I can tell then she know what I'm about to say. For a second, I can see the shame she swallow ever day, working in that house. The fear. I feel embarrassed to ask her.

But Yule May say it before I have to. "I know about the stories you're working on. With that friend of Miss Hilly's."

"It's alright, Yule May. I know you can't do it."

"It's just . . . a risk I can't afford to take right now. We so close to getting enough money together."

"I understand," I say and I smile, let her know she off the hook. But Yule May don't move away.

"The names . . . you're changing them, I heard?"

This the same question everbody ask, cause they curious.

"That's right. And the name a the town, too."

She look down at the floor. "So I'd tell my stories about being a maid and she'd write them down? Edit them or . . . something like that?"

I nod. "We want a do all kind a stories. Good things and bad. She working with . . . another maid right now."

Yule May lick her lips, look like she imagining it, telling what it's like to work for Miss Hilly.

"Could we…talk about this some more? When I have more time?"

"A course," I say, and I see, in her eyes, she ain't just being nice.

"I'm sorry, but Henry and the boys are waiting on me," she says. "But may I call you? And talk in private?"

"Anytime. Whenever you feel like it."

She touch my arm and look me straight in the eyes again. I can't believe what I see. It's like she been waiting on me to ask her all this time.

Then she gone out the door. I stand in the corner a minute, drinking coffee too hot for the weather. I laugh and mutter to myself, even though everbody gone think I'm even crazier for it.

MINNY

CHAPTER 17

G O ON out a here so I can do my cleaning."

Miss Celia draws the covers up around her chest like she's afraid I might jerk her out of bed. Nine months here and I still don't know if she's sick in the body or fried up her wits with the hair coloring. She does look better than when I started. Her tummy's got a little fat on it, her cheeks aren't so hollow as they were, out here starving her and Mister Johnny to death.

For a while, Miss Celia was working in the backyard all the time but now that crazy lady's back to sitting around the bed again. I used to be glad she stayed holed up in her room. Now that I've met Mister Johnny, though, I'm ready to *work*. And damn it, I'm ready to get Miss Celia in shape too.

"You driving me crazy hanging around this house twenty-five hours a day. Get. Go chop down that poor mimosa tree you hate so much," I say, because Mr. Johnny never did chop that thing down.

But when Miss Celia doesn't move from that mattress, I know it's time to pull out the big guns. "When you gone tell Mister Johnny about me?" Because that always gets her moving. Sometimes I just ask it for my own entertainment.

I can't believe the charade has gone on this long, with Mister Johnny knowing about me, and Miss Celia walking around like a ding-a-ling, like she's still pulling her trick. It was no surprise when the Christmas deadline came and she begged for more time. Oh I railed her about it, but then the fool started boo-hooing so I let her off the hook just so she'd shut up, told her it was her Christmas present. She ought to get a stocking chock full of coal for all the lies she's told.

Thank the Lord Miss Hilly hasn't showed up here to play bridge, even though Mister Johnny tried to set it up again just two weeks ago. I know because Aibileen told me she heard Miss Hilly and Miss Leefolt laughing about it. Miss Celia got all serious, asking me what to cook if they come over. Ordered a book in the mail to learn the game, *Bridge for the Beginner*. Ought to call it *Bridge for the Brainless*. When it came this morning in the mailbox, she didn't read it for two seconds before she asked, "Will you teach me to play, Minny? This bridge book doesn't make a lick of sense."

"I don't know how to play no bridge," I said.

"Yes, you do."

"How you know what I can do?" I started banging pots around, irritated just by the looks of that stupid red cover. I finally got Mister Johnny out the way and now I have to worry about Miss Hilly coming over and ratting me out. She'll tell Miss Celia what I did for sure. Shoot. I'd fire my own self for what I did.

"Because Missus Walters told me you used to practice with her on Saturday mornings."

I started scrubbing the big pot. My knuckles hit the sides, making a clanging noise.

"Playing cards is the devil's game," I said. "And I got too much to do already."

"But I'll get all flustered with those girls over here trying to teach me. Won't you just show me a little?"

"No."

Miss Celia hummed out a little sigh. "It's cause I'm such a bad cook, isn't it? You think I can't learn anything now."

"What you gone do if Miss Hilly and them ladies tell your husband you got a maid out here? Ain't that gone blow your cover?"

"I've already worked that out. I'll tell Johnny I'm bringing in some help for the day so it'll look proper and all for the other ladies."

"Mm-hmm."

"Then I'll tell him I like you so much I want to hire you full-time. I mean, I could tell him that...in a few months."

I started to sweat then. "When you think them ladies is coming over for your bridge party?"

"I'm just waiting for Hilly to call me back. Johnny told her husband I'd be calling. I left her two messages, so I'm sure she'll call me back anytime now."

I stand there trying to think of something to stop this from happening. I look at the phone, pray it never rings again.

THE NEXT MORNING, when I get in for work, Miss Celia comes out of her bedroom. I think she's about to sneak upstairs, which she's started to do again, but then I hear her on the kitchen telephone asking for Miss Hilly. I get a sick, sick feeling.

"I was just calling again to see about getting a bridge game together!" she says all cheerful and I don't move until I know it's Yule May, Hilly's maid, she's talking to and not Miss Hilly herself. Miss Celia spells out her telephone number like a floor-mopping jingle, "Emerson two-sixty-six-oh-nine!"

And half a minute later, she's calling up another name from the back of that stupid paper, like she's gotten into the habit of doing every other day. I know what that thing is, it's the newsletter from the Ladies League, and from the looks of it she found it in the parking lot of that ladies' club. It's rough as sandpaper and wilted, like it sat through a rainstorm after blowing out of somebody's pocketbook.

So far, not one of those girls has ever called her back, but every time that phone rings, she jumps on it like a dog on a coon. It's always Mister Johnny.

"Alright...just...tell her I called again," Miss Celia says into the phone.

I hear her hang it up real soft. If I cared, which I don't, I'd tell her those ladies ain't worth it. "Those ladies ain't worth it, Miss Celia," I hear myself saying. But she acts like she can't hear me. She goes back to the bedroom and closes the door.

I think about knocking, seeing if she needs anything. But I've got more important things to worry about than if Miss Celia's won the damn popularity contest. What with Medgar Evers shot on his own doorstep and Felicia clammering for her driver's license, now that she's turned fifteen—she's a good girl but I got pregnant with Leroy Junior when I wasn't much older than her and a Buick had something to do with it. And on top of all that, now I've got Miss Skeeter and her stories to worry about.

AT THE END OF JUNE, a heat wave of a hundred degrees moves in and doesn't budge. It's like a hot water bottle plopped on top of the colored neighborhood, making it ten degrees worse than the rest of Jackson. It's so hot, Mister Dunn's rooster walks in my door and squats his red self right in front of my kitchen fan. I come in to find him looking at me like *I ain't moving nowhere, lady.* He'd rather get beat with a broom than go back out in that nonsense.

Out in Madison County, the heat officially makes Miss Celia the laziest person in the U. S. of A. She won't even get the mail out the box anymore, I have to do it. It's even too hot for Miss Celia to sit out at the pool. Which is a problem for me.

See, I think if God had intended for white people and colored people to be this close together for so much of the day, he would've made us color-blind. And while Miss Celia's grinning and "good morning" and "glad to see"-ing me, I'm wondering, how did she get this far in life without knowing where the lines are drawn? I mean, a floozy calling the society ladies is bad enough. But she has sat down and eaten lunch with me every single day since I started working here. I don't mean in the same room, I mean at the same *table.* That little one up under the window. Every white woman I've ever worked for ate in the dining room as far away from the colored help as they could. And that was fine with me.

"But why? I don't want to eat in there all by myself when I could eat in here with you," Miss Celia said. I didn't even try to explain it to her. There are so many things Miss Celia is just plain *ignorant* about.

Every other white woman also knows that there is a time of the month when you do *not* to talk to Minny. Even Miss Walters knew when the Min-O-Meter was running hot. She'd smell the caramel cooking and cane herself right out the door. Wouldn't even let Miss Hilly come over.

Last week, the sugar and butter had filled Miss Celia's whole house with the smell of Christmas even though it was the crying shame of June. I was tense, as usual, turning my sugar to caramel. I asked her three times, *very politely,* if I couldn't do this by myself, but she wanted to be in there with me. Said she was getting lonely being in her bedroom all the day long.

I tried to ignore her. Problem was, I have to talk to myself when I make a caramel cake or else I get too jittery.

I said, "Hottest day in June history. A hundred and four outside."

And she said, "Do you have air-conditioning? Thank goodness we have it here cause I grew up without it and I know what it's like being hot."

And I said, "Can't afford no air-conditioning. Them things eat current like a boll weevil on cotton." And I started stirring hard because the brown was just forming on the top and that's when you've really got to watch it and I say, "We already late on the light bill," because I'm not thinking straight and do you know what she said? She said, "Oh, Minny, I wish I could loan you the money, but Johnny's been asking all these funny questions lately," and I turned to inform her that every time a Negro complained about the cost of living didn't mean she was begging for money, but before I could say a word, I'd burned up my damn caramel.

At SUNDAY CHURCH SERVICE, Shirley Boon gets up in front of the congregation. With her lips flapping like a flag, she reminds us that the "Community Concerns" meeting is Wednesday night, to discuss a sit-in at the Woolworth's lunch counter on Amite Street. Big nosy Shirley points her finger at us and says, "The meeting is at seven so be on time. No excuses!" She reminds me of a big, white, ugly schoolteacher. The kind that nobody ever wants to marry.

"You coming on Wednesday?" asks Aibileen. We're walking home in the three o'clock heat. I've got my funeral fan in my fist. I'm waving it so fast it looks like it's got a motor on it.

"I ain't got time," I say.

"You gone make me go by myself again? Come on, I'm on bring some gingerbread and some—"

"I *said* I can't go."

Aibileen nods, says, "Alright then." She keeps walking.

"Benny...might get the asthma again. I don't want a leave him."

"Mm-hmm," Aibileen says. "You'n tell me the real reason when you ready."

We turn on Gessum, walk around a car that's plumb died of heat stroke in the road. "Oh, fore I forget, Miss Skeeter wants to come over early Tuesday night," Aibileen says. "Bout seven. You make it then?"

"Lord," I say, getting irritated all over again. "What am I doing? I must be crazy, giving the sworn secrets a the colored race to a white lady."

"It's just Miss Skeeter, she ain't like the rest."

"Feel like I'm talking behind my own back," I say. I've met with Miss Skeeter at least five times now. It's not getting any easier.

"You want a stop coming?" Aibileen asks. "I don't want you to feel like you have to." I don't answer her.

"You still there, M?" she says.

"I just...I want things to be better for the kids," I say. "But it's a sorry fact that it's a white woman doing this."

"Come to the community meeting with me on Wednesday. We talk more about it then," Aibileen says with a little smile.

I knew Aibileen wouldn't drop it. I sigh. "I got in trouble, alright?"

"With who?"

"Shirley Boon," I say. "Last meeting everybody was holding hands and praying they gone let blacks in the white bathroom and talking about how they gone set down on a stool at Woolworth's and not fight back and they all smiling like this world gone be a shiny new place and I just...I popped. I told Shirley Boon her ass won't fit on no stool at Woolworth's anyway."

"What Shirley say?"

I pull out my teacher lady voice. *"'If you can't say nothing nice, then you ought not say nothing at all.'"*

When we get to her house, I look over at Aibileen. She's holding down a laugh so hard she's gone purple.

"It ain't funny," I say.

"I am glad you're my friend, Minny Jackson." And she gives me a big hug until I roll my eyes and tell her I have to go.

I keep walking and turn at the corner. I didn't want Aibileen to know that. I don't want anybody to know how much I need those Skeeter stories. Now that I can't come to the Shirley Boon meetings anymore, that's pretty much all I've got. And I am not saying the Miss Skeeter meetings are fun. Every time we meet, I complain. I moan. I get mad and throw a hot potato fit. But here's the thing: I like telling my stories. It feels like I'm doing something about it. When I leave, the concrete in my chest has loosened, melted down so I can breathe for a few days.

And I know there are plenty of other "colored" things I could do besides telling my stories or going to Shirley Boon's meetings—the mass meetings in town, the marches in Birmingham, the voting rallies upstate. But truth is, I don't care that much about voting. I don't care about eating at a counter with white people. What I care about is, if in ten years, a white lady will call my girls dirty and accuse them of stealing the silver.

At home that night, I get the butter beans simmering, the ham in the skillet.

"Kindra, get everbody in here," I say to my six-year-old. "We ready to eat."

"Suuuupppperrrrr," Kindra yells, not moving an inch from where she's standing.

"You go get your daddy the proper way," I yell. "What I tell you about yelling in my house?"

Kindra rolls her eyes at me like she's just been asked to do the stupidest thing in the world. She stamps her feet down the hall. *"Suuupperrr!"*

"Kindra!"

The kitchen is the only room in the house we can all fit in together. The rest are set up as bedrooms. Me and Leroy's room is in the back, next to that is a little room for Leroy Junior and Benny, and the front living room's been turned into a bedroom for Felicia, Sugar, and Kindra. So all that leaves is the kitchen. Unless it's crazy cold outside, our back door stays open with the screen shut to keep out the flies. All the time there's the roar of kids and cars and neighbors and dogs barking.

Leroy comes in and sits at the table next to Benny, who's seven. Felicia fills up the glasses with milk or water. Kindra carries a plate of beans and ham to her daddy and comes back to the stove for more. I hand her another plate.

"This one for Benny," I say.

"Benny, get up and help your mama," Leroy says.

"Benny got the asthma. He don't need to be doing nothing." But my sweet boy gets up anyway, takes the plate from Kindra. My kids know how to work.

They all set at the table except me. Three children are home tonight. Leroy Junior, who's a senior at Lenier High, is bagging groceries at the Jitney 14. That's the white grocery store over in Miss Hilly's neighborhood. Sugar, my oldest girl, in tenth grade, babysits for our neighbor Tallulah who works late. When Sugar's finished, she'll walk home and drive her daddy to the late shift at the pipe-fitting plant, then pick up Leroy Junior from the grocery. Leroy Senior will get a ride from the plant at four in the morning with Tallulah's husband. It all works out.

Leroy eats, but his eyes are on the *Jackson Journal* next to his plate. He's not exactly known for his sweet nature when he wakes up. I glance over from the stove and see the sit-in at Brown's Drug Store is the front-page news. It's not Shirley's group, it's people from Greenwood. A bunch of white teenagers stand behind the five protesters on their stools, jeering and jabbing, pouring ketchup and mustard and salt all over their heads.

"How they do that?" Felicia points at the picture. "Sit there without fighting back?"

"That's what they supposed to do," says Leroy.

"I feel like spitting looking at that picture," I say.

"We talk about it later." Leroy folds the paper in quarters and tucks it under his thigh.

Felicia says to Benny, not quiet enough, "Good thing Mama wasn't up on one a them stools. Else none a them white folks had any teeth left."

"And Mama be in the Parchman jail," says Benny for everybody to hear.

Kindra props her arm on her hip. "Nuh-uh. Ain't nobody putting my mama in jail. I beat those white people with a stick till they bleed."

Leroy points his finger at every one of them. "I don't want to hear a word about it outside this house. It's too dangerous. You hear me, Benny? Felicia?" Then he points his finger at Kindra. "You hear me?"

Benny and Felicia nod their heads, look down at their plates. I'm sorry I started all this and give Kindra the keep-it-shut look. But Little Miss Something slaps her fork down on the table, climbs out of her chair. "I hate white people! And I'm on tell everbody if I want to!"

I chase her down the hall. When I catch her, I potato sack her back to the table.

"I'm sorry, Daddy," Felicia says because she's the kind that's going to take the blame for everyone every time. "And I look after Kindra. She don't know what she saying."

But Leroy smacks his hand on the table. "Nobody's getting in that mess! Y'all hear me?" And he stares his children down. I turn to the stove so he can't see my face. Lord help me if he finds out what I'm doing with Miss Skeeter.

ALL THE NEXT WEEK, I hear Miss Celia on her bedroom phone, leaving messages at Miss Hilly's house, Elizabeth Leefolt's house, Miss Parker's house, both Caldwell sisters, and ten other society ladies. Even Miss Skeeter's house, which I don't like one bit. I told Miss Skeeter myself: *Don't even think about calling her back. Don't tangle up this web any more than it already is.*

The irritating part is, after Miss Celia makes these stupid calls and hangs up the phone, she picks that receiver right back up. She listens for a dial tone in case the line doesn't go free.

"Ain't nothing wrong with that phone," I say. She just keeps smiling at me like she's been doing for a month now, like she's got a pocketful of paper money.

"Why you in such a good mood?" I finally ask her. "Mister Johnny being sweet or something?" I'm loading up my next "When you gone tell" but she beats me to it.

"Oh, he's being sweet alright," she says. "And it's not gonna be much longer until I tell him about you."

"Good," I say and I mean it. I am sick of this lying game. I imagine how she must smile at Mister Johnny when she hands him my pork chops, how that nice man has to act like he's so proud of her when he knows it's me doing the cooking. She's making a fool of herself, a fool of her nice husband, and a liar out of me.

"Minny, would you mind fetching the mail for me?" she asks even though she's sitting here all dressed and I've got butter on my hands and a wash in the machine and a motor blender going. She's like a Philistine on a Sunday, the way she won't take but so many steps a day. Except every day's Sunday around here.

I clean off my hands and head out to the box, sweat half a gallon on the way. I mean, it's only ninety-nine degrees outside. There's a two-foot package sitting next to the mailbox, in the grass. I've seen her with these big brown boxes before, figure it's some kind of beauty cream she's ordering. But when I pick it up, it's heavy. Makes a tinkling sound like I'm toting Co-Cola bottles.

"You got something, Miss Celia." I plop the box on the floor of the kitchen.

I've never seen her jump up so fast. In fact, the only thing fast about Miss Celia is the way she dresses. "It's just my..." She mumbles something. She heaves the box all the way to her bedroom and I hear the door slam.

An hour later, I go back in the bedroom to suck the rugs. Miss Celia's not laying down and she's not in the bathroom. I know she's not in the kitchen or the living room or out at the pool and I just dusted fancy parlor number one and number two and vacuumed the bear. Which means she must be upstairs. In the creepy rooms.

Before I got fired for accusing Mr. White Manager of wearing a hair piece, I used to clean the ballrooms at the Robert E. Lee Hotel. Those big, empty rooms with no peoples and the lipsticked napkins and the leftover smell of perfume gave me chills. And so does the upstairs of Miss Celia's house. There's even an antique cradle with Mister Johnny's old baby bonnet and silver rattle that I swear I can hear tinkling sometimes on its own accord. And it's thinking of that tinkling sound that makes me wonder if those boxes don't have something to do with her sneaking up to those rooms every other day.

I decide it's time I go up there and take a look for myself.

I KEEP AN EYE ON Miss Celia the next day, waiting for her to sneak upstairs so I can see what she's up to. Around two o'clock, she sticks her head in the kitchen and gives me a funny smile. A minute later, I hear the squeak in the ceiling.

Real easy, I head for the staircase. Even though I tiptoe, the dishes in the sideboard jangle, the floorboards groan. I walk so slowly up the stairs, I can hear my own breathing. At the top, I turn down the long hall. I pass wide open bedroom doors, one, two, three. Door number four, down on the end, is closed except for an inch. I move in a little closer. And through the crack, I spot her.

She's sitting on the yellow twin bed by the window and she's not smiling. The package I toted in from the mailbox is open and on the bed are a dozen bottles filled with brown liquid. It's a slow burn that rises up my bosoms, my chin, my mouth. I know the look of those flat bottles. I nursed a worthless pint drinker for twelve years and when my lazy, life-sucking daddy finally died, I swore to God with tears in my eyes I'd never marry one. And then I did.

And now here I am nursing another goddamn drinker. These aren't even store-bought bottles, these have a red wax top like my Uncle Toad used to cap his moonshine with. Mama always told me the real alcoholics, like my daddy, drink the homemade stuff because it's stronger. Now I know she's as much a fool as my daddy was and as Leroy is when he gets on the Old Crow, only she doesn't chase me with the frying pan.

Miss Celia picks a bottle up and looks at it like it's Jesus in there and she can't wait to get saved. She uncorks it, sips it, and sighs. Then she drinks three hard swallows and lays back on her fancy pillows.

My body starts to shake, watching that ease cross her face. She was so eager to get to her juice, she didn't even close the damn door. I have to grit my teeth so I don't scream at her. Finally I force my way back down the stairs.

When Miss Celia comes back downstairs ten minutes later, she sits at the kitchen table, asks me if I'm ready to eat.

"There's pork chops in the icebox and I'm not eating lunch today," I say and stomp out of the room.

That afternoon Miss Celia's in her bathroom sitting on the toilet lid. She's got the hair dryer on the back tank and the hood pulled over her bleached head. With that contraption on she wouldn't hear the A-bomb explode.

I go upstairs with my oil rags and I open that cupboard for myself. Two dozen flat whiskey bottles are hidden behind some ratty old blankets Miss Celia must've toted with her from Tunica County. The bottles don't have any labels fastened to them, just the stamp OLD KENTUCKY in the glass. Twelve are full, ready for tomorrow. Twelve are empty from last week. Just like all these damn bedrooms. No wonder the fool doesn't have any kids.

ON THE FIRST THURSDAY of July, at twelve noon, Miss Celia gets up from the bed for her cooking lesson. She's dressed in a white sweater so tight it'd make a hooker look holy. I swear her clothes get tighter every week.

We settle in our places, me at the stovetop, her on her stool. I've hardly spoken word one to her since I found those bottles last week. I'm not mad. I'm irate. But I have sworn every day for the past six days that I would follow Mama's Rule Number One. To say something would mean I cared about her and I don't. It's not my business or my concern if she's a lazy, drunk fool.

We lay the battered raw chicken on the rack. Then I have to remind the ding-dong for the bobillionth time to wash her hands before she kills us both.

I watch the chicken sizzle, try to forget she's there. Frying chicken always makes me feel a little better about life. I almost forget I'm working for a drunk. When the batch is done, I put most of it in the refrigerator for supper that night. The rest goes on a plate for our lunch. She sits down across from me at the kitchen table, as usual.

"Take the breast," she says, her blue eyes bugging out at me. "Go ahead."

"I eat the leg and the thigh," I say, taking them from the plate. I thumb through the *Jackson Journal* to the Metro section. I pop up the spine of my newspaper in front of my face so I don't have to look at her.

"But they don't have hardly any meat on them."

"They good. Greasy." I keep reading, trying to ignore her.

"Well," she says, taking the breast, "I guess that makes us perfect chicken partners then." And after a minute she says, "You know, I'm lucky to have you as a friend, Minny."

I feel thick, hot disgust rise up in my chest. I lower my paper and just look at her. "No ma'am. We ain't friends."

"Well...sure we are." She smiles, like she's doing me a big favor.

"No, Miss Celia. We ain't."

She blinks at me with her fake eyelashes. *Stop it, Minny,* my insides tell me. But I already know I can't. I know by the fists in my hands that I can't hold this in another minute.

"Is it..." She looks down at her chicken. "Because you're colored? Or because you don't...want to be friends with me?"

"So many reasons, you white and me colored just fall somewhere in between."

She's not smiling at all now. "But...why?"

"Because when I tell you I'm late on my light bill, I ain't asking you for money," I say.

"Oh Minny—"

"Because you don't even give me the courtesy a telling your husband I'm working here. Because you in this house twenty-four hours a day driving me insane."

"You don't understand, I *can't*. I can't leave."

"But all that is nothing compared to what I know now."

Her face goes a shade paler under her makeup.

"All this time, there I was thinking you were dying a the cancer or sick in the head. Poor Miss Celia, all day long."

"I know it's been hard..."

"Oh, I know you ain't sick. I seen you with them bottles upstairs. And you ain't fooling me another second."

"Bottles? Oh God, Minny, I—"

"I ought to pour them things down the drain. I ought to tell Mister Johnny right now—"

She stands up, knocking her chair over. "Don't you dare tell—"

"You act like you want kids but you drinking enough to poison a elephant!"

"If you tell him, I'll fire you, Minny!" She's got tears in her eyes. "If you touch those bottles, I'll fire you right now!"

But the blood's running too hot in my head to stop now. "Fire me? Who else gone come out here and work in secret while you hang around the house drunk all day?"

"You think I can't fire you? You finish your work today, Minny!" She's boo-hooing and pointing her finger at me. "You eat your chicken and then you go home!"

She picks up her plate with the white meat and charges through the swinging door. I hear it clatter down on the long fancy dining room table, the chair legs scraping against the floor. I sink down in my seat because my knees are shaking, and stare down at my chicken.

I just lost another damn job.

I WAKE UP SATURDAY MORNING at seven a.m. to a clanging headache and a raw tongue. I must've bitten down on it all night long.

Leroy looks at me through one eye because he knows something's up. He knew it last night at supper and smelled it when he walked in at five o'clock this morning.

"What's eating you? Ain't got trouble at work, do you?" he asks for the third time.

"Nothing eating me except five kids and a husband. Y'all driving me up a wall."

The last thing I need him to know is that I've told off another white lady and lost another job. I put on my purple housedress and stomp to the kitchen. I clean it like it's never been cleaned.

"Mama, where you going?" yells Kindra. "I'm hungry."

"I'm going to Aibileen's. Mama need to be with somebody not pulling on her for five minutes." I pass Sugar sitting on the front steps. "Sugar, go get Kindra some breakfast."

"She already ate. Just a half hour ago."

"Well, she hungry again."

I walk the two blocks to Aibileen's house, across Tick Road onto Farish Street. Even though it's hot as sin and steam's already rising off the blacktop, kids are throwing balls, kicking cans, skipping rope. "Hey there, Minny," someone says to me about every fifty feet. I nod, but I don't get friendly. Not today.

I cut through Ida Peek's garden. Aibileen's kitchen door is open. Aibileen's sitting at her table reading one of those books Miss Skeeter got her from the white library. She looks up when she hears the screen door whine. I guess she can tell I'm angry.

"Lord have mercy, who done what to you?"

"Celia Rae Foote, that's who." I sit down across from her. Aibileen gets up and pours me some coffee.

"What she do?"

I tell her about the bottles I found. I don't know why I hadn't told her a week and a half ago when I found them. Maybe I didn't want her to know something so awful about Miss Celia. Maybe I felt bad because Aibileen was the one who got me the job. But now I'm so mad I let it all spill out.

"And then she fired me."

"Oh, Law, Minny."

"Say she gone find another maid. But who gone work for that lady? Some nappy-headed country maid already living out there, won't know squat about serving from the left, clearing from the right."

"You thought about apologizing? Maybe you go in Monday morning, talk to—"

"I ain't apologizing to no drunk. I never apologized to my daddy and I sure ain't apologizing to her."

We're both quiet. I throw back my coffee, watch a horsefly buzz against Aibileen's screen door, knocking with its hard ugly head, *whap, whap, whap,* until it falls down on the step. Spins around like a crazy fool.

"Can't sleep. Can't eat," I say.

"I tell you, that Celia must be the worst one you *ever* had to tend to."

"They all bad. But she the worst of all."

"Ain't they? You remember that time Miss Walter make you pay for the crystal glass you broke? Ten dollars out a your pay? Then you find out them glasses only cost three dollars apiece down at Carter's?"

"Mm-hmm."

"Oh, and you remember that crazy Mister Charlie, the one who always call you nigger to your face like he think it's funny. And his wife, the one who make you eat lunch outside, even in the middle a January? Even when it snowed that time?"

"Make me cold just thinking bout it."

"And what—" Aibileen is chuckling, trying to talk at the same time. "What about that Miss Roberta? Way she make you sit at the kitchen table while she try out her new hair dye solution on you?" Aibileen wipes at her eyes. "Lord, I never seen blue hair on a black woman before or since. Leroy say you look like a cracker from outer space."

"Ain't nothing funny bout that. Took me three weeks and twenty-five dollars to get my hair black again."

Aibileen shakes her head, breathes out a high-keyed "Huhhhhm," takes a sip of her coffee.

"Miss Celia though," she says. "Way she treat you? How much she paying you to put up with Mister Johnny and the cooking lessons? Must be less than all of em."

"You know she paying me double."

"Oh, that's right. Well, anyway, with all her friends coming over, specting you to clean up after em all the time."

I just look at her.

"And them ten kids she got too." Aibileen presses her napkin to her lips, hides her smile. "Must drive you insane the way they screaming all day, messing up that big old house."

"I think you done made your point, Aibileen."

Aibileen smiles, pats me on the arm. "I'm sorry, honey. But you my best friend. And I think you got something pretty good out there. So what if she take a nip or two to get through the day? Go talk to her Monday."

I feel my face crinkle up. "You think she take me back? After everthing I said?"

"Nobody else gone wait on her. And she know it."

"Yeah. She dumb." I sigh. "But she ain't stupid."

I go on home. I don't tell Leroy what's bothering me, but I think about it all day and all weekend long. I've been fired more times than I have fingers. I pray to God I can get my job back on Monday.

CHAPTER 18

O N MONDAY MORNING, I drive to work rehearsing the whole way. *I know I mouthed off...* I walk into her kitchen. *And I know I was out of place...* I set my bag down in the chair, *and...and...* This is the hard part. *And I'm sorry.*

I brace myself when I hear Miss Celia's feet padding through the house. I don't know what to expect, if she'll be mad or cold or just flat out re-fire me. All I know is, I'm doing the talking *first.*

"Morning," she says. Miss Celia's still in her nightgown. She hasn't even brushed her hair, much less put the goo on her face.

"Miss Celia, I got to...tell you something..."

She groans, flattens her hand against her stomach.

"You...feel bad?"

"Yeah." She puts a biscuit and some ham on a plate, then takes the ham back off.

"Miss Celia, I want you to know—"

But she walks right out while I'm talking and I know I am in some kind of trouble.

I go ahead and do my work. Maybe I'm crazy to act like the job's still mine. Maybe she won't even pay me for today. After lunch, I turn on Miss Christine on *As the World Turns* and do the ironing. Usually, Miss Celia comes in and watches with me, but not today. When the program's over, I wait on her awhile in the kitchen, but Miss Celia doesn't even come in for her lesson. The bedroom door stays closed, and by two o'clock I can't think of anything else to do except clean their bedroom. I feel a dread like a frying pan in my stomach. I wish I'd gotten my words in this morning when I had the chance.

Finally, I go to the back of the house, look at that closed door. I knock and there's no answer. Finally, I take a chance and open it.

But the bed is empty. Now I've got the shut bathroom door to contend with.

"I'm on do my work in here," I call out. There's no answer, but I know she's in there. I can feel her behind that door. I'm sweating. I want to get this damn conversation over with.

I go around the room with my laundry sack, stuffing a weekend's worth of clothes inside. The bathroom door stays closed with no sound. I know that bathroom in there's a mess. I listen for some life as I pull the sheets up taut on the bed. The pale yellow bolster pillow is the ugliest thing I've ever seen, packaged on the ends like a big yellow hotdog. I smack it down on the mattress, smooth the bedspread out.

I wipe down the bedside table, stack the *Look* magazines on her side, the bridge book she ordered. I straighten the books on Mister Johnny's. He reads a lot. I pick up *To Kill a Mockingbird* and turn it over.

"Well look a there." A book with black folks in it. It makes me wonder if, one day, I'll see Miss Skeeter's book on a bedside table. Not with my real name in it, that's for sure.

Finally, I hear a noise, something scruff against the bathroom door. "Miss Celia," I call out again, "I'm out here. Just want you to know."

But there's nothing.

"That ain't none a my business whatever's going on in there," I say to myself. Then I holler, "Just gone do my work and get out a here before Mister Johnny gets home with the pistol." I'm hoping that'll draw her out. It doesn't.

"Miss Celia, they's some Lady-a-Pinkam under the sink. Drink that up and come out so I can do my work in there."

Finally, I just stop, stare at the door. Am I fired or am I ain't? And if I ain't, then what if she's so drunk, she can't hear me? Mister Johnny asked me to look after her. I don't think this would qualify as looking after if she's drunk in the bathtub.

"Miss Celia, just say something so I know you still alive in there."

"I'm fine."

But she does not sound fine to me.

"It's almost three o'clock." I stand in the middle of the bedroom, waiting. "Mister Johnny be home soon."

I need to know what's going on in there. I need to know if she's laid out drunk. And if I ain't fired, then I need to clean that bathroom so Mister Johnny doesn't think the secret maid is slacking and fire me a second time.

"Come on, Miss Celia, you mess up the hair coloring again? I helped you fix it last time, remember? We got it back real pretty."

The knob turns. Slowly, the door opens. Miss Celia's sitting on the floor, to the right of the door. Her knees are drawn up inside her nightgown.

I step a little closer. From the side, I can see her complexion is the color of fabric softener, a flat milky blue.

I can also see blood in the toilet bowl. A lot of it.

"You got the cramps, Miss Celia?" I whisper. I feel my nostrils flare.

Miss Celia doesn't turn around. There's a line of blood along the hem of her white nightgown, like it dipped down into the toilet.

"You want me to call Mister Johnny?" I say. I try, but I can't stop myself from looking at that red full bowl. Because there's something else deep down in that red liquid. Something...solid-looking.

"No." Miss Celia says, staring at the wall. "Fetch me... my phone book."

I hurry to the kitchen, snatch the book from the table, rush back. But when I try to hand it to Miss Celia, she waves it away.

"Please, you call," she says. "Under T, for Doctor Tate. I can't do it again."

I skip through the thin pages of the book. I know who Doctor Tate is. He doctors most of the white women I've waited on. He also gives his "special treatment" to Elaine Fairley every Tuesday when his wife is at her hair appointment. *Taft... Taggert... Tann. Thank the Lord.*

My hands tremble around the rotary dial. A white woman answers.

"Celia Foote, on Highway Twenty-Two out Madison County," I tell her as best I can without yacking on the floor. "Yes ma'am, lots and lots a blood coming out...Do he know how to get here?" She says yes, of course, and hangs up.

"He's coming?" asks Celia.

"He coming," I say. Another wave of nausea sneaks up on me. It'll be a long time until I can scrub that toilet again without gagging.

"You want a Co-Cola? I'm on get you a Co-Cola."

In the kitchen, I get a bottle of Coca-Cola from the refrigerator. I come back and set it on the tile and back away. As far from that red-filled pot as I can without leaving Miss Celia alone.

"Maybe we should get you up in the bed, Miss Celia. You think you can stand up?"

Miss Celia leans forward, tries to push herself up. I step in to help her and see that the blood has soaked through the seat of her nightgown, stained the blue tile with what looks like red glue, embedded in the grout. Stains that won't be easy to get up.

Just as I raise her to her feet, Miss Celia slips in a spot of blood, catches the edge of toilet bowl to steady herself. "Let me stay—I want to stay here."

"Alright then." I back away, into the bedroom. "Doctor Tate be here real soon. They calling him up at home."

"Come and set with me, Minny? Please?"

But there's a waft of warm, wretched air coming off that toilet. After some figuring, I sit with half my bottom in the bathroom, half out. And at eye-level, I can really smell it. It smells like meat, like hamburger defrosting on the counter. I kind of panic when I put that one together.

"Come on out of here, Miss Celia. You need some air."

"I can't get the blood on the...rug or Johnny will see it." The veins on Miss Celia's arm look black under her skin. Her face is getting whiter.

"You getting funny-looking. Drink you a little a this Co-Cola."

She takes a sip, says, "Oh Minny."

"How long you been bleeding?"

"Since this morning," she says and starts crying into the crook of her arm.

"It's alright, you gone be fine," I say and I sound real soothing, real confident, but inside my heart is pounding. Sure, Doctor Tate's coming to help Miss Celia, but what about the thing in the toilet? What am I supposed to do, flush it? What if it gets stuck in the pipes? It'll have to be fished up. Oh Lord, how am I going to make myself do that?

"There's so much blood," she moans, leaning against me. "Why's there so much blood this time?"

I raise my chin and look, just a little, in the bowl. But I have to look down again quick.

"Don't let Johnny see it. Oh God, when . . . what time is it?"

"Five to three. We got some time."

"What should we do about it?" asks Miss Celia.

We. God forgive me, but I wish there wasn't a "we" mixed up in this.

I shut my eyes, say, "I guess one a us is gone have to pull it out."

Miss Celia turns to me with her red-rimmed eyes. "And put it where?"

I can't look at her. "I guess . . . in the garbage pail."

"Please, do it now." Miss Celia buries her head in her knees like she's ashamed.

There's not even a *we* now. Now it's will *you* do it. Will *you* fish my dead baby out of that toilet bowl.

And what choice do I have?

I hear a whine come out of me. The tile floor is smashing against my fat. I shift, grunt, try to think it through. I mean, I've done worse than this, haven't I? Nothing comes to mind, but there has to be something.

"Please," Miss Celia says, "I can't . . . look at it no more."

"Alright." I nod, like I know what I'm doing. "I'm on take care a this thing."

I stand up, try to get practical. I know where I'll put it—in the white garbage pail next to the toilet. Then throw the whole thing out. But what will I use to get it out with? My hand?

I bite my lip, try to stay calm. Maybe I should just wait. Maybe . . . maybe the doctor will want to take it with him when he comes! Examine it. If I can get Miss Celia off it a few minutes, maybe I won't have to deal with it at all.

"We look after it in a minute," I say in that reassuring voice. "How far along you think you was?" I ease closer to the bowl, don't dare stop talking.

"Five months? I don't know." Miss Celia covers her face with a washrag. "I was taking a shower and I felt it pulling down, hurting. So I set on the toilet and it slipped out. Like it wanted *out of me*." She starts sobbing again, her shoulders jerking forward over her body.

Carefully, I lower the toilet lid down and settle back on the floor.

"Like it'd rather be dead than stand being inside me another second."

"Now you look a here, that's just God's way. Something ain't going right in your innards, nature got to do something about it. Second time, you gone catch." But then I think about those bottles and feel a ripple of anger.

"That was ... the second time."

"Oh Lordy."

"We got married cause I was pregnant," Miss Celia says, "but it ... it slipped out too."

I can't hold it in another second. "Then why in the heck are you drinking? You know you can't hold no baby with a pint of whiskey in you."

"Whiskey?"

Oh please. I can't even look at her with that "what-whiskey?" look. At least the smell's not as bad with the lid closed. When is that fool doctor coming?

"You thought I was ..." She shakes her head. "It's catch tonic." She closes her eyes. "From a Choctaw over in Feliciana Parish ..."

"Choctaw?" I blink. She is stupider than I ever imagined. "You can't trust them Indians. Don't you know we poisoned their corn? What if she trying to poison you?"

"Doctor Tate said it's just molasses and water," she cries down into her towel. "But I had to try it. I *had* to."

Well. I'm surprised by how loose my body goes, how relieved I am by this. "There's nothing wrong with taking your time, Miss Celia. Believe me, I got five kids."

"But Johnny wants kids now. Oh Minny." She shakes her head. "What's he going to do with me?"

"He gone get over it, that's what. He gone forget these babies cause mens is real good at that. Get to hoping for the next one."

"He doesn't know about this one. Or the one before."

"You said that's why he married you."

"That first time, he knew." Miss Celia lets out a big sigh. "This time's really the . . . fourth."

She stops crying and I don't have any good things left to say. For a minute, we're just two people wondering why things are the way they are.

"I kept thinking," she whispers, "if I was real still, if I brought somebody in to do the house and the cooking, maybe I could hold on to this one." She cries down into her towel. "I wanted this baby to look just like Johnny."

"Mister Johnny a good-looking man. Got good hair . . ."

Miss Celia lowers the towel from her face.

I wave my hand in the air, realize what I've just done. "I got to get some air. Hot in here."

"How do you know . . . ?"

I look around, try to think of a lie, but finally I just sigh. "He knows. Mister Johnny came home and found me."

"What?"

"Yes'm. He tell me not to tell you so you go right on thinking he's proud a you. He love you so much, Miss Celia. I seen it in his face how much."

"But . . . how long has he known?"

"A few . . . months."

"Months? Was he—was he upset that I'd lied?"

"Heck no. He even call me up at home a few weeks later to make sure I didn't have no plans to quit. Say he afraid he gone starve if I left."

"Oh Minny," she cries. "I'm sorry. I'm real sorry about everything."

"I been in worse situations." I'm thinking about the blue hair dye. Eating lunch in the freezing cold. And right now. There's still the baby in the toilet that someone's going to have to deal with.

"I don't know what to do, Minny."

"Doctor Tate tell you to keep trying, then I guess you keep trying."

"He hollers at me. Says I'm wasting my time in bed." She shakes her head. "He's a mean, awful man."

She presses the towel hard against her eyes. "I can't do this anymore." And the harder she cries, the whiter she turns.

I try to feed her a few more sips of Co-Cola but she won't take it. She can't hardly lift her hand to wave it away.

"I'm going to...be sick. I'm—"

I grab the garbage can, watch as Miss Celia vomits over it. And then I feel something wet on me and I look down and the blood's coming so fast now, it's leaked over to where I'm sitting. Everytime she heaves, the blood pushes out of her. I know she losing more than a person can handle.

"Sit up, Miss Celia! Get a good breath, now," I say, but she's slumping against me.

"Nuh-uh, you don't want a lay down. Come on." I push her back up but she's gone limp and I feel tears spring up in my eyes because that damn doctor should be here by now. He should've sent an ambulance and in the twenty-five years I've been cleaning houses nobody ever tells you what to do when your white lady keels over dead on top of you.

"Come on, Miss Celia!" I scream, but she's a soft white lump next to me, and there is nothing I can do but sit and tremble and wait.

Many minutes pass before the back bell rings. I prop Miss Celia's head on a towel, take off my shoes so I don't track the blood over the house, and run for the door.

"She done passed out!" I tell the doctor, and the nurse pushes past me and heads to the back like she knows her way around. She pulls the smelling salts out and puts them under Miss Celia's nose and Miss Celia jerks her head, lets out a little cry, and opens her eyes.

The nurse helps me get Miss Celia out of her bloody nightgown. She's got her eyes open but can hardly stand up. I put old towels down in the bed and we lay her down. I go in the kitchen where Doctor Tate's washing his hands.

"She in the bedroom," I say. *Not the kitchen, you snake.* He's in his fifties, Doctor Tate, and tops me by a good foot and a half. He has real white skin and this long, narrow face that shows no feelings at all. Finally he goes back to the bedroom.

Just before he opens the door, I touch him on the arm. "She don't want her husband to know. He ain't gone find out, is he?"

He looks at me like I'm a nigger and says, "You don't think it's his business?" He walks into the bedroom and shuts the door in my face.

I go to the kitchen and pace the floor. Half an hour passes, then an hour, and I'm worrying so hard that Mister Johnny's going to come home and find out, worrying Doctor Tate will call him, worrying they're going to leave that baby in the bowl for me to deal with, my head's throbbing. Finally, I hear Doctor Tate open the door.

"She alright?"

"She's hysterical. I gave her a pill to calm her down."

The nurse walks around us and out the back door carrying a white tin box. I breathe out for what feels like the first time in hours.

"You watch her tomorrow," he says and hands me a white paper bag. "Give her another pill if she gets too agitated. There'll be more bleeding. But don't call me up unless it's heavy."

"You ain't really gone tell Mister Johnny bout this, are you, Doctor Tate?"

He lets out a sick hiss. "You make sure she doesn't miss her appointment on Friday. I'm not driving all the way out here just because she's too lazy to come in."

He waltzes out and slams the door behind him.

The kitchen clock reads five o'clock. Mister Johnny's going to be home in half an hour. I grab the Clorox and the rags and a bucket.

MISS SKEETER

CHAPTER 19

IT IS 1963. The Space Age they're calling it. A man has circled the earth in a rocketship. They've invented a pill so married women don't have to get pregnant. A can of beer opens with a single finger instead of a can opener. Yet my parents' house is still as hot as it was in 1899, the year Great-grandfather built it.

"Mama, please," I beg, "when are we going to get air-conditioning?"

"We have survived this long without electric cool and I have no intentions of setting one of those tacky contraptions in my window."

And so, as July wanes on, I am forced from my attic bedroom to a cot on the screened back porch. When we were kids, Constantine used to sleep out here with Carlton and me in the summer, when Mama and Daddy went to out-of-town weddings. Constantine slept in an old-fashioned white nightgown up to her chin and down to her toes even though it'd be hot as Hades. She used to sing to us so we'd go to sleep. Her voice was so beautiful I couldn't understand how she'd never had lessons. Mother had always told me a person can't learn anything without proper lessons. It's just unreal to me that she was here, right here on this porch, and now she's not. And no one will tell me a thing. I wonder if I'll ever see her again.

Next to my cot, now, my typewriter sits on a rusted, white enamel washtable. Underneath is my red satchel. I take Daddy's hankie and wipe my forehead, press salted ice to my wrists. Even on the back porch, the Avery Lumber Company temperature dial rises from 89 to 96 to a nice round 100 degrees. Luckily, Stuart doesn't come over during the day, when the heat is at its worst.

I stare at my typewriter with nothing to do, nothing to write. Minny's stories are finished and typed already. It's a wretched feeling. Two weeks ago, Aibileen told me that Yule May, Hilly's maid, might help us, that she shows a little more interest every time Aibileen talks to her. But with Medgar Evers's murder and colored people getting arrested and beat by the police, I'm sure she's scared to death by now.

Maybe I ought to go over to Hilly's and ask Yule May myself. But no, Aibileen's right, I'd probably scare her even more and ruin any chance we have.

Under the house, the dogs yawn, whine in the heat. One lets out a half-hearted woof as Daddy's field workers, five Negroes, pull up in a truckbed. The men jump from the tailgate, hoofing up dust when they hit the dirt. They stand a moment, dead-faced, stupefied. The foreman drags a red cloth across his black forehead, his lips, his neck. It is so recklessly hot, I don't know how they can stand baking out there in the sun.

In a rare breeze, my copy of *Life* magazine flutters. Audrey Hepburn smiles on the cover, no sweat beading on her upper lip. I pick it up and finger the wrinkled pages, flip to the story on the Soviet Space Girl. I already know what's on the next page. Behind her face is a picture of Carl Roberts, a colored schoolteacher from Pelahatchie, forty miles from here. "In April, Carl Roberts told Washington reporters what it means to be a black man in Mississippi, calling the governor 'a pathetic man with the morals of a street-walker.' Roberts was found cattle-branded and hung from a pecan tree."

They'd killed Carl Roberts for speaking out, for *talking*. I think about how easy I thought it would be, three months ago, to get a dozen maids to talk to me. Like they'd just been waiting, all this time, to spill their stories to a white woman. How stupid I'd been.

When I can't take the heat another second, I go sit in the only cool place on Longleaf. I turn on the ignition and roll up the windows, pull my dress up around my underwear and let the bi-level blow on me full blast. As I lean my head back, the world drifts away, tinged by the smell of Freon and

Cadillac leather. I hear a truck pull up into the front drive but I don't open my eyes. A second later, my passenger door opens.

"Damn it feels good in here."

I push my dress down. "What are you doing here?"

Stuart shuts the door, kisses me quickly on the lips. "I only have a minute. I have to head down to the coast for a meeting."

"For how long?"

"Three days. I've got to catch some fella on the Mississippi Oil and Gas Board. I wish I'd known about it sooner."

He reaches out and takes my hand and I smile. We've been going out twice a week for two months now if you don't count the horror date. I guess that's considered a short time to other girls. But it's the longest thing that's ever happened to me, and right now it feels like the best.

"Wanna come?" he says.

"To Biloxi? Right now?"

"Right now," he says and puts his cool palm on my leg. As always, I jump a little. I look down at his hand, then up to make sure Mother's not spying on us.

"Come on, it's too damn hot here. I'm staying at the Edgewater, right on the beach."

I laugh and it feels good after all the worrying I've done these past weeks. "You mean, at the Edgewater . . . together? In the same room?"

He nods. "Think you can get away?"

Elizabeth would be mortified by the thought of sharing a room with a man before she was married, Hilly would tell me I was stupid to even consider it. They'd held on to their virginity with the fierceness of children refusing to share their toys. And yet, I consider it.

Stuart moves closer to me. He smells like pine trees and fired tobacco, expensive soap the likes of which my family's never known. "Mama'd have a fit, Stuart, plus I have all this other stuff to do . . ." But God, he smells good. He's looking at me like he wants to eat me up and I shiver under the blast of Cadillac air.

"You sure?" he whispers and he kisses me then, on the mouth, not so politely as before. His hand is still on the upper quarter of my thigh and I find myself wondering again if he was like this with his fiancée, Patricia. I don't even know if they went to bed together. The thought of them touching makes me feel sick and I pull back from him.

"I just...I can't," I say. "You know I couldn't tell Mama the truth..."

He lets out a long sorry sigh and I love that look on his face, that disappointment. I understand now why girls resist, just for that sweet look of regret. "Don't lie to her," he says. "You know I hate lies."

"Will you call me from the hotel?" I ask.

"I will," he says. "I'm sorry I have to leave so soon. Oh, and I almost forgot, in three weeks, Saturday night. Mother and Daddy want y'all to come have supper."

I sit up straighter. I've never met his parents before. "What do you mean...y'all?"

"You and your parents. Come into town, meet my family."

"But...why all of us?"

He shrugs. "My parents want to meet them. And I want them to meet you."

"But..."

"I'm sorry, baby," he says and pushes my hair behind my ear, "I have to go. Call you tomorrow night?"

I nod. He climbs out into the heat and drives off, waving to Daddy walking up the dusty lane.

I'm left alone in the Cadillac to worry. Supper at the state senator's house. With Mother there asking a thousand questions. Looking desperate on my behalf. Bringing up cotton trust funds.

THREE EXCRUCIATINGLY LONG, hot nights later, with still no word from Yule May or any other maids, Stuart comes over, straight from his meeting on the coast. I'm sick of sitting at the typewriter typing nothing but newsletters and Miss Myrna. I run down the steps and he hugs me like it's been weeks.

Stuart's sunburned beneath his white shirt, the back wrinkled from driving, the sleeves rolled up. He wears a perpetual, almost devilish smile. We both sit straight up on opposite sides of the relaxing room, staring at each other. We're waiting for Mother to go to bed. Daddy went to sleep when the sun went down.

Stuart's eyes hang on mine while Mother waxes on about the heat, how Carlton's finally met "the one."

"And we're thrilled about dining with your parents, Stuart. Please do tell your mother I said so."

"Yes ma'am. I sure will."

He smiles over at me again. There are so many things I love about him. He looks me straight in the eye when we talk. His palms are callused but his nails are clean and trimmed. I love the rough feeling on my neck. And I'd be lying if I didn't admit that it's nice to have someone to go to weddings and parties with. Not to have to endure the look in Raleigh Leefolt's eyes when he sees that I'm tagging along again. The sullen daze when he has to carry my coat with Elizabeth's, fetch me a drink too.

Then there is Stuart at the house. From the minute he walks in, I am protected, exempt. Mother won't criticize me in front of him, for fear he might notice my flaws himself. She won't nag me in front of him because she knows that I'd act badly, whine. Short my chances. It's all a big game to Mother, to show only one side of me, that the real me shouldn't come out until after it's "too late."

Finally, at half past nine, Mother smoothes her skirt, folds a blanket slowly and perfectly, like a cherished letter. "Well, I guess it's time for bed. I'll let you young people alone. Eugenia?" She eyes me. "Not too late, now?"

I smile sweetly. I am twenty-three goddamn years old. "Of course not, Mama."

She leaves and we sit, staring, smiling.

Waiting.

Mother pads around the kitchen, closes a window, runs some water. A few seconds pass and we hear the clack-click of her bedroom door shutting. Stuart stands and says, "Come *here*," and he's on my side of the room in one stride and he claps my hands to his hips and kisses my mouth like I am the drink he's been dying for all day and I've heard girls say it's like melting, that feeling. But I think it's like rising, growing even taller and seeing sights over a hedge, colors you've never seen before.

I have to make myself pull away. I have things to say. "Come here. Sit down."

We sit side by side on the sofa. He tries to kiss me again, but I back my head away. I try not to look at the way his sunburn makes his eyes so blue. Or the way the hairs on his arms are golden, bleached.

"Stuart—" I swallow, ready myself for the dreaded question. "When you were engaged, were your parents disappointed? When whatever happened with Patricia...happened?"

Immediately a stiffness forms around his mouth. He eyes me. "Mother was disappointed. They were close."

Already I regret having brought it up, but I have to know. "How close?"

He glances around the room. "Do you have anything in the house? Bourbon?"

I go to the kitchen and pour him a glass from Pascagoula's cooking bottle, top it off with plenty of water. Stuart made it clear the first time he showed up on my porch his fiancée was a bad subject. But I need to know what this thing was that happened. Not just because I'm curious. I've never been in a relationship. I need to know what constitutes breaking up forever. I need to know how many rules you can break before you're thrown out, and what those rules even are in the first place.

"So they were good friends?" I ask. I'll be meeting his mother in two weeks. Mother's already set on our shopping trip to Kennington's tomorrow.

He takes a long drink, frowns. "They'd get in a room and swap notes on flower arrangements and who married who." All traces of his mischievous smile are gone now. "Mother was pretty shook up. After it...fell apart."

"So...she'll be comparing me to Patricia?"

Stuart blinks at me a second. "Probably."

"Great. I can hardly wait."

"Mother's just...protective is all. She's worried I'll get hurt again." He looks off.

"Where is Patricia now? Does she still live here or—"

"No. She's gone. Moved to California. Can we talk about something else now?"

I sigh, fall back against the sofa.

"Well, do your parents at least know what happened? I mean, am I allowed to know that?" Because I feel a flash of anger that he won't tell me something as important as this.

"Skeeter, I told you, I hate talking..." But then he grits his teeth, lowers his voice. "Dad only knows part of it. Mother knows the real story, so do Patricia's parents. And of course *her*." He throws back the rest of the drink. "She knows what she did, that's for goddamn sure."

"Stuart, I only want to know so I don't do the same thing."

He looks at me and tries to laugh but it comes out more like a growl. "You would never in a million years do what she did."

"What? What did she do?"

"Skeeter." He sighs and sets his glass down. "I'm tired. I better just go on home."

I WALK IN THE STEAMY kitchen the next morning, dreading the day ahead. Mother is in her room getting ready for our shopping trip to outfit us both for supper at the Whitworths'. I have on blue jeans and an untucked blouse.

"Morning, Pascagoula."

"Morning, Miss Skeeter. You want your regular breakfast?"

"Yes, please," I say.

Pascagoula is small and quick on her feet. I told her last June how I liked my coffee black and toast barely buttered and she never had to ask again. She's like Constantine that way, never forgetting things for us. It makes me wonder how many white women's breakfasts she has ingrained in her brain. I wonder how it would feel to spend your whole life trying to remember other people's preferences on toast butter and starch amounts and sheet changing.

She sets my coffee down in front of me. She doesn't hand it to me. Aibileen told me that's not how it's done, because then your hands might touch. I don't remember how Constantine used to do it.

"Thank you," I say, "very much."

She blinks at me a second, smiles weakly. "You…welcome." I realize this the first time I've ever thanked her sincerely. She looks uncomfortable.

"Skeeter, you ready?" I hear Mother call from the back. I holler that I am. I eat my toast and hope we can get this shopping trip over quickly. I am ten years too old to have my mother still picking out clothes for me. I look over and notice Pascagoula watching me from the sink. She turns away when I look at her.

I skim the *Jackson Journal* sitting on the table. My next Miss Myrna column won't come out until next Monday, unlocking the mystery of hard-water stains. Down in the national news section, there's an article on a new pill, the "Valium" they're calling it, "to help women cope with everyday challenges." God, I could use about ten of those little pills right now.

I look up and am surprised to see Pascagoula standing right next to me.

"Are you…do you need something, Pascagoula?" I ask.

"I need to tell you something, Miss Skeeter. Something bout that—"

"You cannot wear dungarees to Kennington's," Mother says from the doorway. Like vapor, Pascagoula disappears from my side. She's back at the sink, stretching a black rubber hose from the faucet to the dishwasher.

"You go upstairs and put on something appropriate."

"Mother, this is what I'm wearing. What's the point of getting dressed up to buy new clothes?"

"Eugenia, please let's don't make this any harder than it is."

Mother goes back to her bedroom, but I know this isn't the end of it. The *whoosh* of the dishwasher fills the room. The floor vibrates under my bare feet and the rumble is soothing, loud enough to cover a conversation. I watch Pascagoula at the sink.

"Did you need to tell me something, Pascagoula?" I ask.

Pascagoula glances at the door. She's just a slip of a person, practically half of me. Her manner is so timid, I lower my head when I talk to her. She comes a little closer.

"Yule May my *cousin*," Pascagoula says over the whir of the machine. She's whispering, but there's nothing timid about her tone now.

"I...didn't know that."

"We close kin and she come out to my house ever other weekend to check on me. She told me what it is you doing." She narrows her eyes and I think she's about to tell me to leave her cousin alone.

"I...we're changing the names. She told you that, right? I don't want to get anybody in trouble."

"She tell me Saturday she gone help you. She try to call Aibileen but couldn't get her. I'd a tole you earlier but..." Again she glances at the doorway.

I'm stunned. "She is? She *will*?" I stand up. Despite my better thinking, I can't help but ask. "Pascagoula, do you...want to help with the stories too?"

She gives me a long, steady look. "You mean tell you what it's like to work for...your mama?"

We look at each other, probably thinking the same thing. The discomfort of her telling, the discomfort of me listening.

"Not Mother," I say quickly. "Other jobs, ones you've had before this."

"This my first job working domestic. I use to work at the Old Lady Home serving lunch. Fore it move out to Flowood."

"You mean Mother didn't mind this being your first house job?"

Pascagoula looks at the red linoleum floor, timid again. "Nobody else a work for her," she says. "Not after what happen with Constantine."

I place my hand carefully on the table. "What did you think about... that?"

Pascagoula's face turns blank. She blinks a few times, clearly outsmarting me. "I don't know nothing about it. I just wanted to tell you what Yule May say." She goes to the refrigerator, opens it and leans inside.

I let out a long, deep breath. One thing at a time.

SHOPPING WITH MOTHER isn't as unbearable as usual, probably because I'm in such a good mood from hearing about Yule May. Mother sits in a chair in the dressing lounge and I choose the first Lady Day suit I try

on, light blue poplin with a round-collar jacket. We leave it at the store so
they can take down the hem. I'm surprised when Mother doesn't try on
anything. After only half an hour, she says she's tired, so I drive us back to
Longleaf. Mother goes straight to her room to nap.

When we get home, I call Elizabeth's house, my heart pounding, but
Elizabeth picks up the phone. I don't have the nerve to ask for Aibileen.
After the satchel scare, I promised myself I'd be more careful.

So I wait until that night, hoping Aibileen's home. I sit on my can of
flour, fingers working a bag of dry rice. She answers on the first ring.

"She'll help us, Aibileen. Yule May said yes!"

"Say what? When you find out?"

"This afternoon. Pascagoula told me. Yule May couldn't reach you."

"Law, my phone was disconnected cause I's short this month. You talk
to Yule May?"

"No, I thought it would be better if you talked to her first."

"What's strange is I call over to Miss Hilly house this afternoon from
Miss Leefolt's, but she say Yule May don't work there no more and hang up.
I been asking around but nobody know a thing."

"Hilly fired her?"

"I don't know. I's hoping maybe she quit."

"I'll call Hilly and find out. God, I hope she's alright."

"And now that my phone's back on, I keep trying to call Yule May."

I call Hilly's house four times but the phone just rings. Finally I call
Elizabeth's and she tells me Hilly's gone to Port Gibson for the night. That
William's father is ill.

"Did something happen...with her maid?" I ask as casually as I can.

"You know, she mentioned something about Yule May, but then she said
she was late and had to pack up the car."

I spend the rest of the night on the back porch, rehearsing questions,
nervous about what stories Yule May might tell about Hilly. Despite our
disagreements, Hilly is still one of my closest friends. But the book, now
that it is going again, is more important than anything.

I lay on the cot at midnight. The crickets sing outside the screen. I let my
body sink deep into the thin mattress, against the springs. My feet dangle

off the end, dance nervously, relishing relief for the first time in months. It's not a dozen maids, but it's one more.

THE NEXT DAY, I'm sitting in front of the television set watching the twelve o'clock news. Charles Warring is reporting, telling me that sixty American soldiers have been killed in Vietnam. It's so sad to me. Sixty men, in a place far away from anyone they loved, had to die. I think it's because of Stuart that this bothers me so, but Charles Warring looks eerily thrilled by it all.

I pick up a cigarette and put it back down. I'm trying not to smoke, but I'm nervous about tonight. Mother's been nagging me about my smoking and I know I should stop, but it's not like it's going to kill me. I wish I could ask Pascagoula more about what Yule May said, but Pascagoula called this morning and said she had a problem and wouldn't be coming in until this afternoon.

I can hear Mother out on the back porch, helping Jameso make ice cream. Even in the front of the house, I can hear the rumbly noise of ice cracking, the salt crunching. The sound is delicious, makes me wish for some now, but it won't be ready for hours. Of course, no one makes ice cream at twelve noon on a hot day, it's a night chore, but Mother has it in her mind that she's going to make peach ice cream and the heat be damned.

I go out on the back porch and look. The big silver ice-cream maker is cold and sweating. The porch floor vibrates. Jameso's sitting on an upside-down bucket, knees on either side of the machine, turning the wooden crank with gloved hands. Steam rises from the well of dry ice.

"Has Pascagoula come in yet?" Mama asks, feeding more cream into the machine.

"Not yet," I say. Mother is sweating. She pushes a loose strand of hair behind her ear. "I'll pour the cream awhile, Mama. You look hot."

"You won't do it right. I have to do it," she says and shoos me back inside.

On the news, now Roger Sticker is reporting in front of the Jackson post office with the same stupid grin as the war reporter. "...this modern postal addressing system is called a Z-Z-ZIP code, that's right, I said

Z-Z-ZIP code, that's five numbers to be written along the bottom of your envelope..."

He's holding up a letter, showing us where to write the numbers. A man in overalls with no teeth says, "Ain't nobody gonna use them there numbers. Folks is still trying to get used to using the tellyphone."

I hear the front door close. A minute passes and Pascagoula comes in the relaxing room.

"Mother's out on the back porch," I tell her but Pascagoula doesn't smile, doesn't even look up at me. She just hands me a small envelope.

"She was gone mail it but I told her I just carry it to you."

The front of the envelope is addressed to me, no return name on it. Certainly no ZIP code. Pascagoula walks off toward the back porch.

I open the letter. The handwriting is in black pen, written on the straight blue lines of school paper:

> Dear Miss Skeeter,
>
> I want you to know how sorry I am that I won't be able to help you with your stories. But now I can't and I want to be the one to tell you why. As you know, I used to wait on a friend of yours. I didn't like working for her and I wanted to quit many times but I was afraid to. I was afraid I might never get another job once she'd had her say.
>
> You probably don't know that after I finished high school, I went on to college. I would've graduated except I decided to get married. It's one of my few regrets in life, not getting my college degree. I have twin boys that make it all worthwhile, though. For ten years, my husband and I have saved our money to send them to Tougaloo College, but as hard as we worked, we still didn't have enough for both. My boys are equally as smart, equally eager for an education. But we only had the money for one and I ask you, how do you choose which of your twin sons should go to college and which should take a job spreading tar? How do you tell one that you love him just as much as the other, but you've decided he won't be the one to get a chance in life? You don't. You find a way to make it happen. Any way at all.
>
> I suppose you could look at this as a confession letter. I stole from that

*woman. An ugly ruby ring, hoping it would cover the rest of the tuition.
Something she never wore and I felt she owed me for everything I'd been
through working for her. Of course now, neither of my boys will be going to
college. The court fine is nearly as much as we had saved.*

   Sincerely,
   Yule May Crookle
   Women's Block 9
   Mississippi State Penitentiary

The *penitentiary.* I shudder. I look around for Pascagoula but she's left the
room. I want to ask her when this happened, how it happened so goddamn
fast? What can be done? But Pascagoula's gone outside to help Mother. We
can't talk out there. I feel sick, nauseous. I switch off the television.

I think about Yule May, sitting in a jail cell writing this letter. I bet I
even know what ring Yule May's talking about—Hilly's mother gave it to
her for her eighteenth birthday. Hilly had it appraised a few years ago and
found out it wasn't even a ruby, just a garnet, hardly worth anything. Hilly
never wore it again. My hands turn to fists.

The sound of the ice cream churning outside sounds like bones crunching. I go to the kitchen to wait for Pascagoula, to get answers. I'll tell Daddy.
I'll see if there's anything he can do. If he knows any lawyers who would be
willing to help her.

I WALK UP AIBILEEN'S STEPS at eight o'clock that night. This was supposed
to be our first interview with Yule May and even though I know that's not
going to happen, I've decided to come anyway. It's raining and blowing hard
and I hold my raincoat tight around me and the satchel. I kept thinking I'd
call Aibileen to talk about the situation, but I couldn't bring myself to do it.
Instead, I practically dragged Pascagoula upstairs so Mother wouldn't see
us talking and asked her everything. "Yule May had her a real good lawyer,"
Pascagoula said. "But everybody saying the judge wife be good friends with
Miss Holbrook and how a regular sentence be six months for petty stealing,

but Miss Holbrook, she get it pushed up to four years. That trial was done fore it even started."

"I could ask Daddy. He could try and get her a...white lawyer."

Pascagoula shakes her head, says, "He *was* a white lawyer."

I knock on Aibileen's door, feel a rush of shame. I shouldn't be thinking about my own problems when Yule May is in jail, but I know what this means for the book. If the maids were afraid to help us yesterday, I'm sure they're terrified today.

The door opens and a Negro man stands there looking at me, his white clerical collar gleaming. I hear Aibileen say, "It's okay, Reverend." He hesitates, but then moves back for me to come in.

I step inside and see at least twenty people packed in the tiny living room and hallway. I cannot see the floor. Aibileen's brought out the kitchen chairs, but most people stand. I spot Minny in the corner, still in her uniform. I recognize Lou Anne Templeton's maid, Louvenia, next to her, but everyone else is a stranger.

"Hey Miss Skeeter," whispers Aibileen. She's still in her white uniform and white orthopedic shoes.

"Should I..." I point behind me. "I'll come back later," I whisper.

Aibileen shakes her head. "Something awful happen to Yule May."

"I know," I say. The room is quiet except for a few coughs. A chair creaks. Hymn books are stacked on the small wooden table.

"I just find out today," Aibileen says. "She arrested on Monday, in the pen on Tuesday. They say the whole trial took fifteen minutes."

"She sent me a letter," I say. "She told me about her sons. Pascagoula gave it to me."

"She tell you she only short seventy-five dollars for that tuition? She ask Miss Hilly for a loan, you know. Say she'd pay her back some ever week, but Miss Hilly say no. That a true Christian don't give charity to those who is well and able. Say it's kinder to let them learn to work things out theyselves."

God, I can just imagine Hilly giving that goddamn speech. I can hardly look Aibileen in the face.

"The churches got together though. They gone send both them boys to college."

The room is dead quiet, except for Aibileen and my whispering. "Do you think there's anything I can do? Any way I can help? Money or..."

"No. Church already set up a plan to pay the lawyer. To keep him on for when she come up for parole." Aibileen lets her head hang. I'm sure it's out of grief for Yule May, but I suspect she also knows the book is over. "They gone be seniors by the time she get out. Court give her four years and a five hundred dollar fine."

"I'm so sorry, Aibileen," I say. I glance around at the people in the room, their heads bowed as if looking at me might burn them. I look down.

"She evil, that woman!" Minny barks from the other side of the sofa and I flinch, hoping she doesn't mean me.

"Hilly Holbrook been sent up here from the devil to ruirn as many lives as she can!" Minny wipes her nose across her sleeve.

"Minny, it's alright," the reverend says. "We'll find something we can do for her." I look at the drawn faces, wondering what that thing could possibly be.

The room goes unbearably quiet again. The air is hot and smells like burned coffee. I feel a profound singularity, here, in a place where I've almost grown comfortable. I feel the heat of dislike and guilt.

The bald reverend wipes his eyes with a handkerchief. "Thank you, Aibileen, for having us in your home for prayer." People begin to stir, telling each other good night with solemn nods. Handbags are picked up, hats are put on heads. The reverend opens the door, letting in the damp outside air. A woman with curly gray hair and a black coat follows close behind him, but then stops in front of me where I'm standing with my satchel.

Her raincoat falls open a little to reveal a white uniform.

"Miss Skeeter," she says, without a smile, "I'm on help you with the stories."

I turn and look at Aibileen. Her eyebrows go up, her mouth opens. I turn back to the woman but she is already walking out the door.

"I'm on help you, Miss Skeeter." This is another woman, tall and lean, with the same quiet look as the first.

"Um, thank...you," I say.

"I am too, Miss Skeeter. I'm on help you." A woman in a red coat walks by quickly, doesn't even meet my eyes.

After the next one, I start counting. Five. Six. Seven. I nod back at them, can say nothing but thank you. Thank you. Yes, thank you, to each one. My relief is bitter, that it took Yule May's internment to bring us to this.

Eight. Nine. Ten. Eleven. No one is smiling when they tell me they want to help. The room clears out, except for Minny. She stands in the far corner, arms clamped across her chest. When everyone is gone, she looks up and meets my gaze for hardly a second then jerks her eyes to the brown curtains, pinned tight across the window. But I see it, the flicker on her mouth, a hint of softness beneath her anger. Minny has made this happen.

WITH EVERYONE TRAVELING, our group hasn't played bridge in a month. On Wednesday, we meet at Lou Anne Templeton's house, greet with hand-patting and good-to-see-yous.

"Lou Anne, you poor thing, in those long sleeves in this heat. Is it the eczema again?" Elizabeth asks because Lou Anne's wearing a gray wool dress in the heat of summer.

Lou Anne looks at her lap, clearly embarrassed. "Yes, it's getting worse."

But I cannot stand to touch Hilly when she reaches out to me. When I back away from her hug, she acts like she doesn't notice. But during the game, she keeps looking at me with narrowed eyes.

"What are you going to do?" Elizabeth asks Hilly. "You're welcome to bring the children over any time, but...well..." Before bridge club, Hilly dropped Heather and William at Elizabeth's for Aibileen to look after while we play bridge. But I already know the message in Elizabeth's sour smile: she worships Hilly, but Elizabeth does not care to share her help with anybody.

"I knew it. I knew that girl was a thief the day she started." As Hilly tells us the story of Yule May, she makes a big circle with her finger to indicate a huge stone, the unimaginable worth of the "ruby."

"I caught her taking the milk after it expired and that's how it starts, you know, first it's washing powder, then they work their way up to towels and coats. Before you know it, they're taking the heirlooms, hocking them for liquor pints. God knows what else she took."

I fight the urge to snap each of her flapping fingers in half, but I hold my tongue. Let her think everything is fine. It is safer for everyone.

After the game, I rush home to prepare for Aibileen's that night, relieved there's not a soul in the house. I quickly flip through Pascagoula's messages for me—Patsy my tennis partner, Celia Foote, whom I hardly know. Why would Johnny Foote's wife be calling me? Minny's made me swear I'll never call her back, and I don't have the time to wonder. I have to get ready for the interviews.

I SIT AT AIBILEEN'S KITCHEN table at six o'clock that night. We've arranged for me to come over nearly every night until we're finished. Every two days, a different colored woman will knock on Aibileen's back door and sit at the table with me, tell me her stories. Eleven maids have agreed to talk to us, not counting Aibileen and Minny. That puts us at thirteen and Missus Stein asked for a dozen, so I think we're lucky. Aibileen stands in the back of the kitchen, listening. The first maid's name is Alice. I don't ask for last names.

I explain to Alice that the project is a collection of true stories about maids and their experiences waiting on white families. I hand her an envelope with forty dollars from what I've saved from the Miss Myrna column, my allowance, money Mother has forced into my hands for beauty parlor appointments I never went to.

"There's a good chance it may never be published," I tell each individually, "and even if it is, there will be very little money from it." I look down the first time I say this, ashamed, I don't know why. Being white, I feel it's my duty to help them.

"Aibileen been clear on that," several say. "That ain't why I'm doing this."

I repeat back to them what they've already decided among themselves. That they need to keep their identities secret from anyone outside the group. Their names will be changed on paper; so will the name of the town and the families they've worked for. I wish I could slip in, as the last question, "By the way, did you know Constantine Bates?" but I'm pretty sure Aibileen would tell me it's a bad idea. They're scared enough as it is.

"Now, Eula, she gone be like prying a dead clam open." Aibileen preps me before each interview. She's as afraid as I am that I'll scare them off before it even starts. "Don't get frustrated if she don't say much."

Eula, the dead clam, starts talking before she's even sat in the chair, before I can explain anything, not stopping until ten o'clock that night.

"When I asked for a raise they gave it to me. When I needed a house, they bought me one. Doctor Tucker came over to my house himself and picked a bullet out my husband's arm because he was afraid Henry'd catch something at the colored hospital. I have worked for Doctor Tucker and Miss Sissy for forty-four years. They been so good to me. I wash her hair ever Friday. I never seen that woman wash her own hair." She stops for the first time all night, looks lonesome and worried. "If I die before her, I don't know what Miss Sissy gone do about getting her hair washed."

I try not to smile too eagerly. I don't want to look suspicious. Alice, Fanny Amos, and Winnie are shy, need coaxing, keep their eyes down to their laps. Flora Lou and Cleontine let the doors fly open and the words tumble out while I type as fast as I can, asking them every five minutes to please, please, slow down. Many of the stories are sad, bitter. I expected this. But there are a surprising number of good stories too. And all of them, at some point, look back at Aibileen as if to ask, *Are you sure? Can I really tell a white woman this?*

"Aibileen? What's gone happen if…this thing get printed and people find out who we are?" shy Winnie asks. "What you think they do to us?"

Our eyes form a triangle in the kitchen, one looking at the other. I take a deep breath, ready to assure her of how careful we're being.

"My husband cousin…they took her tongue out. A while back it was. For talking to some Washington people about the Klan. You think they gone take our tongues? For talking to you?"

I don't know what to say. *Tongues*…God, this hadn't exactly crossed my mind. Only jail and perhaps fake charges or fines. "I…we're being extremely careful," I say but it comes out thin and unconvincing. I look at Aibileen, but she is looking worried too.

"We won't know till the time comes, Winnie," Aibileen says softly. "Won't be like what you see on the news, though. A white lady do things different than a white man."

I look at Aibileen. She's never shared with me the specifics of what she thinks would happen. I want to change the subject. It won't do us any good to discuss it.

"Naw." Winnie shakes her head. "I reckon not. Fact, a white lady might do worse."

"WHERE ARE YOU GOING?" Mother calls from the relaxing room. I have my satchel and the truck keys. I keep heading for the door.

"To the movies," I call.

"You went to the movies last night. Come here, Eugenia."

I backtrack, stand in the doorway. Mother's ulcers have been acting up. At supper she's been eating nothing but chicken broth, and I feel bad for her. Daddy went to bed an hour ago, but I can't stay here with her. "I'm sorry, Mother, I'm late. Do you want me to bring you anything?"

"What movie and with whom? You've been out almost every night this week."

"Just...some girls. I'll be home by ten. Are you alright?"

"I'm fine," she sighs. "Go on, then."

I head to the car, feeling guilty because I'm leaving Mother alone when she's not feeling well. Thank God Stuart's in Texas because I doubt I could lie to him so easily. When he came over three nights ago, we sat out on the porch swing listening to the crickets. I was so tired from working late the night before, I could barely keep my eyes open, but I didn't want him to leave. I lay with my head in his lap. I reached up and rubbed my hand against the bristles on his face.

"When're you going to let me read something you've written?" he asked.

"You can read the Miss Myrna column. I did a great piece on mildew last week."

He smiled, shook his head. "No, I mean I want to read what you're *thinking*. I'm pretty sure it's not about housekeeping."

I wondered then, if he knew I was hiding something from him. It scared me that he might find out about the stories, and thrilled me that he was even interested.

"When you're ready. I won't push you," he said.

"Maybe sometime I'll let you," I said, feeling my eyes close.

"Go to sleep, baby," he said, stroking my hair back from my face. "Let me just sit here with you for a while."

With Stuart out of town for the next six days, I can concentrate solely on the interviews. I head to Aibileen's every night as nervous as the first time. The women are tall, short, black like asphalt or caramel brown. If your skin is too white, I'm told, you'll never get hired. The blacker the better. The talk turns mundane at times, with complaints of low pay, hard hours, bratty children. But then there are stories of white babies dying in arms. That soft, empty look in their still blue eyes.

"Olivia she was called. Just a tiny baby, with her tiny hand holding on to my finger, breathing so hard," Fanny Amos says, our fourth interview. "Her mama wasn't even home, gone to the store for mentholatum. It was just me and the daddy. He wouldn't let me put her down, told me to hold her till the doctor get there. Baby grew cold in my arms."

There is undisguised hate for white women, there is inexplicable love. Faye Belle, palsied and gray-skinned, cannot remember her own age. Her stories unfold like soft linen. She remembers hiding in a steamer trunk with a little white girl while Yankee soldiers stomped through the house. Twenty years ago, she held that same white girl, by then an old woman, in her arms while she died. Each proclaimed their love as best friends. Swore that death could not change this. That color meant nothing. The white woman's grandson still pays Faye Belle's rent. When she's feeling strong, Faye Belle sometimes goes over and cleans up his kitchen.

Louvenia is my fifth interview. She is Lou Anne Templeton's maid and I recognize her from serving me at bridge club. Louvenia tells me how her grandson, Robert, was blinded earlier this year by a white man, because he used a white bathroom. I recall reading about it in the paper as Louvenia nods, waits for me to catch up on my typewriter. There is no anger in her voice at all. I learn that Lou Anne, whom I find dull and vapid and have never paid much mind to, gave Louvenia two weeks off with pay so she could help her grandson. She brought casseroles to Louvenia's house seven times during those weeks. She rushed Louvenia to the colored hospital when the first call came about Robert and waited there six hours with her, until the operation was over. Lou Anne has never mentioned this to any of us. And I understand completely why she wouldn't.

Angry stories come out, of white men who've tried to touch them. Winnie said she was forced over and over. Cleontine said she fought until his face bled and he never tried again. But the dichotomy of love and disdain living side-by-side is what surprises me. Most are invited to attend the white children's weddings, but only if they're in their uniforms. These things I know already, yet hearing them from colored mouths, it is as if I am hearing them for the first time.

WE CANNOT TALK for several minutes after Gretchen's left.

"Let's just move on," Aibileen says. "We don't got to...count that one."

Gretchen is Yule May's first cousin. She attended the prayer meeting for Yule May that Aibileen hosted weeks ago, but she belongs to a different church.

"I don't understand why she agreed if..." I want to go home. The tendons in my neck have locked tight. My fingers are trembling from typing and from listening to Gretchen's words.

"I'm sorry, I had no idea she gone do that."

"It's not your fault," I say. I want to ask her how much of what Gretchen said is true. But I can't. I can't look Aibileen in the face.

I'd explained the "rules" to Gretchen, just like with the others. Gretchen had leaned back in her chair. I thought she was thinking about a story to tell. But she said, "Look at you. Another white lady trying to make a dollar off of colored people."

I glanced back at Aibileen, not sure how to respond to this. Was I not clear on the money part? Aibileen tilted her head like she wasn't sure she'd heard correctly.

"You think anybody's ever going to read this thing?" Gretchen laughed. She was trim in her uniform dress. She wore lipstick, the same color pink me and my friends wore. She was young. She spoke evenly and with care, like a white person. I don't know why, but that made it worse.

"All the colored women you've interviewed, they've been real nice, haven't they?"

"Yes," I'd said. "Very nice."

Gretchen looked me straight in the eye. "They hate you. You know that, right? Every little thing about you. But you're so dumb, you think you're doing them a favor."

"You don't have to do this," I said. "You volunteered—"

"You know the nicest thing a white woman's ever done for me? Given me the heel on her bread. The colored women coming in here, they're just playing a big trick on you. They'll never tell you the truth, lady."

"You don't have any idea what the other women have told me," I said. I was surprised by how dense my anger felt, and how easily it sprang up.

"Say it, lady, say the word you think every time one of us comes in the door. *Nigger.*"

Aibileen stood up from her stool. "That's enough, Gretchen. You go on home."

"And you know what, Aibileen? You are just as dumb as she is," Gretchen said.

I was shocked when Aibileen pointed to the door and hissed, "*You get out a my house.*"

Gretchen left, but through the screen door, she slapped me with a look so angry it gave me chills.

Two nights later, I sit across from Callie. She has curly hair, mostly gray. She is sixty-seven years old and still in her uniform. She is wide and heavy and parts of her hang over the chair. I'm still nervous from the interview with Gretchen.

I wait for Callie to stir her tea. There's a grocery sack in the corner of Aibileen's kitchen. It's full of clothes, and a pair of white pants hangs over the top. Aibileen's house is always so neat. I don't know why she never does anything with that sack.

Callie begins talking slowly and I start to type, grateful of her slow pace. She stares off as if she can see a movie screen behind me, playing the scenes she's describing.

"I worked for Miss Margaret thirty-eight years. She had her a baby girl with the colic and the only thing that stopped the hurting was to hold her. So I made me a wrap. I tied her up on my waist, toted her around all day with me for a entire year. That baby like to break my back. Put ice packs on it ever night and still do. But I loved that girl. And I loved Miss Margaret."

She takes a sip of her tea while I type her last words. I look up and she continues.

"Miss Margaret always made me put my hair up in a rag, say she know coloreds don't wash their hair. Counted ever piece a silver after I done the polishing. When Miss Margaret die of the lady problems thirty years later, I go to the funeral. Her husband hug me, cry on my shoulder. When it's over, he give me a envelope. Inside a letter from Miss Margaret reading, 'Thank you. For making my baby stop hurting. I never forgot it.'"

Callie takes off her black-rimmed glasses, wipes her eyes.

"If any white lady reads my story, that's what I want them to know. Saying thank you, when you really mean it, when you remember what someone done for you"—she shakes her head, stares down at the scratched table—"it's so good."

Callie looks up at me, but I can't meet her eyes.

"I just need a minute," I say. I press my hand on my forehead. I can't help but think about Constantine. I never thanked her, not properly. It never occurred to me I wouldn't have the chance.

"You feel okay, Miss Skeeter?" Aibileen asks.

"I'm ... fine," I say. "Let's keep going."

Callie goes on to her next story. The yellow Dr. Scholl's shoebox is on the counter behind her, still full of envelopes. Except for Gretchen, all ten women have asked that the money go toward Yule May's boys' education.

CHAPTER 20

THE PHELAN FAMILY stands tense, waiting on the brick steps of State Senator Whitworth's house. The house is in the center of town, on North Street. It is tall and white-columned, appropriately azalea-ed. A gold plaque declares it a historical landmark. Gas lanterns flicker despite the hot six o'clock sun.

"Mother," I whisper because I cannot repeat it enough times. "Please, please don't forget the thing we talked about."

"I said I wouldn't mention it, darling." She touches the pins holding up her hair. "Unless it's appropriate."

I have on the new light blue Lady Day skirt and matching jacket. Daddy has on his black funeral suit. His belt is cinched too tight to be comfortable much less fashionable. Mother is wearing a simple white dress—like a country bride wearing a hand-me-down, I suddenly think, and I feel a rush of panic that we have overdressed, all of us. Mother's going to bring up the ugly girl's trust fund and we look like countryfolk on a big damn visit to town.

"Daddy, loosen your belt, it's hitching your pants up."

He frowns at me and looks down at his pants. Never once have I told my daddy what to do. The door opens.

"Good evening." A colored woman in a white uniform nods to us. "They expecting y'all."

We step into the foyer and the first thing I see is the chandelier, sparkling, gauzy with light. My eyes rise up the hollow twirl of the staircase and it is as if we are inside a gigantic seashell.

"Why, hello there."

I look down from my lollygagging. Missus Whitworth is clicking into the foyer, hands extended. She has on a suit like mine, thankfully, but in crimson. When she nods, her graying-blond hair does not move.

"Hello, Missus Whitworth, I am Charlotte Boudreau Cantrelle Phelan. We thank you so much for having us."

"Delighted," she says and shakes both my parents' hands. "I'm Francine Whitworth. Welcome to our home."

She turns to me. "And you must be Eugenia. Well. It is so nice to finally meet you." Missus Whitworth grasps my arms and looks me in the eyes. Hers are blue, beautiful, like cold water. Her face is plain around them. She is almost my height in her peau de soie heels.

"So nice to meet you," I say. "Stuart's told me so much about you and Senator Whitworth."

She smiles and slides her hand down my arm. I gasp as a prong of her ring scratches my skin.

"There she is!" Behind Missus Whitworth, a tall, bull-chested man lumbers toward me. He hugs me hard to him, then just as quickly flings me back. "Now I told Little Stu a month ago to get this gal up to the house. But frankly," he lowers his voice, "he's still a little gun-shy after that other one."

I stand there blinking. "Very nice to meet you, sir."

The Senator laughs loudly. "You know I'm just teasing you," he says, gives me another drastic hug, clapping me on the back. I smile, try to catch my breath. Remind myself he is a man with all sons.

He turns to Mother, solemnly bows and extends his hand.

"Hello, Senator Whitworth," Mother says. "I'm Charlotte."

"Very nice to meet you, Charlotte. And you call me Stooley. All my friends do."

"Senator," Daddy says and pumps his hand hard. "We thank you for all you did on that farm bill. Made a heck of a difference."

"Shee-oot. That Billups tried to wipe his shoes on it and I told him, I said, Chico, if Mississippi don't have cotton, hell, Mississippi don't have *nothing.*"

He slaps Daddy on the shoulder and I notice how small my father looks next to him.

"Y'all come on in," the Senator says. "I can't talk politics without a drink in my hand."

The Senator pounds his way out of the foyer. Daddy follows and I cringe at the fine line of mud on the back of his shoe. One more swipe of the rag would've gotten it, but Daddy's not used to wearing good loafers on a Saturday.

Mother follows him out and I give one last glance up at the sparkling chandelier. As I turn, I catch the maid staring at me from the door. I smile at her and she nods. Then she nods again, and drops her eyes to the floor.

Oh. My nervousness rises like a trill in my throat as I realize, *she knows.* I stand, frozen by how duplicitous my life has become. She could show up at Aibileen's, start telling me all about serving the Senator and his wife.

"Stuart's still driving over from Shreveport," the Senator hollers. "Got a big deal brewing over there, I hear."

I try not to think about the maid and take a deep breath. I smile like this is fine, just fine. Like I've met so many boyfriends' parents before.

We move into a formal living room with ornate molding and green velvet settees, so full of heavy furniture I can hardly see the floor.

"What can I get y'all to drink?" Mister Whitworth grins like he's offering children candy. He has a heavy, broad forehead and the shoulders of an aging linebacker. His eyebrows are thick and wiry. They wiggle when he talks.

Daddy asks for a cup of coffee, Mother and I for iced tea. The Senator's grin deflates and he looks back at the maid to collect these mundane drinks. In the corner, he pours himself and his wife something brown. The velvet sofa groans when he sits.

"Your home is just lovely. I hear it's the centerpiece of the tour," Mother says. This is what Mother's been dying to say since she found out about this dinner. Mother's been on the dinky Ridgeland County Historic Home Council forever, but refers to Jackson's home tour as "high cotton" compared to theirs. "Now, do y'all do any kind of dress-up or staging for the tours?"

Senator and Missus Whitworth glance at each other. Then Missus Whitworth smiles. "We took it off the tour this year. It was just...too much."

"Off? But it's one of the most important houses in Jackson. Why, I heard Sherman said the house was too pretty to burn."

Missus Whitworth just nods, sniffs. She is ten years younger than my mother but looks older, especially now as her face turns long and prudish.

"Surely you must feel some obligation, for the sake of history..." Mother says, and I shoot her a look to let it go.

No one says anything for a second and then the Senator laughs loudly. "There was kind of a mix-up," he booms. "Patricia van Devender's mother is head of the council so after all that...ruck-a-muck with the kids, we decided we'd just as soon get off the tour."

I glance at the door, praying Stuart will get here soon. This is the second time *she* has come up. Missus Whitworth gives the Senator a deafening look.

"Well, what are we gonna do, Francine? Just never talk about her again? We had the damn gazebo built in the backyard for the wedding."

Missus Whitworth takes a deep breath and I am reminded of what Stuart said to me, that the Senator only knows part of it, but his mother, she knows all. And what she knows must be much worse than just "ruck-a-muck."

"Eugenia"—Missus Whitworth smiles—"I understand you aim to be a writer. What kinds of things do you like to write?"

I put my smile back on. From one good subject to the next. "I write the Miss Myrna column in the *Jackson Journal*. It comes out every Monday."

"Oh, I think Bessie reads that, doesn't she, Stooley? I'll have to ask her when I go in the kitchen."

"Well, if she doesn't, she sure as hell will now." The Senator laughs.

"Stuart said you were trying to get into more serious subjects. Anything particular?"

Now everyone is looking at me, including the maid, a different one from the door, as she hands me a glass of tea. I don't look at her face, terrified of what I'll see there. "I'm working on a . . . a few—"

"Eugenia is writing about the life of Jesus Christ," Mother pops in and I recall my most recent lie to cover my nights out, calling it "research."

"Well," Missus Whitworth nods, looks impressed by this, "that's certainly an honorable subject."

I try to smile, disgusted by my own voice. "And such an . . . important one." I glance at Mother. She's beaming.

The front door slams, sending all the glass lamps into a furious tinkle.

"Sorry I'm so late." Stuart strides in, wrinkled from the car, pulling on his navy sportscoat. We all stand up and his mother holds out her arms to him but he heads straight for me. He puts his hands on my shoulders and kisses my cheek. "Sorry," he whispers and I breathe out, finally relax half an inch. I turn and see his mother smiling like I just snatched her best guest towel and wiped my dirty hands all over it.

"Get yourself a drink, son, sit down," the Senator says. When Stuart has his drink, he settles next to me on the sofa, squeezes my hand and doesn't let go.

Missus Whitworth gives one glance at our hand-holding and says, "Charlotte, why don't I give you and Eugenia a tour of the house?"

For the next fifteen minutes, I follow Mother and Missus Whitworth from one ostentatious room to the next. Mother gasps over a genuine Yankee bullethole in the front parlor, the bullet still lodged in the wood. There are letters from Confederate soldiers lying on a Federal desk, strategically placed antique spectacles and handkerchiefs. The house is a shrine to the War Between the States and I wonder what it must've been like for Stuart, growing up in a home where you can't touch anything.

On the third floor, Mother gaggles over a canopy bed where Robert E. Lee slept. When we finally come down a "secret" staircase, I linger over family pictures in the hallway. I see Stuart and his two brothers as babies, Stuart holding a red ball. Stuart in a christening gown, held by a colored woman in white uniform.

Mother and Missus Whitworth move down the hall, but I keep looking, for there is something so deeply dear in Stuart's face as a young boy. His cheeks were fat and his mother's blue eyes shone the same as they do now.

His hair was the whitish-yellow of a dandelion. At nine or ten, he stands with a hunting rifle and a duck. At fifteen, next to a slain deer. Already he is good-looking, rugged. I pray to God he never sees my teenage pictures.

I walk a few steps and see high school graduation, Stuart proud in a military school uniform. In the center of the wall, there is an empty space without a frame, a rectangle of wallpaper just the slightest shade darker. A picture has been removed.

"Dad, that is enough about—" I hear Stuart say, his voice strained. But just as quickly, there is silence.

"Dinner is served," I hear a maid announce and I weave my way back into the living room. We all trail into the dining room to a long, dark table. The Phelans are seated on one side, the Whitworths on the other. I am diagonal from Stuart, placed as far as possible from him. Around the room, the wainscoting panels have been painted to depict scenes of pre–Civil War times, happy Negroes picking cotton, horses pulling wagons, white-bearded statesmen on the steps of our capitol. We wait while the Senator lingers in the living room. "I'll be right there, y'all go ahead and start." I hear the clink of ice, the clop of the bottle being set down two more times before he finally comes in and sits at the head of the table.

Waldorf salads are served. Stuart looks over at me and smiles every few minutes. Senator Whitworth leans over to Daddy and says, "I came from nothing, you know. Jefferson County, Mississippi. My daddy dried peanuts for eleven cents a pound."

Daddy shakes his head. "Doesn't get much poorer than Jefferson County."

I watch as Mother cuts off the tiniest bite of apple. She hesitates, chews it for the longest time, winces as it goes down. She wouldn't allow me to tell Stuart's parents about her stomach problem. Instead, Mother ravishes Missus Whitworth with degustationary compliments. Mother views this supper as an important move in the game called "Can My Daughter Catch Your Son?"

"The *young people* so enjoy each other's company." Mother smiles. "Why, Stuart comes out to see us at the house nearly twice a week."

"Is that right?" says Missus Whitworth.

"We'd be delighted if you and the Senator could drive out to the plantation for supper sometime, take a walk around the orchard?"

I look at Mother. *Plantation* is an outdated term she likes to use to gloss up the farm, while the "orchard" is a barren apple tree. A pear tree with a worm problem.

But Missus Whitworth has stiffened around the mouth. "Twice a week? Stuart, I had no idea you came to town that often."

Stuart's fork stops in midair. He casts a sheepish look at his mother.

"Y'all are so young." Missus Whitworth smiles. "Enjoy yourselves. There's no need to get serious so quickly."

The Senator leans his elbows on the table. "From a woman who practically proposed to the other one herself, she was in such a hurry."

"*Dad,*" Stuart says through gritted teeth, banging his fork against his plate.

The table is silent, except for Mother's thorough, methodical chewing to try to turn solid food into paste. I touch the scratch, still pink along my arm.

The maid lays pressed chicken on our plates, tops it with a perky dollop of mayonnaisey dressing, and we all smile, glad for the mood breaker. As we eat, Daddy and the Senator talk about cotton prices, boll weevils. I can still see the anger on Stuart's face from when the Senator mentioned Patricia. I glance at him every few seconds, but the anger doesn't seem to be fading. I wonder if that's what they'd argued about earlier, when I was in the hall.

The Senator leans back in his chair. "Did you see that piece they did in *Life* magazine? One before Medgar Evers, about what's-'is-name— Carl...Roberts?"

I look up, surprised to find the Senator is aiming this question at me. I blink, confused, hoping it's because of my job at the newspaper. "It was...he was lynched. For saying the governor was..." I stop, not because I've forgotten the words, but because I remember them.

"*Pathetic,*" the Senator says, now turning to my father. "*With the morals of a streetwalker.*"

I exhale, relieved the attention is off me. I look at Stuart to gauge his reaction to this. I've never asked him his position on civil rights. But I don't think he's even listening to the conversation. The anger around his mouth has turned flat and cold.

My father clears his throat. "I'll be honest," he says slowly. "It makes me sick to hear about that kind of brutality." Daddy sets his fork down silently. He looks Senator Whitworth in the eye. "I've got twenty-five Negroes working my fields and if anyone so much as laid a hand on them, or any of their families…" Daddy's gaze is steady. Then he drops his eyes. "I'm ashamed, sometimes, Senator. Ashamed of what goes on in Mississippi."

Mother's eyes are big, set on Daddy. I am shocked to hear this opinion. Even more shocked that he'd voice it at this table to a politician. At home, newspapers are folded so the pictures face down, television channels are turned when the subject of race comes up. I'm suddenly so proud of my daddy, for many reasons. For a second, I swear, I see it in Mother's eyes too, beneath her worry that Father has obliterated my future. I look at Stuart and his face registers concern, but in which way, I do not know.

The Senator has his eyes narrowed on Daddy.

"I'll tell you something, Carlton," the Senator says. He jiggles the ice around in his glass. "Bessie, bring me another drink, would you please." He hands his glass to the maid. She quickly returns with a full one.

"Those were not wise words to say about our governor," the Senator says.

"I agree one hundred percent," Daddy says.

"But the question I've been asking myself lately is, are they true?"

"Stooley," Missus Whitworth hisses. But then just as quickly she smiles, straightens. "Now, Stooley," she says like she's talking to a child, "our guests here don't want to get into all your politicking during—"

"Francine, let me speak my mind. God knows I can't do it from nine to five, so let me speak my mind in my own home."

Missus Whitworth's smile does not waver, but the slightest bit of pink rises in her cheeks. She studies the white Floradora roses in the center of the table. Stuart stares at his plate with the same cold anger as before. He hasn't looked at me since the chicken course. Everyone is quiet and then someone changes the subject to the weather.

WHEN SUPPER IS FINALLY OVER, we're asked to retire out on the back porch for after-dinner drinks and coffee. Stuart and I linger in the hallway. I touch his arm, but he pulls away.

"I knew he'd get drunk and start in on everything."

"Stuart, it's fine," I say because I think he's talking about his father's politics. "We're all having a good time."

But Stuart is sweating and feverish-looking. "It's Patricia this and Patricia that, all night long," he says. "How many times can he bring her up?"

"Just forget about it, Stuart. Everything's okay."

He runs a hand through his hair and looks everywhere but at me. I start to get the feeling that I'm not even here to him. And then I realize what I've known all night. He is looking at me but he is thinking about . . . *her.* She is everywhere. In the anger in Stuart's eyes, on Senator and Missus Whitworth's tongues, on the wall where her picture must've hung.

I tell him I need to go to the bathroom.

He steers me down the hall. "Meet us out back," he says, but does not smile. In the bathroom, I stare at my reflection, tell myself that it's just tonight. Everything will be fine once we're out of this house.

After the bathroom, I walk by the living room, where the Senator is pouring himself another drink. He chuckles at himself, dabs at his shirt, then looks around to see if anyone's seen him spill. I try to tiptoe past the doorway before he spots me.

"There you are!" I hear him holler as I slip by. I back up slowly into the doorway and his face lights up. "Wassa matter, you lost?" He walks out into the hallway.

"No sir, I was just . . . going to meet everybody."

"Come here, gal." He puts his arm around me and the smell of bourbon burns my eyes. I see the front of his shirt is saturated with it. "You having a good time?"

"Yessir. Thank you."

"Now, Stuart's mama, don't you let her scare you off. She's just protective, is all."

"Oh no, she's been . . . very nice. Everything's fine." I glance down the hall, where I can hear their voices.

He sighs, stares off. "We've had a real hard year with Stuart. I guess he told you what happened."

I nod, feeling my skin prickle.

"Oh, it was bad," he says. "So bad." Then suddenly he smiles. "Look a here! Look who's coming to say hello to you." He scoops up a tiny white dog, drapes it across his arm like a tennis towel. "Say hello, Dixie," he croons, "say hello to Miss Eugenia." The dog struggles, strains its head away from the reeking smell of the shirt.

The Senator looks back at me with a blank stare. I think he's forgotten what I'm doing here.

"I was just headed to the back porch," I say.

"Come on, come in here." He tugs me by the elbow, steers me through a paneled door. I enter a small room with a heavy desk, a yellow light shining sickishly on the dark green walls. He pushes the door shut behind me and I immediately feel the air change, grow close and claustrophobic.

"Now, look, everybody says I talk too much when I've had a few but..." the Senator narrows his eyes at me, like we are old conspirators, "I want to tell you something."

The dog's given up all struggle, sedated by the smell of the shirt. I am suddenly desperate to go talk to Stuart, like every second I'm away I'm losing him. I back away.

"I think—I should go find—" I reach for the door handle, sure I'm being terribly rude, but not able to stand the air in here, the smell of liquor and cigars.

The Senator sighs, nods as I grip the handle. "Oh. You too, huh." He leans back against the desk, looking defeated.

I start to open the door but it's the same lost look on the Senator's face as the one Stuart had when he showed up on my parents' porch. I feel like I have no choice but to ask, "Me too what...sir?"

The Senator looks over at the picture of Missus Whitworth, huge and cold, mounted on his office wall like a warning. "I see it, is all. In your eyes." He chuckles bitterly. "And here I was hoping you might be the one who halfway liked the old man. I mean, if you ever joined this old family."

I look at him now, tingling from his words...*joined this old family.*

"I don't...dislike you, sir," I say, shifting in my flats.

"I don't mean to bury you in our troubles, but things have been pretty hard here, Eugenia. We were worried sick after all that mess last year. With the other one." He shakes his head, looks down at the glass in his hand. "Stuart, he just up and left his apartment in Jackson, moved everything out to the camp house in Vicksburg."

"I know he was very...upset," I say, when truthfully, I know almost nothing at all.

"Dead's more like it. Hell, I'd drive out to see him and he'd just be sitting there in front of the window, cracking pecans. Wasn't even eating em, just pulling off the shell, tossing em in the trash. Wouldn't talk to me or his mama for...for *months*."

He crumples in on himself, this gigantic bull of a man, and I want to escape and reassure him at the same time, he looks so pathetic, but then he looks up at me with his bloodshot eyes, says, "Seems like ten minutes ago I was showing him how to load his first rifle, wring his first dove-bird. But ever since the thing with that girl, he's...different. He won't tell me anything. I just want to know, is my son alright?"

"I...I think he is. But honestly, I don't...really know." I look away. Inside, I'm starting to realize that I don't know Stuart. If this damaged him so much, and he can't even speak to me about it, then what am I to him? Just a diversion? Something sitting beside him to keep him from thinking about what's really tearing him up inside?

I look at the Senator, try to think of something comforting, something my mother would say. But it's just a dead silence.

"Francine would have my hide if she knew I was asking you this."

"It's alright, sir," I say. "I don't mind that you did."

He looks exhausted by it all, tries to smile. "Thank you, darlin'. Go on and see my son. I'll see y'all out there in a while."

I ESCAPE TO THE BACK PORCH and stand next to Stuart. Lightning bursts in the sky, giving us a flash of the eerily brilliant gardens, then the darkness sucks it all back in. The gazebo, skeleton-like, looms at the end of the garden path. I feel nauseous from the glass of sherry I drank after supper.

The Senator comes out, looking curiously more sober, in a fresh shirt, plaid and pressed, exactly the same as the last one. Mother and Missus

Whitworth stroll a few steps, pointing at some rare rose winding its neck up onto the porch. Stuart puts his hand on my shoulder. He is somehow better, but I am growing worse.

"Can we…?" I point inside and Stuart follows me inside. I stop in the hallway with the secret staircase.

"There's a lot I don't know about you, Stuart," I say.

He points to the wall of pictures behind me, the empty space included. "Well, here it all is."

"Stuart, your daddy, he told me…" I try to find a way to put it.

He narrows his eyes at me. "Told you what?"

"How bad it was. How hard it was on you," I say. "With Patricia."

"He doesn't know *anything*. He doesn't know who it was or what it was about or…"

He leans back against the wall and crosses his arms and I see that old anger again, deep and red. He is wrapped in it.

"Stuart. You don't have to tell me now. But sometime, we're going to have to talk about this." I'm surprised by how confident I sound, when I certainly don't feel it.

He looks me deep in the eyes, shrugs. "She slept with someone else. There."

"Someone…you know?"

"No one knew him. He was one of those leeches, hanging around the school, cornering the teachers to do something about the integration laws. Well, she did something alright."

"You mean…he was an activist? With the civil rights…?"

"That's it. Now you know."

"Was he…colored?" I gulp at the thought of the consequences, because even to me, that would be horrific, disastrous.

"*No*, he wasn't colored. He was scum. Some Yankee from New York, the kind you see on the T.V. with the long hair and the peace signs."

I am searching my head for the right question to ask but I can't think of anything.

"You know the really crazy part, Skeeter? I could've gotten over it. I could've forgiven her. She asked me to, told me how sorry she was. But I knew, if it ever got out who he was, that Senator Whitworth's daughter-in-law got in bed with a Yankee goddamn activist, it would ruin him. Kill his career like that." He snaps his fingers with a crack.

"But your father, at the table. He said he thought Ross Barnett was wrong."

"You know that's not the way it works. It doesn't matter what he believes. It's what Mississippi believes. He's running for the U.S. Senate this fall and I'm unfortunate enough to know that."

"So you broke up with her because of your father?"

"No, I broke up with her because she cheated." He looks down at his hands and I can see the shame eating away at him. "But I didn't take her back because of...my father."

"Stuart, are you...still in love with her?" I ask, and I try to smile as if it's nothing, just a question, even though I feel all my blood rushing to my feet. I feel like I will faint asking this.

His body slumps some, against the gold-patterned wallpaper. His voice softens.

"You'd never do that. Lie that way. Not to me, not to anybody."

He has no idea how many people I'm lying to. But it's not the point. "Answer me, Stuart. Are you?"

He rubs his temples, stretching his hand across his eyes. Hiding his eyes is what I'm thinking.

"I think we ought to quit for a while," he whispers.

I reach over to him out of reflex, but he backs away. "I need some time, Skeeter. Space, I guess. I need to go to work and drill oil and...get my head straight awhile."

I feel my mouth slide open. Out on the porch, I hear the soft calls of our parents. It is time to leave.

I walk behind Stuart to the front of the house. The Whitworths stop in the spiraling foyer while we three Phelans head out the door. In a cottony coma I listen as everyone pledges to do it again, out at the Phelans next time. I tell them all goodbye, thank you, my own voice sounding strange to me. Stuart waves from the steps and smiles at me so our parents can't tell that anything has changed.

CHAPTER 21

WE STAND in the relaxing room, Mother and Daddy and I, staring at the silver box in the window. It is the size of a truck engine, nosed in knobs, shiny with chrome, gleaming with modern-day hope. *Fedders*, it reads.

"Who are these Fedders anyway?" Mother asks. "Where are their people from?"

"Go on and turn the crank, Charlotte."

"Oh I can't. It's too tacky."

"Jesus, Mama, Doctor Neal said you need it. Now stand back." My parents glare at me. They do not know Stuart broke up with me after the Whitworth supper. Or the relief I long for from this machine. That every minute I feel so hot, so goddamn singed and hurt, I think I might catch on fire.

I flip the knob to "1." Overhead, the chandelier bulbs dim. The whir climbs slowly like it's working its way up a hill. I watch a few tendrils of Mother's hair lift gently into the air.

"Oh...*my*," Mother says and closes her eyes. She's been so tired lately and her ulcers are getting worse. Doctor Neal said keeping the house cool would at least make her more comfortable.

"It's not even on full blast," I say and I turn it up a notch, to "2." The air blows a little harder, grows colder, and we all three smile, our sweat evaporating from our foreheads.

"Well, heck, let's just go all the way," Daddy says, and turns it up to "3," which is the highest, coldest, most wonderful setting of all, and Mother giggles. We stand with our mouths open like we could eat it. The lights brighten again, the whir grows louder, our smiles lift higher, and then it all stops dead. Dark.

"What...happened?" Mama says.

Daddy looks up at the ceiling. He walks out into the hall.

"Damn thing blew the current."

Mother fans her handkerchief on her neck. "Well, good heavens, Carlton, go fix it."

For an hour, I hear Daddy and Jameso throwing switches and clanking tools, boots knocking on the porch. After they've fixed it and I sit through a lecture from Daddy to never turn it to "3" again or it will blow the house to pieces, Mother and I watch as an icy mist grows on the windows. Mother dozes in her blue Queen Anne chair, her green blanket pulled to her chest. I wait until she is asleep, listening for the soft snore, the pucker of her forehead. On tiptoe, I turn out all the lamps, the television, every electricity sucker downstairs save the refrigerator. I stand in front of the window and unbutton my blouse. Carefully, I turn the dial to "3". Because I long to feel nothing. I want to be frozen inside. I want the icy cold to blow directly on my heart.

The power blows out in about three seconds.

FOR THE NEXT TWO WEEKS, I submerge myself in the interviews. I keep my typewriter on the back porch and work most of the day long and into the night. The screens give the green yard and fields a hazy look. Sometimes I catch myself staring off at the fields, but I am not here. I am in the old Jackson kitchens with the maids, hot and sticky in their white uniforms. I feel the gentle bodies of white babies breathing against me. I feel what Constantine felt when Mother brought me home from the hospital and handed me over to her. I let their colored memories draw me out of my own miserable life.

"Skeeter, we haven't heard from Stuart in weeks," Mother says for the eighth time. "He's not cross with you, now, is he?"

At the moment, I am writing the Miss Myrna column. Once ahead by three months, somehow I've managed to almost miss my deadline. "He's fine, Mother. He doesn't have to call every minute of the day." But then I soften my voice. Every day she seems thinner. The sharpness of her collarbone is enough to tamp down my irritation at her comment. "He's just traveling is all, Mama."

This seems to placate her for the moment and I tell the same story to Elizabeth, with a few more details to Hilly, pinching my arm to bear her insipid smile. But I do not know what to tell myself. Stuart needs "space" and "time," as if this were physics and not a human relationship.

So instead of feeling sorry for myself every minute of the day, I work. I type. I sweat. Who knew heartbreak would be so goddamn hot. When Mother's lying down on her bed, I pull my chair up to the air conditioner and stare into it. In July, it becomes a silver shrine. I find Pascagoula pretending to dust with one hand, while holding up her hairbraids at the thing with the other. It's not as if it's a new invention, air-conditioning, but every store in town that has it puts a sign in the window, prints it on its ads because it is so vital. I make a cardboard sign for the Phelan house, place it on the front doorknob, NOW AIR-CONDITIONED. Mother smiles, but pretends she's not amused.

On a rare evening home, I sit with Mother and Daddy at the dinner table. Mother nibbles on her supper. She spent the afternoon trying to keep me from finding out she'd been vomiting. She presses her fingers along the top of her nose to hold back her headache and says, "I was thinking about the twenty-fifth, do you think that's too soon to have them over?" and I still cannot bring myself to tell her that Stuart and I have broken up.

But I can see it on her face, that Mother feels worse than bad tonight. She is pale and trying to sit up longer than I know she wants to. I take her hand and say, "Let me check, Mama. I'm sure the twenty-fifth will be fine." She smiles for the first time all day.

. . .

AIBILEEN SMILES AT THE STACK of pages on her kitchen table. It's an inch thick, double-spaced, and starting to look like something that can sit on a shelf. Aibileen is as exhausted as I am, surely more since she works all day and then comes home to the interviews at night.

"Look a that," she says. "That thing's almost a *book*."

I nod, try to smile, but there is so much work left to do. It's nearly August and even though it's not due until January, we still have five more interviews to sort through. With Aibileen's help, I've molded and cut and arranged five of the women's chapters including Minny's, but they still need work. Thankfully, Aibileen's section is done. It is twenty-one pages, beautifully written, simple.

There are several dozen made-up names, both white and colored, and at times, it is hard to keep them all straight. All along, Aibileen has been Sarah Ross. Minny chose Gertrude Black, for what reason I don't know. I have chosen Anonymous, although Elaine Stein doesn't know this yet. Niceville, Mississippi, is the name of our town because it doesn't exist, but we decided a real state name would draw interest. And since Mississippi happens to be the worst, we figured we'd better use it.

A breeze blows through the window and the top pages flutter. We both slam our palms down to catch them.

"You think...she gone want a print it?" asks Aibileen. "When it's done?"

I try to smile at Aibileen, show some false confidence. "I hope so," I say as brightly as I can manage. "She seemed interested in the idea and she...well, the march is coming up and..."

I hear my own voice taper off. I truly don't know if Missus Stein will want to print it. But what I do know is, the responsibility of the project lays on my shoulders and I see it in their hardworking, lined faces, how much the maids want this book to be published. They are scared, looking at the back door every ten minutes, afraid they'll get caught talking to me. Afraid they'll be beaten like Louvenia's grandson, or, hell, bludgeoned in their front yard like Medgar Evers. The risk they're taking is proof they want this to get printed and they want it bad.

I no longer feel protected just because I'm white. I check over my shoulder often when I drive the truck to Aibileen's. The cop who stopped me a few months back is my reminder: I am now a threat to every white family in town. Even though so many of the stories are good, celebrating the bonds of women and family, the bad stories will be the ones that catch the white people's attention. They will make their blood boil and their fists swing. We must keep this a perfect secret.

I'M DELIBERATELY FIVE MINUTES LATE for the Monday night League meeting, our first in a month. Hilly's been down at the coast, wouldn't dare allow a meeting without her. She's tan and ready to lead. She holds her gavel like a weapon. All around me, women sit and smoke cigarettes, tip them into glass ashtrays on the floor. I chew my nails to keep from smoking one. I haven't smoked in six days.

Besides the cigarette missing from my hand, I'm jittery from the faces around me. I easily spot seven women in the room who are related to someone in the book, if not in it themselves. I want to get out of here and get back to work, but two long, hot hours pass before Hilly finally bangs her gavel. By then, even she looks tired of hearing her own voice.

Girls stand and stretch. Some head out, eager to attend to their husbands. Others dawdle, the ones with a kitchen full of kids and help that has gone home. I gather my things quickly, hoping to avoid talking to anyone, especially Hilly.

But before I can escape, Elizabeth catches my eye, waves me over. I haven't seen her for weeks and I can't avoid speaking to her. I feel guilty that I haven't been to see her. She grabs the back of her chair and raises herself up. She is six months pregnant, woozy from the pregnancy tranquilizers.

"How are you feeling?" I ask. Everything on her body is the same except her stomach is huge and swollen. "Is it any better this time?"

"God, no, it's awful and I still have three months to go."

We're both quiet. Elizabeth burps faintly, looks at her watch. Finally, she picks up her bag, about to leave, but then she takes my hand. "I heard," she whispers, "about you and Stuart. I'm so sorry."

I look down. I'm not surprised she knows, only that it took this long for anyone to find out. I haven't told anyone, but I guess Stuart has. Just this morning, I had to lie to Mother and tell her the Whitworths would be out of town on the twenty-fifth, Mother's so-called date to have them over.

"I'm sorry I didn't tell you," I say. "I don't like talking about it."

"I understand. Oh shoot, I better go on, Raleigh's probably having a fit by himself with her." She gives a last look at Hilly. Hilly smiles and nods her excusal.

I gather my notes quickly, head for the door. Before I make it out, I hear her.

"Wait a sec, would you, Skeeter?"

I sigh, turn around and face Hilly. She's wearing the navy blue sailor number, something you'd dress a five-year-old in. The pleats around her hips are stretched open like accordion bellows. The room is empty except for us now.

"Can we discuss this, please, ma'am?" She holds up the most recent newsletter and I know what's coming.

"I can't stay. Mother's sick—"

"I told you *five months ago* to print my initiative and now another week has passed and you still haven't followed my instructions."

I stare at her and my anger is sudden, ferocious. Everything I've kept down for months rises and erupts in my throat.

"I will *not* print that initiative."

She looks at me, holding very still. "I want that initiative in the newsletter before election time," she says and points to the ceiling, "or I'm calling upstairs, missy."

"If you try to throw me out of the League, I will dial up Genevieve von Hapsburg in New York City myself," I hiss, because I happen to know Genevieve's Hilly's hero. She's the youngest national League president in history, perhaps the only person in this world Hilly's afraid of. But Hilly doesn't even flinch.

"And tell her what, Skeeter? Tell her you're not doing your job? Tell her you're carrying around Negro activist materials?"

I'm too angry to let this unnerve me. "I want them *back*, Hilly. You took them and they don't belong to you."

"Of course I took them. You have no business carrying around something like that. What if somebody saw those things?"

"Who are you to say what I can and cannot carry ar—"

"It is my job, Skeeter! You know well as I do, people won't buy so much as a slice of pound cake from an organization that harbors racial integrationists!"

"Hilly." I just need to hear her say it. "Just *who* is all that pound cake money being raised for, anyway?"

She rolls her eyes. "The Poor Starving Children of Africa?"

I wait for her to catch the irony of this, that she'll send money to colored people overseas, but not across town. But I get a better idea. "I'm going to call up Genevieve right now. I'm going to tell her what a hypocrite you are."

Hilly straightens. I think for a second I've tapped a crack in her shell with those words. But then she licks her lips, takes a deep, noisy sniff.

"You know, it's no wonder Stuart Whitworth dropped you."

I keep my jaw clenched so that she cannot see the effect these words have on me. But inside, I am a slow, sliding scale. I feel everything inside of me slipping down into the floor. "I want those laws back," I say, my voice shaking.

"Then print the initiative."

I turn and walk out the door. I heave my satchel into the Cadillac and light a cigarette.

MOTHER'S LIGHT IS OFF when I get home and I'm grateful. I tiptoe down the hall, onto the back porch, easing the squeaky screen door closed. I sit down at my typewriter.

But I cannot type. I stare at the tiny gray squares of the back porch screen. I stare so hard, I slip through them. I feel something inside me crack open then. I am vaporous. I am crazy. I am deaf to that stupid, silent phone. Deaf to Mother's retching in the house. Her voice through the window, "I'm fine, Carlton, it's passed." I hear it all and yet, I hear nothing. Just a high buzzing in my ears.

I reach in my satchel and pull out the page of Hilly's bathroom initiative. The paper is limp, already damp with humidity. A moth lands in the corner then flutters away, leaving a brown smudge of wing chalk.

With slow, deliberate strokes, I start typing the newsletter: Sarah Shelby to marry Robert Pryor; please attend a baby-clothes showing by Mary Katherine Simpson; a tea in honor of our loyal sustainers. Then I type Hilly's initiative. I place it on the second page, opposite the photo ops. This is where everyone will be sure to see it, after they look at themselves at the Summer Fun Jamboree. All I can think while I'm typing is, *What would Constantine think of me?*

AIBILEEN

CHAPTER 22

"HOW OLD A YOU TODAY, big girl?"

Mae Mobley still in bed. She hold out two sleepy fingers and say, "Mae Mo Two."

"Nuh-uh, we three today!" I move up one a her fingers, chant what my daddy used to say to me on my birthdays, "Three little soldiers, come out the doe, two say stop, one say go."

She in a big-girl bed now since the nursery getting fixed up for the new baby. "Next year, we do four little soldiers, they looking for something to eat."

Her nose wrinkle up cause now she got to remember to say she Mae Mobley Three, when her whole life she can remember, she been telling people she Mae Mobley *Two*. When you little, you only get asked two questions, what's your name and how old you is, so you better get em right.

"I am Mae Mobley Three," she say. She scramble out a bed, her hair in a rat's nest. That bald spot she had as a baby, it's coming back. Usually I can brush over it and hide it for a few minutes, but not for long. It's thin and she's losing them curls. It gets real stringy by the end a the day. It don't trouble me that she ain't cute, but I try to fix her up nice as I can for her mama.

"Come on to the kitchen," I say. "We gone make you a birthday breakfast."

Miss Leefolt off getting her hair done. She don't care bout being there on the morning her only child wakes up on the first birthday she remember. But least Miss Leefolt got her what she want. Brung me back to her bedroom and point to a big box on the floor.

"Won't she be happy?" Miss Leefolt say. "It walks and talks and even cries."

Sho nuff they's a big pink polky-dot box. Got cellophane across the front, and inside they's the doll baby tall as Mae Mobley. Name Allison. She got blond curly hair and blue eyes. Frilly pink dress on. Evertime the commercial come on the tee-vee Mae Mobley run over to the set and grab the box on both sides, put her face up to the screen and stare so serious. Miss Leefolt look like she gone cry herself, looking down at that toy. I reckon her mean old mama never got her what she wanted when she little.

In the kitchen, I fix some grits without no seasoning, and put them baby marshmallows on top. I toast the whole thing to make it a little crunchy. Then I garnish it with a cut-up strawberry. That's all a grit is, a vehicle. For whatever it is you rather be eating.

The three little pink candles I done brought from home is in my pocketbook. I bring em out, undo the wax paper I got em in so they don't turn out bent. After I light em, I bring them grits over to her booster chair, at the white linoleum table in the middle a the room.

I say, "Happy birthday, Mae Mobley Two!"

She laugh and say, "I am Mae Mobley Three!"

"You sure is! Now blow out them candles, Baby Girl. Fore they run up in you grits."

She stare at the little flames, smiling.

"Blow it, big girl."

She blow em clean over. She suck the grits off the candles and start eating. After while, she smile up at me, say, "How old are you?"

"Aibileen's fifty-three."

Her eyes get real wide. I might as well be a thousand.

"Do you...get birthdays?"

"Yeah." I laugh. "It's a pity, but I do. My birthday be next week." I can't believe I'm on be fifty-four years old. Where do it go?

"Do you have some babies?" she ask.

I laugh. "I got seventeen of em."

She ain't quite got up to seventeen in her numbers yet, but she know this be a big one.

"That's enough to fill up this whole kitchen," I say.

Her brown eyes is so big and round. "Where are the babies?"

"They all over town. All the babies I done looked after."

"Why don't they come play with me?"

"Cause most of em grown. Lot of em already having babies a they own."

Lordy, she look confuse. She doing her figuring, like she be trying to count it all up. Finally I say, "You one of em, too. All the babies I tend to, I count as my own."

She nod, cross up her arms.

I start washing the dishes. The birthday party tonight just gone be the family and I got to get the cakes made. First, I'm on do the strawberry one with the strawberry icing. Every meal be strawberry, if it was up to Mae Mobley. Then I do the other one.

"Let's do a chocolate cake," say Miss Leefolt yesterday. She seven months pregnant and love eating chocolate.

Now I done planned this last week. I got everything ready. This too important to be occurring to me the day before. "Mm-hmm. What about strawberry? That be Mae Mobley's favorite, you know."

"Oh no, she wants chocolate. I'm going to the store today and get every- thing you need."

Chocolate my foot. So I figured I'd just go on and make both. At least then she get to blow out two sets a candles.

I clean up the grits plate. Give her some grape juice to drink. She got her old baby doll in the kitchen, the one she call Claudia, with the painted-on hair and the eyes that close. Make a pitiful whining sound when you drop it on the floor.

"There's your baby," I say and she pats its back like she burping it, nods.

Then she say, "Aibee, you're my real mama." She don't even look at me, just say it like she talking about the weather.

I kneel down on the floor where she playing. "Your mama's off getting her hair fixed. Baby Girl, you know who your mama is."

But she shake her head, cuddling that doll to her. "I'm *your* baby," she say.

"Mae Mobley, you know I's just teasing you, about all them seventeen kids being mine? They ain't really. I only had me one child."

"I know," she say. "I'm your real baby. Those other ones you said are pretend."

Now I had babies be confuse before. John Green Dudley, first word out a that boy's mouth was Mama and he was looking straight at me. But then pretty soon he calling everybody including hisself Mama, and calling his daddy Mama too. Did that for a long time. Nobody worry bout it. Course when he start playing dress-up in his sister's Jewel Taylor twirl skirts and wearing Chanel Number 5, we all get a little concern.

I looked after the Dudley family for too long, over six years. His daddy would take him to the garage and whip him with a rubber hose-pipe try-ing to beat the girl out a that boy until I couldn't stand it no more. Treelore near bout suffocated when I'd come home I'd hug him so hard. When we started working on the stories, Miss Skeeter asked me what's the worst day I remember being a maid. I told her it was a stillbirth baby. But it wasn't. It was every day from 1941 to 1947 waiting by the screen door for them beat-ings to be over. I wish to God I'd told John Green Dudley he ain't going to hell. That he ain't no sideshow freak cause he like boys. I wish to God I'd filled his ears with good things like I'm trying to do Mae Mobley. Instead, I just sat in the kitchen, waiting to put the salve on them hose-pipe welts.

Just then we hear Miss Leefolt pulling into the carport. I get a little ner-vous a what Miss Leefolt gone do if she hear this Mama stuff. Mae Mobley nervous too. Her hands start flapping like a chicken. "Shhh! Don't tell!" she say. "She'll spank me."

So she already done had this talk with her mama. And Miss Leefolt didn't like it one bit.

When Miss Leefolt come in with her new hairdo, Mae Mobley don't even say hello, she run back to her room. Like she scared her mama can hear what's going on inside her head.

· · ·

MAE MOBLEY'S BIRTHDAY PARTY GOES fine, least that's what Miss Leefolt tell me the next day. Friday morning, I come in to see three-quarters of a chocolate cake setting on the counter. Strawberry all gone. That afternoon, Miss Skeeter come by to give Miss Leefolt some papers. Soon as Miss Leefolt waddle off to the bathroom, Miss Skeeter slip in the kitchen.

"We on for tonight?" I ask.

"We're on. I'll be there." Miss Skeeter don't smile much since Mister Stuart and her ain't steady no more. I heard Miss Hilly and Miss Leefolt talking about it plenty.

Miss Skeeter get herself a Co-Cola from the icebox, speak in a low voice. "Tonight we'll finish Winnie's interview and this weekend I'll start sorting it all out. But then I can't meet again until next Thursday. I promised Mama I'd drive her to Natchez Monday for a DAR thing." Miss Skeeter kind a narrow her eyes up, something she do when she thinking about something important. "I'll be gone for three days, okay?"

"Good," I say. "You need you a break."

She head toward the dining room, but she look back, say, "Remember. I leave Monday morning and I'll be gone for three days, okay?"

"Yes ma'am," I say, wondering why she think she got to say this twice.

IT AIN'T BUT EIGHT THIRTY on Monday morning but Miss Leefolt's phone already ringing its head off.

"Miss Leefolt res—"

"*Put Elizabeth on the phone!*"

I go tell Miss Leefolt. She get out a bed, shuffle in the kitchen in her rollers and nightgown, pick up the receiver. Miss Hilly sound like she using a megaphone not a telephone. I can hear every word.

"*Have you been by my house?*"

"What? What are you talk—?"

"*She put it in the newsletter about the toilets. I specifically said old coats are to be dropped off at my house not—*"

"Let me get my . . . mail, I don't know what you're—"

"When I find her I will kill her myself."

The line crash down in Miss Leefolt's ear. She stand there a second staring at it, then throw a housecoat over her nightgown. "I've got to *go*," she says, scrambling round for her keys. "I'll be back."

She run all pregnant out the door and tumble in her car and speed off. I look down at Mae Mobley and she look up at me.

"Don't ask me, Baby Girl. I don't know either."

What I do know is, Hilly and her family drove in this morning from a weekend in Memphis. Whenever Miss Hilly gone, that's all Miss Leefolt talk about is where she is and when she coming back.

"Come on, Baby Girl," I say after while. "Let's take a walk, find out what's going on."

We walk up Devine, turn left, then left again, and up Miss Hilly's street, which is Myrtle. Even though it's August, it's a nice walk, ain't too hot yet. Birds is zipping around, singing. Mae Mobley holding my hand and we swinging our arms having a good ole time. Lots a cars passing us today, which is strange, cause Myrtle a dead end.

We turn the bend to Miss Hilly's great big white house. And there they is.

Mae Mobley point and laugh. "Look. Look, Aibee!"

I have never in my life seen a thing like this. Three dozen of em. Pots. Right smack on Miss Hilly's lawn. All different colors and shapes and sizes. Some is blue, some is pink, some is white. Some ain't got no ring, some ain't got no tank. They's old ones, young ones, chain on top, and flush with the handle. Almost look like a crowd a people the way some got they lids open talking, some with they lids closed listening.

We move over into the drain ditch, cause the traffic on this little street's starting to build up. People is driving down, circling round the little island a grass at the end with they windows down. Laughing out loud saying, "Look at Hilly's house," "Look at those things." Staring at them toilets like they never seen one before.

"One, two, three," Mae Mobley start counting em. She get to twelve and I got to take over. "Twenty-nine, thirty, thirty-one. Thirty-two commodes, Baby Girl."

We get a little closer and now I see they ain't just all over the yard. They's two in the driveway side-by-side, like they a couple. They's one up on the front step, like it's waiting for Miss Hilly to answer the door.

"Ain't that one funny with the—"

But Baby Girl done broke off from my hand. She running in the yard and get to the pink pot in the middle and pull up the lid. Before I know it, she done pulled down her panties and tinkled in it and I'm chasing after her with half a dozen horns honking and a man in a hat taking pictures.

Miss Leefolt's car's in the drive behind Miss Hilly's, but they ain't in sight. They must be inside yelling about what they gone do with this mess. Curtains is drawn and I don't see no stirring. I cross my fingers, hope they didn't catch Baby Girl making potty for half a Jackson to see. It's time to go on back.

The whole way home, Baby Girl is asking questions bout them pots. Why they there? Where they come from? Can she go see Heather and play with them toilets some more?

When I get back to Miss Leefolt's, the phone rings off the hook the rest a the morning. I don't answer it. I'm waiting for it to stop long enough so I can call Minny. But when Miss Leefolt slam into the kitchen, she get to yapping on the phone a million miles a hour. Don't take me long to get the story pieced together listening to her.

Miss Skeeter done printed Hilly's toilet announcement in the newsletter alright. The list a them reasons why white folk and colored folk can't be sharing a seat. And then, below that, she follow with the alert about the coat drive too, or at least that's what she was supposed to do. Stead a coats though, it say something like "Drop off your old toilets at 228 Myrtle Street. We'll be out of town, but leave them in front by the door." She just get one word mixed up, that's all. I spec that's what she gone say, anyway.

TOO BAD FOR MISS HILLY there wasn't no other news going on. Nothing on Vietnam or the draft. They already say all they can about the church blown up in Alabama, killing those poor colored girls. Next day, Miss Hilly's house with all them pots makes the front page a the *Jackson Journal*.

I got to say, it is a funny-looking sight. I just wish it was in color so you could compare all them shades a pink and blue and white. Desegregation of the toilet bowls is what they should a call it.

The headline say, COME ON BY, HAVE A SEAT! They ain't no article to go with it. Just the picture and a little caption saying, "The home of Hilly and William Holbrook, of Jackson, Mississippi, was a sight to see this morning."

And I don't mean nothing going on just in Jackson, I mean nothing in the entire United States. Lottie Freeman, who work at the governor's mansion where they get all the big papers, told me she saw it in the Living section a *The New York Times*. And in every one of em it read, "Home of Hilly and William Holbrook, Jackson, Mississippi."

AT MISS LEEFOLT'S, they's lots a extra talking on the telephone that week, lot a head-nodding like Miss Leefolt getting a earful from Miss Hilly. Part a me want a laugh about them pots, other part want a cry. It was a awful big risk for Miss Skeeter to take, turning Miss Hilly against her. She coming home tonight from Natchez, and I hope she call. I reckon now I know why she went.

On Thursday morning, I still ain't heard from Miss Skeeter. I set up my ironing in the living room. Miss Leefolt come home with Miss Hilly and they set at the dining room table. I ain't seen Miss Hilly over here since before the pots. I reckon she ain't leaving the house so much. I turn the tee-vee set down low, keep my ear turned up.

"Here it is. Here's what I told you about." Miss Hilly got a little booklet opened up. She running her finger along the lines. Miss Leefolt shaking her head.

"You know what this means, don't you? She wants to change these laws. Why else would she be carrying them around?"

"I can't believe this," say Miss Leefolt.

"I can't prove she put those pots in my yard. But this"—she holds up the book and taps it—"this is solid proof she's up to something. And I intend to tell Stuart Whitworth, too."

"But they're not steady anymore."

"Well, he still needs to know. In case he has any inclination of patching things up with her. For the sake of Senator Whitworth's career."

"But maybe it really was a mistake, the newsletter. Maybe she—"

"Elizabeth." Hilly cross her arms up. "I'm not talking about pots. I am talking about the laws of this great state. Now, I want you to ask yourself, do you want Mae Mobley sitting next to a colored boy in English class?" Miss Hilly glance back at me doing my ironing. She lower her voice but Miss Hilly never knew how to whisper good. "Do you want Nigra people living right here in this neighborhood? Touching your bottom when you pass on the street?"

I look up and see it's starting to sink in on Miss Leefolt. She straighten up all prim and proper.

"William had a fit when he saw what she did to our house and I can't soil my name hanging around her anymore, not with the election coming up. I've already asked Jeanie Caldwell to take Skeeter's place in bridge club."

"You kicked her out of bridge club?"

"I sure did. And I thought about kicking her out of the League, too."

"Can you even do that?"

"Of course I can. But I've decided I want her to sit in that room and see what a fool she's made of herself." Miss Hilly nods. "She needs to learn that she can't carry on this way. I mean, around us it's one thing, but around some other people, she's going to get in big trouble."

"It's true. There are some racists in this town," Miss Leefolt say.

Miss Hilly nod her head, "Oh, they're out there."

After while, they get up and drive off together. I am glad I don't have to see they faces for a while.

AT NOONTIME, Mister Leefolt come home for lunch, which is rare. He set down at the little breakfast table. "Aibileen, make me up some lunch, would you please." He lift the newspaper, pop the spine to get it straight. "I'll have some roast beef."

"Yessir." I set down a placemat and a napkin and some silverware for him. He tall and real thin. Won't be too long fore he all bald. Got a black ring round his head and nothing on top.

"You staying on to help Elizabeth with the new baby?" he asks, reading his paper. Generally, he don't ever pay me no mind.

"Yessir." I say.

"Because I hear you like to move around a lot."

"Yessir," I say. It's true. Most maids stay with the same family all they lives, but not me. I got my own reasons for moving on when they about eight, nine years old. Took me a few jobs to learn that. "I work best with the babies."

"So you don't really consider yourself a maid. You're more of a nurse-type for the children." He puts his paper down, looks at me. "You're a specialist, like me."

I don't say nothing, just nod a little.

"See, I only do taxes for businesses, not every individual that's filing a tax return."

I'm getting nervous. This the most he ever talk to me and I been here three years.

"Must be hard finding a new job every time the kids get old enough for school."

"Something always come along."

He don't say nothing to that, so I go head and get the roast out.

"Got to keep up good references, moving around to different clientele like you do."

"Yessir."

"I hear you know Skeeter Phelan. Old friend of Elizabeth's."

I keep my head down. Real slow, I get to slicing, slicing, slicing the meat off that loin. My heart's pumping triple speed now.

"She ask me for cleaning tips sometimes. For the article."

"That right?" Mister Leefolt say.

"Yessir. She just ask me for tips."

"I don't want you talking to that woman anymore, not for cleaning tips, not to say hello, you hear?"

"Yessir."

"I hear about you two talking and you'll be in a heap of trouble. You understand?"

"Yessir," I whisper, wondering what this man know.

Mister Leefolt pick up his newspaper again. "I'll have that meat in a sandwich. Put a little mayonnaise on it. And not too toasted, I don't want it dry now."

THAT NIGHT, me and Minny's setting at my kitchen table. My hands started shaking this afternoon and ain't quit since.

"That ugly white fool," Minny say.

"I just wish I knew what he thinking."

They's a knock on the back door and Minny and me both look at each other. Only one person knock on my door like that, everbody else just come on in. I open it and there Miss Skeeter. "Minny here," I whisper, cause it's always safer to know when you gone walk in a room with Minny.

I'm glad she here. I got so much to tell her I don't even know where to start. But I'm surprised to see Miss Skeeter got something close to a smile on her face. I guess she ain't talk to Miss Hilly yet.

"Hello, Minny," she say when she step inside.

Minny look over at the window. "Hello, Miss Skeeter."

Fore I can get a word in, Miss Skeeter set down and start right in.

"I had some ideas while I was away. Aibileen, I think we should lead with your chapter first." She pull some papers out a that tacky red satchel. "And then Louvenia's we'll switch with Faye Belle's story, since we don't want three dramatic stories in a row. The middle we'll sort out later, but Minny, I think your section should definitely come last."

"Miss Skeeter . . . I got some things to tell you," I say.

Minny and me look at each other. "I'm on go," Minny say, frowning like her chair gotten too hard to sit in. She head for the door, but on her way out, she give Miss Skeeter a touch on the shoulder, real quick, keep her eyes straight like she ain't done it. Then she gone.

"You been out a town awhile, Miss Skeeter." I rub the back a my neck.

Then I tell her that Miss Hilly pulled that booklet out and showed it to Miss Leefolt. And Law knows who else she passing it around town to now.

Miss Skeeter nod, say, "I can handle Hilly. This doesn't implicate you, or the other maids, or the book at all."

And then I tell her what Mister Leefolt say, how he real clear that I ain't to talk to her no more about the cleaning article. I don't want a tell her these things, but she gone hear em and I want her to hear em from me first.

She listen careful, ask a few questions. When I'm done, she say, "He's full of hot air, Raleigh. I'll have to be extra careful, though, when I go over to Elizabeth's. I won't come in the kitchen anymore," and I can tell, this ain't really hitting her, what's happening. The trouble she in with her friends. How scared we need to be. I tell her what Miss Hilly say about letting her suffer through the League. I tell her she been kicked out a bridge club. I tell her that Miss Hilly gone tell Mister Stuart all about it, just in case he get any "inclination" to mend things with her.

Skeeter look away from me, try to smile. "I don't care about any of that ole stuff, anyway." She kind a laugh and it hurts my heart. Cause everbody care. Black, white, deep down we all do.

"I just...I rather you hear it from me than in town," I say. "So you know what's coming. So you can be real careful."

She bite her lip, nod. "Thank you, Aibileen."

CHAPTER 23

T HE SUMMER rolls behind us like a hot tar spreader. Ever colored person in Jackson gets in front a whatever tee-vee set they can find, watches Martin Luther King stand in our nation's capital and tell us he's got a dream. I'm in the church basement watching. Our own Reverend Johnson went up there to march and I find myself scanning the crowd for his face. I can't believe so many peoples is there—two-hundred-fifty *thousand*. And the ringer is, sixty thousand a them is *white*.

"Mississippi and the world is two very different places," the Deacon say and we all nod cause ain't it the truth.

We get through August and September and ever time I see Miss Skeeter, she look thinner, a little more skittish in the eyes. She try to smile like it ain't that hard on her that she ain't got no friends left.

In October, Miss Hilly sets at Miss Leefolt's dining room table. Miss Leefolt so pregnant she can't barely focus her eyes. Meanwhile, Miss Hilly got a big fur around her neck even though it's sixty degrees outside. She stick her pinky out from her tea glass and say, "Skeeter thought she was so clever, dumping all those toilets in my front yard. Well, they're working out just fine. We've already installed three of them in people's garages and sheds. Even William said it was a blessing in disguise."

I ain't gone tell Miss Skeeter this. That she ended up supporting the cause she fighting against. But then I see it don't matter cause Miss Hilly say, "I decided I'd write Skeeter a thank-you note last night. Told her how she's helped move the project along faster than it ever would've gone."

WITH MISS LEEFOLT SO BUSY making clothes for the new baby, Mae Mobley and me spend pretty much ever minute a the day together. She getting too big for me to carry her all the time, or maybe I'm too big. I try and give her a lot a good squeezes instead.

"Come tell me my secret story," she whisper, smiling so big. She always want her secret story now, first thing when I get in. The secret stories are the ones I be making up.

But then Miss Leefolt come in with her purse on her arm, ready to leave. "Mae Mobley, I'm leaving now. Come give Mama a big hug."

But Mae Mobley don't move.

Miss Leefolt, she got a hand on her hip, waiting for her sugar. "Go on, Mae Mobley," I whisper. I nudge her and she go hug her mama real hard, kinda desperate-like, but Miss Leefolt, she already looking in her purse for her keys, kind a wiggle off. It don't seem to bother Mae Mobley so much, though, like it used to, and that's what I can't hardly look at.

"Come on, Aibee," Mae Mobley say to me after her mama gone. "Time for my secret story."

We go on in her room, where we like to set. I get up in the big chair and she get up on me and smile, bounce a little. "Tell me, tell me bout the brown wrapping. And the present." She so excited, she squirming. She has to jump off my lap, squirm a little to get it out. Then she crawl back up.

That's her favorite story cause when I tell it, she get two presents. I take the brown wrapping from my Piggly Wiggly grocery bag and wrap up a little something, like piece a candy, inside. Then I use the white paper from my Cole's Drug Store bag and wrap another one just like it. She take it real serious, the unwrapping, letting me tell the story bout how it ain't the color a the wrapping that count, it's what we is inside.

"We doing a different story today," I say, but first I go still and listen, just to make sure Miss Leefolt ain't coming back cause she forgot something. Coast is clear.

"Today I'm on tell you bout a man from outer space." She just loves hearing about peoples from outer space. Her favorite show on the tee-vee is *My Favorite Martian*. I pull out my antennae hats I shaped last night out a tinfoil, fasten em on our heads. One for her and one for me. We look like we a couple a crazy people in them things.

"One day, a wise Martian come down to Earth to teach us people a thing or two," I say.

"Martian? How big?"

"Oh, he about six-two."

"What's his name?"

"Martian Luther King."

She take a deep breath and lean her head down on my shoulder. I feel her three-year-old heart racing against mine, flapping like butterflies on my white uniform.

"He was a real nice Martian, Mister King. Looked just like us, nose, mouth, hair up on his head, but sometime people looked at him funny and sometime, well, I guess sometime people was just downright mean."

I could get in a *lot* a trouble telling her these little stories, especially with Mister Leefolt. But Mae Mobley know these our "secret stories."

"Why Aibee? Why was they so mean to him?" she ask.

"Cause he was green."

Two TIMES THIS MORNING, Miss Leefolt's phone rung and two times I missed it. Once cause I was chasing Baby Girl nekkid in the backyard and another cause I was using the bathroom in the garage and what with Miss Leefolt being three—yes, *three*—weeks late to have this baby, I don't expect her to run for no phone. But I don't expect her to snap at me cause I couldn't get there, neither. Law, I should a known when I got up this morning.

Last night Miss Skeeter and I worked on the stories until a quarter to midnight. I am bone tired, but we done finished number eight and that means we still got four more to go. January tenth be the deadline and I don't know if we gone make it.

It's already the third Wednesday a October, so it's Miss Leefolt's turn to host bridge club. It's all changed up now that Miss Skeeter been thrown out. It's Miss Jeanie Caldwell, the one who call everybody honey, and Miss Lou Anne who replaced Miss Walter, and everybody's real polite and stiff and they just agree with each other for two hours. They ain't much fun listening to anymore.

I'm pouring the last ice tea when the doorbell go *ding-dong*. I get to the door real quick, show Miss Leefolt I ain't as slow as she accused me a being.

When I open it, the first word that pop in my head is *pink*. I never even seen her before but I've had enough conversations with Minny to know it's her. Cause who else around here gone fit extra-large bosoms in a extra-small sweater?

"Hello there," she say, licking her lipsticky lips. She raise her hand out to me and I think she giving me something. I reach out to take whatever it is and she give me a funny little handshake.

"My name is Celia Foote and I am here to see Miss Elizabeth Leefolt, please."

I'm so mesmerized by all that pink, it takes a few seconds to hit me how bad this could turn out for me. And Minny. It was a long time ago, but that lie stuck.

"I...she..." I'd tell her nobody's home but the bridge table's five feet behind me. I look back and all four a them ladies is staring at the door with they mouths open like they catching flies. Miss Caldwell whisper something to Miss Hilly. Miss Leefolt stagger up, slap on a smile.

"Hello, Celia," Miss Leefolt say. "It's certainly been a long time."

Miss Celia clears her throat and says kind a too loud, "Hello, Elizabeth. I'm calling on you today to—" Her eyes flicker back to the table where the other ladies is setting.

"Oh no, I'm interrupting. I'll just...I'll come on back. Another time."

"No, no, what can I do for you?" Miss Leefolt say.

Miss Celia takes a deep breath in that tight pink skirt and for a second I guess we all think she gone pop.

"I'm here to offer my help for the Children's Benefit."

Miss Leefolt smile, say, "Oh. Well, I . . ."

"I got a real knack for arranging flowers, I mean, everybody back in Sugar Ditch said so, even my maid said so, right after she said I'm the worst cook she's ever laid eyes on." She giggle at this a second and I suck in my breath at the word *maid*. Then she snap back to serious. "But I can address things and lick stamps and—"

Miss Hilly get up from the table. She lean in, say, "We really don't need any more help, but we'd be delighted if you and Johnny would attend the Benefit, Celia."

Miss Celia smile and look so grateful it'd break anybody's heart. Who had one.

"Oh thank you," she say. "I'd *love* to."

"It's on Friday night, November the fifteenth at the—"

"—the Robert E. Lee Hotel," Miss Celia finish. "I know all about it."

"We'd love to sell you some tickets. Johnny'll be coming with you, won't he? Go get her some tickets, Elizabeth."

"And if there's anything I can do to help—"

"No, no." Hilly smile. "We've got it all taken care of."

Miss Leefolt come back with the envelope. She fish out a few tickets, but then Miss Hilly take the envelope away from her.

"While you're here, Celia, why don't you buy some tickets for your friends?"

Miss Celia be frozen for a second. "Um, alright."

"How about ten? You and Johnny and eight friends. Then you'd have a whole table."

Miss Celia smiling so hard it starts to tremble. "I think just the two will be fine."

Miss Hilly take out two tickets and hand the envelope back to Miss Leefolt, who goes in the back to put it away.

"Lemme just get my check writ out. I'm lucky I have this big ole thing with me today. I told my maid Minny I'd pick up a hambone for her in town."

Miss Celia struggle to write that check on her knee. I stay still as I can, hoping to God Miss Hilly didn't hear what she just said. She hand the check to her but Miss Hilly all wrinkled up, thinking.

"Who? Who'd you say your maid was?"

"Minny Jackson. Aw! Shoot." Miss Celia pop her hand over her mouth. "Elizabeth made me swear I'd never tell she recommended her and here I am blabbing my mouth off."

"Elizabeth...recommended Minny Jackson?"

Miss Leefolt come back in from the bedroom. "Aibileen, she's up. Go on and get her now. I can't lift a nail file with my back."

I go real quick to Mae Mobley's room but soon as I peek in, Mae Mobley's done fallen asleep again. I rush back to the dining room. Miss Hilly's shutting the front door closed.

Miss Hilly set down, looking like she just swallowed the cat that ate the canary.

"Aibileen," Miss Leefolt say, "go on and get the salads ready now, we're all waiting."

I go in the kitchen. When I come back out, the salad plates is rattling like teeth on the serving tray.

"...mean the one who stole all your mama's silver and..."

"...thought everybody in town knew that Nigra was a thief..."

"...I'd never in a million years recommend..."

"...you see what she had on? Who does she..."

"I'm going to figure this out if it kills me," Miss Hilly say.

MINNY

CHAPTER 24

I'M AT THE KITCHEN SINK waiting for Miss Celia to come home. The rag I've been pulling on is in shreds. That crazy woman woke up this morning, squoze into the tightest pink sweater she has, which is saying something, and hollered, "I'm going to Elizabeth Leefolt's. Right now, while I got the nerve, Minny." Then she drove off in her Bel Aire convertible with her skirt hanging out the door.

I was just jittery until the phone rang. Aibileen was hiccupping she was so upset. Not only did Miss Celia tell the ladies that Minny Jackson is working for her, she informed them that Miss Leefolt was the one who "recommended" me. And that was all the story Aibileen heard. It'll take those cackling hens about five minutes to figure this out.

So now, I have to wait. Wait to find out if, Number One, my best friend in the entire world gets fired for getting me a job. And Number Two, if Miss Hilly told Miss Celia those lies that I'm a thief. And Number Two and a half, if Miss Hilly told Miss Celia how I got back at her for telling those lies that I'm a thief. I'm not sorry for the Terrible Awful Thing I done to her. But now that Miss Hilly put her own maid in jail to rot, I wonder what that lady's going to do to me.

It's not until ten after four, an hour past my time to leave, that I see Miss

Celia's car pull in. She jiggles up the walk like she's got something to say. I hitch up my hose.

"Minny, it's so late!" she yells.

"What happened with Miss Leefolt?" I'm not even trying to be coy. I want to know.

"Go, please! Johnny's coming home any minute." She's pushing me to the washroom where I keep my things.

"We'll talk tomorrow," she says, but for once, I don't want to go home, I want to hear what Miss Hilly said about me. Hearing your maid's a thief is like hearing your kid's teacher's a twiddler. You don't give them the benefit of the doubt, you just get the hell rid of em.

But Miss Celia won't tell me anything. She's shooing me out so she can keep up her charade, so twisted it's like kudzu. Mister Johnny knows about me. Miss Celia knows Mister Johnny knows about me. But Mister Johnny doesn't know that Miss Celia knows he knows. And because of that ridiculousness, I have to leave at four-oh-ten and worry about Miss Hilly for the entire night.

THE NEXT MORNING BEFORE WORK, Aibileen calls my house.

"I call poor Fanny early this morning cause I know you been stewing about it all night." Poor Fanny's Miss Hilly's new maid. Ought to call her Fool Fanny for working there. "She heard Miss Leefolt and Miss Hilly done decided you made the whole recommendation thing up so Miss Celia would give you the job."

Whew. I let out a long breath. "Glad you ain't gone get in trouble," I say. Still, now Miss Hilly calling me a liar *and* a thief.

"Don't you worry bout me," Aibileen says. "You just keep Miss Hilly from talking to your boss lady."

When I get to work, Miss Celia's rushing out to go buy a dress for the Benefit next month. She says she wants to be the first person in the store. It's not like the old days when she was pregnant. Now she can't wait to get out the door.

I stomp out to the backyard and wipe down the lawn chairs. The birds all twitter up in a huff when they see me coming, making the camellia bush rattle. Last spring Miss Celia was always nagging at me to take those flowers home. But I know camellias. You bring a bunch inside, thinking how it's so fresh it looks like it's moving and as soon as you go down for a sniff, you see you've brought an army full of spider mites in the house.

I hear a stick break, then another, behind the bushes. I prickle inside, hold still. We're out in the middle of nowhere and nobody would hear us call for miles. I listen, but I don't hear anything else. I tell myself it's just the old dregs of waiting for Mister Johnny. Or maybe I'm paranoid because I worked with Miss Skeeter last night on the book. I'm always jittery after talking to her.

Finally, I go back to cleaning pool chairs, picking up Miss Celia's movie magazines and tissues the slob leaves out here. The phone rings inside. I'm not supposed to answer the phone what with Miss Celia trying to keep up the big fat lie with Mister Johnny. But she's not here and it might be Aibileen with more news. I go inside, lock the door behind me.

"Miss Celia residence." Lord, I hope it's not Miss Celia calling.

"This is Hilly Holbrook speaking. Who is this?"

My blood whooshes down from my hair to my feet. I'm an empty, bloodless shell for about five seconds.

I lower my voice, make it deep like a stranger. "This Doreena. Miss Celia's help." *Doreena? Why I use my sister's name!*

"Doreena. I thought Minny Jackson was Miss Foote's maid."

"She...quit."

"Is that right? Let me speak to Missus Foote."

"She...out a town. Down at the coast. For a—a—" My mind's pedaling a thousand miles an hour trying to come up with details.

"Well, when is she coming back?"

"Looong time."

"Well, when she gets back, you tell her I called. Hilly Holbrook, Emerson three sixty-eight forty?"

"Yes ma'am. I tell her." In about a hundred years.

I hold on to the counter edge, wait for my heart to stop hammering. It's not that Miss Hilly can't find me. I mean, she could just look up Minny Jackson on Tick Road in the phone book and get my address. And it's not like I couldn't tell Miss Celia what happened, tell her I'm not a thief. Maybe she'd believe me after all. But it's the Terrible Awful that ruins it all.

Four hours later, Miss Celia walks in with five big boxes stacked on top of each other. I help her tote them back to her bedroom and then I stand very still outside her door to hear if she'll call up the society ladies like she does every day. Sure enough, I hear her pick up the phone. But she just hangs it back up again. The fool's listening for the dial tone again, in case someone tries to call.

EVEN THOUGH IT'S THE third week of October, the summer beats on with the rhythm of a clothes dryer. The grass in Miss Celia's yard is still a full-blown green. The orange dahlias are still smiling drunk up at the sun. And every night, the damn mosquitoes come out for their blood hunt, my sweat pads went up three cents a box, and my electric fan is broke dead on my kitchen floor.

On this October morning, three days after Miss Hilly called, I walk into work half an hour early. I've got Sugar seeing the kids to school. The coffee grinds go in the fancy percolator, the water goes in the pot. I lean my bottom against the counter. Quiet. It's what I've been waiting for all night long.

The Frigidaire picks up a hum where it left off. I put my hand on it to feel its vibration.

"You're awful early, Minny."

I open the refrigerator and bury my head inside. "Morning," I say from the crisper. All I can think is, *Not yet.*

I fiddle with some artichokes, the cold spines prickling my hand. Bent over like this, my head pounds even harder. "I'm on fix you and Mister Johnny a roast and I'm on…fix some…" But the words go all high-pitched on me.

"*Minny,* what happened?" Miss Celia has made her way around the refrigerator door without me even realizing it. My face bunches up. The cut on my eyebrow breaks open again, the hot blood stinging like a razor. Usually my bruises don't show.

"Honey, set down. Did you take a spill?" She props her hand on the hip of her pink nightgown. "Did you trip on the fan cord again?"

"I'm fine," I say, trying to turn so she can't see me. But Miss Celia's moving with me, bug-eyeing the cut like she's never seen anything so awful. I had a white lady tell me once that blood looks redder on a colored person. I take a wad of cotton from my pocket, hold it to my face.

"It's nothing," I say. "I banged it in the bathtub."

"Minny, that thing's bleeding. I think you need you some stitches. Let me get Doctor Neal over here." She grabs the phone from the wall, then bangs it back. "Oh, he's up at the hunting camp with Johnny. I'll call Doctor Steele, then."

"Miss Celia, I don't need no doctor."

"You need medical attention, Minny," she says, picking the phone back up.

Do I really have to say it? I grit my teeth to get it out. "Them doctors ain't gone work on no colored person, Miss Celia."

She hangs the phone up again.

I turn and face the sink. I keep thinking, *This ain't nobody's business, just do your work,* but I haven't had a minute's sleep. Leroy screamed at me all night, threw the sugar bowl upside my head, threw my clothes out on the porch. I mean, when he's drinking the Thunderbird, it's one thing, but . . . *oh.* The shame is so heavy I think it might pull me to the floor. Leroy, he wasn't on the Thunderbird this time. This time he beat me stone-cold sober.

"Go on out a here, Miss Celia, let me get some work done," I say because I just need some time alone. At first, I thought Leroy had found out about my working with Miss Skeeter. It was the only reason I could come up with while he was beating me with his hand. But he didn't say a thing about it. He was just beating me for the pure pleasure of it.

"Minny?" Miss Celia says, eyeing the cut again. "Are you sure you did that in the bathtub?"

I run the water just to get some noise in the room. "I told you I did and I did. Alright?"

She gives me a suspicious look and points her finger at me. "Alright, but I'm fixing you a cup of coffee and I want you to just take the day off, okay?" Miss Celia goes to the coffee percolator, pours two cups, but then stops. Looks at me kind of surprised.

"I don't know how you take your coffee, Minny."

I roll my eyes. "Same as you."

She drops two sugars into both mugs. She gives me my coffee and then she just stands, staring out the back window with her jaw set tight. I start washing last night's dishes, wishing she'd just leave me be.

"You know," she says kind of low, "You can talk to me about anything, Minny."

I keep washing, feel my nose start to flare.

"I've seen some things, back when I lived in Sugar Ditch. In fact..."

I look up, about to give it to her for getting in my business, but Miss Celia says in a funny voice, "We've got to call the police, Minny."

I put my coffee cup down so hard it splashes. "Now look a here, I don't want no police getting involved—"

She points out the back window. "There's a man, Minny! Out there!"

I turn to where's she's looking. A man—a *naked* man—is out by the azaleas. I blink to see if it's real. He's tall, mealy-looking and white. He's standing with his back to us, about fifteen feet away. His brown tangled hair is long like a hobo. Even from the back I can tell he's touching himself.

"Who is he?" Miss Celia whispers. "What's he doing here?"

The man turns to face front, almost like he heard us. Both our jaws drop. He's holding it out like he's offering us a po'boy sandwich.

"Oh... *God*," Miss Celia says.

His eyes search the window. They land right on mine, staring a dark line across the lawn. I shiver. It's like he knows me, Minny Jackson. He's staring with his lip curled like I deserved every bad day I've ever lived, every night I haven't slept, every blow Leroy's ever given. Deserved it and more.

And his fist starts punching his palm with a slow rhythm. Punch. Punch. Punch. Like he knows exactly what he's going to do with me. I feel the throb in my eye start again.

"We've got to call the police!" whispers Miss Celia. Her wide eyes dart to the phone on the other side of the kitchen, but she doesn't move an inch.

"It'll take em forty-five minutes just to find the house," I say. "He could break the door down by then!"

I run to the back door, flip the lock on. I dart to the front door and lock it, ducking down when I pass the back window. I stand up on my tiptoes, peek through the little square window on the back door. Miss Celia peeks around the side of the big window.

The naked man's walking real slow up toward the house. He comes up the back steps. He tries the doorknob and I watch it jiggle, feeling my heart whapping against my ribs. I hear Miss Celia on the phone, saying, "Police? We're getting intruded! There's a man! A naked man trying to get in the—"

I jump back from the little square window just in time for the rock to smash through, feel the sprinkle of shards hit my face. Through the big window, I see the man backing up, like he's trying to see where to break in next. *Lord,* I'm praying, *I don't want to do this, don't make me have to do this . . .*

Again, he stares at us through the window. And I know we can't just sit here like a duck dinner, waiting for him to get in. All he has to do is break a floor-to-ceiling window and step on in.

Lord, I know what I have to do. I have to go out there. I have to get him *first.*

"You stand back, Miss Celia," I say and my voice is shaking. I go get Mister Johnny's hunting knife, still in the sheath, from the bear. But the blade's so short, he'll have to be awful close for me to cut him, so I get the broom too. I look out and he's in the middle of the yard, looking up at the house. Figuring things out.

I open the back door and slip out. Across the yard, the man smiles at me, showing a mouth with about two teeth. He stops punching and goes back to stroking himself, smoothly, evenly now.

"Lock the door," I hiss behind me. "Keep it locked." I hear the click.

I tuck the knife in the belt of my uniform, make sure it's tight. And I grip the broom with both hands.

"You get on out a here, you fool!" I yell. But the man doesn't move. I take a few steps closer. And then so does he and I hear myself praying, *Lord protect me from this naked white man...*

"I got me a knife!" I holler. I take some more steps and he does too. When I get seven or eight feet from him, I'm panting. We both stare.

"Why, you're a fat nigger," he calls in a strange, high voice and gives himself a long stroke.

I take a deep breath. And then I rush forward and swing with the broom. *Whoosh!* I've missed him by inches and he dances away. I lunge again and the man runs toward the house. He heads straight for the back door, where Miss Celia's face is in the window.

"Nigger can't catch me! Nigger too fat to run!"

He makes it to the steps and I panic that he's going to try and bust down the door, but then he flips around and runs along the sideyard, holding that gigantic flopping po'boy in his hand.

"You get out a here!" I scream after him, feeling a sharp pain, knowing my cut's ripping wider.

I rush him hard from the bushes to the pool, heaving and panting. He slows at the edge of the water and I get close and land a good swing on his rear, *thwak!* The stick snaps and the brush-end flies off.

"Didn't hurt!" He jiggles his hand between his legs, hitching up his knees. "Have a little pecker pie, nigger? Come on, get you some pecker pie!"

I dive around him back to the middle of the yard, but the man is too tall and too fast and I'm getting slower. My swings are flying wild and soon I'm hardly even jogging. I stop, lean over, breathing hard, the short broken-off broom in my hand. I look down and the knife—it is *gone*.

As soon as I look back up, *whaaam!* I stagger. The ringing comes harsh and loud, making me totter. I cover my ear but the ringing gets louder. He's punched me on the same side as the cut.

He comes closer and I close my eyes, knowing what's about to happen to me, knowing I've got to move away but I can't. Where is the knife? Does he have the knife? The ringing's like a nightmare.

"You get out a here before I kill you," I hear, like it's in a tin can. My hearing's half gone and I open my eyes. There's Miss Celia in her pink satin nightgown. She's got a fire poker in her hand, heavy, sharp.

"White lady want a taste a pecker pie, too?" He flops his penis around at her and she steps closer to the man, slow, like a cat. I take a deep breath while the man jumps left, then right, laughing and chomping his toothless gums. But Miss Celia just stands still.

After a few seconds he frowns, looks disappointed that Miss Celia isn't doing anything. She's not swinging or frowning or hollering. He looks over at me. "What about you? Nigger too tired to—"

Crack!

The man's jaw goes sideways and blood bursts out of his mouth. He wobbles around, turns, and Miss Celia whacks the other side of his face too. Like she just wanted to even him up.

The man stumbles forward, looking nowhere in particular. Then he falls face flat.

"Lordy, you...you got him..." I say, but in the back of my head, there's this voice asking me, real calm, like we're just having tea out here, *Is this really happening?* Is a white woman really beating up a white man to save me? Or did he shake my brain pan loose and I'm over there dead on the ground...

I try to focus my eyes. Miss Celia, she's got a snarl on her lips. She raises her rod and *ka-wham!* across the back of his knees.

This ain't happening, I decide. This is just too damn strange.

Ka-wham! She hits him across his shoulders, making a *ugh* sound every time.

"I—I said you got him now, Miss Celia," I say. But evidently, Miss Celia doesn't think so. Even with my ears ringing, it sounds like chicken bones cracking. I stand up straighter, make myself focus my eyes before this turns into a homicide. "He down, he down, Miss Celia," I say. "Fact, he"—I struggle to catch the poker—"he might be dead."

I finally catch it and she lets go and the poker flies into the yard. Miss Celia steps back from him, spits in the grass. Blood's spattered across her pink satin nightgown. The fabric's stuck to her legs.

"He ain't dead," Miss Celia says.

"He close," I say.

"Did he hit you hard, Minny?" she asks, but she's staring down at him. "Did he hurt you bad?"

I can feel blood running down my temple but I know it's from the sugar bowl cut that's split open again. "Not as bad as you hurt him," I say.

The man groans and we both jump back. I grab the poker and the broom handle from the grass. I don't give her either one.

He rolls halfway over. His face is bloody on both sides, his eyes are swelling shut. His jaw's been knocked off its hinge and somehow he still brings himself to his feet. And then he starts to walk away, a pathetic wobbly thing. He doesn't even look back at us. We just stand there and watch him hobble through the prickly boxwood bushes and disappear in the trees.

"He ain't gone get far," I say, and I keep my grip on that poker. "You whooped him pretty good."

"You think?" she says.

I give her a look. "Like Joe Louis with a tire iron."

She brushes a clump of blond hair out of her face, looks at me like it kills her that I got hit. Suddenly I realize I ought to thank her, but truly, I've got no words to draw from. This is a brand-new invention we've come up with.

All I can say is, "You looked mighty...sure a yourself."

"I used to be a good fighter." She looks out along the boxwoods, wipes off her sweat with her palm. "If you'd known me ten years ago..."

She's got no goo on her face, her hair's not sprayed, her nightgown's like an old prairie dress. She takes a deep breath through her nose and I see it. I see the white trash girl she was ten years ago. She was strong. She didn't take no shit from nobody.

Miss Celia turns and I follow her back to the house. I see the knife in the rosebush and snatch it up. Lord, if that man had gotten hold of this, we'd be dead. In the guest bathroom, I clean the cut, cover it with a white bandage. The headache is bad. When I come out, I hear Miss Celia on the phone, talking to the Madison County police.

I wash my hands, wonder how an awful day could turn even worse. It seems like at some point you'd just run out of awful. I try to get my mind on real life again. Maybe I'll stay at my sister Octavia's tonight, show Leroy I'm not going to put up with it anymore. I go in the kitchen, put the beans on to simmer. Who am I fooling? I already know I'll end up at home tonight.

I hear Miss Celia hang up with the police. And then I hear her perform her usual pitiful check, to make sure the line is free.

THAT AFTERNOON, I do a terrible thing. I drive past Aibileen walking home from the bus stop. Aibileen waves and I pretend I don't even see my own best friend on the side of the road in her bright white uniform.

When I get to my house, I fix an icepack for my eye. The kids aren't home yet and Leroy's asleep in the back. I don't know what to do about anything, not Leroy, not Miss Hilly. Never mind I got boxed in the ear by a naked white man this morning. I just sit and stare at my oily yellow walls. Why can't I ever get these walls clean?

"Minny *Jackson*. You too good to give old Aibileen a ride?"

I sigh and turn my sore head so she can see.

"Oh," she says.

I look back at the wall.

"Aibileen," I say and hear myself sigh. "You ain't gone believe my day."

"Come on over. I make you some coffee."

Before I walk out, I peel that glaring bandage off, slip it in my pocket with my icepack. On some folks around here, a cut-up eye wouldn't even get a comment. But I've got good kids, a car with tires, and a refrigerator freezer. I'm proud of my family and the shame of the eye is worse than the pain.

I follow Aibileen through the sideyards and backyards, avoiding the traffic and the looks. I'm glad she knows me so well.

In her little kitchen, Aibileen puts the coffeepot on for me, the tea kettle for herself.

"So what you gone do about it?" Aibileen asks and I know she means the eye. We don't talk about me leaving Leroy. Plenty of black men leave their families behind like trash in a dump, but it's just not something the colored woman do. We've got the kids to think about.

"Thought about driving up to my sister's. But I can't take the kids, they got school."

"Ain't nothing wrong with the kids missing school a few days. Not if you protecting yourself."

I fasten the bandage back, hold the icepack to it so the swelling won't be so bad when my kids see me tonight.

"You tell Miss Celia you slip in the bathtub again?"

"Yeah, but she know."

"Why, what she say?" Aibileen ask.

"It's what she did." And I tell Aibileen all about how Miss Celia beat the naked man with the fire poker this morning. Feels like ten years ago.

"That man a been black, he be dead in the ground. Police would a had a all-points alert for fifty-three states," Aibileen say.

"All her girly, high-heel ways and she just about kill him," I say.

Aibileen laughs. "What he call it again?"

"Pecker pie. Crazy Whitfield fool." I have to keep myself from smiling because I know it'll make the cut split open again.

"Law, Minny, you have had some things happen to you."

"How come she ain't got no problem defending herself from that crazy man? But she chase after Miss Hilly like she just begging for abuse?" I say this even though Miss Celia getting her feelings hurt is the least of my worries right now. It just feels kind of good to talk about someone else's screwed-up life.

"Almost sounds like you care," Aibileen says, smiling.

"She just don't see em. The *lines*. Not between her and me, not between her and Hilly."

Aibileen takes a long sip of her tea. Finally I look at her. "What you so quiet for? I know you got a opinion bout all this."

"You gone accuse me a philosophizing."

"Go ahead," I say. "I ain't afraid a no philosophy."

"It ain't true."

"Say what?"

"You talking about something that don't exist."

I shake my head at my friend. "Not only is they lines, but you know good as I do where them lines be drawn."

Aibileen shakes her head. "I used to believe in em. I don't anymore. They in our heads. People like Miss Hilly is always trying to make us believe they there. But they ain't."

"I know they there cause you get punished for crossing em," I say. "Least I do."

"Lot a folks think if you talk back to you husband, you crossed the line. And that justifies punishment. You believe in that line?"

I scowl down at the table. "You know I ain't studying no line like that."

"Cause that line ain't there. Except in Leroy's head. Lines between black and white ain't there neither. Some folks just made those up, long time ago. And that go for the white trash and the so-ciety ladies too."

Thinking about Miss Celia coming out with that fire poker when she could've hid behind the door, I don't know. I get a twinge. I want her to understand how it is with Miss Hilly. But how do you tell a fool like her?

"So you saying they ain't no line between the help and the boss either?"

Aibileen shakes her head. "They's just positions, like on a checkerboard. Who work for who don't mean nothing."

"So I ain't crossing no line if I tell Miss Celia the truth, that she ain't good enough for Hilly?" I pick my cup up. I'm trying hard to get this, but my cut's thumping against my brain. "But wait, if I tell her Miss Hilly's out a her league... then ain't I saying they *is* a line?"

Aibileen laughs. She pats my hand. "All I'm saying is, kindness don't have no boundaries."

"Hmph." I put the ice to my head again. "Well, maybe I'll try to tell her. Before she goes to the Benefit and makes a big pink fool a herself."

"You going this year?" Aibileen asks.

"If Miss Hilly gone be in the same room as Miss Celia telling her lies about me, I want a be there. Plus Sugar wants to make a little money for Christmas. Be good for her to start learning party serving."

"I be there too," says Aibileen. "Miss Leefolt done asked me three months ago would I do a lady-finger cake for the auction."

"That old bland thing again? Why them white folks like the lady-fingers so much? I can make a dozen cakes taste better 'n that."

"They think it be real European." Aibileen shakes her head. "I feel bad for Miss Skeeter. I know she don't want a go, but Miss Hilly tell her if she don't, she lose her officer job."

I drink down the rest of Aibileen's good coffee, watch the sun sink. The air turns cooler through the window.

"I guess I got to go," I say, even though I'd rather spend the rest of my life right here in Aibileen's cozy little kitchen, having her explain the world to me. That's what I love about Aibileen, she can take the most complicated things in life and wrap them up so small and simple, they'll fit right in your pocket.

"You and the kids want a come stay with me?"

"No." I untack the bandage, slip it back in my pocket. "I want him to see me," I say, staring down at my empty coffee cup. "See what he done to his wife."

"Call me on the phone if he gets rough. You hear me?"

"I don't need no phone. You'll hear him screaming for mercy all the way over here."

THE THERMOMETER by Miss Celia's kitchen window sinks down from seventy-nine to sixty to fifty-five in less than an hour. At last, a cold front's moving in, bringing cool air from Canada or Chicago or somewhere. I'm picking the lady peas for stones, thinking about how we're breathing the same air those Chicago people breathed two days ago. Wondering if, for no good reason I started thinking about Sears and Roebuck or Shake 'n Bake, would it be because some Illinoian had thought it two days ago. It gets my mind off my troubles for about five seconds.

It took me a few days, but I finally came up with a plan. It's not a good one, but at least it's something. I know that every minute I wait is a chance for Miss Celia to call up Miss Hilly. I wait too long and she'll see her at the Benefit next week. It makes me sick thinking about Miss Celia running up to those girls like they're best friends, the look on her made-up face when she hears about me. This morning, I saw the list by Miss Celia's bed. Of what else she needs to do for the Benefit: Get fingernails done. Go to pantyhose store. Get tuxedo Martinized and pressed. Call Miss Hilly.

"Minny, does this new hair color look cheap?"

I just look at her.

"Tomorrow I am marching down to Fanny Mae's and getting it recolored." She's sitting at the kitchen table and holds up a handful of sample strips, splayed out like playing cards. "What do you think? Butterbatch or Marilyn Monroe?"

"Why you don't like you own natural color?" Not that I have any idea what that might be. But it's sure not the brass-bell or the sickly white on those cards in her hand.

"I think this Butterbatch is a little more festive, for the holidays and all. Don't you?"

"If you want your head to look like a Butterball turkey."

Miss Celia giggles. She thinks I'm kidding. "Oh and I have to show you this new fingernail polish." She scrambles in her purse, finds a bottle of something so pink it looks like you could eat it. She opens the bottle and starts painting on her nails.

"Please, Miss Celia, don't do that mess on the table, it don't come—"

"Look, isn't it the thing? And I've found two dresses to match it just exactly!"

She scoots off and comes back holding two hot pink gowns, smiling all over them. They're long to the floor, covered in sparkles and sequins, slits up the leg. Both hang by straps thin as chickenwire. They are going to tear her up at that party.

"Which one do you like better?" asks Miss Celia.

I point to the one without the low-cut neckline.

"Oh, see now, I would've chosen this other one. Listen to the little rattle it makes when I walk." She swishes the dress from side to side.

I think about her rattling around the party in that thing. Whatever the white version of a juke joint hussy is, that's what they'll be calling her. She won't even know what's happening. She'll just hear the hissing.

"You know, Miss Celia," I speak kind of slow like it's just now coming to me. "Instead a calling them other ladies, maybe you should call up Miss Skeeter Phelan. I heard she real nice."

I asked Miss Skeeter this favor a few days ago, to try and be nice to Miss Celia, steer her away from those ladies. Up to now, I've been telling Miss Skeeter not to dare call Miss Celia back. But now, it's the only option I have.

"I think you and Miss Skeeter would get along just fine," I say and I crank out a big smile.

"Oh no." Miss Celia looks at me all wide-eyed, holding up those saloon-looking gowns. "Don't you know? The League members can't *stand* Skeeter Phelan anymore."

My hands knuckle into fists. "You ever met her?"

"Oh, I heard all about it at Fanny Mae's setting under the heating hood. They said she's the biggest embarrassment this town's ever seen. Said she was the one who put all those toilets on Hilly Holbrook's front yard. Remember that picture that showed up in the paper a few months ago?"

I grind my teeth together to keep my real words in. "I *said*, have you ever met her?"

"Well, no. But if all those girls don't like her, then she must be...well she..." Her words trail off like it's just hitting her what she's saying.

Sickedness, disgust, disbelief—it all wraps together in me like a ham roll. To keep myself from finishing that sentence for her, I turn to the sink. I dry my hands to the point of hurting. I knew she was stupid, but I never knew she was a hypocrite.

"Minny?" Miss Celia says behind me.

"Ma'am."

She keeps her voice quiet. But I hear the shame in it. "They didn't even ask me in the house. They made me stand out on the steps like a vacuum salesman."

I turn around and her eyes are down to the floor.

"Why, Minny?" she whispers.

What can I say? Your clothes, your hair, your boobies in the size-nothing sweaters. I remember what Aibileen said about the lines and the kindness. I remember what Aibileen heard at Miss Leefolt's, of why the League ladies don't like her. It seems like the kindest reason I can think of.

"Because they know about you getting pregnant that first time. And it makes them mad you getting knocked up and marrying one a their mens."

"They *know* about that?"

"And especially since Miss Hilly and Mister Johnny went steady for so long."

She just blinks at me a second. "Johnny said he used to date her but...was it really for that long?"

I shrug like I don't know, but I do. When I started working at Miss Walters' eight years ago, all Miss Hilly talked about was how she and Johnny were going to get married someday.

I say, "I reckon they broke up right around the time he met you."

I'm waiting for it to hit her, that her social life is doomed. That there's no sense in calling the League ladies anymore. But Miss Celia looks like she's doing high math, the way she's got her brow scrunched up. Then her face starts to clear like she's figured something out.

"So Hilly...she probably thinks I was fooling around with Johnny while they were still going steady then."

"Probably. And from what I hear, Miss Hilly still sweet on him. She never got over him." I'm thinking, any normal person would automatically fie on a woman biding for her husband. But I forgot Miss Celia is not a normal person.

"Well, no wonder she can't stand me!" she says, grinning with all she's got. "They don't hate *me*, they hate what they think I did."

"What? They hate you cause they think you white trash!"

"Well, I'm just going to have to explain it to Hilly, let her know I am not a boyfriend stealer. In fact, I'll tell Hilly on Friday night, when I see her at the Benefit."

She's smiling like she just discovered the cure for polio, the way she's worked out a plan to win Miss Hilly over.

At this point, I am too tired to fight it.

.   .   .

On Benefit Friday, I work late cleaning that house top to bottom. Then I fry up a plate of pork chops. The way I figure it, the shinier the floors, the clearer the windowpanes, the better my chances are of having a job on Monday. But the smartest thing I can do, if Mister Johnny's got a say in this, is plant my pork chop in his hand.

He's not supposed to be home until six tonight, so at four-thirty I wipe the counters one last time, then head to the back where Miss Celia's been getting ready for the past four hours. I like to do their bed and bathroom last so it's clean for when Mister Johnny gets home.

"Miss Celia, now what is going on in here?" I mean, she's got stockings dangling from chairs, pocketbooks on the floor, enough costume jewelry for a whole family of hookers, forty-five pairs of high-heel shoes, underthings, overcoats, panties, brassieres, and a half-empty bottle of white wine on the chifforobe with no coaster under it.

I start picking up all her stupid silky things and piling them on the chair. The least I can do is run the Hoover.

"What time is it, Minny?" Miss Celia says from the bathroom. "Johnny'll be home at six, you know."

"Ain't even five yet," I say, "but I got to go soon." I have to pick up Sugar and get us to the party by six-thirty to serve.

"Oh Minny, I'm so excited." I hear Miss Celia's dress swishing behind me. "What do you think?"

I turn around. "Oh my Lord." I might as well be Little Stevie Wonder I am so blinded by that dress. Hot pink and silver sequins glitter from her extra-large boobies all the way to her hot pink toes.

"Miss Celia," I whisper. "Tuck yourself in fore you lose something."

Miss Celia shimmies the dress up. "Isn't it gorgeous? Ain't it just the prettiest thing you've ever seen? I feel like I'm a Hollywood movie star."

She bats her fake-lashed eyes. She is rouged, painted, and plastered with makeup. The Butterbatch hairdo is poufed up around her head like an Easter bonnet. One leg peeks out in a high, thigh-baring slit and I turn away, too embarrassed to look. Everything about her oozes sex, sex, and more sex.

"Where you get them fingernails?"

"At the Beauty Box this morning. Oh Minny, I'm so nervous, I've got butterflies."

She takes a heavy swig from her wineglass, kind of teeters a little in her high heels.

"What you had to eat today?"

"Nothing. I'm too nervous to eat. What about these earrings? Are they dangly enough?"

"Take that dress off, let me fix you some biscuits right quick."

"Oh no, I can't have my stomach poking out. I can't eat anything."

I head for the wine bottle on the gozillion-dollar chifforobe but Miss Celia gets to it before me, dumps the rest into her glass. She hands me the empty and smiles. I pick up her fur coat she's got tossed on the floor. She's getting pretty used to having a maid.

I saw that dress four days ago and I knew it looked hussified—of course she had to pick the one with the low neckline—but I had no idea what would happen when she stuffed herself inside it. She's popping out like a corn cob in Crisco. With twelve Benefits under my belt, I've hardly seen so much as a bare elbow there, much less bosoms and shoulders.

She goes in the bathroom and dabs some more rouge on her gaudy cheeks.

"Miss Celia," I say, and I close my eyes, praying for the right words. "Tonight, when you see Miss Hilly..."

She smiles into the mirror. "I got it all planned. When Johnny goes to the bathroom, I'm just going to tell her. That they were over with by the time me and Johnny started getting together."

I sigh. "That ain't what I mean. It's...she might say some things about...me."

"You want me to tell Hilly you said hi?" she says, coming out of the bathroom. "Since you worked all those years for her mama?"

I just stare at her in her hot pink getup, so full of wine she's almost cross-eyed. She burps up a little. There really isn't any use telling her now, in this state.

"No ma'am. Don't tell her nothing." I sigh.

She gives me a hug. "I'll see you tonight. I'm so glad you'll be there so I'll have somebody to talk to."

"I'll be in the kitchen, Miss Celia."

"Oh and I've got to find that little doo-hickey pin..." She teeters over to the dresser, yanks out all the things I just put away.

Just stay home, fool, is what I want to say to her, but I don't. It's too late. With Miss Hilly at the helm, it is too late for Miss Celia, and Lord knows, it is too late for me.

THE BENEFIT

CHAPTER 25

THE JACKSON JUNIOR LEAGUE Annual Ball and Benefit is known simply as "the Benefit" to anyone who lives within a ten-mile radius of town. At seven o'clock on a cool November night, guests will arrive at the Robert E. Lee Hotel bar for the cocktail hour. At eight o'clock, the doors from the lounge will open to the ballroom. Swags of green velvet have been hung around the windows, adorned with bouquets of real holly berries.

Along the windows stand tables with auction lists and the prizes. The goods have been donated by members and local shops, and the auction is expected to generate more than six thousand dollars this year, five hundred more dollars than last year. The proceeds will go to the Poor Starving Children of Africa.

In the center of the room, beneath a gigantic chandelier, twenty-eight tables are dressed and ready for the sit-down dinner to be served at nine. A dance floor and bandstand are off to the side, opposite the podium where Hilly Holbrook will give her speech.

After the dinner, there will be dancing. Some of the husbands will get drunk, but never the member wives. Every member there considers herself a hostess and will be heard asking one another, "Is it going alright? Has Hilly said anything?" Everyone knows it is Hilly's night.

At seven on the dot, couples begin drifting through the front doors, handing their furs and overcoats to the colored men in gray morning suits. Hilly, who's been there since six o'clock sharp, wears a long taffeta maroon-colored dress. Ruffles clutch at her throat, swathes of material hide her body. Tight-fitted sleeves run all the way down her arms. The only genuine parts of Hilly you can see are her fingers and her face.

Some women wear slightly saucier evening gowns, with bare shoulders here and there, but long kid-leather gloves ensure they don't have more than a few inches of epidermis exposed. Of course, every year some guest will show up with a hint of leg or a shadow of cleavage. Not much is said, though. They aren't members, those kind.

Celia Foote and Johnny arrive later than they'd planned, at seven twenty-five. When Johnny came home from work, he stopped in the doorway of the bedroom, squinted at his wife, briefcase still in his hand. "Celia, you think that dress might be a little bit too...um...open at the top?"

Celia had pushed him toward the bathroom. "Oh Johnny, you men don't know the first thing about fashion. Now hurry up and get ready."

Johnny gave up before he even tried to change Celia's mind. They were already late as it was.

They walk in behind Doctor and Missus Ball. The Balls step left, Johnny steps right, and for a moment, it is just Celia, standing under the holly berries in her sparkling hot pink gown.

In the lounge, the air seems to still. Husbands drinking their whiskeys stop in mid-sip, spotting this pink thing at the door. It takes a second for the image to register. They stare, but don't see, not yet. But as it turns real—real skin, real cleavage, perhaps not-so-real blond hair—their faces slowly light up. They all seem to be thinking the same thing—*Finally*...But then, feeling the fingernails of their wives, also staring, digging into their arms, their foreheads wrinkle. Their eyes hint remorse, as marriages are scorned (she never lets me do anything fun), youth is remembered (why didn't I go to California that summer?), first loves are recalled (Roxanne...). All of this happens in a span of about five seconds and then it is over and they are left just staring.

William Holbrook tips half his gin martini onto a pair of patent-leather shoes. The shoes are attached to the feet of his biggest campaign contributor.

"Oh, Claiborne, forgive my clumsy husband," says Hilly. "William, get him a handkerchief!" But neither man moves. Neither, frankly, really cares to do more than just stare.

Hilly's eyes follow the trail of gazes and finally land on Celia. The inch of skin showing on Hilly's neck grows taut.

"Look at the chest on that one," an old geezer says. "Feel like I'm not a year over seventy-five looking at those things."

The geezer's wife, Eleanor Causwell, an original founder of the League, frowns. "Bosoms," she announces, with a hand to her own, "are for bedrooms and breastfeeding. Not for occasions with dignity."

"Well, what do you want her to do, Eleanor? Leave them at home?"

"I *want* her to cover. Them. Up."

Celia grabs for Johnny's arm as they make their way into the room. She teeters a bit as she walks, but it's not clear if it's from alcohol or the high heels. They drift around, talking to other couples. Or at least Johnny talks; Celia just smiles. A few times she blushes, looks down at herself. "Johnny, do you think I might've overdressed a little for this thing? The invitation said formal, but these girls here all look like they're dressed for church."

Johnny gives her a sympathetic smile. He'd never tell her "I told you so," and instead whispers, "You look gorgeous. But if you're cold, you can put my jacket on."

"I can't wear a man's jacket with a ball gown." She rolls her eyes at him, sighs. "But thanks, honey."

Johnny squeezes her hand, gets her another drink from the bar, her fifth, although he doesn't know this. "Try and make some friends. I'll be right back." He heads for the men's room.

Celia is left standing alone. She tugs a little at the neckline of her dress, shimmies down deeper into the waist.

"*. . . there's a hole in the buck-et dear Liza, dear Liza. . .*" Celia sings an old county fair song softly to herself, tapping her foot, looking around the room for somebody she recognizes. She stands on tiptoe and waves over the crowd. "Hey Hilly, yoo-hoo."

Hilly looks up from her conversation a few couples away. She smiles, gives a wave, but as Celia comes toward her, Hilly heads off into the crowd.

Celia stops where she is, takes another sip of her drink. All around her, tight little groups have formed, talking and laughing, she guesses, about all those things people talk and laugh about at parties.

"Oh, hey there, Julia," Celia calls. They'd met at one of the few parties Celia and Johnny attended when they first got married.

Julia Fenway smiles, glances around.

"It's Celia. Celia Foote. How are you? Oh, I just love that dress. Where'd you get that? Over at the Jewel Taylor Shoppe?"

"No, Warren and I were in New Orleans a few months ago…" Julia looks around, but there is no one near enough to save her. "And you look very…glamorous tonight."

Celia leans closer. "Well, I asked Johnny, but you know how men are. Do you think I'm a tad overdressed?"

Julia laughs, but not once does she look Celia in the eye. "Oh no. You're just *perfect*."

A fellow Leaguer squeezes Julia on the forearm. "Julia, we need you over here a second, excuse us." They walk away, heads leaned close together, and Celia is alone again.

Five minutes later, the doors to the dining room slide open. The crowd moves forward. Guests find their tables using the tiny cards in their hands as oohs and aahs come from the bidding tables along the walls. They are full of silver pieces and hand-sewn daygowns for infants, cotton handkerchiefs, monogrammed hand towels, a child's tea set imported from Germany.

Minny is at a table in the back polishing glasses. "Aibileen," she whispers. "There she is."

Aibileen looks up, spots the woman who knocked on Miss Leefolt's door a month ago. "Ladies better hold on to they husbands tonight," she says.

Minny jerks the cloth around the rim of a glass. "Let me know if you see her talking to Miss Hilly."

"I will. I been doing a super power prayer for you all day."

"Look, there Miss Walters. Old bat. And there Miss Skeeter."

Skeeter has on a long-sleeved black velvet dress, scooped at the neck, setting off her blond hair, her red lipstick. She has come alone and stands in a pocket of emptiness. She scans the room, looking bored, then spots Aibileen and Minny. They all look away at once.

One of the other colored helpers, Clara, moves to their table, picks up a glass. "Aibileen," she whispers, but keeps her eyes on her polishing. "That the one?"

"One what?"

"One who taking down the stories bout the colored help. What she doing it for? Why she interested? I hear she been coming over to your house ever week."

Aibileen lowers her chin. "Now look, we got to keep her a secret."

Minny looks away. No one outside the group knows she's part of this. They only know about Aibileen.

Clara nods. "Don't worry, I ain't telling nobody nothing."

Skeeter jots a few words on her pad, notes for the newsletter article about the Benefit. She looks around the room, taking in the swags of green, the holly berries, red roses and dried magnolia leaves set as centerpieces on all the tables. Then her eyes land on Elizabeth, a few feet away, ticking through her handbag. She looks exhausted, having had her baby only a month ago. Skeeter watches as Celia Foote approaches Elizabeth. When Elizabeth looks up and sees who she's been surrounded by, she coughs, draws her hand up to her throat as if she's shielding herself from some kind of attack.

"Not sure which way to turn, Elizabeth?" asks Skeeter.

"What? Oh, Skeeter, how are you?" Elizabeth offers a quick, wide smile. "I was...feeling so warm in here. I think I need some fresh air."

Skeeter watches Elizabeth rush away, at Celia Foote rattling after Elizabeth in her awful dress. *That's the real story,* Skeeter thinks. *Not the flower arrangements or how many pleats are around the rear end of Hilly's dress. This year, it's all about The Celia Foote Fashion Catastrophe.*

Moments later, dinner is announced and everyone settles into their assigned seats. Celia and Johnny have been seated with a handful of out-of-town couples, friends of friends who aren't really friends of anyone at all. Skeeter is seated with a few local couples, not President Hilly or even Secretary Elizabeth this year. The room is full of chatter, praise for the party, praise for the Chateaubriand. After the main course, Hilly stands behind the podium. There is a round of applause and she smiles at the crowd.

"Good evening. I sure do thank y'all for coming tonight. Everybody enjoying their dinner?"

There are nods and rumbles of consent.

"Before we start the announcements, I'd like to go ahead and thank the people who are making tonight such a success." Without turning her head from the audience, Hilly gestures to her left, where two dozen colored women have lined up, dressed in their white uniforms. A dozen colored men are behind them, in gray-and-white tuxedos.

"Let's give a special round of applause to the help, for all the wonderful food they cooked and served, and for the desserts they made for the auction." Here, Hilly picks up a card and reads, "In their own way, they are helping the League reach its goal to feed the Poor Starving Children of Africa, a cause, I'm sure, dear to their own hearts as well."

The white people at the tables clap for the maids and servers. Some of the servers smile back. Many, though, stare at the empty air just above the crowd's heads.

"Next we'd like to thank those nonmembers in this room who have given their time and help, for it's you who made our job that much easier."

There is light applause, some cold smiles and nods between members and nonmembers. *Such a pity*, the members seem to be thinking. *Such a shame you girls haven't the gentility to join our club.* Hilly goes on, thanking and recognizing in a musical, patriotic voice. Coffee is served and the husbands drink theirs, but most of the women keep rapt attention on Hilly. "...thanks to Boone Hardware...let us not forget Ben Franklin's dime store..." She concludes the list with, "And of course we thank our anonymous contributor of, ahem, *supplies*, for the Home Help Sanitation Initiative."

A few people laugh nervously, but most turn their heads to see if Skeeter has had the gall to show up.

"I just wish instead of being so shy, you'd step up and accept our gratitude. We honestly couldn't have accomplished so many installations without you."

Skeeter keeps her eyes on the podium, her face stoic and unyielding. Hilly gives a quick, brilliant smile. "And finally, a special thanks to my husband, William Holbrook, for donating a weekend at his deer camp." She smiles down at her husband, adds in a lower tone, "And don't forget, voters. Holbrook for State Senate."

The guests offer an amicable laugh at Hilly's plug.

"What's that, Virginia?" Hilly cups her ear, then straightens. "No, I'm not running with him. But congressmen with us tonight, if you don't straighten this thing out with the separate schools, don't think I won't come down there and do it myself."

There is more laughter at this. Senator and Missus Whitworth, seated at a table in the front, nod and smile. At her table in the back, Skeeter looks down at her lap. They spoke earlier, during the cocktail hour. Missus Whitworth steered the Senator away from Skeeter before he could give her a second hug. Stuart didn't come.

Once the dinner and the speech have ended, people get up to dance, husbands head for the bar. There is a scurry to the auction tables for last-minute bids. Two grandmothers are in a bidding war over the child's antique tea set. Someone started the rumor that it had belonged to royalty and had been smuggled out via donkey cart across Germany until it eventually wound up in the Magnolia Antique Store on Fairview Street. The price shot up from fifteen dollars to eighty-five in no time.

In the corner by the bar, Johnny yawns. Celia's brow is scrunched together. "I can't believe what she said about nonmembers helping. She told me they didn't need any help this year."

"Well, you can help out next year," Johnny says.

Celia spots Hilly. For the moment, Hilly has only a few people around her.

"Johnny, I'll be right back," Celia says.

"And then let's get the hell out of here. I'm sick of this monkey suit."

Richard Cross, who's a member of Johnny's duck camp, slaps Johnny's back. They say something, then laugh. Their gazes sweep across the crowd.

Celia almost makes it to Hilly this time, only to have Hilly slip behind the podium table. Celia backs away, as if she's afraid to approach Hilly where she'd seemed so powerful a few minutes ago.

As soon as Celia disappears into the ladies room, Hilly heads for the corner.

"Why Johnny Foote," Hilly says. "I'm surprised to see you here. Everybody knows you can't stand big parties like this." She squeezes the crook of his arm.

Johnny sighs. "You are aware that doe season opens tomorrow?"

Hilly gives him an auburn-lipsticked smile. The color matches her dress so perfectly, it must have been searched out for days.

"I am so tired of hearing that from everybody. You can miss one day of hunting season, Johnny Foote. You used to for me."

Johnny rolls his eyes. "Celia wouldn't have missed this for anything."

"Where *is* that wife of yours?" she asks. Hilly's still got her hand tucked in the crook of Johnny's arm and she gives it another pull. "Not at the LSU game serving hot dogs, is she?"

Johnny frowns down at her, even though it's true, that's how they met.

"Oh, now you know I'm just teasing you. We dated long enough to where I can do that, can't I?"

Before Johnny can answer, Hilly's shoulder is tapped and she glides over to the next couple, laughing. Johnny sighs when he sees Celia headed toward him. "Good," he says to Richard, "we can go home. I'm getting up in," he looks at his watch, "five hours."

Richard keeps his eyes locked on Celia as she strides toward them. She stops and bends down to retrieve her dropped napkin, offering a generous view of her bosoms. "Going from Hilly to Celia must've been quite the change, Johnny."

Johnny shakes his head. "Like living in Antarctica all my life and one day moving to Hawaii."

Richard laughs. "Like going to bed in seminary and waking up at Ole Miss," Richard says, and they both laugh.

Then Richard adds in a lower voice, "Like a kid eating ice cream for the very first time."

Johnny gives him a look. "That's my wife you're talking about."

"Sorry, Johnny," Richard says, lowering his eyes. "No harm meant."

Celia walks up, sighs with a disappointed smile.

"Hey Celia, how are you?" Richard says. "You sure are looking nice tonight."

"Thanks, Richard." Celia lets out a loud hiccup and she frowns, covers her mouth with a tissue.

"You getting tipsy?" asks Johnny.

"She's just having fun, aren't you, Celia?" Richard says. "In fact, I'm fixing to get you a drink you're gonna love. It's called an Alabama Slammer."

Johnny rolls his eyes at his friend. "And then we're going home."

Three Alabama Slammers later, the winners of the silent auction are announced. Susie Pernell stands behind the podium while people mill about drinking or smoking at the tables, dancing to Glenn Miller and Frankie Valli songs, talking over the din of the microphone. As names are read, items are received with the excitement of someone winning a real contest, as if the booty were free and not paid for at three, four, or five times the store value. Tablecloths and nightgowns with the lace tatted by hand bring in high bids. Odd sterling servers are popular, for spooning out deviled eggs, removing pimentos from olives, cracking quail legs. Then there are the desserts: cakes, slabs of pralines, divinity fudge. And of course, Minny's pie.

"...and the winner of Minny Jackson's world-famous chocolate custard pie is...Hilly Holbrook!"

There is a little more applause for this one, not just because Minny's known for her treats, but because the name *Hilly* elicits applause on any occasion.

Hilly turns from her conversation. "What? Was that my name? I didn't bid on anything."

She never does, Skeeter thinks, sitting alone, a table away.

"Hilly, you just won Minny Jackson's pie! Congratulations," says the woman to her left.

Hilly scans the room, eyes narrowed.

Minny, having heard her name called in the same sentence as Hilly's, is suddenly very alert. She is holding a dirty coffee cup in one hand, a heavy silver tray in the other. But she stands stock-still.

Hilly spots her, but doesn't move either, just smiles very slightly. "Well. Wasn't that sweet? Someone must've signed me up for that pie."

She doesn't take her eyes off Minny and Minny can feel it. She stacks the rest of the cups on the tray, and heads for the kitchen as fast as she can.

"Why congratulations, Hilly. I didn't know you were such a fan of Minny's pies!" Celia's voice is shrill. She's come up from behind without Hilly noticing. As she trots toward Hilly, Celia stumbles over a chair leg. There are sideline giggles.

Hilly stands very still, watching her approach. "Celia, is this some kind of joke?"

Skeeter moves in closer too. She's bored to death by this predictable evening. Tired of seeing embarrassed faces of old friends too scared to come and speak to her. Celia's the only interesting thing to happen all night.

"Hilly," Celia says, grasping Hilly's arm, "I've been trying to talk to you all night. I think there's been some kind of miscommunication between us and I just think if I *explained*..."

"What have you done? Let me go—" Hilly says between gritted teeth. She shakes her head, tries to walk off.

But Celia clutches Hilly's long sleeve. "No, wait! Hang on, you got to listen—"

Hilly pulls away, but still Celia doesn't let go. There's a moment of determination between them—Hilly trying to escape, Celia holding on, and then a ripping sound cuts through the air.

Celia stares at the red material in her fingers. She's torn the auburn cuff clear off Hilly's arm.

Hilly looks down, touches her exposed wrist. "What are you trying to do to me?" she says in a low growl. "Did that Nigra maid put you up to this? Because whatever she told you and whatever you've blabbed to anyone else here—"

Several more people have gathered around them, listening, all looking at Hilly with frowns of concern.

"Blabbed? I don't know what you—"

Hilly grabs Celia's arm. "*Who* did you tell?" she snarls.

"Minny told me. I know why you don't want to be friends with me." Susie Pernell's voice over the microphone announcing the winners grows louder, forcing Celia to raise her own voice. "I know you think me and Johnny went behind your back," she yells, and there is laughter from the front of the room over some comment, and more applause. Just as Susie Pernell pauses over the microphone to look at her notes, Celia yells, "—but I got pregnant *after* you broke up." The room echoes with the words. All is silent for a few long seconds.

The women around them wrinkle their noses, some start to laugh. "Johnny's wife is *d-r-u-n-k*," someone says.

Celia looks around her. She wipes at the sweat that's beading on her makeuped forehead. "I don't blame you for not liking me, not if you thought Johnny cheated on you with me."

"Johnny never would've—"

"—and I'm sorry I said that, I thought you'd be tickled you won that pie."

Hilly bends over, snatches her pearl button from the floor. She leans closer to Celia so no one else can hear. "You tell your Nigra maid if she tells anybody about that pie, I will make her suffer. You think you're real cute signing me up for that auction, don't you? What, you think you can blackmail your way into the League?"

"What?"

"You tell me right this *minute* who else you've told ab—"

"I didn't tell nobody nothing about a pie, I—"

"You *liar*," Hilly says, but she straightens quickly and smiles. "There's Johnny. Johnny, I think your wife needs your *attention*." Hilly flashes her eyes at the girls around them, as if they're all in on a joke.

"Celia, what's wrong?" Johnny says.

Celia scowls at him, then scowls at Hilly. "She's not making sense, she called me a—a liar, and now she's accusing me of signing her name on that pie and…" Celia stops, looks around like she recognizes no one around her. She has tears in her eyes. Then she groans and convulses. Vomit splatters onto the carpet.

"Oh shit!" Johnny says, pulling her back.

Celia pushes Johnny's arm off her. She runs for the bathroom and he follows her.

Hilly's hands are in fists. Her face is crimson, nearly the color of her dress. She marches over and grabs a waiter's arm. "Get that cleaned up before it starts to smell."

And then Hilly is surrounded by women, faces upturned, asking questions, arms out like they are trying to protect her.

"I heard Celia's been battling with drinking, but this problem with lying now?" Hilly tells one of the Susies. It's a rumor she'd intended to spread about Minny, in case the pie story ever got out. "What do they call that?"

"A compulsive liar?"

"That's it, a compulsive liar." Hilly walks off with the women. "Celia trapped him into that marriage, telling him she was pregnant. I guess she was a compulsive liar even back then."

After Celia and Johnny leave, the party winds down quickly. Member wives look exhausted and tired of smiling. There is talk of the auction, of babysitters to get home to, but mostly of Celia Foote retching in the middle of it all.

When the room is nearly empty, at midnight, Hilly stands at the podium. She flips through the sheets of silent bids. Her lips move as she calculates. But she keeps looking off, shaking her head. Then she looks back down and curses because she has to start all over again.

"Hilly, I'm headed on back to your house."

Hilly looks up from tallying. It is her mother, Missus Walters, looking even frailer than usual in her formalwear. She wears a floor-length gown, sky blue and beaded, from 1943. A white orchid wilts at her clavicle. A colored woman in a white uniform is attached to her side.

"Now, Mama, don't you get in that refrigerator tonight. I won't have you keeping me up all night with your indigestion. You go right to bed, you hear?"

"I can't even have some of Minny's pie?"

Hilly narrows her eyes at her mother. "That *pie* is in the garbage."

"Well, why'd you throw it out? I won it just for you."

Hilly is still a moment, letting this sink in. "*You?* You signed me up?"

"I may not remember my name or what country I live in, but you and that pie is something I will never forget."

"You—you old, useless..." Hilly throws down the papers she's holding, scattering them everywhere.

Missus Walters turns and hobbles toward the door, the colored nurse in tow. "Well, call the papers, Bessie," she says. "My daughter's mad at me again."

MINNY

ON SATURDAY MORNING, I get up tired and sore. I walk in the kitchen where Sugar's counting out her nine dollars and fifty cents, the money she earned at the Benefit last night. The phone rings and Sugar's on it quicker than a grease fire. Sugar's got a boyfriend and she doesn't want her mama to know.

"Yessir," Sugar whispers and hands me the phone.

"Hello?" I say.

"It's Johnny Foote," he says. "I'm up at deer camp but I just want you to know, Celia's real upset. She had a rough time at the party last night."

"Yessir, I know."

"You heard, then, huh?" He sighs. "Well, keep an eye on her next week, will you, Minny? I'll be gone and— I don't know. Just call me if she doesn't perk up. I'll come home early if I need to."

"I look after her. She gone be alright."

I didn't see myself what happened at the party, but I heard about it while I was doing dishes in the kitchen. All the servers were talking about it.

"You see that?" Farina said to me. "That big pink lady you work for, drunk as a Injun on payday."

I looked up from my sink and saw Sugar headed straight for me with her hand up on her hip. "Yeah, Mama, she upchuck all over the floor. And *everbody* at the whole party see!" Then Sugar turned around, laughing with the others. She didn't see the *whap* coming at her. Soapsuds flew through the air.

"You shut your mouth, Sugar." I yanked her to the corner. "Don't you never let me hear you talking bad about the lady who put food in your mouth, clothes on your back! You hear me?"

Sugar, she nodded and I went back to my dishes, but I heard her muttering. "*You* do it, all the *time.*"

I whipped around and put my finger in her face. "I got a right to. I earn it every day working for that crazy fool."

WHEN I GET TO WORK on Monday, Miss Celia's still laid up in bed with her face buried under the sheets.

"Morning, Miss Celia."

But she just rolls over and won't look at me.

At lunchtime, I take a tray of ham sandwiches to the bed.

"I'm not hungry," she says and throws the pillow over her head.

I stand there looking at her, all mummified in the sheets.

"What you gone do, just lay there all day?" I ask, even though I've seen her do it plenty of times before. But this is different. There's no goo on her skin or smile on her face.

"Please, just leave me alone."

I start to tell her she needs to just get up, put on her tacky clothes, and forget about it, but the way she's laying there so pitiful and poor, I keep quiet. I am not her psychiatrist and she's not paying me to be one.

On Tuesday morning, Miss Celia's still in the bed. Yesterday's lunch tray's on the floor without a single bite missing. She's still in that ratty blue night-gown that looks left over from her Tunica County days, the gingham ruffle torn at the neck. Something that looks like charcoal stains on the front.

"Come on, lemme get to them sheets. Show bout to come on and Miss Julia gone be in trouble. You ain't gone believe what that fool done yester-day with Doctor Bigmouth."

But she just lays there.

Later on, I bring her a tray of chicken pot pie. Even though what I really want to do is tell Miss Celia to pull herself together and go in the kitchen and eat proper.

"Now, Miss Celia, I know it was terrible what happened at the Benefit. But you can't set in here forever feeling sorry for yourself."

Miss Celia gets up and locks herself in the bathroom.

I start stripping the bed. When I'm done, I pick up all the wet tissues and glasses off the nightstand. I see a stack of mail. At least the woman's gotten up to go to the mailbox. I pick it up to wipe the table and there I see the letters H W H across the top of a card. Before I know it, I've read the whole note:

> *Dear Celia,*
>
> *In lieu of reimbursing me for my dress you tore, we at the League would gladly receive a donation of no less than two hundred dollars. Furthermore, please withhold from volunteering for any nonmember activities in the future, as your name has been placed on a probationary list. Your cooperation in this matter is appreciated.*
>
> *Do kindly make the check out to the Jackson League Chapter.*
>
> *Sincerely,*
>
> *Hilly Holbrook*
>
> *President and Chairman of Appropriations*

ON WEDNESDAY MORNING, Miss Celia's *still* under the covers. I do my work in the kitchen, try to appreciate the fact that she's not hanging around with me in here. But I can't enjoy it because the phone's been ringing all morning, and for the first time since I started, Miss Celia won't pick it up. After the tenth time, I can't listen to it anymore and finally just grab it and say hello.

I go in her bedroom, tell her, "Mister Johnny on the phone."

"What? He's not supposed to know that I know that he knows about you."

I let out a big sigh to show I don't give a fat rat about that lie anymore. "He called me at *home*. The jig is up, Miss Celia."

Miss Celia shuts her eyes. "Tell him I'm asleep."

I pick up the bedroom line and look Miss Celia hard in the eye and tell him she's in the shower.

"Yessir, she doing alright," I say and narrow my eyes at her.

I hang up the phone and glare down at Miss Celia.

"He want to know how you doing."

"I heard."

"I lied for you, you know."

She puts the pillow back over her head.

By the next afternoon, I can't stand it another minute. Miss Celia's still in the same spot she's been all week. Her face is thin and that Butterbatch is greasy-looking. The room is starting to smell too, like dirty people. I bet she hasn't bathed since Friday.

"Miss Celia," I say.

Miss Celia looks at me, but doesn't smile, doesn't speak.

"Mister Johnny gone be home tonight and I told him I'd look after you. What's he gone think if he find you laid up in that old nasty nightthing you got on?"

I hear Miss Celia sniffle, then hiccup, then start to cry full-on. "None of this would've happened if I'd just stayed where I belonged. He should've married proper. He should've married . . . *Hilly*."

"Come on, Miss Celia. It ain't—"

"The way Hilly looked at me . . . like I was *nothing*. Like I was trash on the side of the road."

"But Miss Hilly don't count. You can't judge yourself by the way that woman see you."

"I'm not right for this kind of life. I don't need a dinner table for twelve people to sit at. I couldn't get twelve people to come over if I begged."

I shake my head at her. Complaining again cause she has too much.

"Why does she hate me so much? She doesn't even know me," Miss Celia cries. "And it's not just Johnny, she called me a liar, accused me of getting her that...*pie.*" She bangs her fists against her knees. "I *never* would a thrown up if it wasn't for that."

"What pie?"

"H-H-Hilly won your pie. And she accused me of signing her up for it. Playing some...trick on her." She wails and sobs. "Why would I do that? Write her name down on a list?"

It comes to me real slow what's going on here. I don't know who signed up Hilly for that pie, but I sure *know* why she'd eat alive anybody she thought did it.

I glance over at the door. That voice in my head says, *Walk away, Minny. Just ease on out a here.* But I look at Miss Celia bawling into her old night-gown, and I get a guilt thick as Yazoo clay.

"I can't do this to Johnny anymore. I've already decided, Minny. I'm going back," she sobs. "Back to Sugar Ditch."

"You gone leave your husband just cause you threw up at some party?" *Hang on,* I think, my eyes opening wide. Miss Celia can't leave Mister Johnny—where in the heck would that leave me?

Miss Celia cries down harder at the reminder. I sigh and watch her, won-dering what to do.

Lord, I reckon it's time. Time I told her the one thing in the world I never want to tell anybody. I'm going to lose my job either way, so I might as well take the chance.

"Miss Celia..." I say and I sit down in the yellow armchair in the corner. I've never sat anywhere in this house but in the kitchen and her bathroom floor, but today calls for extreme measures.

"I know why Miss Hilly got so mad," I say. "About the pie, I mean."

Miss Celia blows a hard, loud honk into a tissue. She looks at me.

"I did something to her. It was Terrible. Awful." My heart starts thump-ing just thinking about it. I realize I can't sit in this chair and tell her this story at the same time. I get up and walk to the end of the bed.

"What?" she sniffs. "What happened, Minny?"

"Miss Hilly, she call me up at home last year, when I's still working for Miss Walters. To tell me she sending Miss Walters to the old lady home. I got scared, I got five kids to feed. Leroy was already working two shifts."

I feel a burn rise up in my chest. "Now I know what I did wasn't Christian. But what kind a person send her own mama to the home to take up with strangers? They's something bout doing wrong to that woman that make it just seem *right*."

Miss Celia sits up in bed, wipes her nose. She looks like she's paying attention now.

"For three weeks, I be looking for work. Ever day after I get off from Miss Walters', I went looking. I go over to Miss Child's house. She pass me up. I go on to the Rawleys' place, they don't want me neither. The Riches, the Patrick Smiths, the Walkers, not even those Catholic Thibodeaux with them seven kids. Nobody do."

"Oh Minny..." says Miss Celia. "That's awful."

I clench my jaw. "Ever since I was a li'l girl, my mama tell me not to go sass-mouthing. But I didn't listen and I got knowed for my mouth round town. And I figure that's what it be, why nobody want to hire me.

"When they was two days left at Miss Walters's and I still didn't have no new job, I start getting real scared. With Benny's asthma and Sugar still in school and Kindra and...we was tight on money already. And that's when Miss Hilly, she come over to Miss Walters's to talk to me.

"She say, 'Come work for me, Minny. I pay you twenty-five more cent a day than Mama did.' A 'dangling carrot' she call it, like I was some kind a plow mule." I feel my fists forming. "Like I'd even consider beating my friend Yule May Crookle out a her job. Miss Hilly think everbody just as two-faced as she is."

I wipe my hand across my face. I'm sweating. Miss Celia's listening with her mouth open, looking dazed.

"I tell her 'No thank you, Miss Hilly.' And so she say she pay me fifty cent more and I say, 'No ma'am. No thank you.' Then she break my back, Miss Celia. She tell me she know bout the Childs and the Rawleys and all them others that turn me down. Said it was cause she'd made sure everbody knew I was a thief. I've never stole a thing in my life but she told everbody I did and wasn't nobody in town gone hire a sass-mouthing thieving Nigra for a maid and I might as well go head and work for her for free.

"And that's how come I did it."

Miss Celia blinks at me. "What, Minny?"

"I tell her to eat my shit."

Miss Celia sits there, still looking dazed.

"Then I go home. I mix up that chocolate custard pie. I puts sugar in it and Baker's chocolate and the real vanilla my cousin bring me from Mexico.

"I tote it over to Miss Walters's house, where I know Miss Hilly be setting round, waiting for the home to come and get her mama, so she can sell that house. Go through her silver. Collect her due.

"Soon as I put that pie down on the countertop, Miss Hilly smiles, thinking it's a peace offering, like that's my way a showing her I'm real sorry bout what I said. And then I watch her. I watch her eat it myself. Two big pieces. She stuff it in her mouth like she ain't ever eaten nothing so good. Then she say, 'I knew you'd change your mind, Minny. I knew I'd get my way in the end.' And she laugh, kind a prissy, like it was all real funny to her.

"That's when Miss Walters, she say she getting a mite hungry too and ask for a piece a that pie. I tell her, 'No ma'am. That one's special for Miss Hilly.'

"Miss Hilly say, 'Mama can have some if she wants. Just a little piece, though. What do you put in here, Minny, that makes it taste so good?'

"I say 'That good vanilla from Mexico' and then I go head. I tell her what else I put in that pie for her."

Miss Celia's still as a stone staring at me, but I can't meet her eyes now.

"Miss Walters, her mouth fall open. Nobody in that kitchen said anything for so long, I could a made it out the door fore they knew I's gone. But then Miss Walters start laughing. Laugh so hard she almost fall out the chair. Say, 'Well, Hilly, that's what you get, I guess. And I wouldn't go tattling on Minny either, or you'll be known all over town as the lady who ate *two* slices of Minny's shit.'"

I sneak a look up at Miss Celia. She's staring wide-eyed, disgusted. I start to panic that I told her this. She'll never trust me again. I walk over to the yellow chair and sit myself down.

"Miss Hilly thought you knew the story. That you were making fun a her. She never would a pounced on you if I hadn't done what I did."

Miss Celia just stares at me.

"But I want you to know, if you leave Mister Johnny, then Miss Hilly done won the whole ball game. Then she done beat me, she beat you..." I shake my head, thinking about Yule May in jail, and Miss Skeeter without any friends left. "There ain't many people left in this town that she ain't beat."

Miss Celia's quiet awhile. Then she looks over at me and starts to say something, but she shuts her mouth back.

Finally, she just says, "Thank you. For... telling me that."

She lays back down. But before I close the door, I can see her eyes are wide smack open.

THE NEXT MORNING, I find Miss Celia's finally managed to get herself out of bed, wash her hair, and put all that makeup on again. It's cold outside so she's back in one of her tight sweaters.

"Glad to have Mister Johnny back home?" I ask. Not that I care, but what I do want to know is if she's still fiddling with the idea of leaving.

But Miss Celia doesn't say much. There's a tiredness in her eyes. She's not so quick to smile at every little thing. She points her finger out the kitchen window. "I think I'll plant a row of rosebushes. Along the back of the property."

"When they gone bloom?"

"We should see something by next spring."

I take this as a good sign, that she's planning for the future. I figure somebody running off wouldn't go to the trouble to plant flowers that won't bloom until next year.

For the rest of the day, Miss Celia works in the flower garden, tending to the mums. The next morning I come in and find Miss Celia at the kitchen table. She's got the newspaper out, but she's staring out at that mimosa tree. It's rainy and chilly outside.

"Morning, Miss Celia."

"Hey, Minny." Miss Celia just sits, looking out at that tree, fiddling with a pen in her hand. It's started to rain.

"What you want for lunch today? We got a roast beef or some a this chicken pie left over..." I lean in the refrigerator. I've got to make a decision about Leroy, tell him how it is. *Either you quit beating on me, or I'm gone. And I'm not taking the kids either.* Which ain't true, about the kids, but that ought to scare him more than anything.

"I don't want anything." Miss Celia stands up, slips off one red high heel, then the other. She stretches her back, still staring out the window at that tree. She cracks her knuckles. And then she walks out the back door.

I see her on the other side of the glass and then I see the axe. I get a little spooked because nobody likes to see a crazy lady with an axe in her hand. She swings it hard through the air, like a bat. A practice chop.

"Lady, you done lost it this time." The rain is pouring down all over Miss Celia, but she doesn't care. She starts chopping at that tree. Leaves are sprinkling down all over her, sticking in her hair.

I set the platter of roast beef down on the kitchen table and watch, hoping this doesn't turn into something. She bunches her mouth up, wipes the rain from her eyes. Instead of getting tired, every chop comes a little harder.

"Miss Celia, come on out the rain," I holler. "Let Mister Johnny do that when he get home."

But she's nothing doing. She's made it halfway through that trunk and the tree's starting to sway a little, drunk as my daddy. Finally I just plop down in the chair where Miss Celia was reading, wait for her to finish the job. I shake my head and look down at the newspaper. That's when I see Miss Hilly's note tucked underneath it and Miss Celia's check for two hundred dollars. I look a little closer. Along the bottom of the check, in the little space for the notes, Miss Celia's written the words in pretty cursive handwriting: *For Two-Slice Hilly.*

I hear a groan and see the tree crash to the ground. Leaves and dead fronds fly through the air, sticking all over her Butterbatch.

Miss Skeeter

CHAPTER 27

I STARE AT THE PHONE in the kitchen. No one's called here in so long, it's like a dead thing mounted to the wall. There's a terrible quiet looming everywhere—at the library, at the drugstore where I pick up Mother's medicine, on High Street where I buy typewriter ink, in our own house. President Kennedy's assassination, less than two weeks ago, has struck the world dumb. It's like no one wants to be the first to break the silence. Nothing seems important enough.

On the rare occasion that the phone does ring lately, it's Doctor Neal, calling with more bad test results, or a relative checking on Mother. And yet, I still think *Stuart* sometimes, even though it's been five months since he's called. Even though I finally broke down and told Mother we'd broken up. Mother looked shocked, as I suspected she would, but thankfully, just sighed.

I take a deep breath, dial zero, and close myself up in the pantry. I tell the local operator the long distance number and wait.

"Harper and Row, Publishers, how may I connect you?"

"Elaine Stein's office, please."

I wait for her secretary to come on the line, wishing I'd done this earlier. But it felt wrong to call the week of Kennedy's death and I heard on the news most offices were closed. Then it was Thanksgiving week and when I called, the switchboard told me no one was answering in her office at all, so now I'm calling more than a week later than I'd planned.

"Elaine Stein."

I blink, surprised it's not her secretary. "Missus Stein, I'm sorry, this is—Eugenia Phelan. In Jackson, Mississippi."

"Yes...Eugenia." She sighs, evidently irritated that she took the chance to answer her own phone.

"I was calling to let you know that the manuscript will be ready right after the new year. I'll be mailing it to you the second week of January." I smile, having delivered my rehearsed lines perfectly.

There is silence, except for an exhale of cigarette smoke. I shift on the flour can. "I'm...the one writing about the colored women? In Mississippi?"

"Yes, I remember," she says, but I can't tell if she really does. But then she says, "You're the one who applied for the senior position. How is that project going?"

"It's almost finished. We just have two more interviews to complete and I was wondering if I should send it directly to your attention or to your secretary."

"Oh no, January is not acceptable."

"Eugenia? Are you in the house?" I hear Mother call.

I cover the phone. "Just a minute, Mama," I call back, knowing if I don't, she'll barge in here.

"The last editor's meeting of the year is on December twenty-first," Missus Stein continues. "If you want a chance at getting this read, I've got to have it in my hands by then. Otherwise it goes in The Pile. You don't want to be in The Pile, Miss Phelan."

"But...you told me January..." Today is December second. That only gives me nineteen days to finish the entire thing.

"December twenty-first is when everyone leaves for vacation and then in the new year we're deluged with projects from our own list of authors and journalists. If you're a nobody, as you are, Miss Phelan, before the twenty-first is your window. Your only window."

I swallow, "I don't know if..."

"By the way, was that your mother you were speaking to? Do you still live at home?"

I try to think of a lie—she's just visiting, she's sick, she's passing through, because I do not want Missus Stein to know that I've done nothing with my life. But then I sigh. "Yes, I still live at home."

"And the Negro woman who raised you, I'm assuming she's still there?"

"No, she's gone."

"Mmm. Too bad. Do you know what happened to her? It's just occurred to me, you'll need a section about your own maid."

I close my eyes, fighting frustration. "I don't . . . know, honestly."

"Well, find out and definitely get that in. It'll add something personal to all this."

"Yes ma'am," I say, even though I have no idea how I'll finish two maids in time, much less write stories about Constantine. Just the thought of writing about her makes me wish, deeply, that she was here now.

"Goodbye, Miss Phelan. I hope you make the deadline," she says, but before she hangs up, she mutters, "and for God's sake, you're a twenty-four-year-old educated woman. Go get an apartment."

I GET OFF THE PHONE, stunned by the news of the deadline and Missus Stein's insistence to get Constantine in the book. I know I need to get to work immediately, but I check on Mother in her bedroom. In the past three months, her ulcers have gotten much worse. She's lost more weight and can't get through two days without vomiting. Even Doctor Neal looked surprised when I brought her in for her appointment last week.

Mother eyes me up and down from her bed. "Don't you have bridge club today?"

"It's canceled. Elizabeth's baby is colicky," I lie. So many lies have been told, the room is thick with them. "How are you feeling?" I ask. The old white enamel bowl is next to her on the bed. "Have you been sick?"

"I'm fine. Don't wrinkle your forehead like that, Eugenia. It's not good for your complexion."

Mother still doesn't know that I've been kicked out of bridge club or that Patsy Joiner got a new tennis partner. I don't get invited to cocktail parties or baby showers anymore, or any functions where Hilly will be there. Except the League. At meetings, girls are short, to the point with me when discussing newsletter business. I try to convince myself I don't care. I fix myself at my typewriter and don't leave most days. I tell myself, that's what you get when you put thirty-one toilets on the most popular girl's front yard. People tend to treat you a little differently than before.

It was almost four months ago that the door was sealed shut between Hilly and me, a door made of ice so thick it would take a hundred Mississippi summers to melt it. It's not as if I hadn't expected consequences. I just hadn't thought they'd last so long.

Hilly's voice over the phone was gravelly sounding, low, like she'd been yelling all morning. "You are sick," she hissed at me. "Do not speak to me, do not look at me. Do not say hello to my children."

"Technically it was a typo, Hilly," was all I could think to say.

"I am going over to Senator Whitworth's house myself and telling him you, Skeeter Phelan, will be a blight on his campaign in Washington. A wart on the face of his reputation if Stuart ever associates with you again!"

I cringed at the mention of his name, even though we'd been broken up for weeks by then. I could imagine him looking away, not caring what I did anymore.

"You turned my yard into some kind of a sideshow," Hilly'd said. "Just how long have you been planning to humiliate my family?"

What Hilly didn't understand was, I hadn't planned it at all. When I started typing out her bathroom initiative for the newsletter, typing words like *disease* and *protect yourself* and *you're welcome!*, it was like something cracked open inside of me, not unlike a watermelon, cool and soothing and sweet. I always thought insanity would be a dark, bitter feeling, but it is drenching and delicious if you really roll around in it. I'd paid Pascagoula's brothers twenty-five dollars each to put those junkyard pots onto Hilly's lawn and they were scared, but willing to do it. I remember how dark the night had been. I remember feeling lucky that some old building had been gutted and there were so many toilets at the junkyard to choose from. Twice I've dreamed I was back there doing it again. I don't regret it, but I don't feel quite as lucky anymore.

"And you call yourself a *Christian*," were Hilly's final words to me and I thought, *God. When did I ever do that?*

This November, Stooley Whitworth won the senator's race for Washington. But William Holbrook lost the local election, to take his state seat. I'm quite sure Hilly blames me for this too. Not to mention all that work she'd put into setting me up with Stuart was for nothing.

A FEW HOURS after talking to Missus Stein over the phone, I tiptoe back to check on Mother one last time. Daddy's already asleep beside her. Mother has a glass of milk on the table. She's propped up on her pillows but her eyes are closed. She opens them as I'm peeking in.

"Can I get you anything, Mama?"

"I'm only resting because Doctor Neal told me to. Where are you going, Eugenia? It's nearly seven o'clock."

"I'll be back in a little while. I'm just going for a drive." I give her a kiss, hoping she doesn't ask any more questions. When I close the door, she's already fallen asleep.

I drive fast through town. I dread telling Aibileen about the new deadline. The old truck rattles and bangs in the potholes. It's in fast decline after another hard cotton season. My head practically hits the ceiling because someone's retied the seat springs too tight. I have to drive with the window down, my arm hanging out so the door won't rattle. The front window has a new smash in it the shape of a sunset.

I pull up to a light on State Street across from the paper company. When I look over, there's Elizabeth and Mae Mobley and Raleigh all crammed in the front seat of their white Corvair, headed home from supper somewhere, I guess. I freeze, not daring to look over again, afraid she'll see me and ask what I'm doing in the truck. I let them drive ahead, watching their taillights, fighting a hotness rising in my throat. It's been a long time since I've talked to Elizabeth.

After the toilet incident, Elizabeth and I struggled to stay friends. We still talked on the phone occasionally. But she stopped saying more than a hello and a few empty sentences to me at League meetings, because Hilly would see her. The last time I stopped by Elizabeth's house was a month ago.

"I can't believe how big Mae Mobley's gotten," I'd said. Mae Mobley had smiled shyly, hid behind her mother's leg. She was taller but still soft with baby fat.

"Growing like a weed," Elizabeth said, looking out the window, and I thought, what an odd thing to compare your child to. A weed.

Elizabeth was still in her bathrobe, hair rollers in, already tiny again after the pregnancy. Her smile stayed tight. She kept looking at her watch, touching her curlers every few seconds. We stood around the kitchen.

"Want to go to the club for lunch?" I asked. Aibileen swung through the kitchen door then. In the dining room, I caught a glimpse of silver and Battenburg lace.

"I can't and I hate to rush you out but…Mama's meeting me at the Jewel Taylor Shoppe." She shot her eyes out the front window again. "You know how Mama hates to wait." Her smile grew exponentially.

"Oh, I'm sorry, don't let me keep you." I patted her shoulder and headed for the door. And then it hit me. How could I be so dumb? It's Wednesday, twelve o'clock. My old bridge club.

I backed the Cadillac down her drive, sorry that I'd embarrassed her so. When I turned, I saw her face stretched up to the window, watching me leave. And that's when I realized: she wasn't embarrassed that she'd made me feel bad. Elizabeth Leefolt was embarrassed to be seen with me.

I PARK ON AIBILEEN'S STREET, several houses down from hers, knowing we need to be even more cautious than ever. Even though Hilly would never come to this part of town, she is a threat to us all now and I feel like her eyes are everywhere. I know the glee she would feel catching me doing this.

I don't underestimate how far she would go to make sure I suffered the rest of my life.

It's a crisp December night and a fine rain is just starting to fall. Head down, I hurry along the street. My conversation this afternoon with Missus Stein is still racing through my head. I've been trying to prioritize everything left to do. But the hardest part is, I have to ask Aibileen, again, about what happened to Constantine. I cannot do a just job on Constantine's story if I don't know what's happened to her. It defeats the point of the book, to put in only part of the story. It wouldn't be telling the truth.

I hurry into Aibileen's kitchen. The look on my face must tell her something's wrong.

"What is it? Somebody see you?"

"No," I say, pulling papers from my satchel. "I talked to Missus Stein this morning." I tell her everything I know, about the deadline, about "The Pile."

"Alright, so..." Aibileen is counting days in her head, the same way I have been all afternoon. "So we got two and a half weeks stead a six weeks. Oh Law, that ain't enough time. We still got to finish writing the Louvenia section and smooth out Faye Belle—and the Minny section, it ain't right yet...Miss Skeeter, we ain't even got a title yet."

I put my head in my hands. I feel like I'm slipping underwater. "That's not all," I say. "She...wants me to write about Constantine. She asked me...what happened to her."

Aibileen sets her cup of tea down.

"I can't write it if I don't know what happened, Aibileen. So if you can't tell me...I was wondering if there's someone else who will."

Aibileen shakes her head. "I reckon they is," she says, "but I don't want nobody else telling you that story."

"Then...will you?"

Aibileen takes off her black glasses, rubs her eyes. She puts them back on and I expect to see a tired face. She's worked all day and she'll be working even harder now to try to make the deadline. I fidget in my chair, waiting for her answer.

But she doesn't look tired at all. She's sitting up straight and gives me a defiant nod. "I'll write it down. Give me a few days. I'll tell you ever thing that happened to Constantine."

I work for fifteen hours straight on Louvenia's interview. On Thursday night, I go to the League meeting. I'm dying to get out of the house, antsy from nerves, jittery about the deadline. The Christmas tree is starting to smell too rich, the spiced oranges sickly decadent. Mother is always cold and my parents' house feels like I'm soaking in a vat of hot butter.

I pause on the League steps, take in a deep breath of clean winter air. It's pathetic, but I'm glad to still have the newsletter. Once a week, I actually feel like I'm a part of things. And who knows, maybe this time will be different, with the holidays starting and all.

But the minute I walk in, backs turn. My exclusion is tangible, as if concrete walls have formed around me. Hilly gives me a smirk, whips her head around to speak to someone else. I go deeper into the crowd and see Elizabeth. She smiles and I wave. I want to talk to her about Mother, tell her I'm getting worried, but before I get too close, Elizabeth turns, head down, and walks away. I go to my seat. This is new, from her, here.

Instead of my usual seat up front, I slip in the back row, angry that Elizabeth wouldn't even say hello. Beside me is Rachel Cole Brant. Rachel hardly ever comes to meetings, with three kids, working on her master's in English from Millsaps College. I wish we were better friends but I know she's too busy. On my other side is damn Leslie Fullerbean and her cloud of hairspray. She must risk her life every time she lights a cigarette. I wonder, if I pushed the top of her head, would aerosol spray out of her mouth.

Almost every girl in the room has her legs crossed, a lit cigarette in her hand. The smoke gathers and curls around the ceiling. I haven't smoked in two months and the smell makes me feel ill. Hilly steps up to the podium and announces the upcoming gimme-drives (coat drive, can drive, book drive, and a plain old money drive), and then we get to Hilly's favorite part of the meeting, the trouble list. This is where she gets to call out the names of anyone late on their dues or tardy for meetings or not fulfilling their philanthropic duties. I'm always on the trouble list nowadays for something.

Hilly's wearing a red wool A-line dress with a cape coat over it, Sherlock Holmes–style, even though it's hot as fire in here. Every once in a while, she tosses back the front flap like it's in her way, but she looks like she enjoys this gesture too much for it to really be a problem. Her helper Mary Nell stands next to her, handing her notes. Mary Nell has the look of a blond lapdog, the Pekingese kind with tiny feet and a nose that perks on the end.

"Now, we have something very exciting to discuss." Hilly accepts the notes from the lapdog and scans over them.

"The committee has decided that our newsletter could use a little updating."

I sit up straighter. Shouldn't I decide on changes to the newsletter?

"First of all, we're changing the newsletter from a weekly to a monthly. It's just too much with stamps going up to six cents and all. And we're adding a fashion column, highlighting some of the best outfits worn by our members, and a makeup column with all the latest trends. Oh, and the trouble list of course. That'll be in there too." She nods her head, making eye contact with a few members.

"And finally, the most exciting change: we've decided to name this new correspondence *The Tattler*. After the European magazine all the ladies over there read."

"Isn't that the cutest name?" says Mary Lou White and Hilly's so proud of herself, she doesn't even bang the gavel at her for speaking out of turn.

"Okay then. It is time to choose an editor for our new, modern monthly. Any nominations?"

Several hands pop up. I sit very still.

"Jeanie Price, what say ye?"

"I say Hilly. I nominate Hilly Holbrook."

"Aren't you the sweetest thing. Alright, any others?"

Rachel Cole Brant turns and looks at me like, *Are you believing this?* Evidently, she's the only one in the room who doesn't know about me and Hilly.

"Any seconds to . . ." Hilly looks down at the podium, like she can't quite remember who's been nominated. "To Hilly Holbrook as editor?"

"I second."

"I third."

Bang-bang goes the gavel and I've I lost my post as editor.

Leslie Fullerbean is staring at me with eyes so wide, I can see there isn't anything back there where her brain should be.

"Skeeter, isn't that *your* job?" Rachel says.

"It *was* my job," I mutter and head straight for the doors when the meeting is over. No one speaks to me, no one looks me in the eye. I keep my head high.

In the foyer, Hilly and Elizabeth talk. Hilly tucks her dark hair behind her ears, gives me a diplomatic smile. She strides off to chat with someone else, but Elizabeth stays where she is. She touches my arm as I walk out.

"Hey, Elizabeth," I murmur.

"I'm sorry, Skeeter," she whispers and our eyes hang together. But then she looks away. I walk down the steps and into the dark parking lot. I thought she had something more to say to me, but I guess I was wrong.

I DON'T GO STRAIGHT HOME after the League meeting. I roll all the Cadillac windows down and let the night air blow on my face. It is warm and cold at the same time. I know I need to go home and work on the stories, but I turn onto the wide lanes of State Street and just drive. I've never felt so empty in my life. I can't help but think of all that's piling on top of me. *I will never make this deadline, my friends despise me, Stuart is gone, Mother is...*

I don't know what Mother is, but we all know it's more than just stomach ulcers.

The Sun and Sand Bar is closed and I go by slow, stare at how dead a neon sign seems when it's turned off. I coast past the tall Lamar Life building, through the yellow blinking street lights. It's only eight o'clock at night but everyone has gone to bed. Everyone's asleep in this town in every way possible.

"I wish I could just leave here," I say and my voice sounds eerie, with no one to hear it. In the dark, I get a glimpse of myself from way above, like in a movie. I've become one of those people who prowl around at night in their cars. God, I am the town's Boo Radley, just like in *To Kill a Mockingbird*.

I flick on the radio, desperate for noise to fill my ears. "It's My Party" is playing and I search for something else. I'm starting to hate the whiny teenage songs about love and nothing. In a moment of aligned wavelengths, I pick up Memphis WKPO and out comes a man's voice, drunk-sounding, singing fast and bluesy. At a dead end street, I ease into the Tote-Sum store parking lot and listen to the song. It is better than anything I've ever heard.

... you'll sink like a stone
For the times they are a-changin'.

A voice in a can tells me his name is Bob Dylan, but as the next song starts, the signal fades. I lean back in my seat, stare out at the dark windows of the store. I feel a rush of inexplicable relief. I feel like I've just heard something from the future.

At the phone booth outside the store, I put in a dime and call Mother. I know she'll wait up for me until I get home.

"Hello?" It's Daddy's voice at eight-fifteen at night.

"Daddy... why are you up? What's wrong?"

"You need to come on home now, darling."

The streetlight suddenly feels too bright in my eyes, the night very cold. "Is it Mama? Is she sick?"

"Stuart's been sitting on the porch for almost two hours now. He's waiting on you."

Stuart? It doesn't make sense. "But Mama... she's..."

"Oh, Mama's fine. In fact, she's brightened up a little. Come on home, Skeeter, and tend to Stuart now."

THE DRIVE HOME has never felt so long. Ten minutes later, I pull in front of the house and see Stuart sitting on the top porch step. Daddy's in a rocking chair. They both stand when I turn off the car.

"Hey, Daddy," I say. I don't look at Stuart. "Where's Mama?"

"She's asleep, I just checked on her." Daddy yawns. I haven't seen him up past seven o'clock in ten years, when the spring cotton froze.

"'Night, you two. Turn the lights out when you're done." Daddy goes inside and Stuart and I are left alone. The night is so black, so quiet, I can't see stars or a moon or even a dog in the yard.

"What are you doing here?" I say and my voice, it sounds small.

"I came to talk to you."

I sit on the front step and put my head down on my arms. "Just say it fast and then go on. I was getting better. I heard this song and almost felt better ten minutes ago."

He moves closer to me, but not so close that we are touching. I wish we were touching.

"I came to tell you something. I came to say that I saw her."

I lift my head up. The first word in my head is *selfish*. You selfish son-of-a-bitch, coming here to talk about Patricia.

"I went out there, to San Francisco. Two weeks ago. I got in my truck and drove for four days and knocked on the door of the apartment house her mama gave me the address to."

I cover my face. All I can see is Stuart pushing her hair back like he used to with me. "I don't want to know this."

"I told her I thought that was the ugliest thing you could do to a person. Lie that way. She looked so different. Had on this prairie-looking dress and a peace sign and her hair was long and she didn't have any lipstick on. And she laughed when she saw me. And then she called me a whore." He rubs his eyes hard with his knuckles. "She, the one who took her clothes off for that guy—said I was a whore to my daddy, a whore to Mississippi."

"Why are you telling me this?" My fists are clenched. I taste metal. I've bitten down on my tongue.

"I drove out there because of you. After we broke up, I knew I had to get her out of my head. And I did it, Skeeter. I drove two thousand miles there and back and I'm here to tell you. It's dead. It's gone."

"Well, good, Stuart," I say. "Good for you."

He moves closer and leans down so I will look at him. And I feel sick, literally nauseated by the smell of bourbon on his breath. And yet I still want to fold myself up and put my entire body in his arms. I am loving him and hating him at the same time.

"Go home," I say, hardly believing myself. "There's no place left inside me for you."

"I don't believe that."

"You're too late, Stuart."

"Can I come by on Saturday? To talk some more?"

I shrug, my eyes full of tears. I won't let him throw me away again. It's already happened too many times, with him, with my friends. I'd be stupid to let it happen again.

"I don't really care what you do."

I WAKE UP AT FIVE A.M. and start working on the stories. With only seventeen days until our deadline, I work through the day and night with a speed and efficiency I didn't know I possessed. I finish Louvenia's story in half the time it took me to write the others and, with an intense burning headache, I turn off the light as the first rays of sun peek through the window. If Aibileen will give me Constantine's story by early next week, I just might be able to pull this off.

And then I realize I do not have seventeen more days. How *dumb* of me. I have ten days, because I haven't accounted for the time it will take to mail it to New York.

I'd cry, if only I had the time to do it.

A few hours later, I wake up and go back to work. At five in the afternoon, I hear a car pull up and see Stuart climb out of his truck. I tear myself away from the typewriter and go out on the front porch.

"Hello," I say, standing in the doorway.

"Hey, Skeeter." He nods at me, shyly I think, compared to his way two nights ago. "Afternoon, Mister Phelan."

"Hey there, son." Daddy gets up from his rocking chair. "I'll let you kids talk out here."

"Don't get up, Daddy. I'm sorry, but I'm busy today, Stuart. You're welcome to sit out here with Daddy as long as you like."

I go back in the house, pass Mother at the kitchen table drinking warm milk.

"Was that Stuart I saw out there?"

I go in the dining room. I stand back from the windows, where I know Stuart can't see me. I watch until he drives away. And then I just keep watching.

THAT NIGHT, AS USUAL, I go to Aibileen's. I tell her about the deadline of only ten days, and she looks like she might cry. Then I hand her Louvenia's chapter to read, the one I've written at lightning speed. Minny is at the kitchen table with us, drinking a Coke, looking out the window. I hadn't known she'd be here tonight and wish she'd leave us to work.

Aibileen puts it down, nods. "I think this chapter is right good. Read just as well as the slow-wrote ones."

I sigh, leaning back in my chair, thinking of what else needs to be done. "We need to decide on the title," I say and rub my temples. "I've been working on a few. I think we should call it *Colored Domestics and the Southern Families for Which They Work.*"

"Say what?" Minny says, looking at me for the first time.

"That's the best way to describe it, don't you think?" I say.

"If you got a corn cob up you butt."

"This isn't fiction, Minny. It's sociology. It has to sound exact."

"But that don't mean it have to sound boring," Minny says.

"Aibileen," I sigh, hoping we can resolve this tonight. "What do you think?"

Aibileen shrugs and I can see already, she's putting on her peace-making smile. It seems she has to smooth things over every time Minny and I are in the same room. "That's a good title. A course you gone get tired a typing all that on top a ever page," she says. I'd told her this is how it has to be done.

"Well, we could shorten it a little…" I say and pull out my pencil.

Aibileen scratches her nose, says, "What you think about just calling it...*Help*?"

"*Help*," Minny repeats, like she's never heard of the word.

"*Help*," I say.

Aibileen shrugs, looks down shyly, like she's a little embarrassed. "I ain't trying to take over your idea, I just...I like to keep things simple, you know?"

"I guess *Help* sound alright to me," Minny says and crosses her arms.

"I like...*Help*," I say, because I really do. I add, "I think we'll still have to put the description underneath, so the category's clear, but I think that's a good title."

"Good is right," Minny says. "Cause if this thing gets printed, Lord knows we gone need some."

ON SUNDAY AFTERNOON, with eight days left, I come downstairs, dizzy and blinking from staring at pica type all day. I was almost glad when I heard Stuart's car pull up the drive. I rub my eyes. Maybe I'll sit with him awhile, clear my head, then go back and work through the night.

Stuart climbs out of his mud-splattered truck. He's still in his Sunday tie and I try to ignore how handsome he looks. I stretch my arms. It's ridiculously warm out, considering Christmas is in two and a half weeks. Mother's sitting on the porch in a rocking chair, swathed in blankets.

"Hello, Missus Phelan. How are you feeling today?" Stuart asks.

Mother gives him a regal nod. "Fair. Thank you for asking." I'm surprised by the coolness in her voice. She turns back to her newsletter and I can't help but smile. Mother knows he's been stopping by but she hasn't mentioned it but once. I have to wonder when it will come.

"Hey," he says to me quietly and we sit on the bottom porch step. Silently, we watch our old cat Sherman sneak around a tree, his tail swaying, going after some creature we can't see.

Stuart puts his hand on my shoulder. "I can't stay today. I'm heading to Dallas right now for an oil meeting and I'll be gone three days," he says. "I just came by to tell you."

"Alright." I shrug, like it makes no difference.

"Alright then," he says and gets back in his truck.

When he has disappeared, Mother clears her throat. I don't turn around and look at her in the rocking chair. I don't want her to see the disappointment in my face that he's gone.

"Go ahead, Mother," I finally mutter. "Say what you want to say."

"Don't you let him cheapen you."

I look back at her, eye her suspiciously, even though she is so frail under the wool blanket. Sorry is the fool who ever underestimates my mother.

"If Stuart doesn't know how intelligent and kind I raised you to be, he can march straight on back to State Street." She narrows her eyes out at the winter land. "Frankly, I don't care much for Stuart. He doesn't know how lucky he was to have you."

I let Mother's words sit like a tiny, sweet candy on my tongue. Forcing myself up from the step, I head for the front door. There is so much work to be done and not nearly enough time.

"Thank you, Mother." I kiss her softly on the cheek and go inside.

I'M EXHAUSTED AND IRRITABLE. For forty-eight hours I've done nothing but type. I am stupid with facts about other people's lives. My eyes sting from the smell of typing ink. My fingers are striped with paper cuts. Who knew paper and ink could be so vicious.

With just six days left, I go over to Aibileen's. She's taken a weekday off from work, despite Elizabeth's annoyance. I can tell she knows what we need to discuss before I even say it. She leaves me in the kitchen and comes back with a letter in her hand.

"Fore I give this to you . . . I think I ought to tell you some things. So you can really understand."

I nod. I am tense in my chair. I want to tear the envelope open and get this over with.

Aibileen straightens her notebook that's sitting on the kitchen table. I watch as she aligns her two yellow pencils. "Remember, I told you Constantine had a daughter. Well, Lulabelle was her name. Law, she come out pale as snow. Grew hair the color a hay. Not curly like yours. Straight it was."

"She was that white?" I ask. I've wondered this ever since Aibileen told me about Constantine's child, way back in Elizabeth's kitchen. I think about how surprised Constantine must've been to hold a white baby and know it was hers.

She nods. "When Lulabelle was four years old, Constantine..." Aibileen shifts in her chair. "She take her to a... orphanage. Up in Chicago."

"An orphanage? You mean...she gave her baby away?" As much as Constantine loved me, I can only imagine how much she must've loved her own child.

Aibileen looks me straight in the eye. I see something there I rarely see—frustration, antipathy. "A lot a colored womens got to give they children up, Miss Skeeter. Send they kids off cause they have to tend to a white family."

I look down, wondering if Constantine couldn't take care of her child because she had to take care of us.

"But most send em off to family. A orphanage is...different altogether."

"Why didn't she send the baby to her sister's? Or another relative?"

"Her sister...she just couldn't handle it. Being Negro with white skin...in Mississippi, it's like you don't belong to nobody. But it wasn't just hard on the girl. It was hard on Constantine. She...folks would look at her. White folks would stop her, ask her all suspicious what she doing toting round a white child. Policeman used to stop her on State Street, told her she need to get her uniform on. Even colored folks...they treat her different, distrustful, like she done something wrong. It was hard for her to find somebody to watch Lulabelle while she at work. Constantine got to where she didn't want to bring Lula...out much."

"Was she already working for my mother then?"

"She'd been with your mama a few years. That's where she met the father, Connor. He worked on your farm, lived back there in Hotstack." Aibileen shakes her head. "We was all surprised Constantine would go and...get herself in the family way. Some folks at church wasn't so kind about it, especially when the baby come out white. Even though the father was black as me."

"I'm sure Mother wasn't too pleased, either." Mother, I'm sure, knew all about it. She's always kept tabs on all the colored help and their situations—

where they live, if they're married, how many children they have. It's more of a control thing than a real interest. She wants to know who's walking around her property.

"Was it a colored orphanage or a white one?" Because I am thinking, I am hoping, maybe Constantine just wanted a better life for her child. Maybe she thought she'd be adopted by a white family and not feel so different.

"Colored. White ones wouldn't take her, I heard. I guess they knew... maybe they seen that kind a thing before.

"When Constantine went to the train station with Lulabelle to take her up there, I heard white folks was staring on the platform, wanting to know why a little white girl was going in the colored car. And when Constantine left her at the place up in Chicago...four is...pretty old to get given up. Lulabelle was screaming. That's what Constantine told somebody at our church. Said Lula was screaming and thrashing, trying to get her mama to come back to her. But Constantine, even with that sound in her ears...she left her there."

As I listen, it starts to hit me, what Aibileen is telling me. If I hadn't had the mother I have, I might not have thought it. "She gave her up because she was...ashamed? Because her daughter was white?"

Aibileen opens her mouth to disagree, but then she closes it, looks down. "A few years later, Constantine wrote the orphanage, told em she made a mistake, she wanted her girl back. But Lula been adopted already. She was gone. Constantine always said giving her child away was the worst mistake she'd ever made in her life." Aibileen leans back in her chair. "And she said if she ever got Lulabelle back, she'd never let her go."

I sit quietly, my heart aching for Constantine. I am starting to dread what this has to do with my mother.

"Bout two years ago, Constantine get a letter from Lulabelle. I reckon she was twenty-five by then, and it said her adoptive parents give her the address. They start writing to each other and Lulabelle say she want a come down and stay with her awhile. Constantine, Law, she so nervous she couldn't walk straight. Too nervous to eat, wouldn't even take no water. Kept throwing it up. I had her on my prayer list."

Two years ago. I was up at school then. Why didn't Constantine tell me in her letters what was going on?

"She took all her savings and bought new clothes for Lulabelle, hair things, had the church bee sew her a new quilt for the bed Lula gone sleep in. She told us at prayer meeting, *What if she hate me? She's gone ask me why I give her away and if I tell her the truth . . . she'll hate me for what I done.*"

Aibileen looks up from her cup of tea, smiles a little. "She tell us, I can't wait for Skeeter to meet her, when she get back home from school. I forgot about that. I didn't know who Skeeter was, back then."

I remember my last letter from Constantine, that she had a surprise for me. I realize now, she'd wanted to introduce me to her daughter. I swallow back tears coming up in my throat. "What happened when Lulabelle came down to see her?"

Aibileen slides the envelope across the table. "I reckon you ought a read that part at home."

AT HOME, I GO UPSTAIRS. Without even stopping to sit down, I open Aibileen's letter. It is on notebook paper, covering the front and back, written in cursive pencil.

Afterward, I stare at the eight pages I've already written about walking to Hotstack with Constantine, the puzzles we worked on together, her pressing her thumb in my hand. I take a deep breath and put my hands on the typewriter keys. I can't waste any more time. I have to finish her story.

I write about what Aibileen told me, that Constantine had a daughter and had to give her up so she could work for our family—the Millers I call us, after Henry, my favorite banned author. I don't put in that Constantine's daughter was high yellow; I just want to show that Constantine's love for me began with missing her own child. Perhaps that's what made it so unique, so deep. It didn't matter that I was white. While she was wanting her own daughter back, I was longing for Mother not to be disappointed in me.

For two days, I write all the way through my childhood, my college years, where we sent letters to each other every week. But then I stop and listen to Mother coughing downstairs. I hear Daddy's footsteps, going to her. I light a cigarette and stub it out, thinking, *Don't start up again.* The toilet water rushes through the house, filled with a little more of my mother's body. I light another cigarette and smoke it down to my fingers. I can't write about what's in Aibileen's letter.

That afternoon, I call Aibileen at home. "I can't put it in the book," I tell her. "About Mother and Constantine. I'll end it when I go to college. I just…"

"Miss Skeeter—"

"I know I should. I know I should be sacrificing as much as you and Minny and all of you. But I can't do that to my mother."

"No one expects you to, Miss Skeeter. Truth is, I wouldn't think real high a you if you did."

THE NEXT EVENING, I go to the kitchen for some tea.

"Eugenia? Are you downstairs?"

I tread back to Mother's room. Daddy's not in bed yet. I hear the television on out in the relaxing room. "I'm here, Mama."

She is in bed at six in the evening, the white bowl by her side. "Have you been crying? You know how that ages your skin, dear."

I sit in the straight cane chair beside her bed. I think about how I should begin. Part of me understands why Mother acted the way she did, because really, wouldn't anyone be angry about what Lulabelle did? But I need to hear my mother's side of the story. If there's anything redeeming about my mother that Aibileen left out of the letter, I want to know.

"I want to talk about Constantine," I say.

"Oh Eugenia," Mother chides and pats my hand. "That was almost two years ago."

"Mama," I say and make myself look into her eyes. Even though she is terribly thin and her collarbone is long and narrow beneath her skin, her eyes are still as sharp as ever. "What happened? What happened with her daughter?"

Mother's jaw tightens and I can tell she's surprised that I know about her. I wait for her to refuse to talk about it, as before. She takes a deep breath, moves the white bowl a little closer to her, says, "Constantine sent her up to Chicago to live. She couldn't take care of her."

I nod and wait.

"They're different that way, you know. Those people have children and don't think about the consequences until it's too late."

They, those people. It reminds me of Hilly. Mother sees it on my face, too.

"Now you look, I was good to Constantine. Oh, she talked back plenty of times and I put up with it. But Skeeter, she didn't give me a choice this time."

"I know, Mother. I know what happened."

"Who told you? Who else knows about this?" I see the paranoia rising in Mother's eyes. It is her greatest fear coming true, and I feel sorry for her.

"I will never tell you who told me. All I can say is, it was no one...important to you," I say. "I can't believe you would do that, Mother."

"How dare you judge me, after what she did. Do you really know what happened? Were you there?" I see the old anger, an obstinate woman who's survived years of bleeding ulcers.

"That girl—" She shakes her knobby finger at me. "She showed up here. I had the entire DAR chapter at the house. You were up at school and the doorbell was ringing nonstop and Constantine was in the kitchen, making all that coffee over since the old percolator burned the first two pots right up." Mother waves away the remembered reek of scorched coffee. "They were all in the living room having cake, ninety-five *people* in the house, and she's drinking coffee. She's talking to Sarah von Sistern and walking around the house like a guest and sticking cake in her mouth and then she's filling out the form to become a *member*."

Again I nod. Maybe I didn't know those details, but they don't change what happened.

"She looked white as anybody, and she knew it too. She knew exactly what she was doing and so I say, *How do you do?* and she laughs and says, *Fine,* so I say, *And what is your name?* and she says, *You mean you don't know? I'm Lulabelle Bates. I'm grown now and I've moved back in with Mama. I got here yesterday morning.* And then she goes over to help herself to another piece of cake."

"Bates," I say, because this is another detail I didn't know, albeit insignificant. "She changed her last name back to Constantine's."

"Thank God nobody heard her. But then she starts talking to Phoebe Miller, the president of the Southern States of the DAR, and I pulled her into the kitchen and I said, *Lulabelle, you can't stay here. You need to go on,* and oh she looked at me haughty. She said, *What, you don't allow colored Negroes in your living room if we're not cleaning up?* That's when Constantine walks in the kitchen and she looks as shocked as I am. I say, *Lulabelle, you get out of this house before I call Mister Phelan,* but she won't budge. Says, when I thought she was white, I treated her fine and dandy. Says up in Chicago, she's part of some black cat group so I tell Constantine, I say, *You get your daughter out of my house right now.*"

Mother's eyes seem more deep-set than ever. Her nostrils are flaring.

"So Constantine, she tells Lulabelle to go on back to their house, and Lulabelle says, *Fine, I was leaving anyway,* and heads for the dining room and of course I stop her. *Oh no,* I say, *you go out the back door, not the front with the white guests.* I was not about to have the DAR find out about this. And I told that bawdy girl, whose own mama we gave ten dollars extra to every Christmas, she was *not* to step foot on this farm *again.* And do you know what she did?"

Yes, I think, but I keep my face blank. I am still searching for the redemption.

"Spit. In my face. A Negro in my home. Trying to act white."

I shudder. Who would ever have the nerve to spit at my mother?

"I told Constantine that girl better not show her face here again. Not to Hotstack, not to the state of Mississippi. Nor would I tolerate her keeping terms with Lulabelle, not as long as your daddy was paying Constantine's rent on that house back there."

"But it was Lulabelle acting that way. Not Constantine."

"What if she stayed? I couldn't have that girl going around Jackson, acting white when she was colored, telling everybody she got into a DAR party at Longleaf. I just thank God nobody ever found out about it. She tried to embarrass me in my own home, Eugenia. Five minutes before, she had Phoebe Miller filling out the form for her to *join*."

"She hadn't seen her daughter in twenty years. You can't... tell a person they can't see their child."

But Mother is caught up in her own story. "And Constantine, she thought she could get me to change my mind. *Miss Phelan, please, just let her stay at the house, she won't come on this side again, I hadn't seen her in so long.*

"And that Lulabelle, with her hand up on her hip, saying, 'Yeah, my daddy died and my mama was too sick to take care of me when I was a baby. She had to give me away. You can't keep us apart.'"

Mother lowers her voice. She seems matter-of-fact now. "I looked at Constantine and I felt so much shame for her. To get pregnant in the first place and then to lie..."

I feel sick and hot. I'm ready for this to be over.

Mother narrows her eyes. "It's time you learned, Eugenia, how things really are. You idolize Constantine too much. You always have." She points her finger at me. "They are not like regular *people*."

I can't look at her. I close my eyes. "And then what happened, Mother?"

"I asked Constantine, just as plain as day, 'Is that what you told her? Is that how you cover your mistakes?'"

This is the part I was hoping wasn't true. This is what I'd hoped Aibileen had been wrong about.

"I told Lulabelle the truth. I told her, 'Your daddy didn't *die*. He left the day after you were born. And your mama hadn't been sick a day in her life. She gave you up because you were too high yellow. She didn't want you.'"

"Why couldn't you let her believe what Constantine told her? Constantine was so scared she wouldn't like her, that's why she told her those things."

"Because Lulabelle needed to know the truth. She needed to go back to Chicago where she belonged."

I let my head sink into my hands. There is no redeeming piece of the story. I know why Aibileen hadn't wanted to tell me. A child should never know this about her own mother.

"I never thought Constantine would go to Illinois with her, Eugenia. Honestly, I was...sorry to see her go."

"You weren't," I say. I think about Constantine, after living fifty years in the country, sitting in a tiny apartment in Chicago. How lonely she must've felt. How bad her knees must've felt in that cold.

"I was. And even though I told her not to write you, she probably would've, if there'd been more time."

"More time?"

"Constantine died, Skeeter. I sent her a check, for her birthday. To the address I found for her daughter, but Lulabelle...sent it back. With a copy of the obituary."

"*Constantine*..." I cry. I wish I'd known. "Why didn't you tell me, Mama?"

Mother sniffs, keeping her eyes straight ahead. She quickly wipes her eyes. "Because I knew you'd blame me when it—it wasn't my fault."

"When did she die? How long was she living in Chicago?" I ask.

Mother pulls the basin closer, hugs it to her side. "Three weeks."

AIBILEEN OPENS HER BACK DOOR, lets me in. Minny is sitting at the table, stirring her coffee. When she sees me, she tugs the sleeve of her dress down, but I see the edge of a white bandage on her arm. She grumbles a hello, then goes back to her cup.

I put the manuscript down on the table with a thump.

"If I mail it in the morning, that still leaves six days for it to get there. We might just make it." I smile through my exhaustion.

"Law, that is something. Look at all them pages." Aibileen grins and sits on her stool. "Two hundred and sixty-six of em."

"Now we just...wait and see," I say and we all three stare at the stack.

"Finally," Minny says, and I can see the hint of something, not exactly a smile, but more like satisfaction.

The room grows quiet. It's dark outside the window. The post office is already closed so I brought it over to show to Aibileen and Minny one last time before I mail it. Usually, I only bring over sections at a time.

"What if they find out?" Aibleen says quietly.

Minny looks up from her coffee.

"What if folks find out Niceville is Jackson or figure out who who."

"They ain't gone know," Minny says. "Jackson ain't no special place. They's ten thousand towns just like it."

We haven't talked about this in a while, and besides Winnie's comment about tongues, we've haven't really discussed the actual consequences besides the maids losing their jobs. For the past eight months, all we've thought about is just getting it written.

"Minny, you got your kids to think about," Aibileen says. "And Leroy... if he find out..."

The sureness in Minny's eyes changes to something darting, paranoid. "Leroy gone be mad. Sho nuff." She tugs at her sleeve again. "Mad then sad, if the white people catch hold a me."

"You think maybe we ought to find a place we could go...in case it get bad?" Aibileen asks.

They both think about this, then shake their heads. "I on know where we'd go," Minny says.

"You might think about that, Miss Skeeter. Somewhere for yourself," Aibileen says.

"I can't leave Mother," I say. I've been standing and I sink down into a chair. "Aibileen, do you really think they'd...hurt us? I mean, like what's in the papers?"

Aibileen cocks her head at me, confused. She wrinkles her forehead like we've had a misunderstanding. "They'd beat us. They'd come out here with baseball bats. Maybe they won't kill us but..."

"But...who exactly would do this? The white women we've written about...they wouldn't hurt us. Would they?" I ask.

"Don't you know, white mens like nothing better than 'protecting' the white womens a their town?"

My skin prickles. I'm not so afraid for myself, but for what I've done to Aibileen, to Minny. To Louvenia and Faye Belle and eight other women. The book is sitting there on the table. I want to put it in my satchel and hide it.

Instead, I look to Minny because, for some reason, I think she's the only one among us who really understands what could happen. She doesn't look back at me, though. She is lost in thought. She's running her thumbnail back and forth across her lip.

"Minny? What do you think?" I ask.

Minny keeps her eyes on the window, nods at her own thoughts. "I think what we need is some *insurance*."

"Ain't no such thing," Aibileen says. "Not for us."

"What if we put the Terrible Awful in the book," Minny asks.

"We can't, Minny," Aibileen says. "It'd give us away."

"But if we put it in there, then Miss Hilly *can't* let anybody find out the book is about Jackson. She don't want *anybody* to know that story's about her. And if they start getting close to figuring it out, she gone steer em the other way."

"Law, Minny, that is too risky. Nobody can predict what that woman gone do."

"Nobody know that story but Miss Hilly and her own mama," Minny says. "And Miss Celia, but she ain't got no friends to tell anyway."

"What happened?" I ask. "Is it really *that* terrible?"

Aibileen looks at me. My eyebrows go up.

"Who she gone admit that to?" Minny asks Aibileen. "She ain't gone want you and Miss Leefolt to get identified either, Aibileen, cause then people gone be just one step away. I'm telling you, Miss Hilly is the best protection we got."

Aibileen shakes her head, then nods. Then shakes it again. We watch her and wait.

"If we put the Terrible Awful in the book and people *do* find out that was you and Miss Hilly, then you in so much trouble"—Aibileen shudders—"there ain't even a name for it."

"That's a risk I'm just gone have to take. I already made up my mind. Either put it in or pull my part out altogether."

Aibileen and Minny's eyes hang on each other's. We can't pull out Minny's section; it's the last chapter of the book. It's about getting fired nineteen times in the same small town. About what it's like trying to keep the anger inside, but never succeeding. It starts with her mother's rules of how to work for white women, all the way up to leaving Missus Walters. I want to speak up, but I keep my mouth shut.

Finally, Aibileen sighs.

"Alright," Aibileen says, shaking her head. "I reckon you better tell her, then."

Minny narrows her eyes at me. I pull out a pencil and pad.

"I'm only telling you for the book, you understand. Ain't nobody sharing no heartfelt secrets here."

"I'll make us some more coffee," Aibileen says.

ON THE DRIVE BACK to Longleaf, I shudder, thinking about Minny's pie story. I don't know if we'd be safer leaving it out or putting it in. Not to mention, if I can't get it written in time to make the mail tomorrow, it will put us yet another day later, shorting our chances to make the deadline. I can picture the red fury on Hilly's face, the hate she still feels for Minny. I know my old friend well. If we're found out, Hilly will be our fiercest enemy. Even if we're not found out, printing the pie story will put Hilly in a rage like we've never seen. But Minny's right—it's our best insurance.

I look over my shoulder every quarter mile. I keep exactly to the speed limit and stay on the back roads. *They will beat us* rings in my ears.

I WRITE ALL NIGHT, grimacing over the details of Minny's story, and all the next day. At four in the afternoon, I jam the manuscript in a cardboard letter box. I quickly wrap the box in brown paper wrapping. Usually it takes seven or eight days, but it will somehow have to get to New York City in six days to make the deadline.

I speed to the post office, knowing it closes at four-thirty, despite my fear of the police, and rush inside to the window. I haven't gone to sleep since night before last. My hair is literally sticking straight up in the air. The postman's eyes widen.

"Windy outside?"

"Please. Can you get this out today? It's going to New York."

He looks at the address. "Out-a-town truck's gone, ma'am. It'll have to wait until morning."

He stamps the postage and I head back home.

As soon as I walk in, I go straight to the pantry and call Elaine Stein's office. Her secretary puts me through and I tell her, in a hoarse, tired voice, I mailed the manuscript today.

"The last editors' meeting is in six days, Eugenia. Not only will it have to get here in time, I'll have to have time to read it. I'd say it's highly unlikely."

There is nothing left to say, so I just murmur, "I know. Thank you for the chance." And I add, "Merry Christmas, Missus Stein."

"We call it Hanukkah, but thank you, Miss Phelan."

CHAPTER 28

AFTER I HANG UP the phone, I go stand on the porch and stare out at the cold land. I'm so dog-tired I hadn't even noticed Doctor Neal's car is here. He must've arrived while I was at the post office. I lean against the rail and wait for him to come out of Mother's room. Down the hall, through the open front door, I can see that her bedroom door is closed.

A little while later, Doctor Neal gently closes her door behind him and walks out to the porch. He stands beside me.

"I gave her something to help the pain," he says.

"The...pain? Was Mama vomiting this morning?"

Old Doctor Neal stares at me through his cloudy blue eyes. He looks at me long and hard, as if trying to decide something about me. "Your mother has cancer, Eugenia. In the lining of the stomach."

I reach for the side of the house. I'm shocked and yet, didn't I know this?

"She didn't want to tell you." He shakes his head. "But since she refuses to stay in the hospital, you need to know. These next few months are going to be...pretty hard." He raises his eyebrows at me. "On her and you too."

"Few months? Is that...all?" I cover my mouth with my hand, hear myself groan.

"Maybe longer, maybe sooner, honey." He shakes his head. "Knowing your mother, though," he glances into the house, "she's going to fight it like the devil."

I stand there in a daze, unable to speak.

"Call me anytime, Eugenia. At the office or at home."

I walk into the house, back to Mother's room. Daddy is on the settee by the bed, staring at nothing. Mother is sitting straight up. She rolls her eyes when she sees me.

"Well, I guess he told you," she says.

Tears drip off my chin. I hold her hands.

"How long have you known?"

"About two months."

"Oh, *Mama*."

"Now stop that, Eugenia. It can't be helped."

"But what can I . . . I can't just sit here and watch you . . ." I can't even say the word. All the words are too awful.

"You most certainly will not just *sit* here. Carlton is going to be a lawyer and you . . ." She shakes her finger at me. "Don't think you can just let yourself go after I'm gone. I am calling Fanny Mae's the minute I can walk to the kitchen and make your hair appointments through 1975."

I sink down on the settee and Daddy puts his arm around me. I lean against him and cry.

THE CHRISTMAS TREE Jameso put up a week ago dries and drops needles every time someone walks into the relaxing room. It's still six days until Christmas, but no one's bothered to water it. The few presents Mother bought and wrapped back in July sit under the tree, one for Daddy that's obviously a church tie, something small and square for Carlton, a heavy box for me that I suspect is a new Bible. Now that everyone knows about Mother's cancer, it is as if she's let go of the few threads that kept her upright. The marionette strings are cut, and even her head looks wobbly on its post. The most she can do is get up and go to the bathroom or sit on the porch a few minutes every day.

In the afternoon, I take Mother her mail, *Good Housekeeping* magazine, church newsletters, DAR updates.

"How are you?" I push her hair back from her head and she closes her eyes like she relishes the feel. She is the child now and I am the mother.

"I'm alright."

Pascagoula comes in. She sets a tray of broth on the table. Mother barely shakes her head when she leaves, staring off at the empty doorway.

"Oh no," she says, grimacing, "I can't eat."

"You don't have to eat, Mama. We'll do it later."

"It's just not the same with Pascagoula here, is it?" she says.

"No," I say. "It's not." This is the first time she's mentioned Constantine since our terrible discussion.

"They say its like true love, good help. You only get one in a lifetime."

I nod, thinking how I ought to go write that down, include it in the book. But, of course, it's too late, it's already been mailed. There's nothing I can do, there's nothing any of us can do now, except wait for what's coming.

CHRISTMAS EVE IS DEPRESSING and rainy and warm. Every half hour, Daddy comes out of Mother's room and looks out the front window and asks, "Is he here?" even if no one's listening. My brother, Carlton, is driving home tonight from LSU law school and we'll both be relieved to see him. All day, Mother has been vomiting and dry heaving. She can barely keep her eyes open, but she cannot sleep.

"Charlotte, you need to be in the hospital," Doctor Neal said that afternoon. I don't know how many times he's said that in the past week. "At least let me get the nurse out here to stay with you."

"Charles Neal," Mother said, not even raising her head from the mattress, "I am not spending my final days in a hospital, nor will I turn my own house into one."

Doctor Neal just sighed, gave Daddy more medicine, a new kind, and explained to him how to give it to her.

"But will it help her?" I heard Daddy whisper out in the hall. "Can it make her better?"

Doctor Neal put his hand on Daddy's shoulder. "No, Carlton."

At six o'clock that night, Carlton finally pulls up, comes in the house.

"Hey there, Skeeter." He hugs me to him. He is rumpled from the car drive, handsome in his college cable-knit sweater. The fresh air on him smells good. It's nice to have someone else here. "Jesus, why's it so hot in this house?"

"She's cold," I say quietly, "all the time."

I go with him to the back. Mother sits up when she sees him, holds her thin arms out. "Oh Carlton, you're home," she says.

Carlton stops still. Then he bends down and hugs her, very gently. He glances back at me and I can see the shock on his face. I turn away. I cover my mouth so I don't cry, because I won't be able to quit. Carlton's look tells me more than I want to know.

When Stuart drops by on Christmas Day, I don't stop him when he tries to kiss me. But I tell him, "I'm only letting you because my mother is dying."

"Eugenia," I hear Mother calling. It is New Year's Eve and I'm in the kitchen getting some tea. Christmas has passed and Jameso took the tree out this morning. Needles still litter the house, but I've managed to put away the decorations and store them back in the closet. It was tiring and frustrating, trying to wrap each ornament the way Mother likes, to get them ready for next year. I don't let myself question the futility of it.

I've heard nothing from Missus Stein and don't even know if the package made it on time. Last night, I broke down and called Aibileen to tell her I've heard nothing, just for the relief of talking about it to someone. "I keep thinking a things to put in," Aibileen says. "I have to remind myself we already done sent it off."

"Me too," I say. "I'll call you as soon as I hear something."

I go in the back. Mother is propped up on her pillows. The gravity of sitting upright, we've learned, helps keep the vomit down. The white enamel bowl is beside her.

"Hey, Mama," I say. "What can I get you?"

"Eugenia, you cannot wear those slacks to the Holbrook New Year's party." When Mother blinks, she keeps her eyes closed a second too long. She's exhausted, a skeleton in a white dressing gown with absurdly fancy ribbons and starched lace. Her neck swims in the neckline like an eighty-pound swan's. She cannot eat unless it's through a straw. She's lost her power of smell completely. Yet she can sense, from an entirely different room, if my wardrobe is disappointing.

"They canceled the party, Mama." Perhaps she is remembering Hilly's party last year. From what Stuart's told me, all the parties were canceled because of the President's death. Not that I'd be invited anyway. Tonight, Stuart's coming over to watch Dick Clark on the television.

Mother places her tiny, angular hand on mine, so frail the joints show through the skin. I was Mother's dress size when I was eleven.

She looks at me evenly. "I think you need to go on and put those slacks on the list, now."

"But they're comfortable and they're warm and—"

She shakes her head, shuts her eyes. "I'm sorry, Skeeter."

There is no arguing, anymore. "Al-right," I sigh.

Mother pulls the pad of paper from under the covers, tucked in the invisible pocket she's had sewn in every garment, where she keeps antivomiting pills, tissues. Tiny dictatorial lists. Even though she is so weak, I'm surprised by the steadiness of her hand as she writes on the "Do Not Wear" list: "Gray, shapeless, mannishly tailored pants." She smiles, satisfied.

It sounds macabre, but when Mother realized that after she's dead, she won't be able to tell me what to wear anymore, she came up with this ingenious postmortem system. She's assuming I'll never go buy new, unsatisfactory clothes on my own. She's probably right.

"Still no vomiting yet?" I ask, because it's four o'clock and Mother's had two bowls of broth and hasn't been sick once today. Usually she's thrown up at least three times by now.

"Not even once," she says but then she closes her eyes and within seconds, she's asleep.

On New Year's Day, I come downstairs to start on the black-eyed peas for good luck. Pascagoula set them out to soak last night, instructed me on how to put them in the pot and turn on the flame, put the ham hock in with them. It's pretty much a two-step process, yet everyone seems nervous about me turning on the stove. I remember that Constantine always used to come by on January first and fix our good-luck peas for us, even though it was her day off. She'd make a whole pot but then deliver one single pea on a plate to everyone in the family and watch us to make sure we ate it. She could be superstitious like that. Then she'd wash the dishes and go back home. But Pascagoula doesn't offer to come in on her holiday and, assuming she's with her own family, I don't ask her to.

We're all sad that Carlton had to leave this morning. It's been nice having my brother around to talk to. His last words to me, before he hugged me and headed back to school, were, "Don't burn the house down." Then he added, "I'll call tomorrow, to see how she is."

After I turn off the flame, I walk out on the porch. Daddy's leaning on the rail, rolling cotton seeds around in his fingers. He's staring at the empty fields that won't be planted for another month.

"Daddy, you coming in for lunch?" I ask. "The peas are ready."

He turns and his smile is thin, starved for reason.

"This medicine they got her on…" He studies his seeds. "I think it's working. She keeps saying she feels better."

I shake my head in disbelief. He can't really believe this.

"She's gone two days and only gotten sick once…"

"Oh, Daddy. No…it's just a…Daddy, she still has it."

But there's an empty look in Daddy's eyes and I wonder if he even heard me.

"I know you've got better places to be, Skeeter." There are tears in his eyes. "But not a day passes that I don't thank God you're here with her."

I nod, feel guilty that he thinks it's a choice I actually made. I hug him, tell him, "I'm glad I'm here too, Daddy."

WHEN THE CLUB REOPENS the first week of January, I put my skirt on and grab my racquet. I walk through the snack bar, ignoring Patsy Joiner, my old tennis partner who dumped me, and three other girls, all smoking at the black iron tables. They lean down and whisper to each other when I pass. I'll be skipping the League meeting tonight, and forever, for that matter. I gave in and sent a letter three days ago with my resignation.

I slam the tennis ball into the backboard, trying my best not to think about anything. Lately I've found myself praying, when I've never been a very religious person. I find myself whispering long, never-ending sentences to God, begging for Mother to feel some relief, pleading for good news about the book, sometimes even asking for some hint of what to do about Stuart. Often I catch myself praying when I didn't even know I was doing it.

When I get home from the club, Doctor Neal pulls up behind me in his car. I take him back to Mother's room, where Daddy's waiting, and they close the door behind them. I stand there, fidgeting in the hall like a kid. I can see why Daddy is hanging on to his thread of hope. Mother's gone four days now without vomiting the green bile. She's eating her oatmeal every day, even asked for more.

When Doctor Neal comes out, Daddy stays in the chair by the bed and I follow Doctor Neal out to the porch.

"She told you?" I ask. "About how she's feeling better?"

He nods, but then shakes his head. "There's no point in bringing her in for an X-ray. It would just be too hard on her."

"But...is she? Could she be improving?"

"I've seen this before, Eugenia. Sometimes people get a burst of strength. It's a gift from God, I guess. So they can go on and finish their business. But that's all it is, honey. Don't expect anything more."

"But did you see her color? She looks so much better and she's keeping the food—"

He shakes his head. "Just try and keep her comfortable."

ON THE FIRST FRIDAY OF 1964, I can't wait any longer. I stretch the phone into the pantry. Mother is asleep, after having eaten a second bowl of oatmeal. Her door is open so I can hear her, in case she calls.

"Elaine Stein's office."

"Hello, it's Eugenia Phelan, calling long-distance. Is she available?"

"I'm sorry, Miss Phelan, but Missus Stein isn't taking any calls regarding her manuscript selection."

"Oh. But…can you at least tell me if she received it? I mailed it just before the deadline and—"

"One moment please."

The phone goes silent, and a minute or so later she comes back.

"I can confirm that we did receive your package at some point during the holidays. Someone from our office will notify you after Missus Stein has made her decision. Thank you for calling."

I hear the line on the other end click.

A FEW NIGHTS LATER, after a riveting afternoon answering Miss Myrna letters, Stuart and I sit in the relaxing room. I'm glad to see him and to eradicate, for a while, the deadly silence of the house. We sit quietly, watching television. A Tareyton ad comes on, the one where the girl smoking the cigarette has a black eye—*Us Tareyton smokers would rather fight than switch!*

Stuart and I have been seeing each other once a week now. We went to a movie after Christmas and once to dinner in town, but usually he comes out to the house because I don't want to leave Mother. He is hesitant around me, kind of respectfully shy. There is a patience in his eyes that replaces my own panic that I felt with him before. We don't talk about anything serious. He tells me stories about the summer, during college, he spent working on the oil rigs in the Gulf of Mexico. The showers were saltwater. The ocean was crystal clear blue to the bottom. The other men were doing this brutal work to feed their families while Stuart, a rich kid with rich parents, had college to go back to. It was the first time, he said, he'd really had to work hard.

"I'm glad I drilled on the rig back then. I couldn't go off and do it now," he'd said, like it was ages ago and not five years back. He seems older than I remember.

"Why couldn't you do it now?" I asked, because I am looking for a future for myself. I like to hear about the possibilities of others.

He furrowed his brow at me. "Because I couldn't leave you."

I tucked this away, afraid to admit how good it was to hear it.

The commercial is over and we watch the news report. There is a skirmish in Vietnam. The reporter seems to thinks it'll be solved without much fuss.

"Listen," Stuart says after a while of silence between us. "I didn't want to bring this up before but...I know what people are saying in town. About you. And I don't care. I just want you to know that."

My first thought is *the book*. He's heard something. My entire body goes tense. "What did you hear?"

"You know. About that trick you played on Hilly."

I relax some, but not completely. I've never talked to anyone about this except Hilly herself. I wonder if Hilly ever called him like she'd threatened.

"And I could see how people would take it, think you're some kind of crazy liberal, involved in all that mess."

I study my hands, still wary of what he might have heard, and a little irritated too. "How do you know," I ask, "what I'm involved in?"

"Because I know you, Skeeter," he says softly. "You're too smart to get mixed up in anything like that. And I told them, too."

I nod, try to smile. Despite what he thinks he "knows" about me, I can't help but appreciate that someone out there cares enough to stand up for me.

"We don't have to talk about this again," he says. "I just wanted you to know. That's all."

ON SATURDAY EVENING, I say good night to Mother. I have a long coat on so she can't see my outfit. I keep the lights off so she can't comment on my hair. Very little has changed with her health. She doesn't seem to be getting any worse—the vomiting is still at bay—but her skin is grayish white. Her hair has started to fall out. I hold her hands, brush her cheek.

"Daddy, you'll call the restaurant if you need me?"

"I will, Skeeter. Go have some fun."

I get in Stuart's car and he takes me to the Robert E. Lee for dinner. The room is gaudy with gowns, red roses, silver service clinking. There is excitement in the air, the feeling that things are almost back to normal since President Kennedy died; 1964 is a fresh, new year. The glances our way are abundant.

"You look...different," Stuart says. I can tell he's been holding in this comment all night, and he seems more confused than impressed. "That dress, it's so...short."

I nod and push my hair back. The way he used to do.

This morning, I told Mother I was going shopping. She looked so tired though, I quickly changed my mind. "Maybe I shouldn't go."

But I'd already said it. Mother had me fetch the big checkbook. When I came back she tore out a blank check and then handed me a hundred-dollar bill she had folded in the side of her wallet. Just the word *shopping* seemed to've made her feel better.

"Don't be frugal, now. And no slacks. Make sure Miss LaVole helps you." She rested her head back in her pillows. "She knows how young girls should dress."

But I couldn't stand the thought of Miss LaVole's wrinkled hands on my body, smelling of coffee and mothballs. I drove right through downtown and got on Highway 51 and headed for New Orleans. I drove through the guilt of leaving Mother for so long, knowing that Doctor Neal was coming by that afternoon and Daddy would be home all day with her.

Three hours later, I walked into Maison Blanche's department store on Canal Street. I'd been there umpteen times with Mother and twice with Elizabeth and Hilly, but I was mesmerized by the vast white marble floors, the miles of hats and gloves and powdered ladies looking so happy, so *healthy*. Before I could ask for help, a thin man said, "Come with me, I have it all upstairs," and whisked me in the elevator to the third floor, to a room called MODERN WOMEN'S WEAR.

"What is all this?" I asked. There were dozens of women and rock-and-roll playing and champagne glasses and bright glittering lights.

"Emilio Pucci, darling. Finally!" He stepped back from me and said, "Aren't you here for the preview? You do have an invitation, don't you?"

"Um, somewhere," I said, but he lost interest as I faked through my handbag.

All around me, clothes looked like they'd sprouted roots and bloomed on their hangers. I thought of Miss LaVole and laughed. No easter-egg suits here. Flowers! Big bright stripes! And hemlines that showed *several inches of thigh*. It was electric and gorgeous and dizzying. This Emilio Pucci character must stick his finger in a socket every morning.

I bought with my blank check enough clothes to fill the back seat of the Cadillac. Then on Magazine Street, I paid forty-five dollars to have my hair lightened and trimmed and ironed straight. It had grown longer over the winter and was the color of dirty dishwater. By four o'clock I was driving back over the Lake Pontchartrain bridge with the radio playing a band called the Rolling Stones and the wind blowing through my satiny, straight hair, and I thought, *Tonight, I'll strip off all this armor and let it be as it was before with Stuart.*

STUART AND I eat our Chateaubriand, smiling, talking. He looks off at the other tables, commenting on people he knows. But no one gets up to tell us hello.

"Here's to new beginnings," Stuart says and raises his bourbon.

I nod, sort of wanting to tell him that all beginnings are new. Instead, I smile and toast with my second glass of wine. I've never really liked alcohol, until today.

After dinner, we walk out into the lobby and see Senator and Missus Whitworth at a table, having drinks. People are around them drinking and talking. They are home for the weekend, Stuart told me earlier, their first since they moved to Washington.

"Stuart, there are your parents. Should we go say hello?"

But Stuart steers me toward the door, practically pushes me outside.

"I don't want Mother to see you in that short dress," he says. "I mean, believe me, it looks great on you, but…" He looks down at the hemline. "Maybe that wasn't the best choice for tonight." On the ride home, I think of Elizabeth, in her curlers, afraid the bridge club would see me. Why is it that someone always seems to be ashamed of me?

By the time we make it back to Longleaf, it's eleven o'clock. I smooth my dress, thinking Stuart is right. It is too short. The lights in my parents' bedroom are off, so we sit on the sofa.

I rub my eyes and yawn. When I open them, he's holding a ring between his fingers.

"Oh…Jesus."

"I was going to do it at the restaurant but…" He grins. "Here is better."

I touch the ring. It is cold and gorgeous. Three rubies are set on both sides of the diamond. I look up at him, feeling very hot all of a sudden. I pull my sweater off my shoulders. I am smiling and about to cry at the same time.

"I have to tell you something, Stuart," I blurt out. "Do you promise you won't tell anyone?"

He stares at me and laughs. "Hang on, did you say yes?"

"Yes, but…" I have to know something first. "Can I just have your word?"

He sighs, looks disappointed that I'm ruining his moment. "Sure, you have my word."

I am in shock from his proposal but I do my best to explain. Looking into his eyes, I spread out the facts and what details I can safely share about the book and what I've been doing over the past year. I leave out everyone's name and I pause at the implication of this, knowing it's not good. Even though he is asking to be my husband, I don't know him enough to trust him completely.

"This is what you've been writing about for the past twelve months? Not…Jesus Christ?"

"No, Stuart. Not…Jesus."

When I tell him that Hilly found the Jim Crow laws in my satchel, his chin drops and I can see that I've confirmed something Hilly already told him about me—something he had the naïve trust not to believe.

"The talk...in town. I told them they were dead wrong. But they were...right."

When I tell him about the colored maids filing past me after the prayer meeting, I feel a swell of pride over what we've done. He looks down into his empty bourbon glass.

Then I tell him that the manuscript has been sent to New York. That if they decide to publish it, it would come out in, my guess is, eight months, maybe sooner. Right around the time, I think to myself, an engagement would turn into a wedding.

"It's been written anonymously," I say, "but with Hilly around, there's still a good chance people will know it was me."

But he's not nodding his head or pushing my hair behind my ear and his grandmother's ring is sitting on Mother's velvet sofa like some ridiculous metaphor. We are both silent. His eyes don't even meet mine. They stay a steady two inches to the right of my face.

After a minute, he says, "I just...I don't understand why you would do this. Why do you even...*care* about this, Skeeter?"

I bristle, look down at the ring, so sharp and shiny.

"I didn't...mean it like that," he starts again. "What I mean is, things are fine around here. Why would you want to go stirring up trouble?"

I can tell, in his voice, he sincerely wants an answer from me. But how to explain it? He is a good man, Stuart. As much as I know that what I've done is right, I can still understand his confusion and doubt.

"I'm not making trouble, Stuart. The trouble is already here."

But clearly, this isn't the answer he is looking for. "I don't know you."

I look down, remembering that I'd thought this same thing only moments ago. "I guess we'll have the rest of our lives to fix that," I say, trying to smile.

"I don't...think I can marry somebody I don't know."

I suck in a breath. My mouth opens but I can't say anything for a little while.

"I had to tell you," I say, more to myself than him. "You needed to know."

He studies me for a few moments. "You have my word. I won't tell anyone," he says, and I believe him. He may be many things, Stuart, but he's not a liar.

He stands up. He gives me one last, lost look. And then he picks up the ring and walks out.

THAT NIGHT, after Stuart has left, I wander from room to room, dry-mouthed, cold. Cold is what I'd prayed for when Stuart left me the first time. Cold is what I got.

At midnight, I hear Mother's voice calling from her bedroom.

"Eugenia? Is that you?"

I walk down the hall. The door is half open and Mother is sitting up in her starchy white nightgown. Her hair is down around her shoulders. I am struck by how beautiful she looks. The back porch light is on, casting a white halo around her entire body. She smiles and her new dentures are still in, the ones Dr. Simon cast for her when her teeth starting eroding from the stomach acid. Her smile is whiter, even, than in her teen pageant pictures.

"Mama, what can I get you? Is it bad?"

"Come here, Eugenia. I want to tell you something."

I go to her quietly. Daddy is a long sleeping lump, his back to her. And I think, I could tell her a better version of tonight. We all know there's very little time. I could make her happy in her last days, pretend that the wedding is going to happen.

"I have something to tell you, too," I say.

"Oh? You go first."

"Stuart proposed," I say, faking a smile. Then I panic, knowing she'll ask to see the ring.

"I know," she says.

"You do?"

She nods. "Of course. He came by here two weeks ago and asked Carlton and me for your hand."

Two weeks ago? I almost laugh. Of course Mother was the first to know something so important. I'm happy she's had so long to enjoy the news.

"And I have something to tell you," she says. The glow around Mother is unearthly, phosphorescent. It's from the porch light, but I wonder why I've never seen it before. She clasps my hand in the air with the healthy grip of a mother holding her newly engaged daughter. Daddy stirs, then sits straight up.

"What?" he gasps. "Are you sick?"

"No, Carlton. I'm fine. I told you."

He nods numbly, closes his eyes, and is asleep before he has even lain down again.

"What's your news, Mama?"

"I've had a long talk with your daddy and I have made a decision."

"Oh God," I sigh. I can just see her explaining it to Stuart when he asked for my hand. "Is this about the trust fund?"

"No, it's not that," she says and I think, *Then it must be something about the wedding.* I feel a shuddering sadness that Mother will not be here to plan my wedding, not only because she'll be dead, but because there is no wedding. And yet, I also feel a horrifyingly guilty relief that I won't have to go through this with her.

"Now I know you've noticed that things have been on the uptick these past few weeks," she says. "And I know what Doctor Neal says, that it's some kind of last strength, some nonsense ab—" She coughs and her thin body arches over like a shell. I give her a tissue and she frowns, dabs at her mouth.

"But as I said, I have made a decision."

I nod, listening, with the same numbness as my father a moment ago.

"I have decided not to die."

"Oh . . . Mama. God, please . . ."

"Too late," she says, waving my hand away. "I've made my decision and that's that."

She slides her palms across each other, as if throwing the cancer away. Sitting straight and prim in her gown, the halo of light glowing around her hair, I can't keep from rolling my eyes. How dumb of me. Of course Mother will be as obstinate about her death as she has been about every detail of her life.

. . .

THE DATE IS FRIDAY, JANUARY 18, 1964. I have on a black A-line dress. My fingernails are all bitten off. I will remember every detail of this day, I think, the way people are saying they'll never forget what kind of sandwich they were eating, or the song on the radio, when they found out Kennedy was shot.

I walk into what has become such a familiar spot to me, the middle of Aibileen's kitchen. It is already dark outside and the yellow bulb seems very bright. I look at Minny and she looks at me. Aibileen edges between us as if to block something.

"Harper and Row," I say, "wants to publish it."

Everyone is quiet. Even the flies stop buzzing.

"You kidding me," says Minny.

"I spoke to her this afternoon."

Aibileen lets out a whoop like I've never heard come out of her before. "Law, I can't believe it!" she hollers, and then we are hugging, Aibileen and me, then Minny and Aibileen. Minny looks in my general direction.

"Sit down, y'all!" Aibileen says. "Tell me what she say? What a we do now? Law, I ain't even got no coffee ready!"

We sit and they both stare at me, leaning forward. Aibileen's eyes are big. I've been waiting at home with the news for four hours. Missus Stein told me, clearly, this is a very small deal. Keep our expectations between low and nonexistent. I feel obligated to communicate this to Aibileen so she doesn't end up disappointed. I've hardly even figured out how I should feel about it myself.

"Listen, she said not to get too excited. That the number of copies they're going to put out is going to be very, *very* small."

I wait for Aibileen to frown, but she giggles. She tries to hide it with her hand.

"Probably only a few thousand copies."

Aibileen presses her hand harder against her lips.

"*Pathetic*... Missus Stein called it."

Aibileen's face is turning darker. She giggles again into her knuckles. Clearly she's not getting this.

"And she said it's one of the smallest advances she's ever seen…" I am trying to be serious but I can't because Aibileen is clearly about to burst. Tears are coming up in her eyes.

"How…small?" she asks behind her hand.

"Eight hundred dollars," I say. "Divided thirteen ways."

Aibileen splits open in laughter. I can't help but laugh with her. But it makes no sense. A few thousand copies and $61.50 a person?

Tears run down Aibileen's face and finally she just lays her head on the table. "I don't know why I'm laughing. It just seem so funny all a sudden."

Minny rolls her eyes at us. "I *knew* y'all crazy. Both a you."

I do my best to tell them the details. I hadn't acted much better on the phone with Missus Stein. She'd sounded so matter-of-fact, almost uninterested. And what did I do? Did I remain businesslike and ask pertinent questions? Did I thank her for taking on such a risky topic? No, instead of laughing, I started blubbering into the phone, crying like a kid getting a polio shot.

"Calm down, Miss Phelan," she'd said, "this is hardly going to be a bestseller," but I just kept crying while she fed me the details. "We're only offering a four-hundred-dollar advance and then another four hundred dollars when it's finished…are you…listening?"

"Ye-yes ma'am."

"And there's definitely some editing you have to do. The Sarah section is in the best shape," she'd said, and I tell Aibileen this through her fits and snorts.

Aibileen sniffs, wipes her eyes, smiles. We finally calm down, drinking coffee that Minny had to get up and put on for us.

"She really likes Gertrude, too," I say to Minny. I pick up the paper and read the quote I'd written so I wouldn't forget it. "'Gertrude is every Southern white woman's nightmare. I adore her.'"

For a second, Minny actually looks me in the eye. Her face softens into a childlike smile. "She say that? Bout me?"

Aibileen laughs. "It's like she know you from five hundred miles away."

"She said it'll be at least six months until it comes out. Sometime in August."

Aibileen is still smiling, completely undeterred by anything I've said. And honestly, I'm grateful for this. I knew she'd be excited, but I was afraid she'd be a little disappointed, too. Seeing her makes me realize, I'm not disappointed at all. I'm just happy.

We sit and talk another few minutes, drinking coffee and tea, until I look at my watch. "I told Daddy I'd be home in an hour." Daddy is at home with Mother. I took a risk and left him Aibileen's number just in case, telling him I was going to visit a friend named Sarah.

They both walk me to the door, which is new for Minny. I tell Aibileen I'll call her as soon as I get Missus Stein's notes in the mail.

"So six months from now, we'll finally know what's gone happen," Minny says, "good, bad, or nothing."

"It might be nothing," I say, wondering if anyone will even buy the book.

"Well, I'm counting on good," Aibileen says.

Minny crosses her arms over her chest. "I better count on bad then. Somebody got to."

Minny doesn't look worried about book sales. She looks worried about what will happen when the women of Jackson read what we've written about them.

AIBILEEN

CHAPTER 29

THE HEAT done seeped into everything. For a week now it's been a hundred degrees and ninety-nine percent humidity. Get any wetter, we be swimming. Can't get my sheets to dry on the line, my front door won't close it done swell up so much. Sho nuff couldn't get a meringue to whip. Even my church wig starting to frizz.

This morning, I can't even get my hose on. My legs is too swollen. I figure I just do it when I get to Miss Leefolt's, in the air-condition. It must be record heat, cause I been tending to white folks for forty-one years and this the first time in history I ever went to work without no hose on.

But Miss Leefolt's house be hotter than my own. "Aibileen, go on and get the tea brewed and...salad plates...wipe them down now..." She ain't even come in the kitchen today. She in the living room and she done pull a chair next to the wall vent, so what's left a the air-condition blowing up her slip. That's all she got on, her full slip and her earrings. I wait on white ladies who walk right out the bedroom wearing nothing but they personality, but Miss Leefolt don't do like that.

Ever once in a while, that air-condition motor go *phheeewww*. Like it just giving up. Miss Leefolt call the repairman twice now and he say he coming, but I bet he ain't. Too hot.

"And don't forget...that silver thingamajig—cornichon server, it's in the..."

But she give up before she finish, like it's too hot to even tell me what to do. And you know that be hot. Seem like everbody in town got the heat-crazies. Go out on the street and it feel real still, eerie, like right before a tornado hit. Or maybe it's just me, jittery cause a the book. It's coming out on Friday.

"You think we ought a cancel bridge club?" I ask her from the kitchen. Bridge club changed to Mondays now and the ladies gone be here in twenty minutes.

"No. Everything's...already done," she say, but I know she ain't thinking straight.

"I'll try to whip the cream again. Then I got to go in the garage. Get my hose on."

"Oh don't worry about it, Aibileen. It's too hot for stockings." Miss Lee-folt finally get up from that wall vent, drag herself on in the kitchen, flapping a Chow-Chow Chinese Restaurant fan. "Oh God, it must be fifteen degrees hotter in the kitchen than it is in the dining room!"

"Oven a be off in a minute. Kids gone out back to play."

Miss Leefolt look out the window at the kids playing in the sprinkler. Mae Mobley down to just her underpants, Ross—I call him Li'l Man—he in his diaper. He ain't even a year old yet and already he walking like a big boy. He never even crawled.

"I don't see how they can stand it out there," Miss Leefolt say.

Mae Mobley love playing with her little brother, looking after him like she his mama. But Mae Mobley don't get to stay home with us all day no more. My Baby Girl go to the Broadmoore Baptist Pre-School ever morning. Today be Labor Day, though, a holiday for the rest a the world, so no class today. I'm glad too. I don't know how many days I got left with her.

"Look at them out there," Miss Leefolt say and I come over to the window where she standing. The sprinkler be blooming up into the treetops, making them rainbows. Mae Mobley got Li'l Man by the hands and they standing under the sprinkles with they eyes closed like they being baptized.

"They are really something special," she say, sighing, like she just now figuring this out.

"They sure is," I say and I spec we bout shared us a moment, me and Miss Leefolt, looking out the window at the kids we both love. It makes me wonder if things done changed just a little. It is 1964 after all. Downtown, they letting Negroes set at the Woolworth counter.

I get a real heartsick feeling then, wondering if I gone too far. Cause after the book come out, if folks find out it was us, I probably never get to see these kids again. What if I don't even get to tell Mae Mobley goodbye, and that she a fine girl, one last time? And Li'l Man? Who gone tell him the story a the Green Martian Luther King?

I already been through all this with myself, twenty times over. But today it's just starting to feel so real. I touch the window pane like I be touching them. If she find out...oh, I'm gone miss these kids.

I look over and see Miss Leefolt's eyes done wandered down to my bare legs. I think she curious, you know. I bet she ain't never seen bare black legs up close before. But then, I see she frowning. She look up at Mae Mobley, give her that same hateful frown. Baby Girl done smeared mud and grass all across her front. Now she decorating her brother with it like he a pig in a sty and I see that old disgust Miss Leefolt got for her own daughter. Not for Li'l Man, just Mae Mobley. Saved up special for her.

"She's ruining the yard!" Miss Leefolt say.

"I go get em. I take care—"

"And I can't have you serving us like that, with your—your legs showing!"

"I tole you—"

"Hilly's going to be here in five minutes and she's messed up *everything*!" she screech. I guess Mae Mobley hear her through the window cause she look over at us, frozen. Smile fades. After a second, she start wiping the mud off her face real slow.

I put a apron on cause I got to hose them kids off. Then I'm on go in the garage, get my stockings on. Book coming out in four days. Ain't a minute too soon.

.   .   .

WE BEEN LIVING IN ANTICIPATION. Me, Minny, Miss Skeeter, all the maids with stories in the book. Feel like we been waiting for some invisible pot a water to boil for the past seven months. After bout the third month a waiting, we just stopped talking about it. Got us too excited.

But for the past two weeks, I've had a secret joy and a secret dread both rattling inside a me that make waxing floors go even slower and washing underwear a uphill race. Ironing pleats turns into a eternity, but what can you do. We all pretty sure nothing's gone be said about it right at first. Just like Miss Stein told Miss Skeeter, this book ain't gone be no best-seller and to keep our "expectations low." Miss Skeeter say maybe don't spec nothing at all, that most Southern peoples is "repressed." If they feel something, they might not say a word. Just hold they breath and wait for it to pass, like gas.

Minny say, "I hope she hold her breath till she explode all over Hinds County." She mean Miss Hilly. I wish Minny was wishing for change in the direction a kindness, but Minny is Minny, all the time.

"YOU WANT YOU A SNACK, Baby Girl?" I ask when she get home from school on Thursday. Oh, she a big girl! Already four years old. She tall for her age—most folks think she five or six. Skinny as her mama is, Mae Mobley still chubby. And her hair ain't looking too good. She decide to give herself a haircut with her construction paper scissors and you know how that turn out. Miss Leefolt had to take her down to the grown-up beauty parlor but they couldn't do a whole lot with it. It still be short on one side with almost nothing in front.

I fix her a little something low-calorie to eat cause that's all Miss Leefolt let me give her. Crackers and tunafish or Jell-O without no whip cream.

"What you learn today?" I ask even though she ain't in real school, just the pretend kind. Other day, when I ask her, she say, "Pilgrims. They came over and nothing would grow so they ate the Indians."

Now I knew them Pilgrims didn't eat no Indians. But that ain't the point. Point is, we got to watch what get up in these kids' heads. Ever week, she still get her Aibileen lesson, her secret story. When Li'l Man get big enough to listen, I'm on tell him too. I mean, if I still got a job here. But I don't think it's gone be the same with Li'l Man. He love me, but he wild, like a animal. Come and hug on my knees so hard then off he shoots to look after something else. But even if I don't get to do this for him, I don't feel too bad. What I know is, I got it started and that baby boy, even though he can't talk a word yet, he listen to everthing Mae Mobley say.

Today when I ask what she learn, Mae Mobley just say, "Nothing," and stick her lip out.

"How you like your teacher?" I ask her.

"She's pretty," she say.

"Good," I say. "You pretty too."

"How come you're colored, Aibileen?"

Now I've gotten this question a few times from my other white kids. I used to just laugh, but I want to get this right with her. "Cause God made me colored," I say. "And there ain't another reason in the world."

"Miss Taylor says kids that are colored can't go to my school cause they're not smart enough."

I come round the counter then. Lift her chin up and smooth back her funny-looking hair. "You think I'm dumb?"

"No," she whispers hard, like she means it so much. She look sorry she said it.

"What that tell you about Miss Taylor, then?"

She blink, like she listening good.

"Means Miss Taylor ain't right all the time," I say.

She hug me around my neck, say, "You're righter than Miss Taylor." I tear up then. My cup is spilling over. Those is new words to me.

AT FOUR O'CLOCK THAT AFTERNOON, I walk as fast as I can from the bus stop to the Church a the Lamb. I wait inside, watch out the window. After ten minutes a trying to breathe and drumming my fingers on the sill, I see the car pull up. White lady gets out and I squint my eyes. This lady looks like one a them hippies I seen on Miss Leefolt's tee-vee. She got on a short white dress and sandals. Her hair's long without no spray on it. The weight of it's worked out the curl and frizz. I laugh into my hand, wishing I could run out there and give her a hug. I ain't been able to see Miss Skeeter in person in six months, since we finished Miss Stein's edits and turned in the final copy.

Miss Skeeter pull a big brown box out the back seat, then carries it up to the church door, like she dropping off old clothes. She stop a second and look at the door, but then she get in her car and drive away. I'm sad she had to do it this way but we don't want a blow it fore it even starts.

Soon as she gone, I run out and tote the box inside and grab out a copy and I just stare. I don't even try not to cry. Be the prettiest book I ever seen. The cover is a pale blue, color a the sky. And a big white bird—a peace dove—spreads its wings from end to end. The title *Help* is written across the front in black letters, in a bold fashion. The only thing that bothers me is the who-it-be-by part. It say *by Anonymous*. I wish Miss Skeeter could a put her name on it, but it was just too much of a risk.

Tomorrow, I'm on take early copies to all the women whose stories we put in. Miss Skeeter gone carry a copy up to the State Pen to Yule May. In a way, she's the reason the other maids even agreed to help. But I hear Yule May probably won't get the box. Them prisoners don't get but one out a ten things sent to em cause the lady guards take it for theyselves. Miss Skeeter say she gone deliver copies ten more times to make sure.

I carry that big box home and take out one copy and put the box under my bed. Then I run over to Minny's house. Minny six months pregnant but you can't even tell yet. When I get there, she setting at the kitchen table drinking a glass a milk. Leroy asleep in the back and Benny and Sugar and Kindra is shelling peanuts in the backyard. The kitchen's quiet. I smile, hand Minny her copy.

She eye it. "I guess the dove bird looks okay."

"Miss Skeeter say the peace dove be the sign for better times to come. Say folks is wearing em on they clothes out in California."

"I don't care bout no peoples in California," Minny say, staring at that cover. "All I care about is what the folks in Jackson, Mississippi, got to say about it."

"Copies gone show up in the bookstores and the libraries tomorrow. Twenty-five hundred in Mississippi, other half all over the United States." That's a lot more than what Miss Stein told us before, but since the freedom rides started and them civil rights workers disappeared in that station wagon here in Mississippi, she say folks is paying more attention to our state.

"How many copies going to the white Jackson library?" Minny ask. "Zero?"

I shake my head with a smile. "Three copies. Miss Skeeter told me on the phone this morning."

Even Minny look stunned. Just two months ago the white library started letting colored people in. I been in twice myself.

Minny open the book and she start reading it right there. Kids come in and she tell them what to do and how to do it without even looking up. Eyes don't even stop moving across the page. I already done read it many a time, working on it over the past year. But Minny always said she don't want a read it till it come out in the hardboard. Say she don't want a spoil it.

I set there with Minny awhile. Time to time she grin. Few times she laugh. And more an once she growl. I don't ask what for. I leave her to it and head home. After I write all my prayers, I go to bed with that book setting on the pillow next to me.

THE NEXT DAY AT WORK, all I can think about is how stores is putting *my* book on the shelves. I mop, I iron, I change diapers, but I don't hear a word about it in Miss Leefolt's house. It's like I ain't even written a book. I don't know what I spected—*some* kind a stirring—but it's just a regular old hot Friday with flies buzzing on the screen.

That night six maids in the book call my house asking has anybody said anything. We linger on the line like the answer's gone change if we breathe into the phone long enough.

Miss Skeeter call last. "I went by the Bookworm this afternoon. Stood around awhile, but nobody even picked it up."

"Eula say she went by the colored bookstore. Same thing."

"Alright," she sigh.

But all that weekend and then into the next week, we don't hear nothing. The same old books set on Miss Leefolt's nightstand: *Frances Benton's Etiquette*, *Peyton Place*, that old dusty Bible she keep by the bed for show. But Law if I don't keep glancing at that stack like a stain.

By Wednesday, they still ain't even a ripple in the water. Not one person's bought a copy in the white bookstore. The Farish Street store say they done sold about a dozen, which is good. Might a just been the other maids, though, buying for they friends.

On Thursday, day seven, before I even left for work, my phone ring.

"I've got news," Miss Skeeter whisper. I reckon she must be locked up in the pantry again.

"What happen?"

"Missus Stein called and said we're going to be on the Dennis James show."

"*People Will Talk*? The tee-vee show?"

"Our book made the book review. She said it'll be on Channel Three next Thursday at one o'clock."

Law, we gone be on WLBT-TV! It's a local Jackson show, and it come on in color, right after the twelve o'clock news.

"You think the review gone be good or bad?"

"I don't know. I don't even know if Dennis reads the books or just says what they tell him to."

I feel excited and scared at the same time. Something *got* to happen after that.

"Missus Stein said somebody must've felt sorry for us in the Harper and Row publicity department and made some calls. She said we're the first book she's handled with a publicity budget of zero."

We laugh, but we both sound nervous.

"I hope you get to watch it at Elizabeth's. If you can't, I'll call you and tell you everything they said."

. . .

ON FRIDAY NIGHT, a week after the book come out, I get ready to go to the church. Deacon Thomas call me this morning and ask would I come to a special meeting they having, but when I ask what about, he get all in a hurry and say he got to go. Minny say she got the same thing. So I iron up a nice linen dress a Miss Greenlee's and head to Minny's house. We gone walk there together.

As usual, Minny's house be like a chicken coop on fire. Minny be hollering, things be flinging around, all the kids squawking. I see the first hint a Minny's belly under her dress and I'm grateful she finally showing. Leroy, he don't hit Minny when she pregnant. And Minny know this so I spec they's gone be a lot more babies after this one.

"Kindra! Get your butt off that floor!" Minny holler. "Them beans better be hot when your daddy wakes up!"

Kindra—she seven now—she sass-walk her way to the stove with her bottom sticking out and her nose up in the air. Pans go banging all over the place. "Why I got to do dinner? It's Sugar's turn!"

"Cause Sugar at Miss Celia's and you want a live to see third grade."

Benny come in and squeeze me round the middle. He grin and show me the tooth he got missing, then run off.

"Kindra, turn that flame down fore you burn the house down!"

"We better go, Minny," I say, cause this could go on all night. "We gone be late."

Minny look at her watch. Shake her head. "Why Sugar ain't home yet? Miss Celia ain't never kept me this late."

Last week, Minny started bringing Sugar to work. She getting her trained for when Minny have her baby and Sugar gone have to fill in for her. Tonight Miss Celia ask Sugar to work late, say she drive her home.

"Kindra, I don't want a see so much as a bean setting in that sink when I get back. Clean up good now." Minny give her a hug. "Benny, go tell Daddy he better get his fool self out a that bed."

"Aww, Mama, why I—"

"Go on, be brave. Just don't stand too close when he come to."

We make it out the door and down to the street fore we hear Leroy hollering at Benny for waking him up. I walk faster so she don't go back and give Leroy what he good for.

"Glad we going to church tonight," Minny sigh. We round Farish Street, start up the steps. "Give me a hour a not thinking about it all."

Soon as we step in the church foyer, one a the Brown brothers slip behind us and he lock the door. I'm about to ask why, would a got scared if I had the time, but then the thirty-odd peoples in the room start clapping. Minny and me start clapping with em. Figure somebody got into college or something.

"Who we clapping for?" I ask Rachel Johnson. She the Reverend wife.

She laugh and it get quiet. Rachel lean in to me.

"Honey, we clapping for you." Then she reach down and pull a copy a the book out a her purse. I look around and now everbody got a copy in they hands. All the important officers and church deacons are there.

Reverend Johnson come up to me then. "Aibileen, this is an important time for you and our church."

"You must a cleaned out the bookstore," I say, and the crowd laugh real polite-like.

"We want you to know, for your safety, this will be the only time the church recognizes you for your achievement. I know a lot of folks helped with this book, but I heard it couldn't have been done without you."

I look over and Minny's smiling, and I know she in on it too.

"A quiet message has been sent throughout the congregation and all of the community, that if anyone knows who's in the book or who wrote it, it's not to be discussed. Except for tonight. I'm sorry"—he smile, shake his head—"but we just couldn't let this go by without some kind of celebration."

He hand me the book. "We know you couldn't put your name in it, so we all signed our own for you." I open up the front cover and there they is, not thirty or forty names, but hundreds, maybe five hundred, in the front pages, the back pages, along the rim a the inside pages. All the peoples in my church and folks from other churches too. Oh, I just break down then. It's like two years a doing and trying and hoping all come out at once. Then everbody get in a line and come by and hug me. Tell me I'm brave. I tell em there are so many others that are brave too. I hate to hog all the attention, but I am so grateful they don't mention no other names. I don't want em in trouble. I don't think they even know Minny's in there.

"There may be some hard times ahead," Reverend Johnson say to me. "If it comes to that, the Church will help you in every way."

I cry and cry right there in front a everbody. I look over at Minny, and she laughing. Funny how peoples show they feelings in different ways. I wonder what Miss Skeeter would do if she was here and it kind a makes me sad. I know ain't nobody in town gone sign a book for her and tell her she brave. Ain't nobody gone tell her they look after her.

Then the Reverend hands me a box, wrapped in white paper, tied with light blue ribbon, same colors as the book. He lays his hand on it as a blessing. "This one, this is for the white lady. You tell her we love her, like she's our own family."

ON THURSDAY, I wake up with the sun and go to work early. Today's a big day. I get my kitchen work done fast. One a clock come and I make sure I got my ironing all set up in front a Miss Leefolt's tee-vee, tuned to Channel Three. Li'l Man taking his nap and Mae Mobley at school.

I try and iron some pleats, but my hands is shaking and they come out all crooked. I spray it wet and start all over, fussing and frowning. Finally, the time comes.

In the box pops Dennis James. He start telling us what we gone discuss today. His black hair is sprayed down so heavy, it don't even move. He is the fastest talking Southern man I ever heard. Make me feel like I'm on a roller-coaster way he make his voice go. I's so nervous I feel like I'm on throw up right here on Mister Raleigh's church suit.

"...and we'll end the show with the book review." After the commercial, he do something on Elvis Presley's jungle room. Then he do a piece on the new Interstate 55 they gone build, going through Jackson all the way to New Orleans. Then, at 1:22 p.m., a woman come set next to him by the name a Joline French. She say she the local book reviewer.

That very second, Miss Leefolt walk in the house. She all dressed up in her League outfit and her noisy high heels and she head straight for the living room.

"I am so glad that heat wave is over I could jump for joy," she say.

Mister Dennis chatting bout some book called *Little Big Man*. I try to agree with her but I feel real stiff in the face all of a sudden. "I'll—I'll just turn this thing off."

"No, keep it on!" say Miss Leefolt. "That's Joline French on the television set! I better call Hilly and tell her."

She clomp to the kitchen and get on the phone with Miss Hilly's third maid in a month. Ernestine ain't got but one arm. Miss Hilly pickings getting slim.

"Ernestine, this is Miss Elizabeth...Oh, she's not? Well, you tell her the minute she walks in that our sorority sister is on the television set...That's right, thank you."

Miss Leefolt rush back in the living room and set on the sofa, but it's a commercial on. I get to breathing hard. What is she doing? We ain't never watched the tee-vee together before. And here a all days she front and center like she be watching herself on screen!

All a sudden the Dial soap commercial over. And there be Mister Dennis with my book in his hand! White bird look bigger than life. He holding it up and poking his finger at the word *Anonymous*. For two seconds I'm more proud than I is scared. I want to yell—*That's my book! That's my book on the tee-vee!* But I got to keep still, like I'm watching something humdrum. I can't barely breathe!

"...called *Help* with testimonies from some of Mississippi's very own housekeepers—"

"Oh, I wish Hilly was home! Who can I call? Look at those cute shoes she's got on, I bet she got those at The Papagallo Shoppe."

Please shut up! I reach down and turn it up a little, but then I wish I hadn't. What if they talk about her? Would Miss Leefolt even recognize her own life?

"...read it last night and now my wife is reading it..." Mister Dennis talking like a auction man, laughing, eyebrows going up and down, pointing at our book. "...and it is truly touching. Enlightening, I'd say, and they used the made-up town of Niceville, Mississippi, but who knows?" He halfway cover his mouth, whisper real loud, "It could be Jackson!"

Say what?

"Now, I'm not saying it is, it could be anywhere, but just in case, you need to go get this book and make sure you aren't in it! Ha-Ha-Ha-Ha—"

I freeze, feel a tingle on my neck. Ain't *nothing* in there that say Jackson. Tell me again it could be anywhere, Mister Dennis!

I see Miss Leefolt smiling at her friend on the tee-vee like the fool can see her, Mister Dennis be laughing and talking, but that sorority sister, Miss Joline, got a face on red as a stop sign.

"—a disgrace to the South! A disgrace to the good Southern women who've spent their lives taking care of their help. I know I personally treat my help like family and every one of my friends does the same—"

"Why is she frowning like that on tee-vee?" Miss Leefolt whine at the box. "Joline!" She lean forward and *tap-tap-tap* her finger on Miss Joline's forehead. "Don't frown! You don't look cute that way!"

"Joline, did you read that ending? About the pie? If my maid, Bessie Mae, is out there listening, Bessie Mae, I have a new respect for what you do every day. And I'll pass on the chocolate pie from now on! *Ha-Ha-Ha*—"

But Miss Joline holding up the book like she want to burn it. "Do not buy this book! Ladies of Jackson, do not support this slander with your husbands' hard-earned—"

"Huh?" Miss Leefolt ask Mister Dennis. And then poof—we on to a Tide commercial.

"What were they talking about?" Miss Leefolt ask me.

I don't answer. My heart's pounding.

"My friend Joline had a book in her hand."

"Yes, ma'am."

"What was it called? *Help* or something like that?"

I press the iron point down in the collar a Mister Raleigh's shirt. I got to call Minny, Miss Skeeter, find out if they heard this. But Miss Leefolt standing there waiting for my answer and I know she ain't gone let up. She never do.

"Did I hear them say it was about Jackson?" she say.

I keep right on staring at my iron.

"I think they said Jackson. But why don't they want us to buy it?"

My hands is shaking. How can this be happening? I keep ironing, try-ing to make what's beyond wrinkled smooth.

A second later, the Tide commercial's over and there's Dennis James again holding up the book and Miss Joline's still all red in the face. "That's all for today," he say, "but y'all be sure and pick up your copy of *Little Big Man* and *Help* from our sponsor, the State Street Bookstore. And see for yourself, is it or is it not about Jackson?" And then the music come on and he holler, "Good day, Mississippi!"

Miss Leefolt look at me and say, "See that? I told you they said it was about Jackson!" and five minutes later, she off to the bookstore to buy her-self a copy a what I done wrote about her.

MINNY

CHAPTER 30

AFTER THE *People Will Talk* show, I grab the Space Command and punch the "Off" button. My stories are about to come on, but I don't even care. Doctor Strong and Miss Julia will just have to turn the world without me today.

I've a mind to call that Dennis James on the phone and say, *Who do you think you are, spreading lies like that?* You can't tell the whole metro area our book is about Jackson! You don't know what town we've written our book about!

I'll tell you what that fool's doing. He's *wishing* it was about Jackson. He's wishing Jackson, Mississippi, was interesting enough to write a whole book on and even though it is Jackson...well, *he* doesn't know that.

I rush to the kitchen and call Aibileen, but after two tries the line's still busy. I hang up. In the living room, I flip on the iron, yank Mister Johnny's white shirt out of the basket. I wonder for the millionth time what's going to happen when Miss Hilly reads the last chapter. She better get to work soon, telling people it's not our town. And she can tell Miss Celia to fire me all afternoon and Miss Celia won't. Hating Miss Hilly's the only thing that crazy woman and I have in common. But what Hilly'll do once that fails, I don't know. That'll be our own war, between me and Miss Hilly. That won't affect the others.

Oh, now I'm in a bad mood. From where I'm ironing, I can see Miss Celia in the backyard in a pair of hoochie pink satin pants and black plastic gloves. She's got dirt all over her knees. I've asked her a hundred times to quit digging dirt in her dress-up clothes. But that lady never listens.

The grass in front of the pool is covered in yard rakes and hand tools. All Miss Celia does now is hoe up the yard and plant more fancy flowers. Never mind that Mister Johnny hired a full-time yardman a few months ago, name of John Willis. He was hoping he'd be some kind of protection after the naked man showed up, but he's so old he's bent up like a paper clip. Skinny as one too. I feel like I have to check on him just to make sure he hasn't stroked in the bushes. I guess Mister Johnny didn't have the heart to send him home for somebody younger.

I spray more starch on Mister Johnny's collar. I hear Miss Celia hollering instructions on how to plant a bush. "Those hydrangeas, let's get us some more iron in the dirt. Okay, John Willis?"

"Yes'm," John Willis hollers back.

"Shut up, lady," I say. The way she hollers at him, he thinks she's the deaf one.

The phone rings and I run for it.

"OH MINNY," Aibileen says on the phone. "They figure out the town, ain't no time fore they figure out the *people*."

"He a fool is what he is."

"How we know Miss Hilly even gone read it?" Aibileen says, her voice turning high. I hope Miss Leefolt can't hear her. "Law, we should a thought this through, Minny."

I've never heard Aibileen like this. It's like she's me and I'm her. "Listen," I say because something's starting to make sense here. "Since Mister James done made such a stink about it, we *know* she gone read it. Everbody in town gone read it now." Even as I'm saying it, I'm starting to realize it's true. "Don't cry yet, cause maybe things is happening just the way they should."

Five minutes after I hang it up, Miss Celia's phone rings. "Miss Celia res—"

"I just talk to Louvenia," Aibileen whisper. "Miss Lou Anne just come home with a copy for herself and a copy for her best friend, Hilly Holbrook."

Here we go.

ALL NIGHT LONG, I swear, I can feel Miss Hilly reading our book. I can hear the words she's reading whispering in my head, in her cool, white voice. At two a.m. I get up from the bed and open my own copy and try to guess what chapter she's on. Is it one or two or ten? Finally I just stare at the blue cover. I've never seen a book such a nice color. I wipe a smudge off the front.

Then I hide it back in the pocket of my winter coat I've never worn, since I've read zero books after I married Leroy and I don't want to make him suspicious with this one. I finally go back to bed, telling myself there's no way I can guess how far Miss Hilly's read. I do know, though, she hasn't gotten to her part at the end. I know because I haven't heard the screaming in my head yet.

By morning, I swear, I'm glad to be going to work. It's floor-scrubbing day and I want to just get my mind off it all. I heave myself into the car and drive out to Madison County. Miss Celia went to see another doctor yesterday afternoon to find out about having kids and I about told her, you can have this one, lady. I'm sure she'll tell me every last detail about it today. At least the fool had the sense to quit that Doctor Tate.

I pull up to the house. I get to park in front now since Miss Celia finally dropped the ruse and told Mister Johnny what he already knew. The first thing I see is Mister Johnny's truck's still home. I wait in my car. He's never once been here when I come in.

I step into the kitchen. I stand in the middle and look. Somebody already made coffee. I hear a man's voice in the dining room. Something's going on here.

I lean close to the door and hear Mister Johnny, home on a weekday at 8:30 in the morning, and a voice in my head says run right back out the door. Miss Hilly called and told him I was a thief. He found out about the pie. He knows about the book. "Minny?" I hear Miss Celia call.

Real careful, I push the swinging door, peek out. There's Miss Celia setting at the head of the table with Mister Johnny setting next to her. They both look up at me.

Mister Johnny looks whiter than that old albino man that lives behind Miss Walters.

"Minny, bring me a glass of water, please?" he says and I get a real bad feeling.

I get him the water and take it to him. When I set the glass down on the napkin, Mister Johnny stands up. He gives me a long, heavy look. Lord, here it comes.

"I told him about the baby," Miss Celia whispers. "All the babies."

"Minny, I would've lost her if it hadn't of been for you," he says, grabbing hold of my hands. "Thank God you were here."

I look over at Miss Celia and she looks dead in the eyes. I already know what that doctor told her. I can see it, that there won't ever be any babies born alive. Mister Johnny squeezes my hands, then he goes to her. He gets down on his kneecaps and lays his head down in her lap. She smoothes his hair over and over.

"Don't leave. Don't ever leave me, Celia," he cries.

"Tell her, Johnny. Tell Minny what you said to me."

Mister Johnny lifts his head. His hair's all mussed and he looks up at me. "You'll always have a job here with us, Minny. For the rest of your life, if you want."

"Thank you, sir," I say and I mean it. Those are the best words I could hear today.

I reach for the door, but Miss Celia says, real soft, "Stay in here awhile. Will you, Minny?"

So I lean my hand on the sideboard because the baby's getting heavy on me. And I wonder how it is that I have so much when she doesn't have any. He's crying. She's crying. We are three fools in the dining room crying.

"I'M TELLING YOU," I tell Leroy in the kitchen, two days later. "You punch the button and the channel change and you don't even have to get up from your chair."

Leroy's eyes don't move from his paper. "That don't make no sense, Minny."

"Miss Celia got it, called Space Command. A box bout half the size of a bread loaf."

Leroy shakes his head. "Lazy white people. Can't even get up to turn a knob."

"I reckon people gone be flying to the moon pretty soon," I say. I'm not even listening to what's coming out of my mouth. I'm listening for the scream again. When is that lady going to finish?

"What's for supper?" Leroy says.

"Yeah, Mama, when we gone eat?" Kindra says.

I hear a car pull in the driveway. I listen and the spoon slips down into the pot of beans. "Cream-a-Wheat."

"I ain't eating no Cream-a-Wheat for supper!" Leroy says.

"I had that for breakfast!" Kindra cries.

"I mean—ham. And beans." I go slam the back door and turn the latch. I look out the window again. The car is backing out. It was just turning around.

Leroy gets up and flings the back door open again. "It's hot as hell in here!" He comes to the stove where I'm standing. "What's wrong with you?" he asks, about an inch from my face.

"Nothing," I say and move back a little. Usually, he doesn't mess with me when I'm pregnant. But he moves closer. He squeezes my arm hard.

"What'd you do this time?"

"I—I didn't do nothing," I say. "I'm just tired."

He tightens his grip on my arm. It's starting to burn. "You don't get tired. Not till the tenth month."

"I didn't do nothing, Leroy. Just go set and lemme get to supper."

He lets go, giving me a long look. I can't meet his eyes.

AIBILEEN

CHAPTER 31

EVER TIME Miss Leefolt go out shopping or in the yard or even to the bathroom, I check her bedside table where she put the book. I act like I'm dusting, but what I really be doing is checking to see if that First Presbyterian Bible bookmark's moved any deeper in the pages. She's been reading it for five days now and I flip it open today and she still on Chapter One, page *fourteen*. She got two hundred and thirty-five pages left. Law, she read slow.

Still, I want to tell her, you reading about Miss Skeeter, don't you know? About her growing up with Constantine. And I'm scared to death, but I want to tell her, keep reading, lady, cause Chapter Two gone be about *you*.

I am nervous as a cat seeing that book in her house. All week long I been tiptoeing around. One time Li'l Man come up from behind and touch me on the leg and I near bout jump out a my workshoes. Especially on Thursday, when Miss Hilly come over. They set at the dining room table and work on the Benefit. Ever once in a while they look up and smile, ask me to fetch a mayonnaise sandwich or some ice tea.

Twice Miss Hilly come in the kitchen and call her maid, Ernestine. "Are you done soaking Heather's smock dress like I told you to? Uh-huh, and have you dusted the half-tester canopy? Oh you haven't, well go on and do that right away."

I go in to collect they plates and I hear Miss Hilly say, "I'm up to Chapter Seven," and I freeze, the plates in my hand clattering. Miss Leefolt look up and wrinkle her nose at me.

But Miss Hilly, she shaking her finger at Miss Leefolt. "And I think they're right, it just *feels* like Jackson."

"You do?" Miss Leefolt ask.

Miss Hilly lean down and whisper. "I bet we even know some of these Nigra maids."

"You really think so?" Miss Leefolt ask and my body go cold. I can barely move a foot toward the kitchen. "I've only read a little…"

"I do. And you know what?" Miss Hilly smile real sneaky-like. "I'm going to figure out every last one of these people."

THE NEXT MORNING, I'm near about hyperventilating at the bus stop thinking about what Miss Hilly gone do when she get to her part, wondering if Miss Leefolt done read Chapter Two yet. And when I walk in her house, there Miss Leefolt is reading my book at the kitchen table. She hand me Li'l Man from her lap without even taking her eyes off the page. Then she wander off to the back reading and walking at the same time. All a sudden, she can't get enough of it now that Miss Hilly done taken a interest in it.

Few minutes later, I go back to her bedroom to get the dirty clothes. Miss Leefolt's in the bathroom, so I open the book at the bookmark. She already on Chapter *Six,* Winnie's chapter. This where the white lady get the old-timer disease and call the police department ever morning cause a colored woman just walked in her house. That means Miss Leefolt read her part and just *kept on going.*

I'm scared but I can't help but roll my eyes. I bet Miss Leefolt ain't got no idea it be about herself. I mean, thank the Lord, but still. She probably shaking her head in bed last night, reading bout this awful woman who don't know how to love her own child.

Soon as Miss Leefolt go to her hair appointment, I call Minny. All we do lately is run up our white lady's phone bill.

"You heard anything?" I ask.

"No, nothing. Miss Leefolt finish yet?" she ask.

"No, but she made it to Winnie last night. Miss Celia still ain't bought a copy?"

"That lady don't look at nothing but trash. *I'm coming*," Minny holler. "The fool's stuck in the hair dryer hood again. I told her not to put her head in there when she got them big rollers in."

"Call me if you hear anything," I say. "I do the same."

"Something's gone happen soon, Aibileen. It's got to."

THAT AFTERNOON, I stomp up to the Jitney to pick up some fruit and cottage cheese for Mae Mobley. That Miss Taylor done it again. Baby Girl get out the carpool today, walked straight to her room and throwed herself on her bed. "What's wrong, Baby? What happen?"

"I colored myself black," she cried.

"What you mean?" I asked. "With the markers you did?" I picked up her hand but she didn't have no ink on her skin.

"Miss Taylor said to draw what we like about ourselves best." I saw then a wrinkled, sad-looking paper in her hand. I turned it over and sure enough, there's my baby white girl done colored herself black.

"She said black means I got a dirty, bad face." She plant her face in her pillow and cried something awful.

Miss Taylor. After all the time I spent teaching Mae Mobley how to love all people, not judge by color. I feel a hard fist in my chest because what person out there don't remember they first-grade teacher? Maybe they don't remember what they learn, but I'm telling you, I done raised enough kids to know, they *matter*.

At least the Jitney's cool. I feel bad I forgot to buy Mae Mobley's snack this morning. I hurry so she won't have to set with her mama for too long. She done hid her paper under her bed so her mama wouldn't see it.

In the can food section, I get two cans a tunafish. I walk over to find the green Jell-O powder and there's sweet Louvenia in her white uniform looking at peanut butter. I'll think a Louvenia as Chapter Seven for the rest a my life.

"How's Robert doing?" I ask, patting her arm. Louvenia work all day for Miss Lou Anne and then come home ever afternoon and take Robert to blind school so he can learn to read with his fingers. And I have never heard Louvenia complain once.

"Learning to get around." She nod. "You alright? Feel okay?"

"Just nervous. You heard anything at all?"

She shake her head. "My boss been reading it, though." Miss Lou Anne's in Miss Leefolt's bridge club. Miss Lou Anne was real good to Louvenia when Robert got hurt.

We walk down the aisle with our handbaskets. There be two white ladies talking by the graham crackers. They kind a familiar looking, but I don't know they names. Soon as we get close, they hush up and look at us. Funny how they ain't smiling.

"Scuse me," I say and move on past. When we not but a foot away, I hear one say, "That's the Nigra waits on Elizabeth…" A cart rattles past us, blocking the words.

"I bet you're right," the other one say. "I bet that's her…"

Me and Louvenia keep walking real quiet, looking dead ahead. I feel prickles up my neck, hearing the ladies' heels clack away. I know Louvenia heard better than I did, cause her ears is ten years younger than mine. At the end a the aisle we start to go in different directions, but then we both turn to look at each other.

Did I hear right? I say with my eyes.

You heard right, Louvenia's say back.

Please, Miss Hilly, *read.* Read like the wind.

MINNY

CHAPTER 32

Another day passes, and still I can hear Miss Hilly's voice talking the words, reading the lines. I don't hear the scream. Not yet. But she's getting close.

Aibileen told me what the ladies in the Jitney said yesterday, but we haven't heard another thing since. I keep dropping things, broke my last measuring cup tonight and Leroy's eyeing me like he knows. Right now he's drinking coffee at the table and the kids are draped all over the kitchen doing their homework.

I jump when I see Aibileen standing at the screen door. She puts her finger to her lips and nods to me. Then she disappears.

"Kindra, get the plates, Sugar, watch the beans, Felicia, get Daddy to sign that test, Mama needs some air." Poof I disappear out the screen door.

Aibileen's standing on the side of the house in her white uniform.

"What happen?" I ask. Inside I hear Leroy yell, "A *Eff*?" He won't touch the kids. He'll yell, but that's what fathers are supposed to do.

"One-arm Ernestine call and say Miss Hilly's talking all over town about who's in the book. She telling white ladies to fire they maids and she ain't even guessing the right ones!" Aibileen looks so upset, she's shaking. She's twisting a cloth into a white rope. I'll bet she doesn't even realize she carried over her real dinner napkin.

"Who she saying?"

"She told Miss Sinclair to fire Annabelle. So Miss Sinclair fired her and then took her car keys away cause she loaned her half the money to buy the car. Annabelle already paid most of it back but it's gone."

"That *witch*," I whisper, grinding my teeth.

"That ain't all, Minny."

I hear bootsteps in the kitchen. "Hurry, fore Leroy catch us whispering."

"Miss Hilly told Miss Lou Anne, 'Your Louvenia's in here. I know she is and you need to fire her. You ought to send that Nigra to jail.'"

"But Louvenia didn't say a single bad thing about Miss Lou Anne!" I say. "And she got Robert to take care of! What Miss Lou Anne say?"

Aibileen bites her lip. She shakes her head and the tears come down her face.

"She say . . . she gone think about it."

"Which one? The firing or the jail?"

Aibileen shrug. "Both, I reckon."

"Jesus Christ," I say, wanting to kick something. Some*body.*

"Minny, what if Miss Hilly don't ever finish reading it?"

"I don't know, Aibileen. I just don't know."

Aibileen's eyes jerk up to the door and there's Leroy, watching us from behind the screen. He stands there, quiet, until I tell Abileen goodbye and come back inside.

AT FIVE-THIRTY THAT MORNING, Leroy falls into bed next to me. I wake up to the squawk of the frame and the stench of the liquor. I grit my teeth, praying he doesn't try to start a fight. I am too tired for it. Not that I was asleep good anyway, worrying about Aibileen and her news. For Miss Hilly, Louvenia would just be another jail key on that witch's belt.

Leroy flops around and tosses and turns, never mind his pregnant wife's trying to sleep. When the fool finally gets settled, I hear his whisper.

"What's the big secret, Minny?"

I can feel him watching me, feel his liquor breath on my shoulder. I don't move.

"You know I'll find out," he hisses. "I always do."

In about ten seconds, his breathing slows to almost dead and he throws his hand across me. *Thank you for this baby*, I pray. Because that's the only thing that saved me, this baby in my belly. And that is the ugly truth.

I lay there grinding my teeth, wondering, worrying. Leroy, he's onto something. And God knows what'll happen to me if he finds out. He knows about the book, everybody does, just not that his wife was a part of it, thank you. People probably assume I don't care if he finds out—oh I know what people think. They think big strong Minny, she sure can stand up for herself. But they don't know what a pathetic mess I turn into when Leroy's beating on me. I'm afraid to hit back. I'm afraid he'll leave me if I do. I know it makes no sense and I get so mad at myself for being so weak! How can I love a man who beats me raw? Why do I love a fool drinker? One time I asked him, "Why? Why are you hitting me?" He leaned down and looked me right in the face.

"If I didn't hit you, Minny, who *knows* what you become."

I was trapped in the corner of the bedroom like a dog. He was beating me with his belt. It was the first time I'd ever really thought about it.

Who *knows* what I could become, if Leroy would stop goddamn hitting me.

THE NEXT NIGHT, I make everybody go to bed early, including myself. Leroy's at the plant until five and I'm feeling too heavy for my time. Lord, maybe it's twins. I'm not paying a doctor to tell me that bad news. All I know is, this baby's already bigger than the others when they came out, and I'm only six months.

I fall into a heavy sleep. I'm dreaming I'm at a long wooden table and I'm at a feast. I'm gnawing on a big roasted turkey leg.

I fly upright in my bed. My breath is fast. "Who there?"

My heart's flinging itself against my chest. I look around my dark bedroom. It's half-past midnight. Leroy's not here, thank God. But something woke me for sure.

And then I realize what it was that woke me. I heard what I've been waiting on. What we've all been waiting on.

I heard Miss Hilly's scream.

MISS SKEETER

CHAPTER 33

My eyes pop open. My chest is pumping. I'm sweating. The green-vined wallpaper is snaking up the walls. What woke me? What *was* that?

I get out of bed and listen. It didn't sound like Mother. It was too high-pitched. It was a scream, like material ripping into two shredded pieces.

I sit back on the bed and press my hand to my heart. It's still pounding. Nothing is going as planned. People know the book is about Jackson. I can't believe I forgot what a slow goddamn reader Hilly is. I'll bet she's telling people she's read more than she has. Now things are spinning out of control, a maid named Annabelle was fired, white women are whispering about Aibileen and Louvenia and who knows who else. And the irony is, I'm gnawing my hands waiting for Hilly to speak up when I'm the only one in this town who doesn't care what she has to say anymore.

What if the book was a horrible mistake?

I take a deep, painful breath. I try to think of the future, not the present. A month ago, I mailed out fifteen résumés to Dallas, Memphis, Birmingham, and five other cities, and once again, New York. Missus Stein told me I could list her as a reference, which is probably the only notable thing on the page, having a recommendation from someone in publishing. I added the jobs I've held for the past year:

Weekly Housekeeping Columnist for the Jackson Journal Newspaper
Editor of the Junior League of Jackson Newsletter
Author of Help, a controversial book about colored housekeepers and
their white employers, Harper & Row

I didn't really include the book, I just wanted to type it out once. But now, even if I did get a job offer in a big city, I can't abandon Aibileen in the middle of this mess. Not with things going so badly.

But God, I have to get out of Mississippi. Besides Mother and Daddy, I have nothing left here, no friends, no job I really care about, no Stuart. But it's not just out of here. When I addressed my résumé to the *New York Post, The New York Times, Harper's Magazine, The New Yorker* magazine, I felt that surge again, the same I'd felt in college, of how much I want to be there. Not Dallas, not Memphis—*New York City*, where writers are supposed to live. But I've heard nothing back from any of them. What if I never leave? What if I'm stuck. Here. Forever?

I lie down and watch the first rays of sun coming through the window. I shiver. That ripping scream, I realize, was *me*.

I'm standing in Brent's Drug Store picking out Mother's Lustre Cream and a Vinolia soap bar, while Mr. Roberts works on her prescription. Mother says she doesn't need the medicine anymore, that the only cure for cancer is having a daughter who won't cut her hair and wears dresses too high above the knee even on Sunday, because who knows what tackiness I'd do to myself if she died.

I'm just grateful Mother's better. If my fifteen-second engagement to Stuart is what spurred Mother's will to live, the fact that I'm single again fueled her strength even more. She was clearly disappointed by our break-up, but then bounced back superbly. Mother even went so far as to set me up with a third cousin removed, who is thirty-five and beautiful and clearly homosexual. "Mother," I'd said when he left after supper, for how could she not see it? "He's..." but I'd stopped. I'd patted her hand instead. "He said I wasn't his type."

Now I'm hurrying to get out of the drugstore before anyone I know comes in. I should be used to my isolation by now, but I'm not. I miss having friends. Not Hilly, but sometimes Elizabeth, the old, sweet Elizabeth back in high school. It got harder when I finished the book and I couldn't even visit Aibileen anymore. We decided it was too risky. I miss going to her house and talking to her more than anything.

Every few days, I speak to Aibileen on the phone, but it's not the same as sitting with her. *Please,* I think when she updates me on what's going on around town, *please let some good come out of this.* But so far, nothing. Just girls gossiping and treating the book like a game, trying to guess who is who and Hilly accusing the wrong people. I was the one who assured the colored maids we wouldn't be found out, and I am the one responsible for this.

The front bell tinkles. I look over and in walk Elizabeth and Lou Anne Templeton. I slip back into beauty creams, hoping they don't see me. But then I peek over the shelves to look. They're heading for the lunch counter, huddled together like schoolgirls. Lou Anne's wearing her usual long sleeves in the summer heat and her constant smile. I wonder if she knows she's in the book.

Elizabeth's got her hair poufed up in front and she's covered the back in a scarf, the yellow scarf I gave her for her twenty-third birthday. I stand there a minute, letting myself feel how strange this all is, watching them, knowing what I know. She has read up to Chapter Ten, Aibileen told me last night, and still doesn't have the faintest idea that she's reading about herself and her friends.

"Skeeter?" Mr. Roberts calls out from his landing above the register. "Your mama's medicine's ready."

I walk to the front of the store, and have to pass Elizabeth and Lou Anne at the lunch counter. They keep their backs to me, but I can see their eyes in the mirror, following me. They look down at the same time.

I pay for the medicine and Mother's tubes and goo and work my way back through the aisles. As I try to escape along the far side of the store, Lou Anne Templeton steps from behind the hairbrush rack.

"Skeeter," she says. "You have a minute?"

I stand there blinking, surprised. No one's asked me for even a second, much less a minute, in over eight months. "Um, sure," I say, wary.

Lou Anne glances out the window and I see Elizabeth heading for her car, a milkshake in hand. Lou Anne motions me closer, by the shampoos and detanglers.

"Your mama, I hope she's still doing better?" Lou Anne asks. Her smile is not quite as beaming as usual. She pulls at the long sleeves of her dress, even though a fine sweat covers her forehead.

"She's fine. Still...in remission."

"I'm so glad." She nods and we stand there awkwardly, looking at each other. Lou Anne takes a deep breath. "I know we haven't talked in a while but," she lowers her voice, "I just thought you should know what Hilly's saying. She's saying you wrote that book...about the maids."

"I heard that book was written anonymously," is my quick answer, not sure I even want to act like I've read it. Even though everyone in town's reading it. All three bookstores are sold out and the library has a two-month waiting list.

She holds up her palm, like a stop sign. "I don't want to know if it's true. But Hilly..." She steps closer to me. "Hilly Holbrook called me the other day and told me to fire my maid Louvenia." Her jaw tightens and she shakes her head.

Please. I hold my breath. *Please don't say you fired her.*

"Skeeter, Louvenia..." Lou Anne looks me in the eye, says, "she's the only reason I can get out of bed sometimes."

I don't say anything. Maybe this is a trap Hilly's set.

"And I'm sure you think I'm just some dumb girl...that I agree with everything Hilly says." Tears come up in her eyes. Her lips are trembling. "The doctors want me to go up to Memphis for...*shock treatment*..." She covers her face but a tear slips through her fingers. "For the depression and the...the tries," she whispers.

I look down at her long sleeves and I wonder if that's what she's been hiding. I hope I'm not right, but I shudder.

"Of course, Henry says I need to shape up or ship out." She makes a marching motion, trying to smile, but it falls quickly and the sadness flickers back into her face.

"Skeeter, Louvenia is the bravest person I know. Even with all her own troubles, she sits down and talks to me. She helps me get through my days. When I read what she wrote about me, about helping her with her grandson, I've never been so grateful in my life. It was the best I'd felt in months."

I don't know what to say. This is the only good thing I've heard about the book and I want her to tell me more. I guess Aibileen hasn't heard this yet, either. But I'm worried too because, clearly, Lou Anne knows.

"If you did write it, if Hilly's rumor is true, I just want you to know, I will never fire Louvenia. I told Hilly I'd think about it, but if Hilly Holbrook ever says that to me again, I will tell her to her face she deserved that pie and more."

"How do—what makes you think that was Hilly?" *Our protection—our insurance, it's gone if the pie secret is out.*

"Maybe it was and maybe it wasn't. But that's the talk." Lou Anne shakes her head. "Then this morning I heard Hilly's telling everybody the book's not even about Jackson. Who knows why."

I suck in a breath, whisper, "Thank God."

"Well, Henry'll be home soon." She pulls her handbag up on her shoulder and stands up straighter. The smile comes back on her face like a mask.

She turns for the door, but looks back at me as she opens it. "And I'll tell you one more thing. Hilly Holbrook's not getting my vote for League president in January. Or ever again, for that matter."

On that, she walks out, the bell tinkling behind her.

I linger at the window. Outside, a fine rain has started to fall, misting the glassy cars and slicking the black pavement. I watch Lou Anne slip away in the parking lot, thinking, *There is so much you don't know about a person.* I wonder if I could've made her days a little bit easier, if I'd tried. If I'd treated her a little nicer. Wasn't that the point of the book? For women to realize, *We are just two people. Not that much separates us. Not nearly as much as I'd thought.*

But Lou Anne, she understood the point of the book before she ever read it. The one who was missing the point this time was me.

. . .

THAT EVENING, I call Aibileen four times, but her phone line is busy. I hang up and sit for a while in the pantry, staring at the jars of fig preserves Constantine put up before the fig tree died. Aibileen told me that the maids talk all the time about the book and what's happening. She gets six or seven phone calls a night.

I sigh. It's Wednesday. Tomorrow I turn in my Miss Myrna column that I wrote six weeks ago. Again, I've stockpiled two dozen of them, because I have nothing else to do. After that, there's nothing left to think about, except worry.

Sometimes, when I'm bored, I can't help but think what my life would be like if I hadn't written the book. Monday, I would've played bridge. And tomorrow night, I'd be going to the League meeting and turning in the newsletter. Then on Friday night, Stuart would take me to dinner and we'd stay out late and I'd be tired when I got up for my tennis game on Saturday. Tired and content and...*frustrated*.

Because Hilly would've called her maid a thief that afternoon, and I would've just sat there and listened to it. And Elizabeth would've grabbed her child's arm too hard and I would've looked away, like I didn't see it. And I'd be engaged to Stuart and I wouldn't wear short dresses, only short hair, or consider doing anything risky like write a book about colored house-keepers, too afraid he'd disapprove. And while I'd never lie and tell myself I actually changed the minds of people like Hilly and Elizabeth, at least I don't have to pretend I agree with them anymore.

I get out of that stuffy pantry with a panicky feeling. I slip on my man huaraches and walk out into the warm night. The moon is full and there's just enough light. I forgot to check the mailbox this afternoon and I'm the only one who ever does it. I open it and there's one single letter. It's from Harper & Row, so it must be from Missus Stein. I'm surprised she would send something here since I have all the book contracts sent to a box at the post office, just in case. It's too dark to read, so I tuck it in the back pocket of my blue jeans.

Instead of walking up the lane, I cut through the "orchard," feeling the soft grass under my feet, stepping around the early pears that have fallen. It is September again and I'm here. Still here. Even Stuart has moved on. An article a few weeks ago about the Senator said that Stuart moved his oil company down to New Orleans so that he can spend time out on the rigs at sea again.

I hear the rumble of gravel. I can't see the car driving up the lane, though, because for some reason, the headlights aren't on.

I watch her park the Oldsmobile in front of the house and turn off the engine, but she stays inside. Our front porch lights are on, yellow and flickering with night bugs. She's leaning over her steering wheel, like she's trying to see who's home. What the hell does she want? I watch a few seconds. Then I think, *Get to her first.* Get to her before she does whatever it is she's planning.

I walk quietly through the yard. She lights a cigarette, throws the match out the open window into our drive.

I approach her car from behind, but she doesn't see me.

"Waiting for someone?" I say at the window.

Hilly jumps and drops her cigarette into the gravel. She scrambles out of the car and slams the door closed, backing away from me.

"Don't you get an inch closer," she says.

So I stop where I am and just look at her. Who *wouldn't* look at her? Her black hair is a mess. A curl on top is floppy, sticking straight up. Half her blouse is untucked, her fat stretching the buttons, and I can see she's gained more weight. And there's a...sore. It's in the corner of her mouth, scabby and hot red. I haven't seen Hilly with one of those since Johnny broke up with her in college.

She looks me up and down. "What are you, some kind of hippie now? God, your poor mama must be so embarrassed of you."

"Hilly, why are you here?"

"To tell you I've contacted my lawyer, Hibbie Goodman, who happens to be the number one expert on the libel laws in Mississippi, and you are in big trouble, missy. You're going to jail, you know that?"

"You can't prove anything, Hilly." I've had this discussion with the legal department of Harper & Row. We were very careful in our obscurity.

"Well, I one-hundred-percent know you wrote it because there isn't anybody else in town as tacky as you. Taking up with Nigras like that."

It is truly baffling that we were ever friends. I think about going inside and locking the door. But there's an envelope in her hand, and that makes me nervous.

"I know there's been a lot of talk, Hilly, and a lot of rumors—"

"Oh, that talk doesn't hurt me. Everyone in town knows it's not Jackson. It's some town you made up in that sick little head of yours, and I know who helped you, too."

My jaw tightens. She obviously knows about Minny, and Louvenia I knew already, but does she know about Aibileen? Or the others?

Hilly waves the envelope at me and it crackles. "I am here to inform your mother of what you've *done*."

"You're going to tell my *mother* on me?" I laugh, but the truth is, Mother doesn't know anything about it. And I want to keep it that way. She'd be mortified and ashamed of me and... I look down at the envelope. What if it makes her sick again?

"I most certainly am." Hilly walks up the front steps, head held high.

I follow quickly behind Hilly to the front door. She opens it and walks in like it's her own house.

"Hilly, I did not invite you in here," I say, grabbing her arm. "You get—"

But then Mother appears from around the corner and I drop my hand.

"Why, *Hilly*," Mother says. She is in her bathrobe and her cane wobbles as she walks. "It's been such a long time, dear."

Hilly blinks at her several times. I do not know if Hilly is more shocked at how my mother looks, or the other way around. Mother's once thick brown hair is now snow white and thin. The trembling hand on her cane probably looks skeletonlike to someone who hasn't seen her. But worst of all, Mother doesn't have all of her teeth in, only her front ones. The hollows in her cheeks are deep, deathly.

"Missus Phelan, I'm—I'm here to—"

"Hilly, are you ill? You look horrendous," Mother says.

Hilly licks her lips. "Well I—I didn't have time to get fixed up before—"

Mother is shaking her head. "Hilly, *darling*. No young husband wants to come home and see this. Look at your hair. And that..." Mother frowns, peering closer at the cold sore. "That is not attractive, dear."

I keep my eye on the letter. Mother points her finger at me. "I'm calling Fanny Mae's tomorrow and I'm going to make an appointment for the both of you."

"Missus Phelan, that's not—"

"No need to thank me," Mother says. "It's the least I can do for you, now that your own dear mother's not around for guidance. Now, I'm off to bed," and Mother hobbles toward her bedroom. "Not too late, girls."

Hilly stands there a second, her mouth hanging open. Finally, she goes to the door and flings it open and walks out. The letter is still in her hand.

"You are in a lifetime of trouble, Skeeter," she hisses at me, her mouth like a fist. "And those Nigras of yours?"

"Exactly who are you talking about, Hilly?" I say. "You don't know anything."

"I don't, do I? That Louvenia? Oh, I've taken care of her. Lou Anne's all set to go on that one." The curl on the top of her head bobs as she nods.

"And you tell that Aibileen, the next time she wants to write about my dear friend Elizabeth, uh-huh," she says, flashing a crude smile. "You remember Elizabeth? She had you in her wedding?"

My nostrils flare. I want to hit her, at the sound of Aibileen's name.

"Let's just say Aibileen ought to've been a little bit smarter and not put in the L-shaped crack in poor Elizabeth's dining table."

My heart stops. The goddamn crack. How stupid could I be to let that slip?

"And don't think I've forgotten Minny Jackson. I have some *big* plans for that Nigra."

"Careful, Hilly," I say through my teeth. "Don't give yourself away now." I sound so confident, but inside I'm trembling, wondering what these plans are.

Her eyes fly open. "That was not me WHO ATE THAT PIE!"

She turns and marches to her car. She jerks the door open. "You tell those Nigras they better keep one eye over their shoulders. They better watch out for what's coming to them."

MY HAND SHAKES AS I dial Aibileen's number. I take the receiver in the pantry and shut the door. The opened letter from Harper & Row is in my other hand. It feels like midnight, but it's only eight thirty.

Aibileen answers and I blurt it out. "Hilly came here tonight and she *knows.*"

"Miss Hilly? Knows what?"

Then I hear Minny's voice in the background. "Hilly? What about Miss Hilly?"

"Minny's...here with me," Aibileen says.

"Well, I guess she needs to hear this too," I say, even though I wish Aibileen could tell her later, without me. As I describe how Hilly showed up here, stormed into the house, I wait while she repeats everything back to Minny. It is worse hearing it in Aibileen's voice.

Aibileen comes back onto the phone and sighs.

"It was the crack in Elizabeth's dining room table...that's how Hilly knew for sure."

"Law, that *crack.* I can't believe I put that in."

"No, *I* should've caught it. I'm so sorry, Aibileen."

"You think Miss Hilly gone tell Miss Leefolt I wrote about her?"

"She can't tell her," Minny hollers. "Then she admitting it's Jackson."

I realize how good Minny's plan was. "I agree," I say. "I think Hilly's terrified, Aibileen. She doesn't know *what* to do. She said she was going to tell my *mother* on me."

Now that the shock of Hilly's words has passed, I almost laugh at this thought. That's the least of our worries. If my mother lived through my broken engagement, then she can live through this. I'll just deal with it when it happens.

"I reckon they's nothing we can do but wait, then," Aibileen says, but she sounds nervous. It's probably not the best time to tell her my other news, but I don't think I can keep myself from it.

"I got a...letter today. From Harper and Row," I say. "I thought it was from Missus Stein, but it wasn't."

"What then?"

"It's a job offer at *Harper's Magazine* in New York. As a...copy editor's assistant. I'm pretty sure Missus Stein got it for me."

"That's so good!" Aibileen says, and then, "Minny, Miss Skeeter got a job offer in New York City!"

"Aibileen, I can't take it. I just wanted to share it with you. I..." I'm grateful to at least have Aibileen to tell.

"What you mean, you can't take it? This what you been dreaming of."

"I can't leave now, right when things are getting bad. I'm not going to leave you in this mess."

"But...them bad things gone happen whether you here or not."

God, to hear her say that, I want to cry. I let out a groan.

"I didn't mean it like that. We don't know what's gone happen. Miss Skeeter, you got to take that job."

I truly don't know what to do. Part of me thinks I shouldn't have even told Aibileen, of course she would tell me to go, but I had to tell someone. I hear her whisper to Minny, "She say she ain't gone take it."

"Miss Skeeter," Aibileen says back on the phone, "I don't mean to be rubbing no salt on your wound but...you ain't got a good life here in Jackson. Your mama's better and—"

I hear muffled words and handling of the receiver and suddenly it's Minny on the phone. "You listen to me, Miss Skeeter. I'm on take care a Aibileen and she gone take care a me. But you got nothing left here but enemies in the Junior League and a mama that's gone drive you to drink. You done burned ever bridge there is. And you ain't *never* gone get another boyfriend in this town and everbody know it. So don't walk your white butt to New York, *run* it."

Minny hangs the phone up in my face, and I sit staring at the dead receiver in one hand and the letter in the other. *Really?* I think, actually considering it for the first time. *Can I really do this?*

Minny is right, and Aibileen is too. I have nothing left here except Mother and Daddy and staying here for my parents will surely ruin the relationship we have, but...

I lean against the shelves, close my eyes. I'm going. I am going to New York.

AIBILEEN

CHAPTER 34

MISS LEEFOLT'S silver service got funny spots on it today. Must be cause the humidity's so high. I go around the bridge club table, polishing each piece again, making sure they all still there. Li'l Man, he's started swiping things, spoons and nickels and hair pins. He stick em in his diaper to hide. Sometimes, changing diapers can be like opening treasure.

The phone ring so I go in the kitchen and answer it.

"Got a little bit a news today," Minny say on the phone.

"What you hear?"

"Miss Renfro say she *know* it was Miss Hilly who ate that pie." Minny cackle but my heart go ten times faster.

"Law, Miss Hilly gone be here in five minutes. She better put that fire out fast." It feel crazy that we rooting for her. It's confusing in my mind.

"I call one-arm Ernest—" but then Minny shuts up. Miss Celia must a walked in.

"Alright, she gone. I call one-arm Ernestine and she say Miss Hilly been screaming in the phone all day. And Miss Clara, she know about Fanny Amos."

"She fire her?" Miss Clara put Fanny Amos's boy through college, one a the good stories.

"Nuh-uh. Just sat there with her mouth open and the book in her hand."

"Thank the Lord. Call me if you hear more," I say. "Don't worry bout Miss Leefolt answering. Tell her it's about my sick sister." And Lord, don't You go getting me for that lie. Last thing I need is a sister getting sick.

A few minutes after we hang up, the doorbell ring and I pretend I don't even hear. I'm so nervous to see Miss Hilly's face after what she said to Miss Skeeter. I can't believe I put in that L-shaped crack. I go out to my bathroom and just set, thinking about what's gone happen if I have to leave Mae Mobley. Lord, I pray, if I have to leave her, give her somebody good. Don't leave her with just Miss Taylor telling her black is dirty and her Granmama pinching the thank-yous out a her and cold Miss Leefolt. The doorbell in the house ring again, but I stay put. I'm on do it tomorrow, I say to myself. Just in case, I'm on tell Mae Mobley goodbye.

WHEN I COME BACK IN, I hear all the ladies at the table talking. Miss Hilly's voice is loud. I hold my ear to the kitchen door, dreading going out there.

"—is *not* Jackson. This book is garbage, is what it is. I'll bet the whole thing was made up by some Nigra—"

I hear a chair scrape and I know Miss Leefolt about to come hunting for me. I can't put it off no more.

I open the door with the ice tea pitcher in my hand. Round the table I go, keeping my eyes to my shoes.

"I heard that Betty character might be Charlene," Miss Jeanie say with big eyes. Next to her, Miss Lou Anne's staring off like she don't care one way or the other. I wish I could pat her shoulder. I wish I could tell her how glad I am she's Louvenia's white lady, without giving nothing away, but I know I can't. And I can't tell nothing on Miss Leefolt cause she just frowning like usual. But Miss Hilly's face, it's purple as a plum.

"And the maid in Chapter Four?" Miss Jeanie going on. "I heard Sissy Tucker saying—"

"The book is *not about Jackson!*" Miss Hilly kind a scream and I jump while I'm pouring. A drop a tea accidentally plops on Miss Hilly's empty plate. She look up at me and like a magnet, my eyes pull to hers.

Low and cool, she say, "You spilled some, Aibileen."

"I'm sorry, I—"

"Wipe it up."

Shaking, I wipe it with the cloth I had on the handle a the pitcher.

She staring at my face. I have to look down. I can feel the hot secret between us. "Get me a new plate. One you haven't soiled with your dirty cloth."

I get her a new plate. She study it, sniff real loud. Then she turn to Miss Leefolt and say, "You can't even *teach* these people how to be clean."

I HAVE TO SIT LATE that night for Miss Leefolt. While Mae Mobley sleeping, I pull out my prayer book, get started on my list. I'm so glad for Miss Skeeter. She call me this morning and say she took the job. She moving to New York in a week! But Law, I can't stop jumping ever time I hear a noise, thinking maybe Miss Leefolt gone walk in the door and say she know the truth. By the time I get home, I'm too jumpy to go to bed. I walk through the pitch-black dark to Minny's back door. She setting at her table reading the paper. This is the only part a her day when she ain't running around to clean something or feed something or make somebody do right. The house be so quiet I figure something wrong.

"Where everbody?"

She shrug, "Gone to bed or gone to work."

I pull out a chair and set down. "I just want a know what's gone happen," I say. "I know I ought a be thankful it ain't all blowed up in my face yet, but this waiting's driving me crazy."

"It's gone happen. Soon enough," Minny say, like we talking about the kind a coffee we drink.

"Minny, how can you be so calm?"

She looks at me, puts her hand on her tummy that's popped out in the last two weeks. "You know Miss Chotard, who Willie Mae wait on? She ask

Willie Mae yesterday if she treats her bad as that awful lady in the book."
Minny kind a snort. "Willie Mae tell her she got some room to grow but
she ain't too bad."

"She really ask her that?"

"Then Willie Mae tell her what all the other white ladies done to her,
the good and the bad, and that white lady listen to her. Willie May say she
been there thirty-seven years and it's the first time they ever sat at the same
table together."

Besides Louvenia, this the first good thing we heard. I try to enjoy it.
But I snap back to now. "What about Miss Hilly? What about what Miss
Skeeter say? Minny, ain't you at least a little nervous?"

Minny put her newspaper down. "Look, Aibileen, I ain't gone lie. I'm
scared Leroy gone kill me if he find out. I'm scared Miss Hilly gone set my
house on fire. But," she shake her head, "I can't explain it. I got this feeling.
That maybe things is happening just how they should."

"Really?"

Minny kind a laugh. "Lord, I'm starting to sound like you, ain't I? Must
be getting old."

I poke her with my foot. But I try to understand where Minny's coming
from. We done something brave and good here. And Minny, maybe she
don't want a be deprived a any a the things that go along with being brave
and good. Even the bad. But I can't pick up on the calm she feeling.

Minny looks back down at her paper but after a little while, I can tell
she ain't reading. She just staring at the words, thinking about something
else. Somebody's car door slam next door and she jump. And I see it then,
the worry she's trying to hide. But why? I wonder. Why she hiding that
from me?

The more I look, the more I start to understand what's going on here,
what Minny's done. I don't know why I'm just now getting this. Minny
made us put the pie story in to protect us. Not to protect herself, but to
protect me and the other maids. She knew it would only make it worse for
herself with Hilly. But she did it anyway, for everbody else. She don't want
anybody to see how scared she is.

I reach over and squeeze her hand. "You a beautiful person, Minny."

She roll her eyes and stick her tongue out like I handed her a plate a dog biscuits. "I knew you was getting senile," she say.

We both chuckle. It's late and we so tired, but she get up and refill her coffee and fix me a cup a tea and I drink it slow. We talk late into the night.

THE NEXT DAY, SATURDAY, we all in the house, the whole Leefolt family plus me. Even Mister Leefolt home today. My book ain't setting on the bedside table no more. For a while, I don't know where she put it. Then I see Miss Leefolt's pocketbook on the sofa, and she got it tucked inside. Means she carried it with her somewhere. I peek over and see the bookmark's gone.

I want to look in her eyes and see what she know, but Miss Leefolt stay in the kitchen most a the day trying to make a cake. Won't let me in there to help. Say it's not like one a my cakes, it's a fancy recipe she got out the *Gourmet* magazine. She hosting a luncheon tomorrow for her church and the dining room's stacked up with party serving stuff. She done borrowed three chafing dishes from Miss Lou Anne and eight settings a Miss Hilly's silver cause they's fourteen people coming and God forbid any a them church folk got to use a regular ole metal fork.

Li'l Man be in Mae Mobley's bedroom playing with her. And Mister Leefolt pacing round the house. Time to time he stop in front a Baby Girl's bedroom, then go to pacing again. Probably thinks he should be playing with his kids with it being Saturday, but I reckon he don't know how.

So that don't leave a whole lot a places for me to go. It's only two o'clock but I already done cleaned the house down to the nubs, polished the bathrooms, washed the clothes. I ironed everthing short a the wrinkles on my face. Been banned from the kitchen and I don't like Mister Leefolt thinking all I do is set around playing with the kids. Finally I just start wandering round too.

When Mister Leefolt dawdling around the dining room, I peek in and see Mae Mobley got a paper in her hand, teaching Ross something new. She love to play school with her little brother.

I go in the living room, start dusting the books for the second time. I guess I ain't gone get to tell her my in-case goodbye today, with this crowd around.

"We're gonna play a game," I hear Mae Mobley call out to her brother. "Now you sit up at the counter cause you're at the Woolworf's and you're colored. And you got to stay there no matter what I do or you go to jail."

I go to her bedroom fast as I can, but Mister Leefolt's already there, watching at the door. I stand behind him.

Mister Leefolt cross his arms up over his white shirt. Cock his head to the side. My heart's beating a thousand miles a hour. I ain't never once heard Mae Mobley mention our secret stories out loud to anybody except me. And that's when her mama ain't home and they ain't nobody but the house to hear. But she so thick in what she doing, she don't know her daddy's listening.

"Okay," Mae Mobley say and she guide his wobbly self up on the chair. "Ross, you gotta stay there at the Woolworf counter. No getting up."

I want to speak, but I can't get nothing to come out my mouth. Mae Mobley be tippy-toeing up behind Ross, pour a box a crayons on his head, and they clatter down. Li'l Man frown, but she look at him stern, say, "You can't move. You got to be brave. And no violets." Then she stick her tongue out at him and start pinging him with baby doll shoes and Li'l Man look at her like *Why am I putting up with this nonsense?* and he crawl off the chair with a whine.

"You lose!" she says. "Now come on, we're playing Back-a-the-Bus and your name is Rosa Parks."

"Who taught you those things, Mae Mobley?" Mister Leefolt say and Baby Girl whip her head around with eyes like she seed a ghost.

I feel my bones go soft on me. Everthing say go in there. Make sure she don't get in trouble, but I can't breathe enough to go. Baby Girl look right at me standing behind her daddy, and Mister Leefolt turn around and see me, then turn back round to her.

Mae Mobley stare up at her daddy. "I don't know." She looks off at a board game laying on the floor, like she might get to playing it again. I seen her do that, I know what she thinking. She think if she get busy with something else and ignore him, he might just go away.

"Mae Mobley, your daddy asked you a question. Where did you learn about things like that?" He bend down to her. I can't see his face, but I know he smiling cause Mae Mobley all shylike, all Baby Girl loves her daddy. And then she say loud and clear:

"*Miss Taylor did.*"

Mister Leefolt straighten up. Goes into the kitchen and I'm following. He turns Miss Leefolt around by the shoulders and says: "Tomorrow. You go down to that school and put Mae Mobley in a different class. No more Miss Taylor."

"What? I can't just change her teacher—"

I hold my breath, pray, *Yes, you can. Please.*

"Just do it." And like mens do, Mister Raleigh Leefolt walk out the door where he don't have to give nobody no explanation about nothing.

ALL DAY SUNDAY, I can't stop thanking God for getting Baby Girl away from Miss Taylor. *Thank you God, thank you God, thank you God* rings in my head like a chant. On Monday morning, Miss Leefolt head off to Mae Mobley's school, all dressed up, and I have to smile, knowing what she going off to do.

While Miss Leefolt's gone, I get to work on Miss Hilly's silver. Miss Leefolt's got it laid out on the kitchen table from the luncheon yesterday. I wash it and spend the next hour polishing it, wondering how one-arm Ernestine do it. Polishing Grand Baroque with all its loops and curls is a two-arm job.

When Miss Leefolt get back, she put her purse up on the table and tsk. "Oh, I meant to return that silver this morning but I had to go to Mae Mobley's school and I just know she's getting a cold because she was sneezing all morning long and now it's almost ten o'clock..."

"Mae Mobley getting sick?"

"Probably." Miss Leefolt roll her eyes. "Oh, I'm late for my hair appointment. When you're finished polishing, go ahead and walk that silver on over to Hilly's for me. I'll be back after lunch."

When I'm done, I wrap all a Miss Hilly's silver up in the blue cloth. I go get Li'l Man out a bed. He just woke up from his nap and he blink at me and smile.

"Come on, Li'l Man, let's get you a new diaper." I put him up on the changing table and take off the wet one and Lord almighty if there ain't three tinker toys and one a Miss Leefolt's bobby pins in there. Thank the Lord it was just a wet diaper and not the other.

"Boy," I laugh, "you like Fort Knox." He grin and laugh. He point at the crib and I go over and poke through the blanket and sho nuff, there's a hair roller, a measuring spoon, and a dinner napkin. Law, we gone have to do something about this. But not now. I got to get over to Miss Hilly's.

I lock Li'l Man in the stroller and push him down the street over to Miss Hilly's house. It's hot and sunny and quiet. We stroll up her drive and Ernestine open the door. She got a skinny little brown nub that poke out the left sleeve. I don't know her well, except she like to talk a fair amount. She go to the Methodist church.

"Hey Aibileen," she say.

"Hey Ernestine, you must a seen me coming."

She nods and looks down at Li'l Man. He watching that nub like he scared it's gone get him.

"I come out here fore she do," Ernestine whisper and then she say, "I guess you heard."

"Heard what?"

Ernestine look behind her, then lean down. "Flora Lou's white lady, Miss Hester? She give it to Flora Lou this morning."

"She fired her?" Flora Lou had some bad stories to tell. She angry. Miss Hester who everbody think is real sweet, she give Flora a special "hand wash" to use ever morning. Ends up it was straight bleach. Flora showed me the burn scar.

Ernestine shake her head. "Miss Hester pull that book out and start yelling, 'Is this me? Is this me you wrote about?' and Flora Lou say, 'No ma'am, I didn't write no book. I ain't even finished the fifth grade' but Miss Hester go into a fit yelling, 'I didn't know Clorox burned the skin, I didn't know the minimum wage was a dollar twenty-five, if Hilly wasn't telling everybody it's not Jackson I'd fire you so quick your head would spin,' so Flora Lou say, 'You mean I'm not fired?' and Miss Hester scream, 'Fired? I can't fire you or people will *know* I'm Chapter Ten. You're stuck working here for the rest of your life.' And then Miss Hester lay her head on the table and tell Flora Lou to finish the dishes."

"Law," I say, feeling dizzy. "I hope...they all turn out that good."

Back in the house, Miss Hilly hollers Ernestine's name. "I wouldn't count on it," Ernestine whisper. I hand Ernestine the heavy cloth full a silver. She reaches out with her good hand to take it, and I guess out a habit, her nub reach out too.

THAT NIGHT, there's a terrible storm. The thunder's booming and I'm at my kitchen table sweating. I'm shaking, trying to write my prayers. Flora Lou got lucky, but what's gone happen next? It's just too much not knowing and worrying and—

Thunk thunk thunk. Somebody knocking on my front door.

Who that? I sit up straight. The clock over the stove say eight thirty-five. Outside, the rain is blowing hard. Anybody who know me good would use the back door.

I tiptoe to the front. They knock again, and I bout jump out a my shoes.

"Who—who is it?" I say. I check that the lock is on.

"It's *me.*"

Law. I let out a breath and open the front door. There's Miss Skeeter, wet and shivering. Her red satchel's under her raincoat.

"Lord have mercy—"

"I couldn't make it to the back door. The yard's so thick with mud I couldn't get through."

She barefoot and holding her muddy shoes in her hand. I close the door quick behind her. "Nobody see you, did they?"

"You can't see a thing out there. I would've called but the phone's out with the storm."

I know something must a happened, but I'm just so glad to see her face before she leaves for New York. We ain't seen each other in person in six months. I give her a good hug.

"Law, let me see your hair." Miss Skeeter pull back her hood, shake out her long hair past her shoulders.

"It is beautiful," I say and I mean it.

She smile like she embarrassed and set her satchel on the floor. "Mother hates it."

I laugh and then take a big breath, trying to get ready for whatever bad thing she got to tell me.

"The stores are asking for more books, Aibileen. Missus Stein called this afternoon." She take my hands. "They're going to do another print run. Five *thousand* more copies."

I just look at her. "I didn't...I didn't even know they could do that," I say and I cover my mouth. Our book is setting in five thousand houses, on they bookshelves, next to they night tables, behind they toilets?

"There'll be more money coming. At least one hundred dollars to each of you. And who knows? Maybe there'll be more."

I put my hand on my heart. I ain't spent a cent a the first sixty-one dollars and now she telling me they's more?

"And there's something else." Miss Skeeter look down at the satchel. "I went to the paper on Friday and quit the Miss Myrna job." She takes a deep breath. "And I told Mr. Golden, I think the next Miss Myrna should be you."

"*Me?*"

"I told him you've been giving me the answers all along. He said he'd think about it and today he called me and said yes, as long as you don't tell anybody and you write the answers like Miss Myrna did."

She pull a blue-cloth notebook out a her satchel, hand it to me. "He said he'll pay you the same as me, ten dollars a week."

Me? Working for the white newspaper? I go to the sofa and open the notebook, see all them letters and articles from past times. Miss Skeeter set beside me.

"Thank you, Miss Skeeter. For this, for *ever*thing."

She smile, take a deep breath like she fighting back tears.

"I can't believe you gone be a New Yorker tomorrow," I say.

"Actually, I'm going to go to Chicago first. Only for one night. I want to see Constantine, her grave."

I nod. "I'm glad."

"Mother showed me the obituary. It's right outside of town. And then I'll go to New York the next morning."

"You tell Constantine Aibileen say hello."

She laugh. "I'm so nervous. I've never been to Chicago or New York. I've never even been on an airplane before."

We set there a second, listening to the storm. I think about the first time Miss Skeeter came to my house, how awkward we was. Now I feel like we family.

"Are you scared, Aibileen?" she asks. "Of what might happen?"

I turn so she can't see my eyes. "I'm alright."

"Sometimes, I don't know if this was worth it. If something happens to you...how am I going to live with that, knowing it was because of me?" She presses her hand over her eyes, like she don't want to see what's gone happen.

I go to my bedroom and bring out the package from Reverend Johnson. She take off the paper and stare at the book, all the names signed in it. "I was gone send it to you in New York, but I think you need to have it now."

"I don't...understand," she say. "This is for me?"

"Yes ma'am." Then I pass on the Reverend's message, that she is part of our family. "You need to remember, ever one a these signatures means it was worth it." She read the thank-yous, the little things they wrote, run her fingers over the ink. Tears fill up her eyes.

"I reckon Constantine would a been real proud a you."

Miss Skeeter smile and I see how *young* she is. After all we written and the hours we spent tired and worried, I ain't seen the girl she still is in a long, long time.

"Are you sure it's alright? If I leave you, with everything so..."

"Go to New York, Miss Skeeter. Go find your life."

She smile, blinking back the tears, and say, *"Thank you."*

THAT NIGHT I lay in bed thinking. I am so happy for Miss Skeeter. She starting her whole life over. Tears run down my temples into my ears, thinking about her walking down them big city avenues I seen on tee-vee with her long hair behind her. Part a me wishes I could have a new start too. The cleaning article, that's new. But I'm not young. My life's about done.

The harder I try to sleep, the more I know I'm on be up most a the night. It's like I can feel the buzz all over town, of people talking about the book. How can anybody sleep with all them bees? I think about Flora Lou, how if Hilly wasn't telling people the book ain't Jackson, Miss Hester would a fired her. Oh Minny, I think. You done something so good. You taking care a everybody except yourself. I wish I could protect you.

It sounds like Miss Hilly's barely hanging on by a thread. Ever day another person say they know it was her that ate that pie and Miss Hilly just fight harder. For the first time in my life, I'm actually wondering who gone win this fight. Before now, I'd always say Miss Hilly but now I don't know. This time, Miss Hilly just might lose.

I get a few hours sleep before dawn. It's funny, but I hardly feel tired when I get up at six. I put on my clean uniform I washed in the tub last night. In the kitchen, I drink a long, cool glass a water from the faucet. I turn off the kitchen light and head for the door and my phone ring. Law, it's early for that.

I pick up and I hear *wailing*.

"Minny? That you? What—"

"They fired Leroy last night! And when Leroy ask why, his boss say Mister William *Holbrook* told him to do it. Holbrook told him it's Leroy's nigger *wife* the reason and Leroy come home and try to kill me with his bare hands!" Minny panting and heaving. "He throw the kids in the yard and lock me in the bathroom and say he gone light the house on fire with me locked inside!"

Law, it's *happening*. I cover my mouth, feel myself falling down that black hole we dug for ourselves. All these weeks a hearing Minny sound so confident and now...

"That *witch*," Minny scream. "He gone kill me cause a her!"

"Where you now, Minny, where the kids?"

"The gas station, I run here in my bare feet! The kids run next door..." She panting and hiccupping and growling. "Octavia coming to get us. Say she gone drive fast as she can."

Octavia's in Canton, twenty minutes north up by Miss Celia. "Minny, I'm on run up there now—"

"No, don't hang up, please. Just stay on the phone with me till she get here."

"Is you okay? You hurt?"

"I can't take this no more, Aibileen. I can't do this—" She break down crying into the phone.

It's the first time I ever heard Minny say that. I take a deep breath, knowing what I need to do. The words is so clear in my head and *right now* is my only chance for her to really hear me, standing barefoot and rock bottom on the gas station phone. "Minny, listen to me. You never gone lose your job with Miss Celia. Mister Johnny told you hisself. And they's more money coming from the book, Miss Skeeter found out last night. Minny, hear me when I say, *You don't have to get hit by Leroy no more.*"

Minny choke out a sob.

"It's time, Minny. Do you hear me? You are *free.*"

Real slow, Minny's crying wind down. Until she dead quiet. If I couldn't hear her breathing, I'd think she hung up the phone. *Please, Minny,* I think. *Please, take this chance to get out.*

She take a deep, shaky breath. She say, "I hear what you saying, Aibileen."

"Let me come to the gas station and wait with you. I tell Miss Leefolt I be late."

"No," she say. "My sister...be here soon. We gone stay with her tonight."

"Minny, is it just for tonight or..."

She let out a long breath into the phone. "No," she say. "I can't. I done took this long *enough.*" And I start to hear Minny Jackson come back into her own self again. Her voice is shaking, I know she scared, but she say, "God help him, but Leroy don't know *what* Minny Jackson about to become."

My heart jumps. "Minny, you can't kill him. Then you gone be in jail right where Miss Hilly want you."

Lord, that silence is a long, terrible one.

"I ain't gone kill him, Aibileen. I promise. We gone go stay with Octavia till we find a place a our own."

I let out a breath.

"She here," she say. "I'll call you tonight."

WHEN I GET TO Miss Leefolt's, the house is real quiet. I reckon Li'l Man still sleeping. Mae Mobley already gone to school. I put my bag down in the laundry room. The swinging door to the dining room is closed and the kitchen is a nice cool square.

I put the coffee on and say a prayer for Minny. She can stay out at Octavia's for a while. Octavia got a fair-size farmhouse, from what Minny's told me. Minny be closer to her job, but it's far from the kids' schools. Still, what's important is, Minny's away from Leroy. I never once heard her say she gone leave Leroy, and Minny don't say things twice. When she do things, they done the first time.

I fix a bottle a milk for Li'l Man and take a deep breath. I feel like my day's already done and it's only eight o'clock in the morning. But I still ain't tired. I don't know why.

I push open the swinging door. And there be Miss Leefolt and Miss Hilly setting down at the dining room table on the same side, looking at me.

For a second, I stand there, gripping the bottle a milk. Miss Leefolt still got her hair curlers in and she in her blue quilted bathrobe. But Miss Hilly's all dressed up in a blue plaid pantsuit. That nasty red sore still on the side a her lip.

"G'morning," I say and start to walk to the back.

"Ross is still sleeping," Miss Hilly say. "No need to go back there."

I stop where I am and look at Miss Leefolt, but she staring at the funny L-shaped crack in her dining room table.

"Aibileen," Miss Hilly says and she lick her lips. "When you returned my silver yesterday, there were three pieces missing out of that felt wrapper. One silver fork and two silver spoons."

I suck in a breath. "Lemme—lemme go look in the kitchen, maybe I left some behind." I look at Miss Leefolt to see if that's what she want me to do, but she keep her eyes on the crack. A cold prickle creeps up my neck.

"You know as well as I do that silver's not in the kitchen, Aibileen," Miss Hilly say.

"Miss Leefolt, you checked in Ross's bed? He been sneaking things and sticking em—"

Miss Hilly scoff real loud. "Do you hear her, Elizabeth? She's trying to blame it on a toddler."

My mind's racing, I'm trying to remember if I counted the silver before I put it back in the felt. I think I did. I always do. Law, tell me she ain't saying what I think she saying—

"Miss Leefolt, did you already check the kitchen? Or the silver closet? Miss Leefolt?"

But she still won't look at me and I don't know what to do. I don't know, yet, how bad this is. Maybe this ain't about silver, maybe this is really about Miss Leefolt and *Chapter Two*...

"Aibileen," Miss Hilly say, "you can return those pieces to me by today, or else Elizabeth is going to press charges."

Miss Leefolt look at Miss Hilly and suck in a breath, like she surprised. And I wonder whose idea this whole thing is, both of em or just Miss Hilly's?

"I ain't stole no silver service, Miss Leefolt," I say and just the words make me want a run.

Miss Leefolt whisper, "She says she doesn't have them, Hilly."

Miss Hilly don't even act like she heard. She raise her eyebrows at me and say, "Then it behooves me to inform you that you are fired, Aibileen." Miss Hilly sniff. "I'll be calling the police. They know me."

"Maa-maaaa," Li'l Man holler from his crib in the back. Miss Leefolt look behind her, then at Hilly, like she ain't sure what to do. I reckon she just now thinking about what it's gone be like if she don't have a maid no more.

"Aaai-beee," Li'l Man call, starting to cry.

"Aai-bee," call another small voice and I realize *Mae Mobley's home.* She must not've gone to school today. I press on my chest. *Lord, please don't let her see this. Don't let her hear what Miss Hilly saying about me.* Down the hall, the door opens and Mae Mobley walks out. She blinks at us and coughs.

"Aibee, my froat hurts."

"I—I be right there, baby."

Mae Mobley coughs again and it sounds bad, like a dog barking, and I start for the hall, but Miss Hilly say, "Aibileen, you stay where you are, Elizabeth can take care of her kids."

Miss Leefolt look at Hilly like, *Do I have to?* But then she get up and trudge down the hall. She take Mae Mobley into Li'l Man's room and shut the door. It's just two of us left now, me and Miss Hilly.

Miss Hilly lean back in her chair, say, "I won't tolerate liars."

My head swimming. I want to set down. "I didn't steal no silver, Miss Hilly."

"I'm not talking about silver," she say, leaning forward. She hissing in a whisper so Miss Leefolt don't hear her. "I'm talking about those things you wrote about Elizabeth. She has no idea Chapter Two is about her and I am too good of a friend to tell her. And maybe I can't send you to jail for what you wrote about Elizabeth, but I can send you to jail for being a thief."

I ain't going to no penitentiary. *I ain't,* is all I can think.

"And your friend, Minny? She's got a nice surprise coming to her. I'm calling Johnny Foote and telling him he needs to fire her right now."

The room getting blurry. I'm shaking my head and my fists is clenching tighter.

"I'm pretty darn close to Johnny Foote. He listens to what I—"

"Miss *Hilly.*" I say it loud and clear. She stops. I bet Miss Hilly ain't been interrupted in ten years.

I say, "I know something about you and don't you forget that."

She narrow her eyes at me. But she don't say nothing.

"And from what I hear, they's a lot a time to write a lot a letters in jail." I'm trembling. My breath feel like fire. "Time to write to ever person in Jackson the truth about you. Plenty a time and the paper is free."

"Nobody would believe something you wrote, Nigra."

"I don't know. I been told I'm a pretty good writer."

She fish her tongue out and touch that sore with it. Then she drop her eyes from mine.

Before she can say anything else, the door flies open down the hall. Mae Mobley runs out in her nightie and she stop in front a me. She hiccupping and crying and her little nose is red as a rose. Her mama must a told her I'm leaving.

God, I pray, *tell me she didn't repeat Miss Hilly's lies.*

Baby Girl grab the skirt a my uniform and don't let go. I touch my hand to her forehead and she burning with fever.

"Baby, you need to get back in the bed."

"Noooo," she bawls. "Don't gooo, Aibee."

Miss Leefolt come out a the bedroom, frowning, holding Li'l Man.

"Aibee!" he call out, grinning.

"Hey...Li'l Man," I whisper. I'm so glad he don't understand what's going on. "Miss Leefolt, lemme take her in the kitchen and give her some medicine. Her fever is real high."

Miss Leefolt glance at Miss Hilly, but she just setting there with her arms crossed. "Alright, go on," Miss Leefolt say.

I take Baby Girl's hot little hand and lead her into the kitchen. She bark out that scary cough again and I get the baby aspirin and the cough syrup. Just being in here with me, she calmed down some, but tears is still running down her face.

I put her up on the counter and crush up a little pink pill, mix it with some applesauce and feed her the spoonful. She swallow it down and I know it hurts her. I smooth her hair back. That clump a bangs she cut off with her construction scissors is growing back sticking straight out. Miss Leefolt can't hardly look at her lately.

"Please don't leave, Aibee," she say, starting to cry again.

"I got to, baby. I am so sorry." And that's when I start to cry. I don't want to, it's just gone make it worse for her, but I can't stop.

"Why? Why don't you want to see me anymore? Are you going to take care of another little girl?" Her forehead is all wrinkled up, just like when her mama fuss at her. Law, I feel like my heart's gone bleed to death.

I take her face in my hands, feeling the scary heat coming off her cheeks. "No, baby, that's not the reason. I don't want a leave you, but…" How do I put this? I can't tell her I'm fired, I don't want her to blame her mama and make it worse between em. "It's time for me to retire. You my last little girl," I say, because this is the truth, it just ain't by my own choosing.

I let her cry a minute on my chest and then I take her face into my hands again. I take a deep breath and I tell her to do the same.

"Baby Girl," I say. "I need you to remember everthing I told you. Do you remember what I told you?"

She still crying steady, but the hiccups is gone. "To wipe my bottom good when I'm done?"

"No, baby, the other. About what you are."

I look deep into her rich brown eyes and she look into mine. Law, she got old-soul eyes, like she done lived a thousand years. And I swear I see, down inside, the woman she gone grow up to be. A flash from the future. She is tall and straight. She is proud. She got a better haircut. And she is *remembering* the words I put in her head. Remembering as a full-grown woman.

And then she say it, just like I need her to. "You is kind," she say, "you is smart. You is important."

"Oh *Law.*" I hug her hot little body to me. I feel like she done just given me a gift. "Thank you, Baby Girl."

"You're welcome," she say, like I taught her to. But then she lay her head on my shoulder and we cry like that awhile, until Miss Leefolt come into the kitchen.

"Aibileen," Miss Leefolt say real quiet.

"Miss Leefolt, are you…sure this what you…" Miss Hilly walk in behind her and glare at me. Miss Leefolt nods, looking real guilty.

"I'm sorry, Aibileen. Hilly, if you want to…press charges, that's up to you."

Miss Hilly sniff at me and say, "It's not worth my time."

Miss Leefolt sigh like she relieved. For a second, our eyes meet and I can see that Miss Hilly was right. Miss Leefolt ain't got no idea Chapter Two is her. Even if she had a hint of it, she'd never admit to herself that was her.

I push back on Mae Mobley real gentle and she looks at me, then over at her mama through her sleepy, fever eyes. She look like she's dreading the next fifteen years a her life, but she sighs, like she is just too tired to think about it. I put her down on her feet, give her a kiss on the forehead, but then she reaches out to me again. I have to back away.

I go in the laundry room, get my coat and my pocketbook.

I walk out the back door, to the terrible sound a Mae Mobley crying again. I start down the driveway, crying too, knowing how much I'm on miss Mae Mobley, praying her mama can show her more love. But at the same time feeling, in a way, that I'm free, like Minny. Freer than Miss Lee-folt, who so locked up in her own head she don't even recognize herself when she read it. And freer than Miss Hilly. That woman gone spend the rest a her life trying to convince people she didn't eat that pie. I think about Yule May setting in jail. Cause Miss Hilly, she in her own jail, but with a lifelong term.

I head down the hot sidewalk at eight thirty in the morning wondering what I'm on do with the rest a my day. The rest a my life. I am shaking and crying and a white lady walk by frowning at me. The paper gone pay me ten dollars a week, and there's the book money plus a little more coming. Still, it ain't enough for me to live the rest a my life on. I ain't gone be able to get no other job as a maid, not with Miss Leefolt and Miss Hilly calling me a thief. Mae Mobley was my last white baby. And here I just bought this new uniform.

The sun is bright but my eyes is wide open. I stand at the bus stop like I been doing for forty-odd years. In thirty minutes, my whole life's...done. Maybe I ought to keep writing, not just for the paper, but something else, about all the people I know and the things I seen and done. Maybe I ain't too old to start over, I think and I laugh and cry at the same time at this. Cause just last night I thought I was finished with everthing new.

ACKNOWLEDGMENTS

Thank you to Amy Einhorn, my editor, without whom the sticky-note business would not be the success it is today. Amy, you are so wise. I am truly lucky to have worked with you.

Thank you to: my agent, Susan Ramer, for taking a chance and being so patient with me; Alexandra Shelley for her tenacious editing and diligent advice; The Jane Street Workshop for being such fine writers; Ruth Stockett, Tate Taylor, Brunson Green, Laura Foote, Octavia Spencer, Nicole Love, and Justine Story for reading and laughing, even at the parts that weren't that funny. Thank you to Grandaddy, Sam, Barbara, and Robert Stockett for helping me remember the old Jackson days. And my deepest thanks to Keith Rogers and my dear Lila, for *everything*.

Thank you to everyone at Putnam for their enthusiasm and hard work. I took liberties with time, using the song "The Times They Are A-Changin,'" even though it was not released until 1964, and Shake 'n Bake, which did not hit the shelves until 1965. The Jim Crow laws that appear in the book were abbreviated and taken from actual legislation that existed, at various times, across the South. Many thanks to Dorian Hastings and Elizabeth Wagner, the incredibly detailed copy editors, for pointing out these, my stubborn discrepancies, and helping me repair many others.

Thank you to Susan Tucker, author of the book *Telling Memories Among Southern Women*, whose beautiful oral accounts of domestics and white employers took me back to a time and place that is long gone.

Finally, my belated thanks to Demetrie McLorn, who carried us all out of the hospital wrapped in our baby blankets and spent her life feeding us, picking up after us, loving us, and, thank God, forgiving us.

TOO LITTLE, TOO LATE

Kathryn Stockett, in her own words

Our family maid, Demetrie, used to say picking cotton in Mississippi in the dead of summer is about the worst pastime there is, if you don't count picking okra, another prickly, low-growing thing. Demetrie used to tell us all kinds of stories about picking cotton as a girl. She'd laugh and shake her finger at us, warning us against it, as if a bunch of rich white kids might fall to the evils of cotton-picking, like cigarettes or hard liquor.

"For days I picked and picked. And then I looked down and my skin had bubbled up. I showed my mama. None a us ever seen sunburn on a black person before. That was for white people!"

I was too young to realize that what she was telling us wasn't very funny. Demetrie was born in Lampkin, Mississippi, in 1927. It was a horrifying year to be born, just before the Depression set in. Right on time for a child to appreciate, in fine detail, what it felt like to be poor, colored, and female on a sharecropping farm.

Demetrie came to cook and clean for my family when she was twenty-eight. My father was fourteen, my uncle seven. Demetrie was stout and dark-skinned and, by then, married to a mean, abusive drinker named Clyde. She wouldn't answer me when I asked questions about him. But besides the subject of Clyde, she'd talk to us all day.

And God, how I loved to talk to Demetrie. After school, I'd sit in my grandmother's kitchen with her, listening to her stories and watching her mix up cakes and fry chicken. Her cooking was outstanding. It was something people discussed at length after they ate at my grandmother's table. You felt *loved* when you tasted Demetrie's caramel cake.

But my older brother and sister and I weren't allowed to bother Demetrie during her own lunch break. Grandmother would say, "Leave her alone now, let her eat, this is her time," and I would stand in the kitchen doorway, itching to get back with her. Grandmother wanted Demetrie to rest so she could finish her work, not to mention, white people didn't sit at the table while a colored person was eating.

That was just a normal part of life, the rules between blacks and whites. As a little girl, seeing black people in the colored part of town, even if they were dressed up or doing fine, I remember pitying them. I am so embarrassed to admit that now.

I didn't pity Demetrie, though. There were several years when I thought she was immensely lucky to have us. A secure job in a nice house, cleaning up after white Christian people. But also because Demetrie had no babies of her own, and we felt like we were filling a void in her life. If anyone asked her how many children she had, she would hold up her fingers and say three. She meant us: my sister, Susan, my brother, Rob, and me.

My siblings deny it, but I was closer to Demetrie than the other kids were. Nobody got cross with me if Demetrie was nearby. She would stand me in front of the mirror and say, "You are beautiful. You a beautiful girl," when clearly I was not. I wore glasses and had stringy brown hair. I had a stubborn aversion to the bathtub. My mother was out of town a lot. Susan and Rob were tired of me hanging around, and I felt left over. Demetrie knew it and took my hand and told me I was fine.

My parents divorced when I was six. Demetrie became even more important to me then. When my mother went on one of her frequent trips, Daddy put us kids in the motel he owned and brought in Demetrie to stay with us. I'd cry and cry on Demetrie's shoulder, missing my mother so bad I'd get a fever from it.

By then, my sister and brother had, in a way, outgrown Demetrie. They'd sit around the motel penthouse playing poker, using bar straws as money, with the front desk staff.

I remember watching them, jealous because they were older, and thinking one time, *I am not a baby anymore. I don't have to take up with Demetrie while the others play poker.*

So I got in the game and of course lost all my straws in about five minutes. And back I went onto Demetrie's lap, acting put out, watching the others play. Yet after only a minute, my forehead was against her soft neck and she was rocking me like we were two people in a boat.

"This where you belong. Here with me," she said, and patted my hot leg. Her hands were always cool. I watched the older kids play cards, not caring as much that Mother was away again. I was where I belonged.

THE RASH OF negative accounts about Mississippi, in the movies, in the papers, on television, have made us natives a wary, defensive bunch. We are full of pride and shame, but mostly pride.

Still, I got out of there. I moved to New York City when I was twenty-four. I learned that the first question anyone asked anybody, in a town so transient, was "Where are you from?" And I'd say, "Mississippi." And then I'd wait.

To people who smiled and said, "I've heard it's beautiful down there," I'd say, "My hometown is number three in the nation for gang-related murders." To people who said, "God, you must be glad to be out of *that* place," I'd bristle and say, "What do you know? It's beautiful down there."

Once, at a roof party, a drunk man from a rich white Metro North–train type of town asked me where I was from and I told him Mississippi. He sneered and said, "I am so sorry."

I nailed down his foot with the stiletto portion of my shoe and spent the next ten minutes quietly educating him on the where-from-abouts of William Faulkner, Eudora Welty, Tennessee Williams, Elvis Presley, B. B. King, Oprah Winfrey, Jim Henson, Faith Hill, James Earl Jones, and Craig Claiborne, the food editor and critic for *The New York Times.* I informed him that Mississippi hosted the first lung transplant and the first heart transplant and that the basis of the United States legal system was developed at the University of Mississippi.

I was homesick and I'd been waiting for somebody like him.

I wasn't very genteel or ladylike, and the poor guy squirmed away and looked nervous for the rest of the party. But I couldn't help it.

Mississippi is like my mother. I am allowed to complain about her all I want, but God help the person who raises an ill word about her around me, unless she is their mother too.

I WROTE *THE HELP* while living in New York, which I think was easier than writing it in Mississippi, staring in the face of it all. The distance added perspective. In the middle of a whirring, fast city, it was a relief to let my thoughts turn slow and remember for a while.

The Help is fiction, by and large. Still, as I wrote it, I wondered an awful lot what my family would think of it, and what Demetrie would have thought too, even though she was long dead. I was scared, a lot of the time, that I was crossing a terrible line, writing in the voice of a black person. I was afraid I would fail to describe a relationship that was so intensely influential in my life, so loving, so grossly stereotyped in American history and literature.

I was truly grateful to read Howell Raines's Pulitzer Prize–winning article, "Grady's Gift":

> *There is no trickier subject for a writer from the South than that of affection between a black person and a white one in the unequal world of segregation. For the dishonesty upon which a society is founded makes every emotion suspect, makes it impossible to know whether what flowed between two people was honest feeling or pity or pragmatism.*

I read that and I thought, *How did he find a way to put it into such concise words?* Here was the same slippery issue I'd been struggling with and couldn't catch in my hands, like a wet fish. Mr. Raines managed to nail it down in a few sentences. I was glad to hear I was in the company of others in my struggle.

Like my feelings for Mississippi, my feelings for *The Help* conflict greatly. Regarding the lines between black and white women, I am afraid I have told too much. I was taught not to talk about such uncomfortable things, that it was tacky, impolite, they might hear us.

I am afraid I have told too little. Not just that life was so much worse for many black women working in the homes in Mississippi, but also that there was so much more love between white families and black domestics than I had the ink or the time to portray.

What I *am* sure about is this: I don't presume to think that I know what it really felt like to be a black woman in Mississippi, especially in the 1960s. I don't think it is something any white woman on the other end of a black woman's paycheck could ever truly understand. But trying to understand is *vital* to our humanity. In *The Help* there is one line that I truly prize:

> Wasn't that the point of the book? For women to realize, *We are just two people. Not that much separates us. Not nearly as much as I'd thought.*

I'm pretty sure I can say that no one in my family ever asked Demetrie what it felt like to be black in Mississippi, working for our white family. It never occurred to us to ask. It was everyday life. It wasn't something people felt compelled to examine.

I have wished, for many years, that I'd been old enough and thoughtful enough to ask Demetrie that question. She died when I was sixteen. I've spent years imagining what her answer would be. And that is why I wrote this book.

Kathryn Stockett was born and raised in Jackson, Mississippi. After graduating from the University of Alabama with a degree in English and creative writing, she moved to New York City, where she worked in magazine publishing and marketing for nine years. She currently lives in Atlanta with her husband and their daughter. This is her first novel.